The Last Daughter of Smoke and Shadows

Of Passions and Thrones Book One

Written by:
Lillie Jean Andrews

This book is dedicated to those who know what it's like to need to escape to another world, I see you.

While this book is a work of fiction and it is my hope that I have treated these subjects with the utmost respect and care, there are themes and subjects in this book that some readers may find triggering.

These subjects include but are not limited to;

-Explicit sexual content

-A main character that deals with anxiety and depression, both past and present

-Death of a parent (backstory)

-Talk of previous physical abuse

-Very brief mention of past sexual assault (not towards or from any main character)

The Fae Realm
Elvoria
Keelmont
Norwood
Shaston
Lorvil
Drailia
Avenell
N
S

Chapter One

I cy roads and one too many shots of Tequila don't mix. That was what Haven was told the night her father died. It never really made sense, he wasn't even coming home from the bar the night he crashed. He had been on his way to pick up some new flowers to be planted in her mothers garden. It was something Haven and her father did once a month, every month. The last Saturday of each month her father would take her to pick out some flowers and together they would plant them in the square beds her mother kept in the backyard.

Haven only ever missed one trip.

The Friday before the crash Haven had gone home unusually sick. When Saturday morning rolled around and she wasn't feeling any better, she told her father to go without her. He offered to wait but Haven had insisted, telling him to use his best judgment to pick out the flowers and that when he got home she would do her best to hobble out to the backyard and help him plant. He never made it home.

That had been a little over two years ago. Now, Haven was in her senior year of high school, soon to graduate and turn nineteen. The upcoming weekend held her birthday and coincidentally the senior trip being put on by her school. Each year the private school she attended paid for the senior class to go on a three day long trip in the mountains of North Carolina where she was from. There would be hiking, swimming and marshmallows roasted over a fire. Exactly where she wanted to spend her birthday. Except, that was the exact opposite of how Haven wanted to spend her birthday.

The activities would be fine, it was the other people that were the problem. Haven always enjoyed nature but only one of her friends would be going and that made her nervous, she had been diagnosed with both anxiety and depression at a young age. Doing things in a large group of people she didn't know, in a place she had never been, always set her anxiety off.

She would be fine, Haven constantly reassured herself. Her mother had encouraged her to go, in fact, she all but insisted. It hadn't been hard for her mom to convince Haven to go but her mothers pressuring almost made her not want to go just out of spite. Haven could be bad that way. She could be spiteful and vengeful when there was absolutely no reason for it. Those feelings and characteristics only heightened after her fathers death.

Haven had gotten mad, her mother grew distant. Even though Haven could tell her mother tried hard to be there for her daughter, she almost always fell short. Haven used to resent her mother for that. Even in those few moments when her mother opened up and spoke of how much her fathers death had hurt, it didn't seem to make much of a difference. It was like Haven's mother hadn't considered that her daughter might also be hurting. It took a little over a year but eventually Haven learned to deal with her feelings better, standing on her own instead of leaning on her mom to help compartmentalize her feelings.

Resentment or no, she loved her mother and their relationship had grown in the time that had passed. She could still see the sadness that grief and loss had caused but the relationship between the two women had gotten much better. They went out for coffee, to the movies, and to their favorite thrift stores. That was where they were now, sitting in their favorite coffee shop going over some designs her mother had drawn for the new garden she wanted to put in. The drawings were lovely, Haven could truly feel the love her mother put into her garden. It was radiating off the page like it had been sprayed with perfume.

The image of the garden her mother had created reminded Haven of the stories her parents used to tell her. Ones of faraway places with magic and fairies so many beautiful things. It looked like something Haven might find in the gardens of the castles they used to describe.

"What do you think Haven?" Her mother asked.

"It looks great mom. I can't wait to see what it'll look like when you're done with it."

"Your father would have loved it."

"I'm sure he would have. Maybe once things get going and the flowers start blooming, we could leave some cut flowers at his grave?"

Her mother looked away for a moment before sliding the drawing into her purse and saying, "How about we head home so you can finish packing for your trip?"

A quick drive and they were home. Haven went up the staircase that led to her room and pulled her not very full backpack off the hooks on the back of her door.

Sighing, she set it down on the bed and shoved the clothes she planned to take into it. Next came the toiletries like her hairbrush and toothpaste. She also gathered her kindle and one of her favorite fantasy novels off her bookshelf. Once she was done, Haven hung it back on the hooks and tossed herself down on the bed. Staring up at the ceiling, she pictured the upcoming weekend. Anxious thoughts of what could happen crept into her mind. She thought of falling off mountain peaks and getting kidnapped by the bus driver. She knew her intrusive thoughts were unlikely to happen but that didn't stop her heart from racing. Haven turned her mind to other things in an attempt to relax. Unfortunately, it landed on her future and she ended up with thoughts of where to go to college and what she was going to do for the rest of her life. Maybe if she had the answers to those questions she wouldn't constantly feel as anxious as she did.

Minutes passed before her heart rate settled enough for Haven to relax. Sleep hadn't been her original goal but it claimed her nonetheless.

Chapter Two

"Hurry up or you'll be late!" Her mother called up the stairs.

Haven rushed out of her room and down the stairs to where her mother stood, arms crossed, keys in hand.

"We never seem to be able to be on time anywhere, can we?" Her mother sighed.

Haven huffed a laugh and rushed out the door, launching herself and bag into the passenger seat with her mother following close behind. Forty-five minutes of driving in silence, save for the radio, had them in the school parking lot where the bus for the senior trip was waiting.

"I'm going to miss you," Her mother hugged her tight as soon as they were out of the car.

"Relax, it's just three days and two nights then I'll be back"

Her mother hugged tighter,

"Alright mom, the bus is going to leave with or without me and I'd rather be on it"

Her mother finally relinquished her hold and Haven stepped towards the bus. She didn't get far before her mother was yanking her backwards for one more hug.

"Okay mom, I'll see you in a few days. I love you."

"I love you too Haven, have a great birthday!" Her mother was tearing up.

Haven loaded herself onto the bus, taking a seat next to her only friend on this trip and contemplating her mother's strange behavior. She had stayed away longer when she was younger for camp and her mother hadn't been that dramatic when saying goodbye.

After everyone was seated, the bus lurched forward, starting their two hour long drive to the mountain camp where she'd be spending her weekend and birthday. Haven leaned her head on Sydney's shoulder and let her eyes close, nerves from her mothers strange behavior and the upcoming weekend tiring her.

***

Haven woke to passing trees on a two-lane road. After she rubbed the sleep from her eyes, Sydney told her they were only fifteen minutes away. The morning light coming through the bus windows was soft and pleasant. Haven was thankful it wouldn't be too hot outside since it was still spring. She was pretty sure the cabins they'd be staying in did not have air conditioning.

Minutes passed and soon they were pulling into what appeared to be a long gravel driveway. Everyone around her began packing their things and preparing to get off the bus. Haven did the same, she had only pulled out her phone so there wasn't much to prepare. Looking around, she found the mountainside mesmerizing. Large, beautiful trees covered the ground and you could see mountain peaks off in the distance. Haven wished she hadn't slept for so much of the trip, she would have loved to see more of the mountainside.

Eventually the bus pulled up to what appeared to be the main house. In the middle of the clearing was a large, old looking log house with a long wrap around porch. A glance to your left or right and you could see several small cabins dotted around the property, likely where the students would be staying. Thanks to the small size of the senior class there would only have to be three or four girls in each cabin. The boys were lucky in that they only had to have two per cabin.

"Alright this is our stop," The bus driver called out.

The two teachers in the front of the bus stood as the driver opened the doors.

I want all of you to be on your best behavior, we have never held the senior trip here and would like to be able to continue it here for years to come. We don't need that screwed up because some of you thought to have a little extra fun." Spoke Ms McElderoy, the female teacher, earning a few snickers from the group.

For years the senior trip had been to a fun amusement park type of place. Everyone had been surprised when they announced that it was now in the middle of the woods. Sure, hiking was fun for some but there definitely were no roller coasters.

Within five minutes everyone was off the bus and gathered in front of the house, watching the bus pull away.

"Oh no, there goes our only way out!" One of the guys joked. The whole group laughed. Although Haven could see a few nervous looking students, Sydney included. Jokes or no, that boy was right. With the bus gone they had no way out of the mountains.

"Silence!" One of the teachers called out as the two older men who ran the camp exited the house. They walked to stand at the top of the stairs connected to the house's porch.

"Welcome" One of the older men called.

"I'm Rodney and this is Sharp, " The man gestured to himself and then the man standing next to him, "We expect all of you to enjoy your stay and be on your best behavior."

With that, the men walked down the small flight of stairs.

"Boys follow me" Rodney spoke

"And girls follow me" Sharp spoke

All of the girls followed Sharp to where he stopped in front of a small grouping of cabins not far from the main house.

"This is where you'll be staying, three girls in each and one group of four."

Sydney linked her arm through Haven's and nodded to another girl Haven was vaguely familiar with. The girl walked over to where Sydney and Haven were standing. Haven was pretty sure her name was Chelsea.

"If that's everyone" Ms McEdleroy called. She began assigning each group of girls their cabins. There was one group of five girls who didn't want to separate and, in the end, Ms McElderoy solved the problem by tossing up her hands and saying,

"Well alright, if you don't mind being cramped." Apparently the girls didn't.

Ms McElderoy walked up to Havens group and said, "You girls will be in cabin five"

A quick scan of the cabins revealed the one in the far right corner to be theirs. Once all the cabins were assigned Ms McElderoy told everyone,

"For now, head to your cabins to unpack and relax. I will come and gather all of you for lunch in an hour. After that, we will be getting a tour of the property and going over the plans for this weekend"

With a wave of her hand the girls dispersed and found their cabins. Haven, Sydney and Chelsea found theirs quickly. Opening the door they found four beds, two on each side with a small dresser next to each and a door to the small bathroom on the back wall. Haven walked to the bed in the back right and set her bag down on the dresser. Sydney and Chelsea claimed their beds and began unpacking their things. It only took a few minutes for each of the girls to completely unpack. After they finished there was a pause of awkward silence that hung in the air until Sydney sarcastically said,

"We're going to have so much fun this weekend, with Ms McElderoy peering over our shoulders and those two creepy old dudes milling about" All three girls laughed.

Haven could always count on Sydney to break the tension in a room or lighten the mood, it was one of the things she liked most about her.

"Oh yeah loads" Chelsea responded with a light laugh and roll of her eyes.

Haven laughed again and sat down on her bed, the other girls doing the same. Soon it was talking trash about the boys they had dated, girls as well in Havens case, making bets about which of their classmates was going to be the first to get in trouble and discussing which activity they were most excited about. Hiking in Haven's case, roasting marshmallows in Chelsea's case and stargazing in Sydneys. The hour till Ms McElderoy came to find them for lunch passed quickly. Haven was feeling incredibly light and more relaxed than she had assumed she'd be.

She enjoyed spending time with people even though it could be emotionally taxing and somewhat overwhelming at times. Thankfully, she wasn't currently feeling that way. In fact, ever since she stepped off the bus she'd been feeling lighter, almost tingly. Haven didn't know why but she was glad of it. She hoped the feeling would continue.

Chapter Three

Ms McElderoy found them for lunch almost exactly on the hour. Haven and her friends were some of the last in the group headed for the main cabin where lunch would be held. Looking around, Haven found that all of her classmates were smiling, laughing and enjoying themselves. Haven wondered if her classmates felt like she did, unusually easy going and happy.

Lunch was spread out on a table to the side of the main cabin. There were large logs placed in rows just beyond the table for the students to sit. There were salads, sandwiches and chips placed on one end of a table and bottled water at the other end. Haven set a sandwich and some chips on a plate, grabbed a bottle of water and followed Chelsea and Sydney to where they were sitting. The logs weren't exactly comfortable but they beat sitting on the ground where dirt would stain her pants and ants would likely find her plate.

"Attention students," One of the owners called from a small slightly raised platform in front of the collection of logs. From where Haven was sitting, she couldn't see through the groups of her classmates milling about to tell which owner had spoken.

The students hustled to sit and gave the two owners their attention. Now that everyone was silent and sitting she could tell that it was Rodney who had spoken.

"This afternoon we will be giving all of you a guided tour of the facility and grounds in preparation for tomorrow's hike. You will have the next hour to eat and then about fifteen minutes to prepare and meet back in front of the main house before the tour. Is this understood?"

Most of the students nodded in response.

The following hour was fun, Haven, Sydney and Chelsea ate lunch and talked with the students sitting on the logs behind them. Chelsea talked about how hard it had been to get into the college she was going to and Haven had to agree, for her getting into college had been no easy feat. Completing high school hadn't been exactly easy either for that matter. But somehow she had managed both. Haven would soon be graduating and continuing onto college in the fall.

Now all she had left to do was to pick, would she go to Duke university or North Carolina state? Both seemed like smart choices but neither felt right. Luckily, she still had until the end of the semester to decide.

Haven was pulled from her thoughts by Tom, a guy in the group they had been talking to,

"What about you Haven, do you like to hike?"

Haven nodded. She enjoyed pretty much anything that had to do with the outdoors. Her favorite teacher, Mrs McKenna, a sophomore English teacher, had held a lot of her classes outside. In truth, she was incredibly excited to go hiking tomorrow. Most of the kids who went on this trip had to be or else they would have stayed home like the rest of her friends did. Haven didn't understand why the school had stopped doing the senior trip at the amusement park when many more students were likely to enjoy being there. She hadn't cared enough to ask but the question still played in her mind as everyone spoke around her.

It wasn't long before conversation with the other students drifted off.

"I guess we should go 'prepare'" Chelsea commented with air quotes around the word prepare.

"I don't know exactly what I'm supposed to be preparing for but we don't want to be late to the main house, that one owner seems kind of strict about that sort of thing," Sydney replied.

"Well then we better get going" Haven remarked as she stood, brushing her hands off on her jeans and throwing away her plate.

The walk to their cabin was quick. Once they reached the cabin and entered, Haven went over to the small dresser beside her bed and pulled her long red hair into a high ponytail. Sydney plopped down onto her bed.

"So that Tom guy was kinda cute" She commented to no one in particular.

Haven and Chelsea shared a quick glance.

"Yeah I guess he was a little cute, why? Are you thinking of getting into some trouble this weekend?" Chelsea asked with a snicker.

"Hmm maybe" Sydney made a show of contemplating, "It's been a while and I could use some fun" She joked.

Both Chelsea and Haven laughed. If Haven was being honest it hadn't really been all that long since she'd had any fun of that sort. Her friend James had thrown a late Christmas party, aka his parents were out of town and he wanted an excuse to drink and have fun. Haven ended up having a little *fun* with her ex-girlfriend Amanda. She probably shouldn't have, Haven had known that when she did it, but at the time she had had a few too many Tequila shots and about as much impulse control as a puppy left alone in the house too long. That was a little over two months ago, so not all that long in the grand scheme of things.

"What about that one newer guy, what's his name?" Sydney paused.

"Roman." Haven answered for her.

"Oh yes, him!" Sydney exclaimed.

"Well I hate to break it to you Syd but he's gay" Chelsea spoke.

Not much else was known about Roman, he joined the school about a month into senior year and no one had gotten particularly close to him except for one guy named Daniel. They had dated on and off and were occasionally caught making out under the football field bleachers. Roman had written an essay for his history class about strong black gay men throughout the last 500 years like civil rights activist Bayard Rustin and how he related to them. That was how they knew he was gay and not bi.

"I guess I'll just have to find some sad soul to befriend this weekend" Sydney sighed dramatically. She wiggled her eyebrows and sent the girls into a fit of laughter. Haven laughed so hard it made her stomach hurt.

"Alright let's get back to the main house." Chelsea stood from where she was sitting on the edge of her bed.

"Maybe you can scope out your prospects on the tour" Haven sarcastically suggested to Sydney as they headed out the door, sending the girls into another fit of laughter.

Luckily, Haven, Sydney and Chelsea were not the last to arrive in front of the main house. That honor fell to a small pack of boys. Mr Chaplin, the male teacher and chaperone, quickly counted heads and assured the two owners that everyone had arrived.

"Okay let's get started" The owner Mr Sharp spoke, clapping his hands together. The owners led the group of students from the main house to where they had had lunch.

"Now, you've already driven past here on your way in and had lunch in this area but I'm sure none of you noticed the entrance to one of our main trails" Mr Sharp pointed towards a section of forest just beyond the lunch area.

He was correct, Haven hadn't noticed the trailhead marked by a small tower of rocks on either side, she was pretty sure none of the other students had either. There was a well worn path that quickly disappeared out of view. If Haven had to guess, she'd say it went up the mountain, circled around the camp and came out somewhere behind the girls cabins.

"This is the path we will hike tomorrow. It will show us some amazing views on the side of the mountain and even a small waterfall," Mr Rodney said.

The waterfall would be pretty cool to see. From what Haven could tell, the camp was fairly deep in the mountains and seemed mostly untouched by outside forces. She absently wondered if she'd be able to see any semblance of a town from the lookout points.

The two men led the group back past the cabins, first the boys and then the girls. Next they showed the group a few more trail heads, a small garden and chicken pen, a volleyball court along with a few other outdoor games hidden behind the main house and finally back to the front of the main house. Once the group of students came to a stop, the owner Mr Sharp spoke,

"You all are free to do as you please until dinner which is in three hours where you all had lunch. No one will come get you, you are responsible for getting yourselves there. Until then, please don't wander down any of the trails or cause any general trouble"

Mr Sharp smiled tightly and walked away followed by Rodney. Five minutes later, the girls were back lounging in their cabin. Sydney, the only one with service, was on her phone and Chelsea was braiding Havens hair.

"You have really soft hair," Chelsea commented.

"Thanks" She responded.

Haven had always taken pride in her hair, it was exactly like her mothers. In fact, she got a lot of her features from her mother; her height, a few freckles, slightly brownish red hair, pale skin and very bright red lips. She often got asked what lipstick she used to which she always responded, "none."

Her father always told her, "Everything but the eyes, those you got from me."

Havens bright emerald green eyes matched her fathers perfectly except for a few small specks of gold. She seemed to be the only one who noticed it. No one had ever commented on it, or maybe it was just that no one had ever cared enough to pay that close of attention.

Chelsea finished and tied off the braid. Going over to her own bed she asked,

"So what do you guys want to do for the remainder of the evening?"

Haven shrugged, Sydney did the same.

"Come on guys, there has to be something"

Chelsea didn't strike Haven as the type that ever sat still very long.

"We could go find Sydney a guy to mess around with" Chelsea said with a few suggestive looks between Sydney and the door.

"Yes but that would require me to get off of this bed, and I am very comfortable!" Sydney exclaimed. All three girls burst out laughing.

"Well then I guess you'll just have to miss dinner" Haven retorted.

"Oh no, food is definitely worth getting out of bed. Boys however..." Sydney trailed off, earning another round of laughs from the group.

"Oh, I almost forgot" Chelsea jumped up, grabbed her bag and pulled out a deck of Uno cards, "Ah ha!"

"Well I guess that could be fun" Sydney spoke, earning a wide smile from Chelsea.

Chapter Four

Trees. Trees everywhere, and a glittering lake with a beautiful castle.

"Come home" A voice whispered,

"Come home"

Haven woke with a start, slightly panicked but not surprised. For the past year or so she had been having these odd sorts of dreams. They started right after her father died but had picked up in frequency over the last year. Originally, there was a car going over a cliff which had to be about her fathers death. Eventually they developed into these weird, all too real feeling, dreams of a place she had never been. It was beautiful, sometimes she saw a sprawling castle, other times she was sitting by a shimmering lake with clear beautiful water.

The only consistent thing was the voice telling her to *'come home'. It was present* even in the ones about her fathers death.

Haven looked around her cabin to assure herself she had not woken her cabin mates. Thankfully, they were both sleeping soundly. Sighing, Haven laid her head back down, hoping to get at least a little more rest before breakfast.

Haven had no guesses as to what was happening in her mind. She hadn't wanted to tell anyone, instead, hoping that whatever it was would sort itself out eventually. With her dreams increasing in both intensity and quantity, she supposed that maybe it was time to admit something was wrong.

After this trip was over, she told herself, she'd tell her mom what was happening and give the therapist's office a call to schedule an appointment. All she had to do was get through this weekend.

A rustling sound pulled Haven from the light sleep she had fallen back into after being woken by her dreams. Turning her head slightly, she could see Chelsea pulling clothes out of her bag.

"Hey, sorry I didn't mean to wake you" She whispered

"It's no problem I usually wake early" Haven lied. She almost never woke early, enjoying being up all hours of the night whenever she could. Chelsea nodded,

"I'm just gonna hop in the shower"

Haven nodded as a response. She sat up in her bed and stretched her arms, yawning as she slid from under the thin blanket. She quickly changed into the simple black leggings and old T-shirt she would be wearing for the hike beginning directly after breakfast. It wasn't long before Sydney was up, Chelsea was out of the shower and the girls were ready to head to breakfast.

Breakfast had been wonderful with plates of eggs presumably laid by the small chicken flock they had seen on the tour yesterday, lots of toast and cups of orange juice. After everyone finished eating, the students gathered in front of the main house to wait for their trail leaders to appear. While they were waiting, Mr Chaplin began informing the students about a slight change of plans,

"Attention students, last night we made the decision to go in two separate groups to cut down the size of the group on the trail. While we wait for our guides to appear I will read off the names of the students in group one, which will be escorted by myself along with our two trail guides" He paused, pulled a small paper from his pocket and began reading,

"Chase, Roman, Sydney, Chelsea, Haven, Sarah" Mr Chaplin announced, he rattled off a few more names Haven didn't recognize before he put the paper back in his pocket. Ms McElderoy began speaking,

"Those of you that were just called will stay here, the rest are free to do as they please, overseen by me for the approximate two hours it should take to complete the hike"

About half of the students accompanied by Ms McElderoy walked off. Some in the direction of the cabins and others back to where everyone had had breakfast.

"Perfect timing" Mr Chaplin stated as the two owners and trail guides walked out of the main house to where the remainder of the students were standing. Haven was glad to be with her friends, she didn't know any of the other people in her group except in passing.

"For this hike I," Mr Sharp pointed to himself, "Will be in the front guiding the hike accompanied by your teacher. Rodney," Mr Sharp pointed to the other owner, "Will be following in the back of the group to make sure we don't lose anyone. Now if all of you will please follow me" He began walking toward the main trailhead that had been pointed out yesterday.

"About halfway through the hike we will stop at a lookout point for a small break, to catch our breaths and get some water" He held up a small bag Haven hadn't noticed he was carrying.

"This bag contains all of the water bottles we could ever need so don't worry, I will be doing all the heavy lifting"

***

They were about thirty minutes into their hike when Sydney looped her arm through Havens. At first, A moment hadn't gone by that someone wasn't saying something. Then about 15 minutes ago the first snake had been spotted and quickly it became a competition to see who could spot the most wildlife. Mr Rodney had pointed out that you were more likely to see something if you were quiet and since then the group hadn't made much sound except for a few of the boys that had been pushing each other around. They had quickly been shushed by the other students, earning a laugh from both trail guides.

Sydney leaned over and with a nod of her head toward Roman, she whispered,

"There really is something about him"

Haven smirked a little and heard Chelsea snicker. Smirks and snickers aside, Sydney was kind of right. There was something about Roman that seemed to draw people in, he had an air about him Haven had never noticed before this trip. Maybe that was why

Sydney seemed a little infatuated, maybe she was feeling the same thing. It helped that he was hot, very tall and clearly muscular with hair cropped close to his dark brown skin and light brown eyes that seemed to say,

"I know something you don't"

Overall, he seemed rather mischievous from the little that Haven had been around him. There was also this thing about him Haven couldn't quite place, it radiated off him. If she didn't know any better, she would say that he had some sort of magical power and it filled the air around him. If only something like that could be true, maybe then magic really would exist and Haven could find out what actually happened to her dad.

The group continued hiking in silence eventually spotting three Blue Jays, another snake and possibly a deer a girl named Sarah swears she saw. The jury was still out on that one. By the time the students reached their break spot the silence had switched from being about not scaring off the wildlife to the fact that everyone had at least one part of their body that was hurting and were all tired.

Silence was quickly replaced with small gasps once everyone paused long enough to look around and take in the scenery.

They found themselves standing in a large clearing adorned with the same log benches from where they ate their meals. Only now, the benches overlooked the edge of a cliff. Right at the edge there was a very old wooden rail that stopped anyone from going too far over the edge, possibly to try to get a better look at the small waterfall off in the distance.

"Be careful, that railing hasn't been replaced in years" Mr Sharp told the group as he handed out water bottles. Haven took one and walked quickly over to the edge where most of the students had gathered. Upon closer inspection, the edge of the cliff didn't drop straight down but was more like a steep hill. It was filled with tall pine trees and some very thorny looking bushes.

Haven sucked in a breath, something about this place felt so different. There was an electric zing in the air that she had felt ever since stepping off the bus. She also noticed that being around a fairly large group of people didn't tire her like it normally did. Haven had no idea what, exactly, she was feeling but it felt as if the woods were calling to her, pulling her in.

For some strange reason, whatever Haven was feeling reminded her of the dreams she had been having.

"We will break here for fifteen minutes before continuing on. The trail leads to a rather impressive view of that waterfall" Mr Sharp pointed as he spoke.

Both Rodney and Mr Sharp went and sat down on some logs. Haven couldn't seem to pull herself away from the point right at the edge of the clearing. Even after almost all the other students had sat down, she was still glued to the railing. Roman was the only student still standing there with her. His eyes were glassy and he had this homesick sort of look on his face.

At the risk of sounding insane Haven leaned over and quietly said to him,

"Can you feel it too?" His eyes met hers and he nodded.

Within the blink of an eye, it was like a dam had broken. Suddenly the ground under her feet was gone. Haven was standing on nothing. No, she wasn't even standing, now she was tumbling, rolling, falling down over the edge of the cliff. Someone was screaming, Haven couldn't tell if it was herself or someone else.

Chapter Five

When Haven came to, she almost wished she was still knocked out. The pounding in her head was worse than any hangover or headache she'd ever experienced.

"What the hell happened?" A deep voice off to her right spoke.

Haven startled and looked over to see that Roman was on the ground only ten feet away. She stood quickly with black spots dotting her vision and tried to get over to where he was, noting the scratch marks up and down her arms and legs as she went. Thankfully nothing felt broken.

As if the ground somehow opening up causing her to fall down the side of a cliff wasn't odd enough, what she was looking at now was worse.

Roman was covered in blood, similar to her but with one small differing factor. Haven had actual cuts and marks, something to show where the blood had come from. Roman did not.

Haven checked over Roman as best she could with no prior medical experience and still not quite believing what she was seeing. While he looked injured, rough and generally in bad shape, there wasn't a single mark to show why he looked that way. Examining his arm, Haven found quite a bit of drying blood but nothing else; no cut, no mark, not even a damn thorn stuck in his skin. Haven had plenty of those.

"Wow I must've really hit my head" She mumbled.

"I'm sure it's fine," Roman reassured her, a dazed look in his eye, "It's probably just the adrenaline confusing you."

Haven took a deep breath and nodded, "That makes sense"

Standing and helping Roman to follow, Haven took a few quick glances around. She quickly decided the first thing they needed to do was figure out where they had landed and which way they had come from. It didn't take long, Haven was pretty sure of the direction they had fallen based on the two trails of broken lower branches, bushes that looked like they had been plowed over and the fact that only one way was uphill.

"There's no way we can climb back up," Roman said, following her gaze.

Haven sighed, he was right. They couldn't even see to old brittle railing they had been standing by before falling, too far down the mountain to even think about attempting to climb back up. Their best bet was probably to wait and hope someone found them before nightfall. Haven looked around again, taking inventory of the area around them. She saw trees, trees and more trees.

Annoyed and unnerved by their situation, Haven kicked at the ground, groaning when the impact made her injuries scream. She was covered in scratches, cuts, thorns and had ripped a few holes in her clothes.

"Are you alright?" Roman asked, no longer leaning on her for support.

"Yeah" She responded. Other than a growing headache, none of her wounds appeared overly severe.

"We should clean that out somehow" Roman pointed to one of the larger gashes on her leg. It looked like the leggings had helped prevent her legs from getting completely torn up but they were only able to do so much. There was a five inch mark on her lower leg, it oozed blood but luckily didn't appear deep or wide enough to require stitches.

"Yeah um, let's look around for our water bottles" Haven spoke. They had been holding them before they fell.

A quick search turned up nothing. Apparently their water bottles had been lucky, staying on the cliff edge high above them. If only the bottles had fallen instead of them.

"Okay then" Haven groaned as she leaned up against a tree.

"Wait here while I take a quick look around" Roman said to her.

"No way. I'm not staying here alone!" She protested, having seen enough horror movies to know that splitting up was never a good idea.

"I'm just going to take a quick look around, see if I see any water sources or a trail. It's possible the owners had trails carved out down here since we should be close to the waterfall. You are more than welcome to follow if you want but it's probably smarter to stay here" Roman stated simply. Haven felt like he was entirely too calm considering the circumstances.

As soon as Roman started to walk away, she made a show of following him. He chuckled a bit and said,

"Alright. I thought it would be better for you to rest your leg but okay." He put his hands up in a mock surrender which caused Haven to laugh a little and be thankful she wasn't stuck out here alone. She may not know Roman much but she'd take a kind acquaintance over being alone in this situation any day.

They picked one direction and headed in it, both pretty sure it was the direction of the waterfall. While walking, Roman brought up the fact that one of the owners had mentioned earlier that the trail the rest of the students would be heading down went right by the waterfall, or at least had a pretty good view of it.

After taking a moment to panic about two students falling over the edge of a small cliff, the rest of the group would most likely be headed back to the main grounds to call for help, maybe even organize a search party. Haven and Roman quickly decided that the best plan was to attempt to run into the group, or at least find some sort of trail to lead them back to the main grounds. This direction also provided their best shot at finding some sort of creek, water source or even the waterfall itself to rinse out some of Havens wounds. If it didn't work, they had been breaking off branches as they went along to lead them back to where they landed at the bottom of the cliff.

After about 15 minutes of walking Haven paused,

"Roman, I think I hear something. Can you hear that?"

He listened for a moment, "Yes, yes I can. I think it's this way, come on" Roman picked up a jog and Haven followed, the pain of her fall numbed by hope.

They followed what had been assumed as the sound of a waterfall for only five minutes before they stopped dead in their tracks,

"Wow" Both Roman and Haven declared, voices full of awe.

They had found the waterfall and it was beautiful.

Chapter Six

Crystal clear water poured from the mountain somewhere high above them. The water gathered in a large pool with several smaller creeks flowing from it. The urge to forego all reason and jump in was incredibly high.

Roman and Haven sat on a cluster of rocks at the edge of the lake. Roman dipped his hand down, running it through the sparkling clear water.

"Damn that's cold" He remarked, drying his hand on the edge of his shirt.

Haven reached down and briefly dipped her fingers in the water. Roman was right, the water was cold, near freezing if she had to guess.

"Okay here we go," Haven sucked in a breath of air and gathered her strength to rinse the wound on her leg with the freezing water. She lowered her leg down to the surface of the lake, straining her muscles to keep it suspended over the water while she splashed some over the gash. Roman grimaced as Haven splashed as much water as she could over her leg before she could no longer stand the bite of the icy water.

"Alright, that's going to have to be good enough," She said, trying to stand.

At least her wounds weren't so full of dirt now, Haven thought. She hoped that that would help stave off any infections. Haven started to ask Roman if he needed any help rinsing off his wounds but then remembered how he hadn't appeared to have any when she looked him over after they fell. Haven still assumed she must have hit her head since it was impossible to survive that fall with little more than a slightly torn shirt. She also hoped that if Roman needed any help, he would ask.

Haven took a minute to admire the waterfall. It was truly gorgeous, easily one of the most beautiful things she had ever seen. It would have been even more beautiful if they weren't currently lost in the woods with it. She stumbled slightly as she moved to walk around, stretching her legs a bit and trying to get her bearings. The adrenaline from the fall was quickly wearing off, leaving Haven feeling especially run down and slightly dizzy.

"Do you need any help?" Roman asked as he stood and reached out to balance her.

"No, I think I'm good," Haven answered.

"Well, let me know if you need anything. You probably lost a decent bit of blood"

Haven nodded. That could help explain the slightly weightless feeling she was now experiencing.

"Not having to spend the night in the woods would make me a whole lot better" She remarked. Roman offered a half smile at her comment but she could tell he fully agreed with her.

"Let's try to find the trail" He said

Minutes passed, all of which turned up nothing. There didn't appear to be any signs of life around other than the broken branches to point them back where they came and more bushes full of thorns like the ones covering the cliffside.

Almost an hour had passed since they had initially fallen, causing feelings of hopelessness to begin to surface in Haven. Luckily she did not have to deal with them for long before Roman shouted,

"Hey look! I think this might be it!"

Havens gaze darted to where he pointed. Across the small lake clearing, about 15 feet from where Roman was standing was what could be a trail covered in overgrown weeds and a tangle of branches that formed a sort of arch. If it was the trail, it hadn't seen people in a long time.

"I'm not sure, it looks kinda iffy " Haven remarked, walking over to where Roman stood.

"I get that but I haven't seen anything else that even remotely looks like a trail and unless you actually want to spend the night out here waiting for rescue, I say we try that way"

Roman spoke with a sort of confidence that helped put Haven at ease. Still, there was something about the trail he had found that set off warning bells in her head. The fact that it looked like something straight out of a fairytale didn't help, the way the branches weaved together, the vines that grew across the arch of branches and draped towards the ground, the vibrant green grass, it was all very whimsical and bizarre.

Haven supposed taking the strange trail was a risk; they could end up even more lost. But they could also end up finding a main trail that could lead them back to the main house or even the group they'd been separated from. It helped that Haven really did not want to spend the night out here.

Giving the lake clearing one last once over and finding nothing, Haven hesitantly agreed,

"Alright, I'll follow you"

Romans answering smile was nothing short of canine. Haven could've sworn she saw the hint of fangs, but she shook her head, telling herself that that was impossible. She knew she must have seriously hit her head to be seeing things like that. Haven hoped they'd find their way out of this forest quickly so she could get herself examined.

Roman walked towards the trail, moving loose branches and vines out of his way as he went. Haven was a bit slower and a few steps behind him. The air seemed to still as Roman took one step under the large arch of branches and disappeared. He simply vanished, Haven couldn't believe what she was seeing, which was nothing, absolutely nothing.

"Roman?" Haven shouted, "Where are you?"

Haven ran the last few steps to where she had seen him, ignoring the slight twinge caused by the gash in her leg. Looking as far down the trail as she could, Haven saw nothing. There was no hint that he had ever even been there at all. Stepping under the shadowy canopy of branches felt like it took hours. Time spun, worlds blended. Haven had the distinct feeling of falling. Of being everywhere and nowhere all at once. The last thing she saw was the shadows of the trail ahead before they engulfed her.

Chapter Seven

"*N*o she's not ready yet, Robert"

"*Yes she is, Morana. We need to tell her the truth!*"

Haven's parents were fighting, as they often did after she went to sleep.

"*I say when she is ready Robert and it is not now!*"

"*Morana she is a teenager, she has a right to know her truth, her history!*" *Havens fathers voice lowered slightly, still with underlying hints of anger.*

"*Fine! Maybe it's me who's not ready yet,*" *Her mother admitted, "I want her to enjoy life for just a little while longer, this life! She'll be starting high school soon, I don't see why this conversation can't wait until she's just a little older." Her mother paused, "I want her to have all the normal experiences. I want her to grow, get her license, go to prom, do all the things normal teenagers do." Her mothers voice carried an air of sadness as she spoke.*

"But she is not a normal teenager my love." Haven's father said, tucking a strand of hair behind her mothers ear. Pulling her mom in close her father finished their conversation with,

"I fear we are running out of time"

***

Haven woke with a start. Lurching forward into a sitting position, she rubbed at her temples. Her parents often had conversations like that, unaware Haven had snuck downstairs to listen. She never understood what her parents meant, at one point she'd asked them about it. They had simply brushed her off and quit having late night conversations in the kitchen. After her father died, Haven tried again to get her mom to explain some of the things she'd heard. Whenever she asked it usually ended with the two of them fighting so she simply quit asking. Why it had been playing in her head while she was passed out, Haven had no idea.

Groaning as a headache pounded through her head, Haven looked around to see where she was. Deja vu hit her when the first thing she noticed was Roman sprawled about five feet from her. Except instead of them finding themselves on the forest floor this time they found themselves sprawled in some sort of meadow.

Immediately scrambling over to where Roman was, she gently shook him and said,

"Roman. Wake up!"

He did not stir.

"Roman" She said again, putting her fingers to his neck to check his pulse. Thankfully it beat strongly underneath her fingertips.

Groaning, Roman finally began to stir. Opening his eyes he said, "Hello"

Haven threw her arms around him. She barely knew the guy but apparently getting lost in the woods and then somehow traveling through a strange archway to god only knows where, could bring two people closer.

"I'm okay" He mumbled.

Haven let go of him and helped him sit up.

"Do you have any idea where we are?" He asked.

Haven shook her head and looked around, they were definitely not in the dark North Carolina woods anymore. Haven and Roman were now surrounded by tall grasses and the occasional wildflower. Trees off to their right were the only hint as to where they might have come from. The fact that the trees appeared to be glowing was another issue entirely.

"Maybe we died and are now in heaven." Haven half joked.

Roman chuffed a laugh at her comment. Off in the distance Haven could see a very small log cabin sitting in a cluster of tall oak trees. Smoke was coming out of the chimney, there was a clothesline and a small garden next to it, along with a well worn path that led to what might be a road. Overall the cabin looked warm and cozy. Hopefully someone there could tell them what had happened and not murder them after they did it.

Haven got to her feet and then helped Roman up. Looking to the small cluster of trees besides them, now fading in their glow, she asked,

"What do you think happened?"

"Hell if I know" Roman responded.

Haven stretched her arms and legs out, testing how sturdy she felt on her feet. Overall, she felt like she had just stepped off of a ride at the fair, dizzy and kind of disoriented. The pounding headache certainly didn't help.

"So, should we go see if whoever lives there can help us or if they're just gonna cook us and eat us?" Roman asked

"Well it appears like we don't have much of a choice. I guess we're just going to have to hope they don't eat queer people" Haven responded

Roman laughed deep, the sound vibrating around them.

"That was a good one, H" He said, clapping her on the shoulder. His laughter was contagious, Haven found herself carrying a small laugh all the way up to the edge of the property that held the cabin.

They paused and quickly examined the structure before them. Now that they were closer, Haven could see a small porch and a few chickens scratching around in the side yard.

"H?" Haven asked, attempting to clear her nerves.

"Yeah, it's your new nickname."

Both appeared slightly nervous, Haven more so than Roman. His lack of nervousness set Haven a little on edge, she wondered why he didn't seem as tense as she was. Havens first guess was that Roman thought he could overpower whoever was inside the cabin if it came down to that. Her second guess was that she was hallucinating and Roman was something her mind had conjured to help her feel less alone. She liked the second answer a lot less than the first.

Attempting to shake off her nerves, Haven took a step forward.

"Let's do this" She said, more to herself than anyone else.

They walked in silence up to the large wood door. Haven took a deep breath and knocked. It took only a moment for someone to open the door.

"Hello" Said the older woman, "My name is Binah, Would you like to come in?"

Haven looked at Roman, he shrugged his shoulders.

"I promise not to harm you" The woman named Binah said.

"That's exactly what someone who wanted to harm us would say" Roman spoke under his breath, eliciting a nervous laugh from Haven.

Binah appeared harmless. A few small wrinkles littered her pale face and gray hair that appeared to have been brown at one time in her life was pulled in a low bun at the nape of her neck. She stood confident with her head held high even though she only came up to Havens shoulders. The older woman didn't exactly scream Ax Murderer but Haven supposed the best ones never did.

"Actually we just need some information if you don't mind," Haven spoke.

Binah nodded her head and asked,

"Of course, what do you need dear?"

Haven glanced at Roman before she said, "Well my friend and I were on a trip and we got lost. I was wondering if you could point us in the direction of Raleigh, North Carolina?" If they could figure out the direction of their state's capital then they should be fine, the town Haven lived in was not too far from there.

Realization seemed to dawn on Binah as she spoke,

"Oh well my dears you are very far from home aren't you"

Both Roman and Haven nodded.

"Alright well why don't you two go have a seat over there and I'll bring you out some tea and we can get this mess all cleared up" Binah pointed to some wrought iron chairs sitting around a small table at the edge of her garden. Roman spoke before Haven had a chance to,

"That sounds good, thank you." He nodded his head and moved to the garden chairs, pulling Haven along with him.

The pair sat down in the chairs and waited for their host to come out of her house. Leg bouncing, Haven took in the space around her. It was truly a cute little house, albeit a bit lonely out here with no neighbors. There were no other houses or buildings as far as the eye could see. Haven wondered where the road leading from the cabin would go if they were to follow it.

The door opened and Binah appeared carrying a tray with some cups and a pitcher full of tea.

"There we are," Bianh said, setting the tray down on the table. She poured Roman and Haven each a cup and handed it to them. Roman drank greedily from his, as did Haven, albeit a bit more hesitantly. The tea was iced and refreshing. Once they had each set their cups down Binah started,

"So you say you are from this, Raleigh?"

Both Roman and Haven nodded.

"Yes, it's in North Carolina," Roman said. Binah held a hand up to hush him before he could continue.

"Yes I know where that is." Binah paused before adding, "I'm afraid you are no longer in North Carolina. In fact, you are not even in that realm"

Chapter Eight

Haven nearly spit out the tea she was drinking.

"I'm sorry what do you mean, *realm*?" She loudly blurted.

"Alright dear lets stay calm, give me a chance to explain" Binah looked startled, as if she wasn't the one who had just told them they were in another realm.

Haven could only try to hold her mouth closed and glance at Roman who looked almost as surprised as she was.

"It is simple" Binah started, "When you were lost in the woods in your North Carolina you must have stumbled through a pathway that brought you here. To the fae realm."

Haven could hardly contain herself, a pathway, a fae realm? None of that made sense. Things like that weren't possible, sure something weird had happened but stumbling through a portal into a *fae* realm? That was absurd.

Haven started to protest, earning a sharp glance from Binah. Roman, to her surprise, kept quiet, "My dear if you let me continue I believe I could explain." Binah said.

Haven nodded, although she wasn't sure what this woman could say that would sound less ridiculous than a fae realm.

"A very long time ago the fae lived among humans. We lived peacefully for a long while until the humans started to fear us, for what we could do" Binah paused, Haven was sure the look on her face was nothing but shock and disbelief.

"A war was started and it lasted many years, thousands died on both sides. Our seven fae rulers came together in an attempt to save what was left of the fae. While some fae had extraordinary powers, we were severely outnumbered. An idea was born to create a world where the fae could live in peace, a world without humans. A new realm."

Haven almost fell out of her chair, this was all so much to take in, yet she found herself clinging to Binahs every word.

"There have always been whispers of other realms so it was not something that seemed impossible. Some time passed before our rulers found a witch who could create a spell to give us the world you see now. But it would come at a cost, like everything does. All but one of the great leaders was willing to pay this cost. In the end, the majority won out and they began the preparations to create our realm."

Binah paused and refilled both Haven and Romans teacups before continuing,

"In total, the creation of the spell took about a month. There were some fae that were hesitant to come to this new world, especially after they heard what the cost would be." Binah paused again. Roman impatiently motioned for her to continue,

"You see, the fae would head into this new world alone, their rulers would be allowed two weeks to visit their new realm and set everything straight before they had to leave back to the human realm. If not, the spell holding our realm together would crumble, destroying our realm and everyone in it. The rulers won over the fae people with the fact that even though they themselves would not be able to lead them into this scary new place, the witch had assured them that their children would in time, take over and rule."

Binah cleared her throat, took a sip from her teacup and continued,

"Even though only three of our seven rulers had children at the time, it was enough to convince the people. The witch had promised that in time, children of the remaining four rulers would be born and find their way to this realm and take over as King or Queen. Several portals were left throughout the human realm for the future fae children to come through. And so, our realm was created, seven lands for the seven rulers."

Haven's jaw was on the ground, she was sure of it. All of this sounded like something straight out of one of her fantasy novels or the bedtime stories her parents had told her as a child.

Binah continued, "Since then, only two rulers have been left without their children taking over, all others have been accounted for and are now ruling in their rightful places. The lands without children from their royal bloodline are being ruled over by those in command at the time our realm was created.

One person rules over both lands, the reasons are unnecessary to get into right now but it is important to understand who holds the power. His official title is crown regent. Unfortunately, since it has been so long with no sign of the missing royals we have presumed them dead, most likely from being away from their magics too long. Which means the crown regent,"

Roman interrupted whatever Binah was going to say by asking,

"Wait, what do you mean, 'being away from their magics'?"

Haven couldn't believe that that was what he was wondering about. Not the fact that there could potentially be a whole other realm that existed and was apparently full of fae? Haven still hadn't decided if this was one big hallucination or not. Maybe she actually died when she fell and this was some sort of twisted afterlife.

"Very good question" Binah said with a nod towards Roman. "When our realm was created it took with it most of the fae magic that had been contained within the human realm. Some fae decided to stay in the human world rather than brave the new realm so trickles of power stayed with them, but for the most part all of our magics and power was transferred into our new realm"

"Oh" Was all Roman had to say.

Binah looked between the two teenagers sitting at the table with her. Haven could see the wheels turning in her head, Binah was clearly trying to decide whether or not to say something, to add one more piece of information into what she had already dumped on them.

"What?" Haven asked.

"Well all of the information brings us to where we are now, here sitting at this table" Binah appeared to be waiting for them to connect the dots.

"Wait, you don't mean?" Haven questioned.

Binah nodded, "Yes my dears. What I have told you and my being here tells us that you are not just some random lost kids, you are fae. In fact, you are more than that, you are fae royalty."

Roman looked like he might pass out. Haven felt exactly how he looked.

Chapter Nine

"**I** don't care what she says," Haven whisper yelled in case there were any spying ears in the grasses around them. Roman and Haven were currently in the field across from the cabin taking some time to process what they had just been told per Binahs suggestion.

"I don't believe her, there's no way I'm some fae royalty!" Haven continued.

In the minutes since Binah had told them that they were not only fae, but fae royalty, Haven had come to terms with the fact that they were definitely not in North Carolina and that they may even be in another realm, but fae royalty? That was a little too over the top.

Binah had assured the pair that more than likely they were the descendants of one of the bloodlines that had already been found and that they wouldn't have to rule in any official capacity if they did not want to. Apparently there was some sort of test to show what bloodline you belonged too and what powers you held. Supposedly, either the first born or the child with the most power was set to rule. Since children for each bloodline except the missing two had already been found it was unlikely that either Haven or Roman would be in a position to rule.

Forgetting the fact that they were supposedly fae, apparently they also had powers! Binah had told them that it was a little more in depth than them just simply having powers and that if they wanted her to, she could explain. At the time the pair had said no, choosing to think over the lot she had already dumped on them.

Haven sat down in the tall grass, Roman sat next to her. He seemed to be taking this whole thing a lot better than she was.

"Suppose I actually believe that I'm not just hallucinating and this is actually real, what would that even mean? What would happen? Would I just be sequestered off to some castle to live out my days as some sad princess? Would I ever see my mom again?"

Roman contemplated for a moment before responding, "Well I suppose you could probably take a portal like the one we came through and forget this ever happened"

Haven almost snorted, "Oh yeah, I travel to some strange land and find out that not only am I a princess but a fae princess, that I'm not even human and have magical powers and then I'm just supposed to forget about it?" Haven paused and shook her head, "How do we know that we're actually royalty and not just some lost kids. I mean, I don't even have the ears! Aren't fae supposed to have pointy ears?"

Roman laughed, "Well as Binah explained, being here with her means that you have to be royalty not simply some lost kid or fae from a family that decided to stay in the human realm. She explained to us that her sole purpose has been to guide the royal fae and that we wouldn't have appeared through the portal where we did if we weren't royal. As for the ear thing," He laughed again, "maybe we should ask her"

Haven smiled, Roman made some good points. They also needed to decide what they were going to do, the sun had started setting and soon it would be dark.

Haven drew her knees up to her chest, rested her head in her hands and asked Roman,

"How are you so calm about this? Isn't your head spinning out of control?"

Roman shrugged,

"I guess it just makes sense. I don't know, something about this seems right. It's like I finally found the missing puzzle piece and now I can see the whole picture."

Roman had a decent point. Right after her father died, Haven had imagined that his death would turn out to be some big mystery and lead her on this amazing adventure. Looking back, that was just a daughters way of coping with the loss of her beloved father. The thing was, this whole situation had the exact same feeling. It felt like this, right here, was leading up to a big adventure. Romans words said it perfectly; somehow, this felt right.

But first, Haven had some questions.

***

Binah was right where they left her, sitting at the table in her garden sipping tea.

"We have some questions" Haven announced

"I am sure you do." Binah responded and gestured for them to sit down. Haven and Roman sat, the latter picking up a small biscuit off a plate Binah must have placed on the table while they were out in the field. The sun beginning to set had Haven a little on edge. She hoped they could get this figured out before the sun went down and all the light disappeared.

"Out with it child" Binah gently insisted, as if Havens momentary pause was keeping the woman from something important.

Haven took a deep breath, "First, why don't we have the pointy ears?"

She gestured to Binahs long pointed ears. When they first met Binah, Haven assumed she had hallucinated them. Now she was almost sure they were real.

Binah chuckled, "Of everything you could ask, that is what you want to know first?"

"Yes." Roman stated. Apparently not having the cool ears was bothering him as well.

Binah sighed, "It's simple, you have lived in the human realm your whole lives. The magic that makes fae the way we are, that gives us our powers, hasn't taken hold in the two of you yet. If you spend enough time in the fae realm, your features will change to what they are supposed to be. Just like how your powers will develop."

Haven had planned to ask how they were supposed to get back home but she got stuck on Binahs words,

"Powers?" She asked.

Binah nodded, "All fae have powers but it can vary from fae to fae. There isn't one rule that determines how powerful a fae may be. For example, you may come from a lineage of incredibly powerful fae that have ruled for centuries, but there is no guarantee you will have even a fraction of their power. Although, the type of powers does usually stay consistent within a line. If both parents are blessed with the ability to bend water, then more often than not, the child will have similar powers."

Haven appeared stunned, Roman slightly less so. This was a lot of information for them to take in at once. Binah must have noticed how overwhelmed the pair had become because she stood and announced,

"I believe the two of you need to rest. We can talk more tomorrow, for tonight I will set you up in the spare rooms in my cabin"

"Wait!" Haven called after her, standing to follow the older woman, "What about my mother? She has to be worried sick! I just disappeared." Haven wasn't entirely sure how long it had been since she and Roman went over that cliff, but surely her mother had to know she was missing by now. Someone from the school must have told her.

Binah gave Haven a pitying look, "My dear I believe she knows exactly where you are. As I told you earlier, you come from fae parents so more than likely when she found out where you were going she would have known where you would end up."

Binah paused for a moment before continuing,

"Most of the fae rulers and those from their lines know where the portals are. She would know what happened as soon as someone told her where you disappeared."

Haven felt faint; to think that not only had her mom had been lying to her, but that she secretly had some other life as a ruler of a magical race of fae? The idea that her mom could have lied about something so big and important made her heart hurt. What about her dad? Did he know? Was he also fae? Was this what those late night fights were about? There were too many questions tumbling through her head.

Haven felt Romans steadying hand on her back. Leaning into him slightly, she simply nodded and followed Binah into the house. All the while wondering how her friend could be so calm about all of this.

Chapter Ten

Startling from a deep sleep, I knew. Down to my bones I knew that the time so many of us had been waiting for was here. *She* was here. I had to alert everyone.

Quickly sliding out of bed, I yanked my shirt over my head and sped out the door. Running down the castle halls, I headed to where he was.

Jostling him into waking, I said,

"It's time"

Of course he knew exactly what I meant. We had been planning this for years. Everything was finally starting to come together, all the pieces of the puzzle were starting to click into place and finally we could see a picture.

He sat up groggily. I knew how much this meant to him. After everything he'd been through at the hands of his father, he deserved a win. One final win to save the realm.

Together we stood and went over to his window that overlooked the sprawling grounds.

Grounds that if all went according to plan, *she* would soon be walking across.

It was quiet and dark, it had been that way for a long time. Even when the sun was shining and birds were chirping there was a suffocating air surrounding this place that had once been so beautiful, not that either of us were ever there to see it.

It was our hope that the two of us, along with others, would be able to bring this place back to what it once was, or was supposed to be. We wouldn't be able to do that without *her*. Hopefully she survived long enough to take her throne and eliminate the poison that had seeped into the walls here.

Unfortunately, neither him, nor I, would likely be around to enjoy the life she'd be able to give our people. Dismantling the horrors of our kingdoms would likely bring us down right along with them.

Chapter Eleven

Binah set Haven and Roman up on two cots in her small spare room. The cots weren't overly comfortable but with a nice blanket they would be more than fine for a night. Haven was just glad they weren't still lost in a forest.

Binah had quickly offered a bite to eat, shown them where the bathroom was and sent them to bed. Haven had been pleasantly surprised to find out that even in another realm indoor plumbing was a thing. Especially seeing as all of Binahs lights were candles and the floor of her cottage was dirt. Binah must have seen the look on Havens face because she smiled and said,

"Tomorrow"

Whatever that meant.

Now, Haven was lying on her cot looking at the candle lit lamp Binah had set on the small wooden dresser next to the door. She had been tossing and turning for what felt like hours. Haven wouldn't be surprised to see the sun start to peek through the window. Blowing out a breath, she crawled from her cot and walked past where Roman was snoring softly. Quietly slipping through the door, she padded down the dim hall to the kitchen intent on getting a sip of water.

Haven paused when she came to the doorway of the kitchen. She had not thought Binah would still be awake at this hour, but there she was, sitting at a small round kitchen table with another candle lamp at its center.

"Hello" Haven spoke softly.

"Hello there, come sit child." Binah gestured to the empty chair across from her.

"I hope I did not wake you, I just couldn't sleep."

Binah responded with a soft smile,

"Nonsense, don't worry about it. I figured you might need a little more guidance before you would be able to rest"

Haven felt like a *little* more guidance might not be the best way to put it. She definitely had a long way to go before she accepted this as something that was actually happening. Even now, she wondered when she was going to wake up, this all having been a very intense dream.

"I just don't understand" Haven mumbled

"What is it that you don't understand?" Binah asked gently, she reached across the table and rested her hand on Havens arm. Her touch was very comforting, already helping to calm Havens anxious mind. Binah's attention felt like what Haven would imagine a grandmothers attention felt like.

"Any of it, all of it" She said, "My parents were perfectly normal. They both had normal jobs, they had date nights, my dad got my mom flowers, we went on family trips; everything about their lives seemed so normal. Until my dad died, everything was perfect. We were friends with our neighbors, I had a big room with a pink canopy over my bed until I was thirteen, my parents bought me whatever books I wanted. I understand that kids don't know everything about their parents, but for them to have not only secret lives, but to not even be *human?* It just seems too crazy to believe."

Something Haven said seemed to have unsettled Binah. Now, she was looking at Haven with a strange look in her eye, as if connecting some dots in her head.

"You say your father died?"

"Yes, about two years ago. It was a car accident."

Binah seemed to consider this for a few moments before saying,

"Well, it appears as though nothing is as it seems"

"What is that supposed to mean?" Haven asked

"Nothing you need to concern yourself with just yet. For now, you should head to bed and try to get some rest. You have a big day tomorrow."

Binah got up swiftly, before Haven could ask anymore questions, and exited the kitchen. Why did she have to be so cryptic? What was so big about tomorrow? Granted, any day spent in a supposed fae realm was a big day for Haven.

Her thoughts had Havens mind spinning in circles as she got up to get the glass of water she had originally come for. She hoped that tomorrow would bring some answers. Although, if Binah continued to be as evasive and cryptic as she was just now, Haven had a feeling those answers might take a while, if she ever got them at all.

Chapter Twelve

After Binah dropped her line about nothing being as it seems and thoroughly freaking Haven out since she would say no more, Haven went back to bed where she eventually fell into a fitful sleep.

"Haven" Roman whispered, shaking her gently.

"I'm up, I'm up!" Haven grumbled.

"Alright I'll leave you alone." Roman laughed a little, "By the way, Binah made breakfast"

That woke Haven right up. Not the offering of breakfast but the reminder of where they were and the idea that she might be able to get more information out of Binah while they ate.

Haven got herself up and made her way into the bathroom where she washed up as much as she could. She was deeply startled to find that most of her scratches and wounds from yesterday had already healed. Normally she healed fairly quickly but nowhere near as fast as the rapidly disappearing scratches up and down her body.

Chasing those thoughts from her mind, Haven rinsed out her mouth as best she could. She hadn't been able to brush her teeth last night since Binah didn't have any spare toothbrushes. At the time, she had just been grateful that Binah knew what those were. Her next thought had been if there was such a thing as a fae dentist and if the sharp canines Binah had needed special maintenance. Haven asked Binah when the older woman was showing them the bathroom and with a slight laugh, Binah told her that there are fae that specialize in healing and if you needed something done with your teeth or *fangs* that was where you went.

As she exited the bathroom, Haven cringed slightly at the film on her teeth from her previous meals and sleeping. Occasionally, when the depression was at its worst and she was mostly staying in bed, her teeth went a day or two without being brushed. It normally didn't bother her quite as much. Being clear headed and not being able to brush her teeth was something else entirely. It was also strange to Haven that her anxiety had yet to bother her. One would think that something like this would cause everything to become ten times worse yet ever since falling into this land, her anxiety had been mostly silent. This place washed a sense of calm over her. Haven had the brief thought that maybe Roman was right and they actually did belong here.

Sighing, Haven pushed those thoughts from her mind and headed down the hall, finding Binah and Roman immersed in conversation. The kitchen table was covered with plates of what appeared to be eggs, bacon and a fancy looking type of fruit. Haven made a plate for herself, grabbed a cup of water and sat down with them.

The topic of conversation was what royal family Binah thought Roman was from. She was telling him all about the five currently in power and the two currently being ruled over by what Binah referred to as an imposter. By the time the conversation ended, Haven gathered that Binah thought Roman descended from Norwood, a small island kingdom across the sea from Drailia, the kingdom they were currently in.

"What about the two missing bloodlines?" Roman asked.

Binah cut an odd glance at Haven, who had a mouth full of bacon. Apparently the woman hadn't completely recovered from whatever Haven had said last night. Haven sighed, at least she wasn't looking at her like she was from outer space anymore.

"Well," Binah paused, "The Montali queen and the Rionach king were the two most powerful fae rulers and evidently, the same ones that no one has been able to find. Shortly after the war ended and our realm was created, our rulers went their separate ways and the two of them dropped off the face of the earth. No one could track their magics and no signs of them showed up for a long while. The crown regent, whose kingdom you are currently in and that took over for Queen Montali, has been sending spies into the human realm ever since they went missing to try to find out what happened. It is common practice for each kingdom to have scouts in the human world that keep up with the times and let us know what is going on over there"

Binah paused, taking a sip of water before continuing,

"It is how we have such similar things as the humans have, such as what you called indoor plumbing" Binah sent a small smile Havens way, "Supposedly, the spies for the crown regent have found no sign of our missing rulers."

"You said, 'supposedly'. What do you mean by that?" Haven asked

"Many believe that the Montali and Rionach bloodlines simply died off when their powers were given over to create the fae world. Others believe that their disappearance is due to who is in control now and has been since they left our realm after it was created. You see, King Rionach left his kingdom in the care of his sister, she was powerful but not nearly as powerful as he. He had a common fire magic that many are also blessed with but none with quite as much strength as he did. When his sister became the top contender to take over in his place, she welcomed the role with open arms.

She turned out to be the wrong choice because about fifty or so years ago, the crown regent that took over in Queen Montalis stead pushed her out of power and took over rule of Shaston, King Rionachs kingdom. She died not long after that. The main issue is who took over in place of Queen Montali."

Binah took another moment to get a sip of water and catch her breath before continuing,

"You see, Queen Montali had no living relatives which meant that the position went to someone of her choosing. She chose her second in power, now known as the crown regent. Before our realm was created, he was known as a passionate man with a thirst for power. That had never been a problem until we came here and he got that power he had been craving. It didn't take long for him to become bitter and cruel. From the outside looking in, you may not notice anything, but if you look close enough you will begin to see things that paint him in a very dark light. Servants that won't look him in the eye, young girls that go missing after an event at the castle, the fact that our relationships with the other kingdoms have been strained ever since he took the power from King Rionachs sister."

Binah shuddered, Haven could tell the words were hard for the older woman to get out but she pushed ahead nonetheless,

"Many believe that he is the true source of evil. There are whispers that he is responsible for his wife's death. He was married for almost twenty years before his wife died giving birth to their second child. The child unfortunately did not make it. Some say the pain of the experience is what killed his wife. Although, the red marks around her throat found on her body might say otherwise.

His first son now lives on in the shadow of his father and is set to take over once the crown regents immortal life ends or he relinquishes control. Some have speculated that he is also responsible for the fact that we haven't heard anything about our two missing royals. Whether it was an assassination that ended them before they were able to have children or he is lying about the fact that there has never been any trace of them, no one knows. The only thing that we can be certain about is that the crown regent is a tricky and bitter man who will not hesitate to end anyone that stands in between him and what he wants."

***

After Binah's eerie words at breakfast that erased all questions from Havens mind and left her thoroughly unsettled, the older woman took them out to help feed her chickens and offered them a choice.

"You may go back to the human realm by way of a portal," She had told them, Otherwise, she would secure travel to the castle here in Drailia where they may be tested to find out what bloodline they came from and what powers they held. Binah had also reaffirmed that more than likely, neither would rank powerful enough to rule unless they had been born from one of the missing bloodlines, therefore having no competition for the throne. Yesterday she had made it seem like that wasn't even an option, like there was no possible way a child had finally come about from the missing bloodlines but today, her words painted a different picture.

Haven sat in the middle of Binah's garden admiring some roses she had planted on a trellis while attempting to decide what she was going to do about Binah's offer. Eventually Roman walked up and sat next to her.

Ten minutes of silence passed before Haven spoke,

"You're going to stay aren't you?"

He nodded, "Yes I am and I think you should too"

"Why? I have nothing here for me"

"And what do you have back in the human realm?" He asked, a slight bite in his tone.

"My mother!" She snapped

Roman took a moment to reign in his temper, Haven did the same. She wondered why he cared if she stayed seeing as it more than likely would not affect him.

"Your mother may be there but think of all you could have here. You'd have a chance to find out who you really are, you'd be able to learn so many things and grow in a way not even possible back home."

Haven started to say something before she was cut off by Roman,

"Think about it, do you really believe that you can go back to the human realm, choose some boring college to go to, celebrate your birthday and simply continue to live as if this never happened?"

Out of everything he said, Haven wondered how he knew today was her birthday. She hadn't told him, seeing as they barely knew each other before they were thrown into this mess together. She decided to let it go seeing as she had much bigger things to worry about. Binah had made it clear that if they decided to go back to the human realm they would be unable to return. Apparently it was some sort of failsafe to prevent someone who was not dedicated to this life one hundred percent from getting ahold of a crown.

"Alright, " Haven sighed. After all, she supposed she'd be able to go back to the human realm if she eventually wanted to. When she really thought about it, Haven couldn't see the harm in staying just a little while longer.

Chapter Thirteen

As soon as Haven and Roman told Binah their decisions, a small horse drawn carriage had shown up fully equipped for the day and a half long trip it would take to get to the castle. There was no roof, it was basically a platform on wheels with some hay, pallets, blankets and a spot at the front for the driver to sit. They had also been told that someone was already awaiting their arrival at the castle.

Haven had chuckled when she saw the carriage pull up less than five minutes after she talked to Binah. The older woman was currently packing them each a sack with some apples and bread for their journey.

"Are you sure you're ready for this H?" Roman asked as they stood watching the horses graze.

"No" She responded, only half joking.

"Oh come on, it'll be fun" Roman nudged her shoulder playfully.

"Mhmm sure" Haven said, looking at Roman where he was standing next to her. He seemed overly excited whereas Havens stomach was churning with nerves.

"Alright royals!" Binah announced as she walked towards them with their packs clutched in her hands. Haven did not particularly like being called that but it was better than children, a word which had been bugging Haven since she'd met the woman.

"This road will take you straight to the castle. Stopping once at an inn to stay the night and rest the horses. You are in very good hands with Trevor over there"

Binah waved to the young boy who would be driving the carriage. He barely looked 13 but Binah assured Haven he would get them to the castle with no problem.

As they walked over to the back of the carriage, Binah handed them each their packs and a cloak for the journey. Havens cloak was dark green and had a few holes but its thickness would certainly keep her warm since she was still only wearing the tattered leggings and shirt she had gone on the hike with.

With the cool breeze in the air around them, Haven was glad to have the cloak. Pausing before climbing into the carriage, Haven gave Binah a hug. No matter what happened with this whole *royal fae* thing she liked the old lady.

"Be safe my dear" Binah whispered

"Will do" Haven whispered back

Taking Romans outstretched hand, Haven climbed onto the carriage and sat with her legs hanging off the back and her pack nestled protectively in her lap. Trevor gathered up the reins. Before they could take off, Haven called to Binah and asked a question that had popped into her brain and refused to leave,

"Binah! What was Queen Montali's power? You said that King Rionach had influence over fire but what about her?"

Binah smiled like she held some sort of secret and said,

"Shadows my dear, she could manipulate shadows"

With that, the carriage took off.

***

It only took half an hour before Haven felt like pacing. She was a ball of nerves sitting next to Roman as the carriage traveled along, her foot was bouncing and she had been picking at her nails. It didn't help that an incredibly annoying strand of hair kept falling in her eyes.

"How much longer till the inn do you think?" She asked

"Probably awhile" Roman responded. He was laying on his back with his feet dangling over the edge of the carriage and looking up at the sky.

"Are you nervous?" She asked

"Not as much as I probably should be." Roman responded, "To be honest, something about this truly does feel right. Even just being here I feel more relaxed than I have in a long while."

Haven tried to avoid admitting that she was feeling the exact same way. Even her earlier anxiety had been nothing compared to what she had dealt with in the past. She may be a ball of nerves about the whole thing, but she couldn't deny that she had never experienced such an overwhelming feeling of being in the exact right place at the exact right time. Even while trying to pick out a college or going on dates or finding the perfect item at a thrift store, nothing ever made her feel as settled as being in this realm did.

"Aren't you worried about your parents?" She asked

Roman shook his head, "I didn't really have much back there"

Haven wanted to ask what Roman what he meant but he immediately changed the subject, the universal code for 'I don't want to talk about it'.

"Are you excited to see a castle?" He asked

Haven smiled and placed her hand back down in her lap, the nail was chewed to the bed but at least it wasn't bleeding.

"Yeah, I am actually. I read a lot of fantasy books when I was younger, before I was so consumed with my fathers death and then trying to focus on school. This feels straight out of one, seeing an actual real life castle kind of solidifies that."

"Hey, look over there!" Roman pointed.

Looking over, Haven immediately saw what he was pointing at. Off in the distance was a small herd of wild horses grazing in some tall grasses.

"Wow" She said, the sight stole the breath straight out of her lungs.

"We have them all over" Trevor spoke up, "Sometimes the farmers have to put up a barrier of some sort to keep them from eating half their crops"

Haven laughed at that, the worst pest problem she had ever encountered was a stray wild bunny nibbling at her mothers plants. As they drove further from the herd, Haven laid down next to

Roman and stared at the sky. Smiling slightly, she found herself truly excited about something for the first time in a long time.

Chapter Fourteen

A few more hours of bouncing down rocky roads had the group arriving at a small inn on the outskirts of what Haven had been told was the city of Inglis. When they first arrived, Trevor told them to go inside and check in while he settled the horses, Binah having already sent word to book their rooms.

Haven was looking forward to learning about whatever kind of magic she used to do that. She'd had the thought that she might be able to use it to get a message to her mom. However Haven assumed it would take strong magic to send something between realms. Haven was hoping that she didn't need to be the one casting the magic. If she even had any, Haven doubted her magic could send a letter five feet, much less to her house in the human realm. She also couldn't believe she'd already gotten used to saying things like,

'human realm'

How long would it take for her to forget about the human realm completely?

Attempting to push the unsettling thought aside, Haven hopped off the carriage, legs wobbly from hours of disuse. She had once read a quote talking about not borrowing the problems of tomorrow. Haven figured that that was particularly useful advice for this situation.

Walking through the wooden doorway, Haven spotted lots of fae in the small dining room adjacent to the inn's entrance hall. Trevor's earlier words flashed through her mind, he had warned them to keep their heads down and not to talk to anyone unless absolutely necessary. Haven hadn't understood what he had meant but he'd walked off before explaining.

After checking in with the kind lady behind the counter, Haven found the small room assigned as hers. While sitting on the twin bed, she began rifling through the pack Binah had sent with her. She hadn't realized Binah had put anything other than snacks in it.

"Wow," Haven said aloud to the empty room. Roman was currently getting settled into the room across the hall from hers. She didn't know where Trevor would be staying.

Along with a small brush, a spare shirt she was sure was called a tunic, a beautiful dagger and a leather canteen with some water, Binah had given her a necklace enclosed in a letter that read,

Haven, this necklace belongs to you. Soon you will figure out what I mean. Until then, please keep this hidden. Do not show it to anyone.

You are so incredibly powerful, I need you to believe this, to believe in yourself. You are in for a lot in these coming weeks. I am afraid it will not be the quiet and easy adventure I told you.

For that I am so sorry.

I have no doubt you will make a wonderful Queen.

I hope they do not get to you before you are able to come into who you are. There is an old diary hidden deep in the castle library that will help explain.

Please be careful and trust no one.

-Binah

The necklace was amazing, clearly handmade and old. A small emerald pendant hung on a gold chain. It was incredibly simple but also one of the most beautiful things Haven had ever held. She just wished it hadn't come with such an eerie letter.

Clasping the necklace behind her and situating it under the clean tunic she had put on, Haven reread the letter. She had no idea what Binah was talking about. Apparently she was powerful, going to become a queen and had people after her, none of which made any sense. Granted, a magical fae realm where Haven not only happened to be royalty but also held magic didn't make any sense either.

Haven reread the letter twice before giving her eyes a break and exhaling a breath laced with confusion. She was no longer feeling that sense of calm she had found while watching the endless sky on the ride here. She was tempted to ask Roman about it and if he somehow recognized the necklace but Binah explicitly said not to show it to anyone. For now, she was going to follow those instructions because clearly the old woman knew something important. Haven could only guess at what, and even guessing was hard seeing as she knew practically nothing about the realm she was now in.

The part in the letter that was really sticking out to Haven was the line about her becoming a queen. When Binah first explained what had happened to them she said that more than likely, Haven and Roman would become a prince and a princess to their respective kingdoms because there was no chance they'd be powerful enough to take the throne from whatever fae already in power.

Haven had been more than fine with that, the idea of becoming a princess but not having to worry about the power and responsibilities that came with being queen sounded perfect to her, an actual fantasy come true.

Binah must have thought Haven was powerful enough to take the throne, not that she exactly wanted it. Her mind spun, would the throne simply be given to her because she might be slightly more powerful than whoever was currently ruling? Would she have to take it? And did she even want it?

None of what Binah wrote made any sense, nor did the fact that the older fae somehow already knew how powerful Haven would be. Haven herself didn't even know that.

A thought popped into Havens head, something that unsettled her. Was it possible she was from one of the missing bloodlines? That would make sense. That way, there would be no competition for the throne, no one to challenge her, practically guaranteeing she would end up as a queen. The only person preventing that would be the crown regent but by law he was supposed to hand over the throne once the true king or queen was able to step into place. Haven had a hard time picturing someone who had been in power for so long simply handing over the throne.

Another thing that didn't make sense was that no one had heard anything about the two missing lineages since they created this realm. Or maybe it was that Binah had been right in that someone was interfering. If Haven's crazy thoughts were right and she was actually from one of the missing bloodlines, that could explain why Binah told her to trust no one and to be careful.

Haven didn't quite believe her thoughts, she knew in her head that there was no possible way she was the daughter of long, sup-posedly dead fae rulers.

She may not believe her thoughts but Haven would heed Binahs words. Because if someone cared enough to make it seem as though the two fae rulers had simply disappeared and were likely dead, they sure wouldn't like that Haven was now in their realm.

Chapter Fifteen

"It's time to get up!" A loud and annoying voice called, startling Haven awake. The voice sounded an awful lot like Roman. Haven could murder him for waking her at what felt like such an early hour. Not that she actually knew what time it was.

The covers were quickly pulled off of Haven, causing her to groan and sputter curses at the intruder. He was lucky she had worn her pants to bed, otherwise, he'd be getting an eyeful and she'd have a valid reason for murder. At least valid in her mind.

Roman repeated to Haven that it was time to get up at least three more times before she finally sat up. Telling Roman she was awake, she shooed him out of her room. After he left and presumably went back into his room across the hall, Haven climbed out of the moderately comfortable bed and slipped her feet into her shoes. Padding to the door, she left her room and entered the small bathroom at the end of the hallway.

After taking care of her needs, Haven looked in the small mirror above the sink basin and grimaced at what she found. Apparently tossing and turning all night with dreams of being chased through a dark forest was not good for a girl's complexion. The bags under her eyes and exhaustion weighing down her shoulders told Haven she clearly did not get enough sleep.

It wasn't hard to figure out why, it was also likely the reason for her dreams about being chased.

Haven could not get used to the idea of possibly hailing from one of the missing royal bloodlines. Nor could she get the thoughts to leave her. Her mind constantly switched between the doubt that was so strong and had almost convinced her she was crazy and the nagging feeling that she might actually be onto something. There was also a possibility Binah was simply messing with her. Although, the necklace was clearly old and while Haven did not know the older fae well, she got the impression that Binah would not take advantage of Haven's naivety of all things fae like that.

Exhaling and heading back into her room, Haven pulled the brush from her bag and braided her hair. She easily twisted the wavy strands until a neat plait laid across her shoulder that she tied off with a small leather band that had been looped around the brush handle.

Roman appeared back in her doorway fully dressed, told her he was heading down to grab some breakfast and that Trevor had said they'd be leaving soon. Haven nodded and he left without another word.

Pulling the note from Binah out of her bag, Haven reread over it. Sleep had not made things any clearer.

Haven made a mental note to start looking for the diary mentioned in the letter as soon as they arrived at the castle. After securing her pack to her back and wrapping her dark green cloak around herself, Haven made her way down to the inns dining room for breakfast.

***

The fact that she looked human had never been so apparent to Haven. Her, Roman and Trevor were situated at the back of the inns dining room waiting for their breakfast. Filling the room around her were fae, all of varying races and ethnicities. Some had gorgeous pale skin with vines that appeared to be crawling across them, others had stunning dark brown skin with flowers braided into their hair. Each fae was different and unique and Haven found every single one of them beautiful.

One of the things that stuck out the most to Haven was that no matter their differences, every single one of them had pointed ears. Some had long and skinny ears, some were short and very sharp but each and every one of them was pointed. The fact that no one else had rounded ears like her and Roman caused Haven to pull up the hood of her cloak and take solace in the fact that Binah had told her that given time she would develop most of the common fae features.

The pointy ears, the fangs, all of that would come. She reminded herself multiple times while waiting for breakfast to arrive. Roman didn't seem at all put off by the fact that he also did not have the pointed ears, if he even noticed at all. The entire short time Haven had been at breakfast he hadn't said one word. Instead, twisting a few sticks of straw into what appeared to be the rough outline of a crow.

Other than Romans complete lack of concern, one fae in particular had captured Havens attention. He had inky dark skin and bright icy eyes. He was truly stunning and while his good looks might have been what caught her attention, what kept it was the snowflakes he kept having to knock off of his exposed arms. Every few minutes some would gather in clusters up and down his forearms, then he would send them tumbling off his arms where they dissipated before they ever hit the floor. A few minutes later more would gather. He seemed to be the only one in here with that sort of problem.

"Some fae with nature like talents have to do things like that" Trevor spoke, pulling Haven from where she was taking mental snapshots of the obvious display of magic.

"Occasionally with the more powerful fae, their powers can take on characteristics of their own. For example, A fae with a power over flame will occasionally leave burn marks where they walk or have little tendrils of flame flitting around them wherever they go. Sometimes the flame will even interact with others." He finished

"That is entirely awesome but sounds kind of inconvenient," Haven responded.

Roman was quiet next to her. Every once in a while he would scan the room with his eyes and then go back to folding the straw in front of him.

Before Haven could ask Trevor to tell her more, a waiter came over and dropped off plates piled high with eggs, bacon and biscuits. Next he picked up glasses of orange juice off his tray, sitting them down in a cluster at the middle of the table before asking if they needed anything else and leaving. Haven was just about to reach for one of the glasses when Trevor pulled all three towards him, picked them up one by one and took what Haven could only describe as a very thorough sniff.

"Checking for poison" Trevor commented sheepishly, a slight blush rising to the kids cheeks. Haven thought it was adorable, although the thought of being poisoned kind of ruined it.

"Find anything?" Haven asked slightly sarcastically.

"Nope." Trevor responded, sliding a glass towards her. It occurred to Haven that Trevor could have easily lied and she would never know until it was too late. She pushed the thought aside and took a sip of the orange juice. It tasted fine to her but she assumed all the best poisons had no taste.

Luckily, Haven didn't keel over and die on the spot after taking a drink so it was unlikely Trevor or anyone else had poisoned her. It wasn't long before breakfast was over and they were back on the road towards the castle. Only a couple of hours, Trevor had told her. Only a couple more hours until she would be in an actual fae castle. The warning from Binah weighed heavily in the pack slung across her back but it hadn't completely kept her from being excited. The big adventure of her life was beginning. It wasn't college and a degree like most expected but she'd taken an actual fantastical adventure over a degree any day.

Chapter Sixteen

After trekking hours by carriage, the packed dirt road turned to cobblestone. After another hour on the cobblestone road, A large castle began coming into view on the horizon.

Haven didn't have words for what was slowly being revealed before her. Beautiful didn't even begin to cover what she was seeing, it was truly glorious.

Nestled against a large glistening lake Haven could only see a part of and a deep green pine forest was a castle fit for a queen.

Made out of some sort of light stone, it was long and rectangular. Two tall spires sat on either side of a large double door connected to the bottom level of the castle. The next three levels sat inset so you could spend time on the flat rooftop of the base level. Haven could see herself spending a lot of time under the sun on that rooftop or stargazing during the night. She'd bet that nights out here would compare to no others. It wasn't just the clear view of the sky or lack of light pollution, it was the magic of such a beautiful sight. It hung in the air even this far away from the castle.

The spires were made up of a darker stone than the main walls and matched the towers that made up the corners of the top three levels. There were vines creeping up some parts of the castle, giving it a whimsical and aged look. Tall rectangular windows could be seen on every level along with many balconies and gables.

While the forest spanned to the left of the castle as far as the eye could see, Haven could only see a sliver of the lake that appeared to wrap around the back of the castle. The parts of it she could see were only in her sight because of the angle they were traveling at. Towards the right was what appeared to be a large, expansive garden with rows of flowers and what could be vegetables. As they got closer, Haven could see people in the gated gardens, some appeared to be tending to the plants, others were just walking. It wasn't hard to assume that the garden alone took up acres and acres of land.

The sight of so many bright and blooming flowers had Haven wearing a bittersweet smile. It reminded her of her mothers garden. She hoped once things settled she could find a way to contact her mother and let her know that she was alright.

Despite what she had been told by Binah about her mother knowing exactly where she was and keeping this world a secret from her, Haven wasn't convinced. It had been just Haven and her mom for so long that the idea of her mother keeping such a huge secret was hard to grasp. Haven hoped to eventually not only get word to her mother but actually get ahold of her so she could get the story from her, because surely she hadn't actually kept so much from her?

The idea that her father had been fae made more sense to Haven. That idea was much easier to grasp. She assumed he had intended to tell her but died before he was able. Haven certainly liked that explanation a whole lot better than the alternative provided by Binah.

As Haven, Roman and Trevor grew closer to the castle, a tightness grew in Havens chest that could only be identified as anxiety. Haven had been dealing with it for so long that the feeling itself was as familiar as breathing.

While the castle that was slowly growing closer was truly beautiful and Haven was more excited than anything else, everything was quickly becoming very real. The sight of it was a physical reminder of everything that was going to happen in the coming days that until now, had felt like more of a dream than reality.

Haven was going to be tested, whatever that meant, find out which royal family she descended from and then begin training to take her place wherever she belonged. Even if Binahs first statements were correct and she ended up as a princess last in line for any sort of throne, surely there'd be expectations to go with that position. And what if Binahs letter held more weight than Haven was letting herself believe and she did end up as a queen, what would a position like that entail?

Anxiety had Havens breath picking up, her heart beat almost painfully against her chest and her fingers subconsciously went back to picking at her nail beds. Before the anxiety could grip Haven fully, Roman reached over and placed his large hands over Havens much smaller ones.

"Haven listen to me and take a breath. It's going to be fine, you are not alone."

Roman began taking long, slow breaths in attempt to have Haven mimic him and slow her own breathing. Haven listened to the deep sounds of his breathing and felt his hands grasping her shaking ones for many long minutes before she began to calm down. Eventually, her breathing returned to normal and the trembling she hadn't noticed before subsided.

"Are you okay now?" Roman asked

Haven nodded, "Yeah, I think it everything just became very real all of a sudden. I didn't even realize what was happening before the anxiety had ahold of me"

"Makes sense," Roman told her, "Remember, you're not doing this alone and no matter what the thoughts in your head tell you, you belong here."

Haven allowed Romans comforting words to wash over her. The reminder that she wasn't the only person going through this helped more than she c. Roman was right there with her and no matter how put together he seemed, Haven knew he was likely just as nervous as she.

Roman slung his arm around Havens shoulders. Fifteen more minutes of the horses at a slow pace had them at the front of the entrance to the castle. Roman hopped off the carriage before holding out his hand and helping Haven down.

"Can you believe this place?" She asked, looking up in amazement.

"I know, it's truly a sight isn't it?" Roman responded, also looking up at the castle.

Haven nodded her agreement and followed him to the front of the carriage where Trevor was unclipping the horses.

"Someone should be out shortly, I'm sure they knew we were coming." Trevor said.

"Who's they?" Haven asked

"The crown regent, he's been ruling in lieu of the descendant of Queen Montali. "

Out of the corner of her eye, Haven caught Romans jaw tightening almost imperceptibly. She couldn't decipher that, or the slightly annoyed look that came over his face when Trevor started speaking about the crown regent. The look was over in less than a second so she chalked it up to him being tired due to recent events and her mind still feeling off after her minor anxiety attack.

Haven watched Trevor finish with the two horses. He started to walk to the left of the building with a lead in each hand, leaving the carriage behind. Haven moved to follow Trevor but he stopped her with a raised hand and said,

"No, you guys wait here. Someone will be out to get you soon."

Haven hesitated before she stepped back next to Roman. Trevor quickly disappeared around the castle and out of view. Deciding to make the best of their wait, she began taking in her surroundings, immediately noticing the fae on the roof of the main level. Almost everyone seemed to be watching the two of them. As they caught Haven looking back at them, most turned away. A few didn't, some outright stared, not caring if Haven caught them. One unsettling thing Havem noticed sent small shivers down her spine. Most of them weren't looking at Roman. Even though he was right next to her, Haven could tell that those who were looking were staring directly at her.

Chapter Seventeen

Trevor had been right, it hadn't taken long for someone to open the large castle doors and usher Haven and Roman inside. Even though there was no indoor lighting, save for some unlit sconces along the walls, the room they entered was bright. There was a colorful rug under their feet and some beautiful artwork on the walls. Haven could see two hallways, each one through an open door on either side of the room. She looked forward to finding out where they went. She could also see what appeared to be a great hall through the third set of doors directly ahead of them.

"Hello, my name is Wendy. I'll be showing you around the castle." The woman who greeted them at the doors spoke. She was short, older with graying blonde hair, light blue eyes and a warm smile that helped put Haven at ease.

Roman introduced himself while shaking her hand and Haven did the same.

"Hello, my name is Haven."

Wendy smiled another warm smile, "It's nice to finally have you here Haven"

Haven didn't know how to respond to that so she simply smiled back at the woman and followed her through the double doors into what she assumed was the great hall, or possibly a ballroom.

"This is the throne room," Wendy said. So not the great hall or ballroom, Haven thought.

"It is also used as our ballroom and great hall"

Haven snickered under her breath.

Looking around the large room, Haven noticed the rows and rows of windows lining the walls. There was a painting in between each, some depicting people, others showed scenes and landscapes. She could see a small door on the left side of the back wall behind a raised platform where a throne sat. She assumed that would be where the queen or king sat if they had one. Haven absently wondered what it would be like to have all that power, to rule.

Binahs words had freaked Haven out at first. But barring her anxiety a few moments ago, now that she'd had some time on the ride here to do nothing other than think, Haven decided that whatever happened, she would be okay with it. Whether she ended up sitting on a throne somewhere, either as the only fae from a missing bloodline or from a bloodline with so many siblings she'd need a notebook to keep them all straight, or if she ended up a no named princess last in line for just about everything, Haven decided that any option would be alright. She'd hope for the best-case scenario and be happy with the worst. She just had to decide what scenario she considered the best.

Wendy led them back out of the throne room and down the hall to their left. Almost immediately there was a set of stairs that the three of them began climbing.

"So," Wendy started, "You've seen the throne room. It takes up the entirety of the first floor, both the passageways off the entry room take you up to the rooftop where you access the rest of the floors. The second level is made up of entertaining rooms where meetings are held, offices, the kitchens, library and store rooms." Haven sucked in a breath at the mention of the library, remembering Binahs words. She hoped to visit that room sooner rather than later.

"The third level is made up of only bedchambers, whether it's for visiting nobles or servants who stay at the castle; that's where you will find their bedchambers" Haven was too lost to her own mind to pay close attention to what Wendy was saying,

"And no one ever enters the fourth level, it is the royal quarters and no one has stayed there since the creation of this realm. It is enchanted to stay clean and no one dares go up there out of respect for our lost royal bloodline" Wendy finished, a slightly sad tone in her voice.

"The crown regent doesn't stay there?" Haven asked, finally snapping out of her thoughts. Apparently she'd been paying closer attention than she realized.

Wendy gasped, "He does not dare"

It seemed a little silly to waste an entire level out of respect for someone that people appeared sure would never show. Haven decided it was best not to say anything else on the subject, based off the offended look on Wendys face.

After exiting the door at the top of the staircase, she found herself standing on the rooftop of the first level with Roman behind her.

The view of the castle had been nice but the view *from* the castle was nothing short of awe inspiring. She could see the sprawling lake situated behind the castle glittering in the sunlight, the forest that encased the entire left side of the castle and circled the backside of the lake.

The gardens were even better to look at from this angle. Haven couldn't see exactly how big they were but she could tell they easily outmatched any garden she'd ever seen. She'd be more than willing to bet they outsized the castle. There appeared to be some sort of hedge maze, people were picking baskets of fruits and vegetables and colorful flowers sprang up every which way.

Haven wondered how amazing it would feel to walk through the gardens just before sunset, during golden hour. It was her favorite time of day. Her mother used to take garden walks during that time and ever since she was old enough to walk, she joined her mom whenever she could. Haven didn't always make those walks a priority. Other things often got in the way, school clubs, trips out with the few friends she had or getting lost in a book. Now that she was faced with the possibility of staying in the fae realm for the foreseeable future, she regretted not making those walks a priority.

For as long as she was here, Haven told herself, she would keep up the tradition as often as she could, walking through the gardens just before sunset and enjoying the moment like her mother always did.

Chapter Eighteen

Wendy showed Haven and Roman the second level, through the kitchens where a large brick oven had been full of flames, past some storerooms where they kept equipment for any events the castle held, to a war room that Wendy told them had never been used and finally to the library. They hadn't been in there long before Wendy rushed them out and towards a staircase that went up to the third level. Haven did her best to memorize the way they had come so she could find her way back to the library later to look for the diary from Binahs letter but there were so many turns she quickly lost track. By the time Wendy showed them to where their rooms would be, Haven's head was spinning.

Wendy made quick work of explaining to Haven and Roman that someone would be by shortly to deliver lunch and supplies and to talk with them about meeting with the crown regent. Wendy showed Roman to where he would be staying down the hall from Haven's room and just like that, Haven was alone. Only a thick wooden door separated her from where she'd be staying in an actual fae castle for the foreseeable future.

Turning to face her door, Haven sucked in a breath. For whatever reason this felt *big*, like fate or destiny or whatever you would call it had been leading up to *this* moment in time. *This* moment and place.

Exhaling, Haven turned the doorknob and entered her room. Or at least, what would be her room until her bloodline was discovered and she was sent to whatever kingdom she originated from. Either way, this felt *right*.

It wasn't something she could explain, it wasn't something Haven could see or hear or touch. It wasn't a tangible feeling, it was simply a humming in her chest that told her that entering this room was exactly what she was supposed to be doing at that moment.

Stepping inside her room, Haven began to take in the world around her. Immediately to the left, on the wall shared with the door, was a decent sized wooden dresser. Next, she noticed the large canopy bed, it had nets that were currently tied back and beautiful soft pink sheets. A small desk and chair shared the wall to her right along with the door to what Haven assumed was the bathroom. Finally, her gaze landed on the doorway to a balcony. Walking over to it, Haven took in another deep breath, attempting to calm her racing heart.

Opening the door and stepping out onto the balcony, she took in the view of the lake, surrounding forest and small courtyard outside the castle before you reached the bank of the lake. She would have preferred a view of the gardens simply because they reminded her of her mom but the lake view was powerful in its own right.

Haven walked to the railing, past a small tea table and chair set to her right and looked around some more. Luckily she wasn't afraid of heights or being out here would be hell.

Taking a moment to gather her thoughts, Haven sat in the small chair accompanying the tea table. So far, she had somehow traveled from her world, been told that not only was she secretly fae royalty, but that she also had magical powers. Next she had been brought to a castle more beautiful than anything she'd ever seen and now here she was, in a room not much bigger than her room in the human world, waiting for someone to show up and tell her about these tests she was expected to take that would tell her what royal bloodline she came from and what powers she held.

The craziest part wasn't the fact that she was sitting here at all, it was the fact that none of this felt wrong or strange. She didn't feel like an outsider to this world. Except for a little bit of skepticism and doubt at the start of this whole thing, Haven had yet to doubt that what was going on was real or the fact that she *belonged* here.

***

Haven hadn't been sitting on the balcony for very long before there was a knock at the door. Standing and walking over to the door, she noticed a folded letter on the ground that had not been there when she first entered the room. Snatching it up quickly, Haven put it away in the drawer of the desk sitting against the wall. She would have to wait until whoever was at the door went away before reading it, just in case its contents was something she didn't want shared.

Opening the door, Haven was met with a stunning woman wearing a bright smile.

"Hello, I'm here to give you some necessities and talk with you a bit"

Haven nodded and opened the door wider so the girl could enter. She took a moment to look her over. She was beautiful, appearing to be about Havens age, possibly slightly older, slightly taller than Haven with pale skin and even paler white hair. Her eyes were an icy blue and she spoke with an accent Haven couldn't place. She was wearing a plain gray gown with corset straps going up the back.

"My name is Astrea but you can call me Rea, all my friends do"

The woman, Astrea, seemed very friendly and Haven liked her instantly.

"Hi, my name is Haven" She reached out and offered her hand. Rea took it instantly.

"I know who you are, the whole kingdom is already alight with the news of your arrival"

"Really?" Haven asked, "We only just got here, the whole kingdom really doesn't have anything better to be talking about?"

Rea smirked, "To be honest, no. There's been some restlessness in the kingdom recently and people are hoping your arrival might change some things"

Confusion twisted Havens face, "I'm sorry, I'm a little confused. When I arrived here the woman I spoke to told me that more than likely I would end up last in line for any throne and with little to no power. I guess I'm just confused as to how I could change much of anything"

Rea turned away from Haven before she spoke but Haven still caught a glimpse of something like hope on Rea's face.

"If sources are correct, you will be so much more than that Haven"

Before she could ask what Rea meant by that, the girl plopped a basket Haven hadn't seen her carrying down on the bed and cheerfully said,

"Let's get things started"

Rea pulled out all sorts of things, a notebook, pencils, string, a small closed pouch, what looked to be soap, some salves, herbs, crystals, a few tins that held something Haven could only guess at and finally, a dark purple candle. Waiting for Rea to explain what all these things were for, Haven sat down on the bed next to a small pile of what looked like dried lavender.

"Before I begin, there are a few things you need to understand about the way our world, and we as fae work." Rea paused and looked to Haven. Haven nodded for her to continue,

"So, down to the basics, every fae has power. No one knows why some fae are more powerful than others but it has been guessed that our bloodlines have something to do with it. You see, we get our power from within ourselves. There are other species of that have to draw their power from other magical things, vampires drink blood, werewolves draw power from the moon, and so on," Haven wanted to interrupt at the mention of vampires and werewolves but Rea held up a hand to silence her before she could interrupt.

"Currently, there are no other magical beings besides fae in our realm. It has been outlawed for the protection of the fae for a long time so that is not something you need to concern yourself with. As fae we get our power from within ourselves. We have no need to draw power from other magical things like vampires do with blood because we ourselves are magical." Rea paused to make sure Haven was keeping up with her before continuing,

"Again, no one knows why we are able to draw power from within ourselves but other magical creatures have to find it elsewhere. This is just the way it has always been.

With that being said, there are objects that have magical properties we can use to draw in more power. For example, a spell cast under certain lunar phases is more powerful than one cast using just the magic we have inside ourselves. Each fae's power is different. I myself have low level influence over snow and water elements while my three brothers and sister all have influence over earth elements like rocks and soil. My brothers used to use their magic to chase me around by pelting tiny rocks at me," Astrea snickered,

"Eventually I got old enough to dose them in freezing water which usually made them quit."

"There is no telling what sort of powers you will have, although our powers are usually that of what bloodline we hail from. You could have influence over water, earth, fire, air or a combination of all of those. There are more uncommon talents like the influence of shadows or the ability to manipulate time. Overall, there are so many different powers and talents that until you take your tests, we won't know what sort of talents you have."

Rea continued on to explain that tomorrow Haven would meet with the crown regent to discuss when she would be able to take her tests. Rea also explained that it was not a written test like Haven had been expecting. In fact, Rea had no clue what Havens test would be like.

Apparently, each test was different and the only way to find out what she would be doing was to do it. That made zero sense to Haven but she hadn't pressured Rea for more answers simply because she was fairly certain Rea had none.

So many things were swirling around in Havens brain that when Rea finally left it was all she could do to keep from collapsing against the door as she closed it behind her.

Instead, she went into what she correctly assumed was her bathroom and splashed some water on her face. After easing closed her balcony doors, Haven tossed herself down on her bed, not even bothering to tuck herself under the covers before drifting off to sleep.

Chapter Nineteen

Haven rested for only half an hour, if the small clock on her desk was anything to go by, before she was pulled from her nap by her rumbling stomach. Stretching her arms above her head and letting out a loud yawn, Haven sat up and rubbed the sleep from her eyes. When she first laid down, Haven had guessed she'd sleep through dinner with how exhausted she was. That was clearly not what happened. Haven didn't know whether to be happy about or not, this meant she'd have to get out of her comfortable bed to go find something to eat.

After a moment, Haven decided to go through the things Astrea left for her and put them away. She'd explained each and every one of the items, there was soap for her body and hair, some salves and ointments for various things like scratches or cramps, a notebook to write in and some crystals that each did something different. One was supposed to help with sleep, another acted as a light when activated, another helped soothe aches and pains when dropped into the bath. Rea had also left a small pouch of things for Havens cycle when it came around.

Rea had explained that Haven would notice fae cycles only came once every four to six months and as her body developed into that of a fae. As her ears gained points and her canines became long and sharp, she would also gain the every four to six month cycle.

Lastly was the large purple candle. When lit, it cast a bubble around the room so that no sound could escape. Haven found that particularly useful. Rea also explained that eventually Haven would be able to cast a bubble like that as she gained control of her powers but for now, the candle would work. The last thing Rea had done before she left was use some string to measure Haven so that she could have a wardrobe made up for her. For now, there were a few dresses and pants in the closet near the door.

Haven entered the bathroom and put away the items on a shelf next to the sink. Overall, there wasn't anything fancy about the space, a simple sink with a mirror above it, a toilet in the right corner of the room and finally a clawfoot tub with a spout coming out of the ceiling directly above it for showers. The shocking part was how modern everything was.

Even though she was in what appeared to be a medieval fae castle, it still had all the comforts of modern architecture, a flushing toilet, indoor lighting and fans on the ceiling that kept the air moving. She wondered if the fae copied those inventions from humans or if they had come up with them on their own.

Before Haven could get too lost in her thoughts there was a knock at the door.

"Who is it?" She called

"Roman"

Haven smiled to herself and went to open the door for him,

"Hey" She greeted

Roman smiled at her,

"I thought you might be hungry so I figured we'd grab an early dinner from the kitchens"

"Yeah that sounds nice" Haven responded, stepping through the door and using the key Rea had given her to lock it behind her. She slipped the key onto a small chain around her neck and moved to follow Roman down the hall.

"How do you know where we're going?" She asked him. Roman shrugged,

"I dunno, I guess I just paid good attention when Wendy was showing us around the place" Haven had thought she paid pretty good attention but apparently not as good as Roman who was currently leading them through the halls like he knew exactly where he was going.

Only five minutes later they were in the kitchens, Roman was grabbing snacks off a shelf and handing them to Haven. Next he opened what appeared to be a large ice chest and tossed her two wrapped sandwiches. He closed the ice chest and then they were walking back out the door.

Roman led them to the rooftop area where they sat down at a table and began to unpack their stolen snacks and sandwiches. There weren't many other fae on the roof with them but the ones that were there were doing a terrible job of concealing their glances towards Roman and Haven. Haven assumed they simply didn't care if they were caught staring.

The unsettling thing was that just like earlier, they all seemed to be staring at her. Haven couldn't tell what their stares held, most seemed to be plain curiosity but if she was right, others held nothing but disdain.

***

The sandwiches had been eaten, the trash was thrown away and now Haven and Roman were taking a walk through the gardens at Haven's request. It was getting late; the sun was dipping behind the horizon illuminating the row of colorful flowers they were walking through. Haven wondered if it was also evening in the human world and whether her mother was doing the same thing as her.

Was her mother worried about her, Haven wondered. Binah had made it seem like her mother had known what was going to happen to Haven and where she'd end up before she left for her trip but Haven wasn't convinced.

Despite Havens slightly dark thoughts, the gardens were absolutely gorgeous. So far they had seen rows and rows of vegetable plants, flowers scattered throughout every row, fruit bearing trees lining the perimeter and then more rows filled with nothing but more flowers. Haven's favorite thing had been a rose arch that led way to the back of the gardens where a tall hedge maze sat. Haven loved the gardens, just like she assumed she would.

Roman eventually broke the relaxed silence they had been walking in by saying,

"I think it's about time we head back to our rooms, I'm exhausted."

Haven had to agree, they turned towards what appeared to be the nearest exit and headed back towards the castle entrance. As the two of them left the gated gardens, they saw the crow Haven was sure had been following them. At almost every turn it had been sitting somewhere nearby, she had seen it too many times for it to be a coincidence. Haven also noticed Roman giving it a few dirty looks.

It squawked at them as they passed by, startling Haven slightly. As it flew away, it made a chattering sound that sounded a whole lot like laughter.

Haven and Roman made it back to their rooms right before the sun fully set. Locking the door behind her, Haven was prepared to take a nice long soak in the bathtub before she passed by the desk and remembered the letter she'd found.

Turning back to her desk and taking a seat in the chair, Haven pulled out the letter. After unfolding it, she found that the letter was no more than a blank sheet of paper. Haven didn't understand why someone would slip a plain sheet of paper under her door. Pondering for a moment, Haven held it up to the lit candle she'd accidentally left burning on her desk. In the firelight text began to appear. Sucking in a breath, Haven moved the note as close to the candle as possible without burning it and read,

Be careful who you trust

That was all the note said. Nothing more, nothing less. Haven tried taking it away from the candle and putting it back but nothing else appeared.

Sighing, Haven slipped the note back into her desk drawer where her own notebook and pencils sat and pondered what the note could mean. Was it some kind of threat? It hadn't felt particularly threatening but it was definitely some kind of warning. Haven wondered who sent it. Maybe Rea had slipped it under the door before she knocked? That seemed likely since she hadn't heard anyone else by her door before Rea had shown up. But why not just say that to Haven?

Haven had just as many questions if not more than before she sat down. She decided to try and forget about it for tonight, take a bath and get some proper rest. Her meeting with the crown regent wasn't until lunchtime tomorrow so hopefully she would be able to find the library in the morning and begin looking for the diary Binah told her to find. She hoped it would offer some answers, or at least, not bring about more questions.

Chapter Twenty

She was finally here in the fae realm. He could barely believe it. This was something him and so many others had been preparing and hoping for, for quite some time. It had taken a lot to get to this point, he'd personally seen some of the sacrifices made to get to this point. And while his friends would never admit it, those sacrifices had left scars.

A nervous laugh erupted from him as he sat alone in his room. Her presence changed not just his life, but the future of everyone in their kingdom, possibly even the realm.

In another life, she would have been his worst enemy. While he may need to treat her that way, the tiny glimpse he'd caught of her through his window while she'd been touring the grounds told him everything he needed to know about his feelings towards her.

These coming weeks were going to be hard, in more way than one. He prayed to whatever gods were left out there to give him the strength needed to do what was necessary.

He was already off to a bad start. Should he have sent her that note? Probably not, but he had to warn her. Now that she was here, things were beginning to happen. The forces currently in control were furious and he knew that if there was a way, they would kill her without a second thought.

He had to stop that from happening. She was their kingdoms only hope.

Chapter Twenty-One

Haven could feel the weight of a large chest pressing down on her, naked skin pressing against hers. The scent of whiskey and sex moved through her room like a haze. Haven ran her hands through the silky strands of his hair, letting out a moan as she shifted under him. Her sounds echoed off the walls around them.

Something didn't seem right about the sound, about the way it echoed around her.

Haven woke with a start. Opening her eyes, a glance around her room told her she was alone. Havens mind reeled with how vivid her dream had been. She'd had sex dreams before but none quite like that. Usually it was leftover memories of times with past partners but this had been something else entirely. It was visceral, like there was actually a man in her room making her feel those things. Even now that she was on her way to being properly awake, there were lingering feelings dancing across her skin.

The throbbing between her legs also lingered, not as vibrant as it had been in her dream but she was sure that if she slipped her hand between her legs she would find herself soaked. Haven briefly thought about doing that and taking the ache away before she bolted upright, having gotten a look at the clock.

Haven cursed herself as she launched out of bed, it was almost time for lunch with the crown regent. She couldn't believe she'd slept that long.

After hastily brushing her teeth and detangling her hair, Haven rushed back into the bedroom. Pausing at her armoire, she couldn't decide what piece to pull out. Haven assumed she would need something fancy for a meeting with the crown regent but all she could find were a few plain dresses, two pairs of leggings, another long nightshirt like the one she was wearing and a few tunics to pair with the leggings.

Just as Haven began to panic, there was a knock on the door.

"Who is it?" She asked.

"Astrea" Called the voice beyond the door. Haven smiled at the sound of her maybe friend, she hoped Rea could help her figure out this outfit situation.

Haven opened the door and beckoned Rea in.

"I brought you something" Rea stated, holding up a garment bag

"Is it for my meeting with the crown regent because if not, I might just have to go naked!"

"Yup" Rea smiled, "It's the only thing the seamstresses were able to get ready in time. The rest of your wardrobe should be delivered sometime tomorrow"

Haven was internally cheering at the idea of a new wardrobe. She didn't need a lot but she did like to have something fancy to wear every once in a while. Smiling, Haven reached out to take the garment bag. Unzipping it, she found a gorgeous soft pink gown with a corset top and puffy off the shoulder sheer sleeves. Walking over to the floor length mirror on the other side of the bed, Haven held it up to herself.

"Wow," She said softly.

"I know" Rea spoke from where she was standing behind Haven, "You're going to look amazing"

Haven slipped off her nightshirt, now in nothing but a cotton pair of underwear and entirely comfortable in her skin in front of Rea. She wasn't usually like that, especially around strangers, but with Rea she felt comfortable. It helped that yesterday Rea had explained she'd be acting as a sort of lady's maid for Haven, helping her dress if she needed and occasionally doing her hair. Rea had also assured Haven that it was no big deal to her to help her change as long as Haven was comfortable. Haven liked the idea of some assistance, especially after seeing the complicated looking corset straps.

Stepping into the gown, Haven pulled it up and slipped her arms into the sleeves. The material was so soft and plush it was like walking around in pajamas. Haven couldn't believe something so pretty could be so soft.

Rea reached forward to tie up the back corset. Thankfully Rea didn't tie it too tight so Haven had some room to breathe.

Pulling her hair out of the back of the dress and laying it across one shoulder, Haven repeated to the mirror,

"Wow"

Haven couldn't remember the last time she felt this nice, this pretty. At first glance, she may not have thought the soft blush color would complement her pale skin and red hair but it did.

Rea smiled at her in the mirror, helped smooth her hair and then patted Haven on the shoulder and told her they had to hurry if Haven wanted her hair done before it was time to leave.

Walking down the castle halls next to Rea with the skirt of her dress fisted in one hand, Haven was a bundle of nerves. She'd never done anything that made her feel this nervous and once in seventh grade, she'd almost had a panic attack after being told she'd have to present a project in front of half the school for the science fair. This meeting brought back similar nerves.

Rea had done Havens hair in a half up look that billowed out in long curls behind her. Haven's hair was always curly, not necessarily a crazy curly but it never quite lost its wave. Haven smiled as she touched a soft curl framing her face.

Her nerves had nothing to do with her outfit, her hair or the light makeup she wore and everything to do with the fact that she was about to come face to face with someone who was supposedly one of the most powerful fae in the kingdom to talk about something that was incredibly important to her future. A future she didn't even know existed a couple of days ago.

Breathe in, breathe out, Haven repeated to herself as she came to a stop outside a large door. Taking in one last big gulp of air, she sent a quick nervous smile Rea's way and knocked.

"Come in" Boomed a voice behind the door

Rea gave her one last encouraging look as Haven cautiously entered the office.

Looking around, there wasn't much to see. A small window-less room held two cushioned chairs in front of a large oak desk, a few cabinets that appeared to hold paperwork and a small table and chair set in the back corner behind the large desk where a man she assumed was the crown regent was pouring a drink.

Haven immediately noticed how tall the man was, easily towering over her with wide shoulders and long, thick legs. He wore his dark blonde hair cropped close to his scalp and when he turned slightly, Haven noticed the brown of his eyes, so dark they were almost black. Haven was instantly glad she dressed as nicely as she did when she took in the luxurious look of the clothes the man was wearing.

The crown regent looked up from where he was pouring himself a drink and said,

"Good afternoon Haven, I am the crown regent. I want to welcome you to our lovely kingdom."

Haven instantly distrusted the man. Something about him put her on edge, she couldn't quite pinpoint what but being in the room with this man was reminiscent of the time she thought she was being followed on the way home from a trip to the store.

"Why don't you have a seat and I can answer some of your questions, I'm sure you have many" The crown regent smiled as he spoke but there was no warmth behind it. Haven also found it interesting that he introduced himself by his title rather than his name thus placing himself in a position of power over her since he knew her name but she did not know his.

The crown regent seemed more robot than fae, emotionless and cold.

Who knew, Haven thought to herself, it was possible he wasn't always like that. After all, she'd known the man for all of five minutes. Although Haven was having a hard time picturing him any other way.

Haven offered him the best smile she could conjure and took a seat in one of the chairs in front of his desk.

"So," He began, "First let me say we are so glad you made your way here"

Haven could tell that was a lie by the way he sneered slightly as he spoke.

"Second, let me be the first to offer you any help you may need. If you run into any trouble just let me know and I will take care of it." She definitely wouldn't be doing that, but she wasn't about to tell him that.

"I will, thank you." Haven responded, offering him another small smile and hoping her distrust was not evident.

"Great!" He clapped his hands together, "Now onto our next order of business, I spoke to your friend Roman this morning, he will be doing his bloodline and talent testing under the light of the next full moon which is three days from now. I assume you will be fine doing it then as well?"

Haven nodded.

"Excellent! I, for one, look forward to getting those results of yours. As I'm sure you do too."

He distractedly scribbled something down on a notepad as he spoke but Haven was too far away to read what it said. She simply nodded again at his words. No matter how uncomfortable this guy made her, she was really looking forward to getting some answers and discovering more about herself.

After the uncomfortable meeting with the crown regent, Haven found Rea waiting outside the door. After telling Rea about what happened in the meeting, save for how uncomfortable the crown regent made Haven, she asked Rea to take her to the library. Rea agreed, they stopped by the kitchens to grab some lunch and then made their way to the grand room. Soon after they arrived, Rea excused herself to tend to some chores and left Haven alone.

There were bookshelves as far as the eye could see, a trim around the edge of the second level made it possible to view part of the first level from the second floor and vice versa. Haven was told there were steps in the back of the stacks directly in front of her that would take her up to the second floor. Haven liked being surrounded by so many books, it made her think of the small library she had at home.

Pulling Binahs note out of her pocket, she touched the necklace that had accompanied the note and read it over, finding nothing helpful about the location of this diary she was supposed to find. Haven huffed a breath, wondering why Binah couldn't have just said,

"This mysterious diary I have told you to find is on row 13, shelf 3 number 7"

She looked up from the letter, deciding to head left and work her way right. There was no way she could even get half her searching done today but at least she could start.

The deeper she headed into the stacks, the darker it got. Reaching the back wall, Haven pulled out the light crystal Rea had given her. Brushing her hand over the rune carved into the top of the crystal to activate it, she held it up in her hand to better see the titles of the books on the shelves. Now that she could see slightly better, Haven began her search.

Almost two whole hours of searching had turned up nothing but dust on the edge of her dress and a slight headache. Haven had no idea what she was even looking for, she had been hoping that something would jump out at her.

She'd eaten all of the snacks her and Rea had grabbed and was currently scanning a high shelf when the distinct feeling of being watched crawled down her spine.

Haven paused and shined her light down the row she was in, it wasn't bright enough to see the whole distance, but it was enough to tell her that there was nothing in this row watching her. At least, nothing she could see. Haven quickly decided that now would be a good time to take a break, she could even head outside for some fresh air and sunlight.

Just as she got to the end of the row, something reached out and grabbed her ankle. Haven bit back a scream as she began to fall forward. Right as she was about to hit the floor, strong hands reached out and grabbed her. Taking in a breath and righting herself, Haven looked up to thank the person who saved her from smacking her face against the hard floor.

Haven was stunned into silence, in front of her was the most gorgeous man she had ever seen. He was just a few inches taller than her, maybe 6'1 or 6'2, with thick hair so brown it was almost black, dark eyes, sharp cheekbones and the softest, fullest looking lips she had ever seen. He smelled slightly like alcohol, maybe bourbon or whiskey. His hands were still on her arms where he'd grabbed her to make sure she didn't fall. Haven unintentionally took a moment to take in the wide expanse of his chest and the tattoos peeking out of his collar.

Haven was pulled from her leering when he said,

"The words are, thank you. It's rude to stare and you should watch where you're going" He immediately released her and strutted past her, knocking into her shoulder and almost sending her tumbling himself.

The whole encounter had only taken a moment but it left her rattled. Just as she was about to open her mouth to thank the guy, he opens his and basically tells her off. Then he almost knocks her down right after keeping her from hitting the floor. Sure, she probably shouldn't have looked him over like that but he hadn't needed to be so rude.

Even though the sight of him had been enough to send electric tingles down her spine, Haven hoped she didn't run into him again anytime soon.

Chapter Twenty-Two

After shaking off her encounter with the rude mystery man in the library, Haven decided to find her way to her room. Thankfully only getting lost twice.

Currently, Haven was sitting at the desk in her room writing her mother a letter. She had no idea how or if it would ever get to her but she hoped someone here would help her find a way.

Dear Mom,

Hi, it's Haven. I wanted to let you know that I'm okay. I'm not lost or dead, I hope you aren't worrying too much. I know you'll probably never believe me, if this letter somehow even finds you, but before I went on that hike I believed that magical things could only ever happen in books.

Now, I'd have to believe that anything is possible because I'm living the impossible. Currently I am sitting at my desk in an actual castle after being told that I am somehow a fae princess. I know that it sounds crazy but I promise it's true. They told me that one or possibly both of my parents were secretly fae royalty that hadn't been able to live in this realm due to the rules used to create it long ago. I know you wouldn't have kept this from me but maybe dad had? Did you know? I won't lie and say that the thought of you guys lying to me for so long doesn't hurt but I'd rather have the truth than another lie.

Anyways, I just wanted to let you know that I am safe and alive. I hope this letter gets to you, I miss you.

All my love, Haven.

Haven couldn't put even half of her feelings into words but she hoped that what she had written would be enough to end the worry she was sure her mom was experiencing. Whenever she saw Rea next she'd decided to ask if there was any way the letter could make it to her mother.

For now, Haven tucked it into her desk drawer and got up to prepare to take a nice long bath and go to bed. The events of the day had been stressful and her whole body screamed with every move she made.

After pouring some of the soap Rea had given her to help calm aches and pains into the bathtub, Haven stretched to undo the back straps on her gorgeous pink dress. Laying the dress across the small vanity stool by the sink, she sunk into the tub.

Haven moaned loudly when the heat from the water combined with the effects of the soap immediately began to soothe away the aches the day had caused. Luckily, Haven had lit the dark purple silencing candle as soon as she entered her room or else anyone within hearing distance would've heard the soft sighs and moans she continued to make as the magic of the water drew away all of her physical pains.

Rea had explained that most fae had supernatural senses like heightened hearing and smell so if you wanted anything kept private you had to find ways around it like the silencing candle. At the time, Rea had also told a story about her parents knowing exactly when she lost her virginity as a teen because she hadn't learned the spell to mask your scent yet. As soon as she had come home from *hanging out* with her girlfriend, her parents immediately called bullshit on the excuse Rea had given them as to where she was. At the time Rea told the story, Haven had turned beet red from the thought of having to go through something like that.

After what had to be at least an hour, the bath water finally turned cold, forcing Haven to get out and dry off. After doing so, Haven dressed in nothing but a loose tank top and underwear and climbed into bed.

Watching the night pass through the windows that made up the doors to the balcony, Havens thoughts turned to the dream she'd had the night before. Immediately the ache between her legs returned, just as strong as during the dream.

Trying to banish those feelings, Haven turned from the windows, shut her eyes and attempted to doze off as best she could to no avail. Minutes passed and the roar between her legs wouldn't settle. Haven had never experienced feelings of lust so strong before, not even in the past when she'd been in a relationship with someone.

Haven waited as long as she could, thinking about anything and everything to sway her mind from its current path, clothes, food, knives, even that terribly embarrassing story Rea had told her. Nothing worked. Another ten minutes went by before Haven finally gave into the pull and slipped her hand down her side under the covers.

She began to circle her clit and allowing the feelings and of the dream to engulf her. Almost immediately, Haven could feel herself building towards an orgasm. Blurred, dream-like scenes played out in her mind as Haven moved her underwear to the side so she could feel herself fully.

Moving a finger down to her entrance, Haven gasped as she felt how soaked she was. Sliding one finger and then two into herself, Haven released a loud moan. With her eyes shut, blurry images were still playing behind them. Broad shoulders and dark hair. She could almost feel the man from the dream towering over her like he was in the room with her.

Quickly, Haven moved her other hand down to move back and forth across her clit while the other pumped in and out. It didn't take more than a moment for Haven to feel the telltale signs of her orgasm. Crying out as she hit her peak, Haven's legs clamped together and shook just slightly.

Settling into the pillows as she came down from her high, the pictures in Havens head slowly became clear. A slight panic rose in her when she recognized the features staring back at her. The dark hair, the bourbon and whiskey kisses. The broad, slightly intimidating shoulders. As the image of his face became clear, Haven recognized him as the mystery man from the library.

Thoroughly unsettled, Haven pulled the blankets up over her head and pondered what the hell just happened. She'd had the dream before she ever ran into the man.

Wondering what this could mean, Haven found herself even more unsettled when no answers came to mind. She gripped the blanket tighter around herself and hoped there wasn't a fae who could read minds. She absolutely did not want this *event* getting out into the realm and she certainly did not want the asshole from the library to find out what she had done, even if she had not known exactly what she was doing while she was doing it, or rather, who she was thinking of while she did it.

Haven would just have to file the memory away in the embarrassing folder in her brain and try her best not to ever think about it again.

Chapter Twenty-Three

The next two days went by rapidly. After a sleepless night plagued with thoughts of the mystery library man, Haven had woken to a small group of older fae women outside her door carrying the wardrobe they made for her. The women must have stayed up all night and all day since Haven arrived to have that many pieces done. She couldn't thank them enough, although she did try. All six of the women waved her off and told her they couldn't wait to see Haven wearing the clothes around the castle.

All of the clothes were spectacular. Ranging from vibrant dresses to thick leather pants the women told her would be for training, whatever that meant, they had thought of everything.

Eventually Rea showed up and explained that no matter what kingdom she was from, what powers she held or where she would be in line for a throne, Haven would take training classes here at the castle. She would be taught things like swordplay and hand to hand combat to politics and fae customs and everything in between. She would also be taught how to use her magic. That was what Haven was most excited for, although learning to use various weapons also sounded like something she would enjoy.

After Rea finished explaining about the training she would receive, Haven asked her about getting the letter to her mom. Before she left, Rea told her she would try to come up with a way to get it sent to her but she made no promises.

Now, Roman was due to show up at her door at any moment. The two of them were going to a dinner being hosted by the crown regent. It was an early celebration for what would be happening tomorrow. Sometime after dark tomorrow night, the two of them would be taking their bloodline and magics test. There was a celebration planned throughout the day for the general population but this dinner was supposed to be just for the two of them, the crown regent, his family and some sort of council they had yet to be introduced to.

Haven was dressed in one of her favorite dresses in her wardrobe, it was a glossy black V-neck with a high slit going up the left leg. The sleeves were nothing more than thin straps and the back dipped low. The dress definitely wasn't the most scandalous thing in the closet but it wasn't the most conserva-tive either.

It was a nice middle, Haven had decided. Especially when paired with a black shawl. Overall, the deep black made her skin seem to glow and her hair extra fiery. It showed off her midsize breasts well and made her feel genuinely confident.

Rea had done Haven's hair and makeup. Loose curls cascaded down her back and a small tiara with glittering black stones sat atop her head. Smokey black eyeshadow and deep red lipstick completed the look.

She felt regal, dangerous even. Haven imagined queens probably felt like this a lot. It bummed her out to consider that she might never be a queen, just a princess somewhere in line for a throne as Binah had initially said. Tomorrow would likely prove that so she was soaking up every little thing she could. No matter what happened, Haven knew that no one could take tonight and the way she felt wearing the tiara and dress, away from her.

A knock at the door pulled Haven from her thoughts. Opening it, she found a smiling Roman on the other side, dressed in all sorts of finery. Whoever made his wardrobe had done an excellent job.

A velvet black suit accompanied a deep red tie that matched the color of Havens lipstick, causing her to briefly wonder if that had somehow been planned. Roman had a glittering silver earring in one ear and she spied a big silver and red ring on one of his fingers.

"You look amazing" She smiled

"As do you" He bowed slightly. Haven giggled at the formal gesture and bowed back at him. Her giggle caused Roman to laugh and within seconds the slight tension Haven barely noticed in the air was gone. Roman offered his arm out for her to take,

"Your highness," He joked.

Haven chuckled and took his arm, locking the door behind them. Haven took a deep breath and mentally began preparing herself to deal with the crown regent. She hadn't seen him since their first meeting, all contact had gone through Astrea, but the thought of him still made her tense more than it probably should.

"That's a nice necklace" Roman commented as they walked through the corridors.

Haven touched the necklace Binah had given her, smiling slightly as she thanked him. She had thought about leaving it behind since the cut of the dress did nothing to hide it and in Binahs letter she had said to keep it hidden but it was just a necklace. She couldn't see a good enough reason to leave it behind. It's not like it could hurt anybody. Besides, Haven had grown quite attached to it.

"Where did you get it?" Roman asked. Haven turned her head briefly to look at him and noticed how tense he seemed. His jaw was tight and the arm he had around her seemed as stiff as a board.

"Oh, it was just in with the jewelry brought with my clothes," She lied.

Somehow, Haven could sense that admitting Binah had given it to her and that it appeared to be special somehow would not be a good thing. Even if she was only telling her friend.

Roman didn't respond, instead he just nodded and continued walking. Even though it seemed like he had dropped the subject, the tightness in his arm and slightly pissed off look on his face did not abate. Haven tried not to think about it, absently wondering if she should take the necklace off since it seemed to bother Roman. Before she could make that decision, they were outside of the dining room where the dinner was set to take place.

There was a guard on either side of the door. Roman removed his arm from hers and nodded to the guard on the left. Haven tried to calm her breathing as the door was opened. Taking one last big deep breath and hoping her nerves weren't showing too badly, she followed Roman through the doorway and into the room.

Immediately Haven noticed the shining chandelier hanging above the long wooden dinner table. It sparkled with some sort of engraved stone and must have held at least twenty lit candles. She was so busy looking at the chandelier that she barely noticed the two men walking towards her. One was the crown regent and the other startled Haven enough that she needed to grab onto Romans arm for balance.

Walking a step behind the crown regent was the man from the library. Now that he was in brighter light, his features were all the more stunning. Those sharp cheekbones, dark bourbon colored eyes, everything about him seemed more handsome now that she could see him properly rather than in the dim library light. In addition to the light making his features more alluring, Haven also noticed a small scar that went through his right eyebrow.

"Hello Haven it's lovely to see you" The crown regent spoke.

"And you yourself" She replied.

"Might I say, you look stunning" The crown regent looked her over, pausing on her necklace and leaving a sick feeling behind when he met her eyes again.

"Thank you" Haven smiled as brightly as she could despite the feeling of the crown regents eyes had left on her.

"Haven, Roman, might I introduce you to my son, Nikolaus. He will be joining us tonight."

Haven tried her best to school in her shock, hoping it wasn't written across her face. The two of them looked nothing alike. His son? She definitely had not seen that coming.

Nikolaus reached out and shook hands with Roman, offering him a smile.

"Please, call me Nik. Most fae do" Just his voice sent shivers down Haven's spine.

Suddenly she was reminded of her dream about him, and what she had done as a result of that dream. Since that night, thoughts of him hadn't bothered her except for a stray reminder when she visited the library to continue looking for the diary. Now she just hoped her face wasn't too flushed.

Nik reached his hand out to shake hers. As he did, his eyes dropped down to the swell of her breasts where the necklace was resting. They only stayed on the necklace for a few seconds before returning to look her in the eye. As he looked back up, a mask of distaste came over his face. Haven couldn't figure out what she had done to already have earned such strong dislike.

The touch of Niks skin as she slid her hand into his set Haven on fire. It warmed her entire body from the inside out. She held onto his hand for longer than was probably appropriate before they broke apart. At least he hadn't yanked his hand away and said another mean thing.

"Where is the council? I was told they'd be here?" Roman asked

"Ah yes, they should all be here soon" The crown regent announced. He clapped his hands together and gestured towards the table. As soon as he did, servants entered from a side door and began placing covered trays along the table before lining up against the far wall. They appeared to be awaiting another order.

Haven stepped up to the table with the others and sat down in the seat marked with a place card that had her name on it. Pulling her shawl tighter against herself, she picked up her water and took a sip to wet her now very dry throat. Somehow Haven already knew, this was going to be a long night.

Chapter Twenty-Four

Haven had just figured out she'd be sat across from Roman, sandwiched between a council member and Nik when the door opened, revealing a guard announcing the councils arrival.

She had been told in preparation of this dinner that the purpose of the council was to advise the king or queen, or in this kingdoms case, the crown regent. Every kingdom had a council whose advice, Rea had told her, was always taken with the utmost respect. If the majority of the council was of the opinion that the current ruler was unfit, they could challenge him or her and dethrone them, causing the majority ruling power to be handed over to their spouse or next in line for the throne.

Haven stood nervously from her seat. Chances were that these fae wouldn't be her advising council but she still wanted to impress them. As she stepped closer to the door to greet the council members slowly entering, she felt a soft caress on the back of her neck. Turning swiftly, she found no one there. The only person anywhere near her was Nik but he was standing at least five feet behind her so it couldn't have been him. Haven shook off the feeling, chalking it up to nerves.

The first council member stepped up to Haven and introduced herself.

"Hello" She held out her hand, "My name is Celia, you must be Haven"

"That would be me, it's great to meet you" Haven smiled

Celia was about the same height as Haven, with smooth dark brown skin, long pointed ears that had piercings going the entire length, almost unnerving pale blue eyes and a small pointed nose. Where the crown regent had immediately set off Havens warning bells, Celia made Haven feel nothing but warm. She liked this woman already even though she had said all of nine words to her.

"Alright, I'm going to find my seat and let you mingle," Celia smiled, brushing Havens arm as she stepped past her.

There were six more council members after Celia and few others were as kind as she had been. Mostly they just skeptically looked over Haven and then moved on to do the same to Roman. Haven was secretly glad it wasn't only her they disliked.

Smiling when she found herself seated next to Celia, Niks presence on her other side dimmed that smile slightly. As soon as they sat down, Nik leaned as far away from her as he could without falling out of his seat. At first, Haven thought she'd imagined it but when she glanced down at her lap, she could see that there was easily four inches of the seat of Niks chair on the side closest to her exposed.

The crown regent, much to Haven's displeasure, stood up from his seat at the head of the table to make a speech as dinner was served.

"Esteemed council members, I am honored to be hosting this dinner in celebration of the realms newest royals." As the crown regent spoke, Haven swore she could hear a slight snicker come from Nik.

"Tomorrow they will begin the biggest journey of their lives by embarking on the tests that will determine what bloodline they hail from and what powers they are blessed with. Then they will train here at our lovely castle to hone their skills before being sent to their respective kingdoms. Let us all raise a glass to honor them,"

The crown regent picked up his glass, as did the entire council and Nik. Haven followed Romans lead and picked up hers.

"To Roman and Haven" Nik spoke loudly, startling her.

"Here here" The council cheered aggressively. Haven didn't miss the slight sneer on the crown regents face that appeared to be directed at his son.

Taking the basket of rolls that had been passed to her, Haven set one down on her plate and passed along the basket before looking over the rest of the spread in front of her. Tension bracketed her shoulders with Nik on one side of her and the crown regent not so sneakily sizing her up from the head of the table. She hoped this dinner would be over quick.

***

The dinner took almost all night. If she didn't know any better, Haven might have guessed that the crown regent was trying to keep them there so they'd be tired for their tests the next day. Haven didn't know what these tests were but she had a feeling that being tired would not help. As it was, she was likely only going to get an hour or two of sleep.

Other than the unnecessary length, the dinner had surprisingly gone well. Some of the other council members appeared to warm to her. Although Roman definitely seemed to have an easier time getting them to like him.

After saying goodnight to Roman, Haven had departed for her room where she found Astrea waiting at her door. Yawning, Haven said,

"What are you doing here? It's the middle of the night"

"I wanted to see if you needed anything, I'm sure dinner was stressful" Rea offered her a conspiratorial smile.

"Are you sure you're not just here for the gossip?" Haven snickered as she unlocked her bedroom door.

"Well, if you're offering."

Both girls laughed as they entered the room. Rea tossed herself down on the bed, her white hair fanning out behind her.

"There really isn't much to tell. The council seemed alright, the crown regent was his usually arrogant self" Haven had shared her feelings about him with Rea yesterday. Rea had told her that most fae felt like that when in his presence and usually tried to ignore it.

"What about the regents son? Did you meet him?" Rea questioned as Haven stepped into the bathroom.

"He's... Alright" Haven responded. Rea laughed aloud at that.

"He's hot!" Rea called through her laughs causing Haven to snicker as well.

"Yeah I guess so, if you like broody assholes" Haven called through the open bathroom door. Problem was, Haven usually did like broody assholes.

Beginning to take off her earrings, Haven looked in the bathroom mirror and cursed loudly at what she found there.

Rea rushed into the bathroom with her, "What is it?" She asked frantically.

"My necklace is gone" Haven cried

It didn't even take her a moment to think before she knew exactly who took it.

Chapter Twenty-Five

Marching down the hall towards his room, Haven huffed. She made Rea tell her exactly how to get where she was going. Rea only told her on the condition that she agreed not to try to kill him. Apparently she'd seen enough fury written on Havens face to understand that she was truly pissed.

Ascending a small set of stairs, Haven walked towards the end of the empty hall and banged on the large wooden door ahead of her. It opened with a creak but no one was on the other side.

Stepping into the room, it was dark and appeared empty. Even better, she thought, she'd slip in, steal back the necklace and be gone. Once Haven got a little further into the large circular room, she realized she could hear the groan of a shower beyond the skinny door to the left of a large dark oak bed. She'd have to be fast.

A quick glance around the dark room revealed a small nightstand next to the large bed straight ahead of her, a matching dresser stood to the left next to a tall rectangular window set into the wall. To her right was a small couch facing a fireplace. Next to the fireplace was another door, Haven assumed it probably led to an office. Overall the room was fairly bare. There was only one pillow taking up space on the large bed.

Creeping up to the nightstand, Haven moved aside a few papers in search of her necklace and found nothing. Next she tried the small drawer, finding it locked. Moving to the dresser, she was careful not to disturb the few knickknacks sitting on top of it. There was a small statue of a wolf and another of a flying crow but no necklace. Haven listened to make sure the shower was still going before attempting to pull open the top drawer.

Cautious in her movements, she pushed aside the soft clothes she found. This drawer looked like it was full of the kind of clothes you'd wear to bed but again, no necklace. Moving to the next drawer, Haven opened it and found nothing but boxers. Right as she went to close it rather than digging through what would probably be nothing but underwear, Havens eye caught on the glint of something at the far back of the drawer.

Just as she closed her fist around the object she'd found, Haven got the same sense she'd had in the library. She was being watched. Before she could spin around, someone grabbed her from behind and forced her up against the wall next to the dresser.

"What the hell are you doing in my room?" He growled into her ear. His grip was loose enough for Haven to turn. When she did, she found him barely a breath away from her.

"Looking for this" Haven held up her necklace she'd managed to snag from his drawer between them and looked Nik dead in the eye as she said,

"Looks like someone's got sticky fingers"

Nik rolled his eyes and pressed himself further into her, his hands on the wall on either side of her head. The slight contact between them was making Havens head spin. Taking a moment to look Nik over, Haven realized he was in nothing but a towel, his chest still gloriously wet from his shower and showcasing a whole array of tattoos. She could also still hear the shower running. He must've left it on so the sound would disguise his footsteps.

Nik leaned in closer to her ear and asked, with disdain dripping from his voice,

"I'll ask you again princess, what are you doing in my room?"

Havens mind tripped on the word princess. How could someone make something said with so much hate also sound so hot?

"And I'll repeat myself *Nik*, I was looking for this" She gestured as much as she could to the necklace currently pinned between them.

"It looked terrible on you, I was doing you a favor. You shouldn't have worn it"

Haven scoffed. Tilting her head back against the wall and rolling her eyes, she said,

"Oh really? That's your excuse? I want the real answer Nik!"

Niks eyes tracked the pulse in her throat that was exposed when she tilted her back against the wall. She watched as his eyes dilated, barely catching the movement in the dim light of the room.

"I told you, you shouldn't have worn it" Nik spoke lowly and aggressively, eyes still on her throat. A speck of truth rung out in that statement but before she could question him further, Nik looked down at the dress from dinner she was still wearing, leaned in close and continued,

"Actually, I think this whole getup looks *terrible* on you."

Haven sucked in a breath, Nik was so close that Haven could feel his breath on her neck. Haven didn't get a second to think as Nik slowly dipped his hand into the slit of her dress.

Parting the fabric, he laid his palm directly on the outside of her soft thigh. Her skin burned where Nik touched her. His hand was barely resting on the outside of her thigh and it was still one of the most erotic things she'd ever felt. Haven struggled to bite back a moan as Nik slowly, so slowly, slid his hand higher, parting the fabric even more. It was dark enough he probably couldn't see the stretch marks on her thighs and she was somewhat thankful for that. She'd always struggled a bit with showing off her body to romantic partners. Her friends usually weren't a problem, just like it had been with Rea, but anyone she was attracted to was an entirely different story. She may dislike the guy but Haven could admit she was most definitely attracted to him.

Thoughts of the necklace were pushed to the very back of her mind when Nik laid a light kiss to the sensitive skin just below her ear. Her heart was pounding in her chest. The ache in her core seemed incessant, it only deepened when Niks lips parted and he ran the tip of his fangs over that same sensitive skin.

Haven reached a hand up and wound it through the thick hair at the base of Nik's skull, tugging slightly. A soft groan sounded from him. Pushing himself impossibly closer to her, Haven could feel the evidence of Niks attraction, especially when he hitched her leg up through the slit in her dress and wound it around his hip.

A sudden voice pulled Haven and Nik from the trance they had found themselves in,

"Am I interrupting?"

Nik threw himself away from her, the loss of contact and wash of cool air brought Haven back into her mind where she realized exactly *what* she'd been doing and exactly *who* she'd been doing it with. Taking the opportunity, Haven darted out the open door behind the stranger. She didn't even bother to greet whoever had interrupted them as she ran, the necklace still clutched in her palm.

Once she was safely down the hall, she let her mind wander over what just happened. Realizing something she cursed, Nik completely distracted her from finding out why he had taken her necklace in the first place. Haven didn't know if it was intentional or not but she had the feeling it was. Embarrassment burned on her face as she thought about how easily she'd been played.

At least she had gotten back her necklace, Haven thought as she made her way back to her room. Unlocking the door, Haven crashed down on her bed, still in her dinner clothes and still feeling the result of being up close and personal with Nik. She quickly decided to hide beneath her covers and try her best to forget about everything that happened tonight. Even if part of her did not want to forget, she would not be listening to *that* part again anytime soon.

Chapter Twenty-Six

S hit, Nik thought. Delroy was going to kick his ass. Turning from where he still was facing the wall, he tried not to let his mind, or body, reel over what just happened. He tried to will his erection away as he turned but no luck. Apparently whatever gods left out there were determined to make Niks life a living hell, something that started long before today.

After doing the best he could and turning, Nik found himself face to face with a very angry Delroy. As he met his friends' eyes, his arousal instantly went away. Nik quickly decided that he would have been better off still facing the wall.

"What the hell were you thinking?" Delroy yelled.

Quickly raising a hand to cast a silencing spell, Nik tried to come up with a reason that might satisfy his best friend. Unfortunately, nothing came to mind.

Still only in a towel, Nik ran a hand through his hair, her touch still on his skin like a flare of heat on the coldest of nights. Nik could tell he needed to try to explain before his friend blew a gasket.

Grabbing some clothes out of the nearest open drawers, Nik tossed them on and did his best to tell his friend what happened without implicating Haven too much. He might want to hate her but that did not mean he wanted an angry Delroy anywhere near her. Nik knew Delroy wouldn't physically hurt her but he could say some seriously mean and awful things once he got going.

"I don't know, okay! I stole something from her at dinner and somehow she figured out it was me and came looking for it. What you saw, it started out as a way to distract her and just sort of spiraled from there"

Nik could tell Delroy was barely containing his anger. Watching his best friend pace back and forth in front of the fireplace, Nik could see the anxiety hounding him.

Delroy had been Niks best friend since they were three. He was two inches taller than Niks six foot two and could probably kick Niks ass if it ever truly came down to that. Years in the royal guard would do that to someone. He was still wearing his uniform, likely just coming off shift. The silver metal of the hooks on his breastplate complemented his dark hair that was shorter on the sides and only slightly longer on the top. Pointed dark brown eyes and light brown skin popped against the crimson red tunic under his armor.

"Well I had come to see how dinner went but I think I just got my answer" Delroy snarked, pulling Nik out of his thoughts.

"Hey, back off. I didn't mean for that to happen, dinner went exactly as planned. Nothing's going to change, she and everyone else will think I hate her. My father will never know anything. It won't happen again" Niks stern words and serious tone seemed to help calm Delroy as he went from pacing to settling into the couch.

"What did you steal from her?" Delroy asked

"A necklace she was wearing," Nik answered. Delroy gave him a confused look prompting Nik to explain more,

"The necklace is very easily recognizable. If someone had realized what it was then dinner probably would have ended in screaming or bloodshed, or both."

Delroy nodded at Niks explanation. He knew as soon as Delroy saw the necklace for himself that he'd understand. Nik just had to hope Haven wouldn't take it out again until after tomorrow. Then the big secret would be out and something as simple as that necklace couldn't completely derail their plans.

"So everything went well?" Delroy asked

Nik nodded,

"I think it went okay. Celia liked her, but that's a given. The rest of the council seemed rather cold towards her but not immediately distrustful or hateful. I think their coldness will help ease my father for awhile" Nik slumped down on the couch next to his friend.

"Good," Delroy looked to Nik as he spoke, "So really, what was that I just walked in on?"

Nik turned away from his friend, feeling heat creeping up his neck and face.

"Honestly, I don't know. Being so close to her I just felt drawn in, I guess. I didn't even realize what I was doing until I was already doing it."

Delroy nodded and said in a stern voice, "I get that, but you can't let it get in the way"

"I won't" Nik promised, he was almost afraid to admit this part, "I almost bit her"

Delroy spun fully toward Nik, eyes wide, "Are you fucking serious?" He breathed, Nik could feel the intensity and concern radiating off of his friend in waves.

Nik nodded. He knew that fact alone could wreck everything they were and had been working towards. He needed to hate her. He needed her to hate him. Nik couldn't have it any other way. For his safety and hers. At least for now, their lives depended on it.

Chapter Twenty-Seven

Bright light filtered in through the balcony doors. After rustling around for probably an hour, determined not to get herself off to images of Nik, Haven had finally fallen asleep. The aches and pains combined with exhaustion in her body told her she hadn't gotten to sleep for long.

Sliding out of bed, Haven began undressing, wincing as the fabric of her dress brushed past her ears. The aches in her body were becoming more and more frequent. Rea had told her it was her body changing into that of a fae and that she'd likely start to see some major changes over the next couple of weeks.

After showering and drying off, Haven wrapped herself in a towel and went to her armoire to pick out an outfit for the day's festivities. She was supposed to be able to come back and change before her tests tonight. So right now, she didn't have to worry about dressing appropriately for her tests, whatever they may be.

Just as she pulled out something she thought suitable for a royal fae festival, there was a knock on her door. Expecting it to be Rea, she called for the fae to come in, having unlocked it earlier in expectation of her friends arrival. It was not Rea who stepped through the door.

Haven gasped lightly. Turning to view the uninvited guest, she recognized him as the fae who'd interrupted her and Nik last night. She didn't know if she should thank him, yell at him to go away or pretend like last night never happened.

Choosing ignorance, Haven offered him a smile and introduced herself,

"Hi, I'm Haven. I'd say it was nice to meet you but since I'm not sure what you're here for, I'll have to hold off on that assumption."

The fae standing in her doorway smirked before holding out his hand and saying,

"I'm Delroy. I came here to talk to you about the events of last night."

Haven blushed and took his outstretched hand. Scanning his features, Haven found light brown skin with hair shaved on the sides and slightly longer on top. Accompanying his dark brown eyes and short pointy ears was a smile that raised the skin on Haven arms. Where Nik appeared harmless at times, even though Haven knew that was definitely not the case, this man was the exact opposite. There was no doubting that a predator had just stepped into the room. Tension bracketed Havens shoulders while she quickly took her hand from his, slipped into the bathroom and covered the towel she was wearing with a bathrobe.

"What can I do for you?" She asked as she exited the bathroom.

"I want you to stay away from my friend" He responded plainly. If Haven didn't know any better, she'd think he was discussing something as simple as the weather. Tone of voice aside, the look on his face told Haven there was definitely a threat not so well concealed in his words.

"Maybe you should tell your friend to stay away from me" She bit back. Delroy huffed a laugh in response, the sound entirely animal.

"Please, if you hadn't been in his room, practically throwing yourself at him I'm sure Nik wouldn't touch you with a ten foot pole"

Haven scoffed at that, "Well I can assure you, the only pole Nik was touching me with was hanging between his legs" Delroy's eyes flared with anger at her response. He was clearly pissed. Why she thought provoking him was a good idea, Haven didn't know but she wasn't about to let some random guy come into her room and walk all over her.

Delroy didn't get a chance to respond because Astrea came breezing through the slightly open door carrying a garment bag.

"Oh hello" She greeted, obviously thrown off by Delroys presence.

He nodded to Rea in response, cast another scathing glare Havens way and exited her room. Rushing to the door Haven called out to him,

"Make sure to tell your little friend not to take things that don't belong to him!"

Slamming the door behind her, Haven turned to Rea.

"What was that about?" She asked

"Don't worry about it." Haven smiled, attempting to focus on something else by grabbing the garment bag in Reas outstretched hand.

"Alrighty then," Rea started, "Let's get you dressed. You're going to love what I have for you!"

Haven smiled, "I'm sure I will! Let's do this!"

After hanging up and opening the garment bag, all Haven could do was gape. The dress was gorgeous. Rea had been right, she did love it, just maybe not for herself.

Keeping with the darker color theme was a cinched waist, halter top dress with black and gold lacing, a keyhole back and a high low skirt that Haven all but drooled over. It truly was a gorgeous dress but it also showed *a lot* of skin. Rea had brought elbow high matching black gloves and black boots but the upper part of her legs, a large part of her back and most of her shoulders and collarbones would be showing thanks to the cut and tightness of the dress. Haven was mostly self conscious about the thickness of her legs and the soft rolls on her sides. This dress would do nothing to hide those things, especially her legs.

Usually she tried not to let her insecurities bother her but she was going out in front of the entire kingdom today. Combining her anxiety about that and a dress that highlighted some of her main insecurities sounded like a recipe for disaster.

"Just try it on and if you don't like it we can find you something different alright?" Rea spoke softly to Haven, sensing her nervousness.

"Alright" Haven nodded and slipped the dress off its hanger.

"I want you to wait to look at yourself until I'm all done with you, okay?" Rea asked with a smile

"Agreed" Haven timidly smiled back

About an hour went by and Haven hadn't looked into the mirror once as she'd promised Rea. The dress fit perfectly and was actually rather comfortable despite its tight fit. Dressed in the gloves, boots, hair and makeup done along with the small dagger Binah had given her strapped to her thigh, Haven felt like a total badass. All that was left were the few finishing touches currently being put on and then it was time to take a look in her floor length mirror.

Taking a deep breath, Haven stood from where she sat at her desk while Rea did her hair and smoothed down her dress. Rea secured a delicate tiara at the top of her head and a black choker necklace with a small gold charm dangling from it.

"Wow you look amazing" Rea told her, tears brimming at the edge of her eyes.

Haven looked down at herself. She had to admit, even though she hadn't seen herself in the mirror yet, she already knew that her anxieties might have gotten the best of her earlier. She may have more weight on her lower body than Rea or some of the girls she'd gone school with but that didn't mean she was any less beautiful. Both girls were wearing their best dresses, Rea having gotten ready before coming to Havens room, and entirely ready to step through the door and have a blast at todays festival.

Stepping up to the mirror, Haven revealed to herself exactly what she'd already known;

She truly looked like a queen.

Chapter Twenty-Eight

Taking a deep breath, Haven stepped through the open door to the ballroom where she was supposed to meet Roman. A few fae were milling about inside, finishing up the decor around the room.

After games, performances, music and lunch at the festival on the castle grounds, Haven and Roman would begin their tests. Haven still didn't know what exactly she'd be doing in her tests and when she'd asked Roman, he didn't know either. Not knowing made Haven nervous but she kept telling herself that she was not the first, nor would she be the last to go into something like this with absolutely no clue as to what was going on. It helped that Haven had always been decent at improvising. Granted, swapping honey for vanilla extract after running out while making banana bread wasn't exactly the same but the premise was there.

After completing their tests, Haven and Roman would be escorted here, to the ballroom, where a ceremony will be taking place to officially welcome them into fae royal society.

Nerves raked down Havens spine when she didn't immediately spot Roman. Rea would wait with her until he arrived but standing around waiting while the fae around you not so subtly sized you up was not Havens idea of a good time.

"Try and relax, enjoy today" Rea nudged her arm and smiled.

"I'll try," Haven promised.

"Are you sure you don't know anything about the tests tonight?" Haven asked again, trying to gain any little tidbit of information she could. She knew Rea really didn't know much and had already told her what she did, but she could know something and not even realize it, at least that's what Haven was hoping.

"No, I don't know much of anything about them, as I already told you. But I assure you, everything will be fine. Royals everywhere like to keep the intricate details about these things very close, but no one has ever gotten hurt."

Haven smiled weakly at that, Rea's words only helping slightly.

"You will be fine" Rea continued to reassure her, "Just think, after today you will know for sure who your parents were, what magics you possess and likely even how far in line for a throne you are. You will get answers to questions you haven't even thought about asking. After today you get to start training with your magic, with weapons, you will learn about the kingdom you will go to and so many other wonderful things." Rea squeezed her arm around Haven as she spoke, offering an additional level of comfort.

"Thank you Rea, you're pretty good at that whole reassurance thing"

Rea's smile brightened, "I know" she joked.

A few more minutes passed before Roman showed up, a short blonde man trailing behind him. Haven assumed he was Romans lady's maid, or whatever the male equivalent of a lady's maid was. Rea walked off as soon as Roman appeared. Haven thought her sudden disappearance was odd but she didn't get any time to dwell on it.

"Wow Haven, you look stunning!" Roman took Havens hand and spun her around, causing a small laugh to bubble up.

"Thank you Roman, you look great as well," She quickly scanned the outfit he was wearing, finding a sharp black tunic with silver etching tucked into dark brown leathers and knee-high black riding boots. A small crown similar to Havens sat atop his freshly cropped black hair. He looked ethereal, like a king preparing to rule a kingdom. Haven could only hope she looked as put together as he.

"Shall we?" Roman extended his arm.

"We shall" Haven nodded and took his arm.

Together they walked across the hall to the open castle entrance doors. Taking another deep breath and putting on her strongest smile, Haven stepped through the doorway with Roman beside her. Exiting the castle, Haven paused at the sight she found displayed before her.

"Wow." She breathed. Roman didn't respond, he didn't say anything at all. Haven knew he was likely also wrapped up in the sight ahead of them,

Sprawled across the front castle grounds were rows and rows of tents, banners and booths. Haven could even spot a stage to the far left. Everywhere she looked something was going on, there was a juggler with flaming knives, a few displays of elemental magic, someone walking through the rows with a mule carrying colorful fabrics. Another lady appeared to be selling different potions and brews. Haven could see countless kids running about, some with food and toys, all with big smiles on their faces. There was so much *life* going on it was impossible not to smile.

"Are you ready?" Roman asked

"Absolutely!" She responded, "Let's do this!"

Together they began walking down the slight slope of the castle grounds to where the festival was in full swing.

Chapter Twenty-Nine

Crowds descended as soon as they made it to the outskirts of the festival. So many people offered Haven and Roman blessings and advice. It was crazy and chaotic but Haven hadn't stopped smiling yet. Back in the human realm, she'd had a bit of a hard time in big crowds but almost all day there had been a lightness hanging around her she hadn't been able to shake, not that she wanted to.

After what had to be hundreds of hellos and dozens of conversations, Haven found herself sitting under the shade of a large tree on the very outskirts of the festival snacking on a turkey and cheese sandwich. For hours she wandered up and down each row, looking at items for sale, listening to speeches, learning about the customs and traditions of the people of Drailia.

Her feet had finally begun hurting after about three hours. The boots she was wearing held the appearance of horse riding boots but had a thick cushion in the soles that thankfully kept her feet from hurting more than she could handle. A soft breeze blew by, blowing a strand of hair into her mouth. She managed to toss the majority of it over her shoulder but a few stray pieces were still sticking to the lip gloss she had on.

"Well that's not very queenly" A sarcastic voice spoke from the other side of the tree. Unfortunately, it was a voice she recognized.

"Well then I guess it's a good thing I'm not a queen" She snapped back

Nik stepped around the tree, looking down at her.

"You could be" He responded.

Rolling her eyes, she asked,

"How long have you been over there?"

"Long enough to wonder if you would moan the same way while I was buried between your thighs as you do when you eat"

Haven scoffed and rolled her eyes, attempting to hide her flush. It was possible she had made a few noises while she was eating but, in her defense, she thought she was alone and the sandwich tasted like heaven.

"Not that it's any of your business but I'm much louder in bed" She snarked back

Nik snickered and lowered himself to sit beside Haven.

"What are you doing?" She asked

"What? Do you own this tree or something? Is no one else allowed to sit under it?"

Haven, again, rolled her eyes.

"I was enjoying a few moments of peace after the chaos that has been this morning"

Nik smiled slightly at that, the hard mask of anger and resentment he normally wore disappearing for only a moment,

"I know how you feel, when the kingdom gets together like this it can be rather crazy"

Leaning her head back against the tree, Haven somehow found herself relaxing in Niks presence. When he wasn't throwing jaded looks at her, saying something rude or turning her on so much she couldn't think straight, Haven found that being in his presence was actually fairly calming. He had this air about him that Haven couldn't help but be drawn into. It was only slightly different than the one surrounding Roman and so far, he was turning out to be one of her closest friends.

Haven casually admired the tattoos peeking out the top of Niks white tunic. She hadn't been able to get a good look at them in the dark of his room the other night but she found herself wanting to know more about them, why he got them and what they meant. Haven thought to herself that maybe it wouldn't be so bad to get to know him.

"You shouldn't let the attention from today go to your head. You aren't special, more than likely you'll turn out to be a nobody princess with little to no power and one of the last in line for whatever throne you end up under"

Or not

Haven recovered quickly, apparently either the guy didn't know how to be nice or for whatever reason, really did not like her. She had a feeling it was the latter.

"Like you?" She responded, distracting herself by picking at some dirt under her nails.

Nik rolled his eyes but Haven could swear she saw the ghost of a smile playing on his lips.

"I have power. Lots of it and I will rule one day. I'll always be one of the most important fae in this realm. My father has made sure of that" He sneered

"Yeah but you hate that don't you?" Haven guessed, she had no evidence to back up her claim but something about the way he spoke had given her that impression. She could practically feel the resentment pouring off of him when he spoke of his father.

"You have no idea what you're talking about" He scoffed. But Haven could see, she'd hit the nail directly on its head. Nik may have power and be the only one directly in line for a throne that wasn't supposed to be his but he didn't want it. He very clearly resented what his father wanted for him. Or maybe, he simply resented his father.

Nik quickly stood and began heading back towards the festival.

"For future reference, I don't take kindly to know it all princesses sticking their noses where they don't belong. Leave me the hell alone." He called over his shoulder as he walked away

"You came up to me asshole!" She shouted back

Nik grumbled something in response but it was too low for Havens not yet fully developed fae hearing to catch. He might have been an asshole but damn he looked good walking away.

***

After her and Niks mostly unpleasant interaction, Haven had gone back into the depths of the festival, met more fae and listened to a speech given by the crown regent about how happy he was to be hosting and training Haven and Roman until they left for their respective kingdoms. The whole speech seemed like bullshit to Haven and if she guessed correctly, she wasn't the only one that thought that. During the crown regents speech Haven spotted at least three other fae roll their eyes, scoff under their breath and generally not pay attention.

Night was quickly approaching. Haven was due to go inside and change into more appropriate apparel for her test that was supposed to be starting sometime in the next hour. She still didn't know what the test involved. No one seemed inclined to tell her either.

As it was, Haven was heading down the path back towards the castle so she could go up to her room and change. Most likely she'd pick out some sort of thick leggings and tunic, something versatile and simple so she'd be able to move and be comfortable no matter what tonight held.

Just as she made it to the castle doors, large hands grabbed Haven from behind, immediately covering her mouth so she couldn't scream for help.

Haven kicked out as she was lifted off the ground, struggling and trying to get away from her captor. The tight dress she was wearing didn't exactly make it easy. The closest festival booth seemed an entire football field away. Surely if she could just get her kidnappers hand away from her mouth she could scream and someone would hear her.

An entire festival full of fae and no one seemed to notice Haven being dragged across the castle grounds towards the forest.

She managed to elbow into the person holding her. She heard a grunt just before something blunt came down against her temple and everything went black.

Chapter Thirty

Haven woke on the cold ground, a throbbing pain echoing through her head where she'd been hit. Putting a hand to her head and feeling a small bump, Haven stood on wobbly legs. A quick glance made it obvious her captor had dumped her deep in a forest. If she had to guess, Haven would say she was in the woods near the castle. She couldn't see anyone else around nor could she see light in any direction.

Why would someone do this, she asked herself. Was someone trying to keep her from taking her bloodline and power tests? Was this a part of the test?

Thoughts tumbled through Havens head as she tried to get her bearings. Her dress was dirty, the small crown atop her head was sitting at an angle and her left glove was ripped. She did her best to dust herself off but unfortunately some of what was on her dress appeared to have already left a stain. Haven hoped Rea and the seamstresses wouldn't be too mad when they saw the dress. Afterall, it wasn't her fault she'd been kidnapped and dumped in a forest.

She reached for the dagger Binah had given her, thankfully finding it still strapped to her thigh.

As Haven tried to remove a small stick from her hair, a rustling sounded to her left. Keeping her hand on her dagger in case this turned out to be some kind of trap, Haven made her way towards where the sound appeared to be coming from. Her legs were still slightly shaky but were getting better by the minute.

Five minutes of walking turned up nothing. Just when Haven was ready to give up her search for the source of the sound a voice called out,

"Help! Can anybody hear me?"

Haven took two more steps in the direction she'd been heading before she saw the source of the voice standing in a small clearing twenty feet away. It was a young fae woman holding a toddler close to her. They were clearly lost and looked terrified.

"What happened to you?" Haven called as she made her way towards them as quickly as she could without tripping and falling.

"Hi! Oh thank the gods!" The woman exclaimed, "I was on my way back home from the festival when a strange man grabbed me and dumped me here! I've been wandering for what feels like hours. Do you know the way back to the castle?"

Haven shook her head, "I don't but I'm sure we can figure it out"

The woman didn't seem so convinced, a few tears fell from her eyes as she pulled the little boy she was holding in her arms closer to her.

"I was supposed to be watching Thomas so his parents could have fun at the festival. What are they going to do if we can't find our way back? We could die out here!"

The young woman was clearly headed towards a full blown panic attack. Haven had been through enough of them to recognize what they looked like. Attempting to reassure the woman, Haven reached out and rested a hand on her arm.

"It'll be alright" Haven told her, using her best calming tone. Before she could tell if she'd calmed the woman at all, an arrow flew past Havens head and lodged itself in the tree next to them earning a piercing scream from the woman Haven did not yet know the name of.

"RUN!" Haven yelled.

Attempting to usher the woman and child the opposite direction the arrow had come from, Haven ran directly behind the two of them in hopes that if any arrows found their marks, they'd hit her and not either of them.

She called to the woman, telling her to run in a zig zag so they weren't such easy targets. Thankfully, the woman listened and immediately began weaving through the forest. Another arrow lodged in the tree directly to their right, causing the group to run left. If Haven had a moment to think she'd probably wonder if the arrows weren't meant to hit them but rather, to corral them.

The woman slammed to a halt, causing the little boy to tumble out of her arms and Haven to run directly into her back. Before she could mumble out an apology and check to see if the boy was okay,

Haven saw what made the woman stop so suddenly. Blocking the path ahead of them was a very large man. He was dressed in all black, almost completely blending into his surroundings.

If it weren't for the full moon illuminating him, she'd never have known he was there.

Quickly whipping around to the front of the woman, Haven cast her arms out in an effort to protect her and the child. She felt the woman crowding as close behind Haven as she could get. The woman must have picked up Thomas from where he had fallen because she felt him pressed up against Havens back, likely cradled in the womans arms.

"What do you want?" She yelled at the man in front of her.

A low chuckle came from him but he didn't answer.

"One will die tonight!" Someone called from the woods to her right. A second later, a man Haven did not recognize stepped out of the shadows with a bow gripped in his hand.

The woman behind her whimpered, Haven knew she had to stall. What appeared to be only a little further ahead, Haven could see what she prayed was the edge of the festival. Hopefully if Haven stalled long enough someone might come across them and help or hear the cries coming from the woman. Haven didn't know exactly how strong the fae's gifted hearing was but she had to hope for the best. If that didn't work then maybe she could find a way for the woman and child to escape and run for help.

"Leave them alone!" She yelled, causing the dark man blocking the path to chuckle again. Somewhere out in the woods, Haven could hear a crows call.

"No can do princess, we have orders. Someone has to die." The man with the bow responded. Since he was the only one talking,

Haven guessed he was the one in charge. Turning to look him in the eye, Haven kept the woman close to her back.

"Why can't you be the one to die?" She snapped

The man chuckled, "Because it doesn't work like that!" He said in an obvious tone. He drew his bow, aiming it directly at Haven.

"Let them go!" She said lowly, "They don't deserve this"

Haven didn't add that she didn't deserve this either, that would probably do nothing more than make the man standing in front of her chuckle again.

Just then, an unnatural gust of wind blew the woman and Thomas away from safety behind her. The man quickly refocused his aim towards them.

"Choose!" He shouted

Haven had only a split second to think, the woman and child didn't deserve this and if Haven could stop them from being killed, she would.

Right as the man loosed his arrow, Haven moved faster than she knew possible, jumping directly in the path of the flying projectile. She heard the woman cry out behind her just as the arrow found its mark, deep in Havens stomach.

Chapter Thirty-One

Haven had never given much thought to how she would die. As she looked down at the arrow protruding from her stomach, she had only one thought,

At least she'd gone out heroically.

Looking up to where the man was still standing a few feet away from her, Haven found him wearing a wide smile,

"Nicely done" He told her

Confusion wracked through Haven as he came to stand in front of her, his footsteps echoing through the forest. Haven hoped the sound of his footsteps wouldn't be the last thing she heard. Gripping the arrow tightly, he leaned in and whispered,

"All hail the Queen"

As soon as he yanked out the arrow, Haven stumbled back in shock. She felt no pain at all. None. Nothing when the man had initially gripped the arrow, nothing when he'd pulled the arrow back out and nothing after the fact. It was as if she'd never been shot at all.

Looking down to where she'd been impaled only seconds ago, Haven found no blood. In fact, as she put a hand to her stomach where she'd thought the arrow had impaled her, she found not even a wound. The only evidence she'd been shot at all was the small hole in her dress from the tip of the arrow.

Havens brows knitted together. Looking up in confusion she asked,

"I don't understand, what's going on?"

"You passed your test" The man told her, still wearing that wide and slightly creepy smile.

After he said it, Haven felt a strange power erupting from her. Gasps rang out from all around her. Somehow, a large group of fae had gathered while she'd been freaking out about being shot. Haven had been so distracted that she hadn't even seen or heard them show up. Their abrupt arrival shocked Haven, although she didn't get much time to dwell because next thing she knew, the air suddenly changed and the fae gathered went from hesitant interest to outright awe.

Feeling heat at her feet, Haven looked down, her own gasp ringing out as she did. An entire circle of ground around her feet was on fire, wisps of flame floated in the air around her like ashes rising with the wind. The fire wasn't even the most shocking part. Every bit of Haven, from the tips of her toes to her fingers and even the curled ends of her hair was wreathed in shadows. They were all over her, circling her arms, flowing through strands of her hair and crawling up her legs. The shadows oddly provided a warmth wherever they touched her skin.

Haven could not believe what she was seeing.

Almost instantly, people began dropping to their knees. A few pointed at her, whispering to themselves. It took her a moment to understand what they were pointing at, sure a woman standing in a ring of fire covered in shadows probably wasn't the most common thing to happen here but these fae were looking at her with so much awe in their eyes you'd think a god was standing before them. As Haven was about to, again, ask what the hell was going on, she felt a pulsing heat right above her heart.

Looking down, it took Haven a second to figure out exactly what she was looking at. Above her heart, hovering close enough to touch the fabric of her dress were two symbols created out of the same fire and shadows currently wrapped around her body and circling her feet. Upon closer inspection, Haven thought she might faint. Those weren't random symbols.

Floating close enough to her to be patches on a uniform were two crests, crests she immediately recognized from her time spent in the library searching the stacks for the diary Binah wanted her to find. Thankfully Haven paid close enough attention to the paintings and various pictures around the library of all the royal crests to not be completely in the dark.

She might recognize the crests but that didn't mean she understood what they were doing floating above her tattered dress.

"What does this mean?" She asked aloud, hoping someone might take pity on her and answer.

A few people called out, "All hail the Queen," which only deepened Havens confusion.

The man that had originally been blocking the path reached up to pull off his hood, he was the only one not currently kneeling. As his hand slid further back and his face was revealed, Haven recognized him. It was the crown regent, Niks father. A few gasps rang out with his reveal. Anyone who made a sound immediately closed their mouth as the crown regent turned to Haven and said,

"It means that you are so much more than we ever could have guessed"

Turning to address the crowd behind him, the crown regent appeared to be excited, maybe even gleeful at this news but Haven could see the barely concealed rage brewing under the surface. It was dark and dangerous and made the hair on the back of Havens neck stand up on end.

No matter what words may come out of his mouth, Haven knew the truth. She could see it in his eyes, sense it in the thinly veiled hostility radiating off of him. He did not find this news good by any stretch of the imagination.

"For almost a century we have believed the Montali and Rionach bloodlines to be lost, but they are lost no longer! I would like to introduce you all to Haven Montali Rionach, daughter of Morana Montali and Robert Rionach. The next great Queen of this kingdom!"

As his last words rang out and fae began clapping, Haven found, possibly for the first time ever, that she was genuinely afraid of what might happen next.

Chapter Thirty-Two

The last hour had been a whirlwind. After the crown regents declaration, Haven had been whisked away to the castle and up to her room where she was promised someone would come and explain things a little more thoroughly. Haven thought she understood most of what happened but the idea of someone coming to her and explaining it, hopefully in plain terms, helped calm her nerves.

Her head was spinning from everything she already knew. Apparently her parents, the people she'd known in the human realm, either weren't her biological parents or they were secretly long lost fae royalty that had been missing for over a century. Also, she apparently held influence over shadows and fire as shown by the shadows that wrapped around her and the fire that burned at her feet. Honestly, while she still didn't quite get that part, it felt like the least of her concerns.

Sighing, Haven tossed herself down on her bed. She was still wearing the tattered dress but she'd taken off her boots and untangled the crown from her hair. What she really needed was a nice hot bath and a good scrub but she didn't want to be indisposed when someone showed up to explain the craziness of tonight. Especially if it was someone she didn't know. Haven might be okay if Rea caught her in the bath but if some stranger walked in while she was scrubbing dirt out of places she didn't want to admit it had gotten into then she wouldn't have to worry about the crown regent because she'd surely die of embarrassment.

Another few minutes passed before there was a soft but persistent knock at the door.

"Come in," Haven called.

Rea poked her head through the door, a large smile plain to see across her face.

"I heard someone is in need of an explanation!" The cheeriness in Astreas voice set Haven on edge. It had been a long day and while she usually loved Rea's ability to brighten things up, she'd rather have a straight and to the point explanation so she could go panic in the bath in peace.

Haven immediately sat up, "You can tell me what the hell's going on?"

"Yup" Rea sat down on the bed next to Haven, still wearing that overly cheery smile. Obviously she hadn't sensed Havens rapidly dampening mood.

"There isn't much to explain really" Rea started, "You already know that the rules of the spell used to create our realm prevented the rulers at that time from staying here longer than two weeks. After that, they'd have to return to the human realm, leaving their offspring to take over. Obviously they did not all have children at the time so it was decreed that in their place a crown regent would rule until they had children. At some point in that child's life, they would find their way here, usually by accident, where they would be tested to see what bloodline they hailed from and what powers, if any, they held."

Haven nodded, she did know all of this already. Getting impatient waiting for Rea to finish her explanation, she began to pick at her fingernails.

Astrea stretched her hand over to Havens, lacing their fingers together and preventing Haven from continuing her nervous habit.

"As time went on, heirs for all the bloodlines except the Montali and Rionach bloodlines were found. Fae were sent into the human world to look for them but no one ever found anything to prove their whereabouts. For almost the last century, many assumed that Robert Rionach and Morana Montali were dead. Fae are practically immortal and based on the amount of time that had passed, most assumed that if a child of either was going to be born it would have happened already." Rea paused, taking a moment to check in with Haven before continuing,

"Eventually our crown regent forcefully convinced the Rionach crown regent to give over her power, thus joining the two kingdoms under one rule. This obviously angered the people of Shaston, the Rionach kingdom, but at the time, there wasn't much they could do to stop it. There has been a lot of resentment growing over the years but I suppose that's not what's important right now."

Haven didn't know anything about the crown regent taking over rule in Shaston.

Although, she supposed if she really was the daughter of both the Montali and Rionach bloodlines than that made whatever was supposed to happen next easier since the people of Shaston were already used to being ruled from beyond their border. Haven immediately felt bad about her thoughts when she considered that people had probably been hurt and even killed when Niks father took over the rule of Shaston, he certainly did not seem like the type to make things peaceful.

Haven squeezed Rea's hand, encouraging her to keep talking and to take Haven's mind off of something that was surely way ahead of herself. After all, she wasn't entirely sure all this meant she'd actually become queen. She also needed to consider whether she even wanted that for herself or if she could handle something as important as ruling a kingdom. Thankfully, Rea saved Haven from diving too deep into her self doubting thoughts by continuing with her explanation,

"It is no surprise that you belong to both Morana Montali and Robert Rionach. It had long been rumored that they were mates. No one could ever prove it and at the time, it was illegal for fae royalty to cross bloodlines. Something about the child being too powerful"

Rea smiled at Haven. A question burned out of Havens mouth before she could stop it,

"So does this mean the people I knew as my parents weren't my biological parents or did they lie to me my whole life?"

"The only person who can answer that is you Haven."

"How?" She asked

"I brought something that will help. It's a copy of a painting made of the royals at the time the original spell was created. It has your biological parents in it. Either you will recognize them as the people you've known your entire life or you won't. It's as simple as that. Are you ready to see it?"

Haven took a breath and nodded. This was the moment of truth, the answer to a question that had been plaguing her since this whole adventure started. Rea leaned down to where a small bag Haven hadn't seen her bring in sat. Reaching into it, she pulled out a small canvas. It fit perfectly in the palm of her hand. Haven took it from her, finding the canvas rough in her hand.

The picture was slightly blurry, in it was a group of fae gathered around a large table.

Havens breathing stalled as she recognized the two people in the middle of the group even through the blurriness.

"That's them," Haven touched the picture, "Those are my parents"

Chapter Thirty-Three

Taking a deep breath, Nik leaned against his shower wall. He always loved taking showers, it was some of the only times he ever felt at peace. The only other time in recent memory where he felt as calm as he did now was when Haven had come into his room looking for her necklace. Even then, that had been an entirely different type of calm. More like the calm before the storm, and she certainly was a storm.

Today in particular had been incredibly stressful for Nik, he'd known exactly what was coming but that didn't mean it hadn't been stressful trying to get through it. Haven was a long lost queen. He'd known about her for years, waiting patiently for her to come to his realm and take the throne from him. As the years passed, he'd grown more and more impatient. Nik could not wait to get away from the throne his father stole for him and more importantly, away from his father.

Speaking of, his father was absolutely furious he hadn't found a way to prevent this from happening. Nik was sure his father had an inkling about who she was, but before tonight, had not known for sure. Nik thanked whatever gods existed in this universe for that.

If his father had known, he would have killed Haven the moment she stepped into this realm and Nik knew there was more than one member of the council who likely would have helped him. Thankfully, because no one dangerous put two and two together before her tests, they missed their chance to take her out of the game before it began.

Part of that was thanks to Nik stealing Havens necklace. It might have seemed shady and pissed Haven off to no end but that only helped further the hate Nik desperately needed from her. If the council had gotten a look at the necklace, they would have recognized her for who she was instantly.

Now that the whole kingdom knew exactly who she was, she couldn't so easily disappear. Hopefully no one would dare hurt her for fear of it falling back onto them. Nik was going to have to rely on that fear to help him sleep for the next little while. The only person crazy enough to even attempt something was his father.

Power was his fathers most favorite thing in all the realms and he did not expect him to hand it over easily. Or at all.

Thankfully, Nik had an idea of a plan his father had hatched. It was a backup plan his father began formulating years ago, only found thanks to the snooping around his fathers office Nik did every so often.

If Nik was correct in his assumptions, he needed to do everything in his power to stop it from happening. For both his sake and Havens. In order to save them both, he needed her to hate him.

The water slowly started to go cold, he'd been standing under it for almost two hours now. The cold water helped bring Nik back to the present and out of his almost always negative thoughts. The cold water may have started goosebumps racing across his arms but it hadn't done anything to make the hardness between his legs go down. Knowing it was the only thing that might make it go away after many many cold showers, Nik reached down and gripped himself. Groaning as he began moving his hand up and down along his cock, Nik allowed himself to get lost in his most private thoughts and fantasies. Bright red hair, piercing green eyes and a smart mouth that could likely sass the armor off a knight.

Her, it was always her.

He might need her to hate him for the sake of both their lives and their kingdom but that didn't mean he didn't want her, didn't desire her. And boy did he want her almost more than anything. The only thing stronger than his desire to take Haven for himself was the need to be rid of his father.

Nik wanted to hate her, everything would be so much easier if he could just hate her.

He couldn't though, no matter how hard he tried. Even before she'd come into this realm, Nik dreamt of Haven. One night, he'd dream of her laugh, the next, her smile. The dreams started just before her father died and only increased in frequency as time passed. By the time she reached the fae realm, Nik was dreaming of her every single night.

The only other person who knew some of what was happening was Delroy. His friend held theories on why these things kept happening but Nik could not bring himself to admit what he knew, he couldn't even say it aloud.

More images invaded his brain as Nik lost himself in the depths of his mind. Haven on her back beneath him, on top of him, on her knees with her lips wrapped around his cock. He wanted her in every position. Every. Single. One.

Nik moved his hand faster and faster as he neared his end. His whole body seemed to ache, desperately needing release.

It was recalling the sounds she had made today during the festival, while eating what must have been the realms best sandwich, that tipped him over the edge. He'd love to find out if she really was louder in bed, like she claimed. Nik had a feeling she was not bluffing about that.

Nik absently wondered if she too was plagued with thoughts like his since meeting, if she also needed to ease the constant ache between her thighs. He wondered if it was thoughts of him she used if- *when,* she did.

Niks breathing slowed as he came down from his high, he needed to try his best to put a stop to thoughts of her like that or he might do something he'd likely regret. That *they'd* likely regret when all was said and done and Nik was as far away from this castle as possible.

Only relatively satisfied, Nik sank down to the tile floor and allowed the harshness of the now freezing water to bring him back to the present where he hated Haven and she hated him. He needed to get these thoughts under control before he doomed them both.

Chapter Thirty-Four

After Astrea left, Haven had taken a quick bath and promptly passed out. She was woken however many hours later by a heavy pounding on the door.

"WHAT?" She yelled, not bothering to disguise the annoyance in her voice.

"I'm coming in!" Called a voice she did not recognize.

Haven looked down at herself, finding nothing but skin. Apparently she'd been too exhausted after her bath to find some night clothes. Haven wrapped herself up in the blanket just as the door opened, reminding her to work on building a habit of locking the door before bed.

"Wake up princess, it is time to start your training"

Peering out from under the blanket, Haven surveyed the woman standing at the foot of her bed. She was tall and muscular, with deep brown skin almost as dark as the long braid trailing down her back.

"Who are you?" Haven asked

"My name is Tasha, I'll be in charge of most of your training"

"What kind of training?"

"We will begin with simple things like conditioning, wielding basic weapons, and of course learning to use your magic"

That caught Havens attention, "I get to learn to use my magic?"

"Of course! Do you think the council would hand over control of the entire kingdom to a girl that doesn't know how to use her magic or even the most basic of weapons?"

Tasha may have said the words kindly but they still gave Haven a headache. She'd been trying not to think about the fact that she was set to inherit two whole kingdoms since she'd found out about it. Dralia, which they were currently in, and Shaston, the neighboring kingdom once ruled by her father. She hadn't had much time to mull over the idea but whenever the thoughts occurred, a deep headache Haven often referred to as self doubt popped into her brain.

"By the time your coronation comes around, I will have whipped you into quite the young warrior. Someone worthy of the crown"

Haven gulped at the mention of her coronation. She knew it was something she'd likely have to endure but it was another one of those things Haven was choosing not to think about.

"When is that supposed to be?" She asked

"Your coronation?" Tasha asked, Haven nodded. "In exactly a month"

"A MONTH?" Haven screeched, "But I've never even held a weapon in my life. I don't know all that much about Dralian customs and I definitely don't know how to rule one kingdom, much less two!" Haven could feel herself beginning to panic, her heart picked up speed and her chest tightened.

Tasha sat down on the edge of the bed and placed a calming hand on the top of Havens foot over the blanket,

"Haven, it'll be alright. In the mornings you will train with me and in the evenings someone will be teaching you all about what it takes to rule our kingdom. We have waited so long for something like this to happen. We aren't going to toss you in the deep end without first teaching you how to swim"

The calm and steady tone Tasha used washed over Haven, helping to calm her almost as much as her words themselves did. Taking a deep breath and battling back the nerves, Haven spoke the words she had only allowed herself to say in her mind,

"I really am going to become Queen?"

"Yes," Tasha nodded, "And you will make an amazing one"

It took Haven over an hour to dress in the training leathers Tasha told her to put on. It wasn't the clothes themselves, rather, what she had seen when she looked into the mirror.

When she first saw them, Haven almost fainted. Somewhere between when she was forced into the woods and when she woke up this morning, her ears had changed into full fae ears, long bodied with pointed tips.

When she first saw them, the gasp that escaped showed Haven that her ears weren't the only thing that changed. Now she also had two sharp fangs. Haven couldn't guess why Fae needed fangs but so far, everyone she'd seen had them. When Haven dragged Tasha back into her room from where she'd been waiting out in the hall, Tasha had simply smiled and said,

"You are a full Fae now Haven"

After taking more than a few minutes to adjust to her new appearance, Haven followed Tasha into the courtyard behind the castle by the lake. People stared, some even bowed. Haven ignored them.

Another new thing was her heightened senses. All along the walk to the courtyard, Haven picked up tidbits of conversations, smells coming from all over and even the warmth of the sunlight on her skin felt stronger. It was going to take some getting used to, but as Haven came to a stop next to Tasha, she took a deep breath and allowed these new feelings and senses to settle inside her. Her life was changing. Haven knew it would likely be uncomfortable for a while, as most change was, but she also knew that she had never felt more like she belonged in her entire life. Here, in this realm, experiencing these new feelings and changes was exactly where Haven was supposed to be. She just had to remember that next time the anxiety and doubt came creeping in.

"Alright," Tasha began, "Every morning we will meet here. First we will run two laps around the entirety of the castle grounds. After our run we will begin your weapons and combat training. We will work on weapons for a few hours before ending our sessions by working on your magic." Tasha paused briefly to make sure Haven was following along,

"Every single day you come out here, Fae will watch you and they will stare. You need to get used to the stares. You need to assure them that you are up to the challenge and that you are fit to take the throne. Not everyone is entirely happy about this new development. The crown regent has been ruling for quite some time and while not everyone likes him, our kingdom has mostly done well under his rule."

"Will people try to stop me from taking over?" Haven asked

"Honestly, I am not sure. I would expect some blowback, people will surely voice their opinions and test you but I don't think anyone would actually try to prevent you from ruling. Old magic binds the spell used to create our realm and I think most are too afraid of what might happen if they were to go against the rules by trying to prevent the last daughter from taking her place"

Haven thought over Tashas words while stretching in preparation for her run. A few specific words stuck out in her mind causing Haven to ask,

"Why did you call me the last daughter?"

Tasha smiled faintly,

"Because you could very well be the last. Besides Roman, no other fae children have made it into our realm in the last fifty years. You complete the circle, the last of the royal lines have officially been found. People have already come up with a title for you."

"What is it?" Haven asked nervously, she hoped it wasn't something stupid that she'd have to hear for the rest of her hopefully long life.

Tasha straightened up from her forward stretch, leaned in close to Haven as if she did not want others to hear and said,

"The Last Daughter of Smoke and Shadows"

Chapter Thirty-Five

Havens whole body burned. She barely made it half a lap before she was out of breath and panting. On the second lap, she collapsed about a third of the way in. Tasha had forced her off the ground and all but dragged her for the rest of their run. After they finished, Tasha shared the news that after a week at their current pace, she would be upping it to three laps each day instead of two. The thought had Haven about ready to cry.

"Watch your feet!" Tasha scolded. Haven immediately attempted to fix her footing.

Tasha was teaching her hand to hand combat with a dagger, or at least she was trying to. The only thing Haven had been relatively good at so far was shooting the bow and arrows. She tried an ax, a sword so heavy she could barely lift it, multiple tiny throwing knives, a crossbow and regular bow. Currently, she held a dagger in her hand. It was longer than the knives but shorter than the sword and had a small emerald inlaid in the hilt. It fit perfectly in Havens hand and while she hadn't had much luck defending herself with it yet, it was her favorite weapon.

Tasha thrusted her sword forward, striking out at Haven. Jumping left, out of the swords path, Haven attempted to close in on Tashas side and knock the sword out of her hand. She had yet to complete this basic move but she was determined to make some sort of progress.

Time seemed to move in slow motion as Haven's wrist closed in on Tasha outstretched arm, the one holding the sword. Just as she managed to make contact, Tasha twisted sideways and used her elbow to shove Haven back.

"Dammit" Haven cursed, earning a laugh from Tasha. The woman seemed to take pleasure in Havens frustrations.

"You'll get there. When you started, you couldn't get anywhere near me. Now look, you were almost close enough to knock the sword out of my hand."

Haven supposed Tasha was right but it still didn't feel great that she hadn't been able to fully complete a single weapons task Tasha had given her.

"I think that is enough of weapons for today" Tasha exclaimed, tossing her sword on the ground near the other discarded weapons. Haven was hesitant to give up her dagger. She really did like it, plus she was pretty sure it was about the same size as the dagger Binah had given her. The green emerald would probably even match the original daggers gold hilt.

"You can keep the dagger when you're able to knock the sword out of my hand" Tasha told Haven, noticing her apprehension to put the dagger away.

"Since I'm to be Queen doesn't that mean it's technically my dagger that I could do whatever I want with" Haven remarked with a smirk, growing a little cocky.

Tasha snorted, "You are not Queen yet, little fae. Which means, until then, technically the dagger belongs to me and the crown regent. Plus, wouldn't it feel better to earn it?"

Of course Tasha was right. Haven nodded, she hadn't been close to disarming Tasha today but she hoped one day she'd be able to. Preferably before her coronation. After that, she'd take the dagger and never let anyone else wield it.

Haven frowned at the strange possessiveness she was feeling.

"It's normal" Tasha told her

Looking up to meet Tasha's eyes, Haven must have worn her confusion because her trainer began to explain,

"What you are feeling, the possessiveness, it's normal. With your body going through so many things while it transforms into its true state, your emotions can go a little crazy. It can lead to small outbursts, feeling things stronger than you normally would. It's almost like a coping mechanism. Your body has never dealt with things like this before, the heightened speed, hearing, sense of smell. You're adjusting to so many new things, it might be a few weeks before things settle down."

Haven nodded. She'd have to keep an eye on herself, she already dealt with wacky emotions thanks to her anxiety and depression. Adding what her body was going through, Haven imagined things could get a little crazy.

Pulling Haven from her thoughts, Tasha stepped towards her and slid the dagger out of her hand. Haven immediately missed the feeling of it.

"Alright, now it's time for magic. There hasn't been another recorded shadow wielder since your mother. We don't know much about your specific type of magic but you should be able to learn the same way others do." Tasha sat down on the grass and motioned for Haven to join her, sitting cross legged facing each other.

"What about the fire?" Haven asked

"Your fire comes from your father. Usually, but not always, the child inherits whatever magic the more powerful parent wielded. Because both your parents were incredibly powerful, you ended up with both their magics. It is important to understand that while each fae tends to hold a main power they have influence over, they can also perform spells, similar to witches. For now, we are going to focus on gaining control over the elements you have influence over" Haven nodded, taking in every word out of Tashas mouth and committing them to memory.

"Hold your hands out in front of you, palms up" Tasha demonstrated what she was asking. Haven quickly copied her.

"Now you need to internally reach inside yourself. Since your powers have been dormant for nineteen years, your fire or shadows won't be right there on the surface. You need to dig deep and when you find that thread, give it a tug. Try to pull something to the surface, it can be either fire or a shadow."

Haven closed her eyes, attempting to ignore the curious stares from the fae loitering in the courtyard around them. It didn't take long for Haven to find what Tasha was talking about. Haven expected to have to dig deep, as Tasha said, but she didn't. Her power was right there, waiting right below the surface. She could feel the fire and shadows coursing through her veins. It was like they wanted to escape, like they had been waiting for Haven all this time.

Haven tugged slightly, instinctively imagining a small ball of flames in her outstretched hands. The warm feeling gathering in her fingertips caused Haven to open her eyes, a wide smile growing on her face.

Cupped between her two palms was a ball of flames roughly the size of a baseball. Haven watched as a few flames took on a life of their own, twining around her fingers and dancing up her arms. When they tried to crawl across the ground towards Tasha, Haven panicked slightly and pulled them back inside her. The flames hadn't hurt Haven but she didn't know if they could hurt someone else. Her powers seemed to whine like a toddler when she pulled them back.

"Good," Tasha smiled, "Now the shadows"

Haven nodded, closing her eyes again. She easily reached the thread tying her to her powers. Giving it a little tug, she found that the shadows fought back more than the fire had. She tugged harder, trying to imagine a small ball of shadows in her hand like she had done with the flames.

Shadows erupted from her, shooting every which way. People ducked and gasped but none were hit with them. Haven immediately tried to contain them by pulling them back towards her. Haven grimaced as they slowly inched back towards her before dissipating completely.

"Well at least we know your shadows can be a bit stubborn" Tasha remarked. Haven could tell she was entertained and not even slightly fazed by the small outburst.

"Another important thing to remember is that the more power you have, the harder it can be to get under control. When you cast, some of your fire or shadows will respond to you, some will not, as you saw with the shadows. The easiest way to explain it is that there are two types of magic that rise when you cast, magic that is purely yours and will always listen to you and the second kind, this kind of magic is tricky. You may have seen fae walking around with snow or flames flitting around them,"

Haven nodded, her mind drifting back to the fae she saw when they stopped to eat on the journey to the castle, the one that had snowflakes buzzing around him,

"That is the second kind of magic. At times, it can seem to take on a mind of its own, kind of like a pet. You can tell it what to do but there isn't a guarantee it'll always listen. Over time you will learn to cast a certain type of magic so that there's no chance it won't listen to you but for now, I wouldn't worry much about discerning the two"

Tasha stood off the ground, offering a hand to Haven to help her up.

"Some fae find that if you let a little magic out all the time, the magic that doesn't always listen will be more cooperative. It is up to you to find what you feel comfortable with. We can work on more tomorrow, for now go inside and find some lunch. Someone will come for you in a little while to begin the second half of your training"

Haven thanked Tasha, promised she'd be back tomorrow to continue their lessons and headed for the castle door, passing a crow she swore was following her and a few whispering fae. This was only day one and her head already seemed to be stuffed full.

Haven hoped the rest of her day would go by easily. Knowing her luck, just because she wanted an easy day, the universe would make it a mission to make the rest of her day hell.

As she walked through the halls, Havens attention turned to some of the fae she passed. Most of them were whispering, some offering her kind smile, others outright sizing her up. If she tried hard enough she could probably hear whatever they were saying but in that moment, Haven was too tired and hungry to care.

Chapter Thirty-Six

Lunch passed quickly, Haven had grabbed a sandwich in the kitchens and headed to the library to use whatever amount of time she had to continue searching for the journal from Binahs letter. Again, she found nothing. Two and a half hours in the library turned out to be a large waste of time. Eventually, she began wandering the castle.

After multiple trips back and forth through the halls, Haven felt like she had a much better grip on the layout of the large castle. Another hour passed before a short gray haired woman found her looking over the paintings in the great hall. The older woman introduced herself as Elanor, Havens new instructor. Elanor proceeded to grab ahold of Havens wrist and all but force her back to the library. Once seated in the library, Elanor sat Haven down at a desk and began a rapid but easy to follow lesson on politics of the fae realm and the basics of what Haven would be learning in her time spent with the older woman.

Seven royal founders, seven kingdoms, seven members of each council, apparently the fae really liked the number seven.

Another two hours passed before Havens lesson ended. After gathering a few papers Elanor told her to look over before they met again the next day, Haven used her newfound familiarity of the castle halls and staircases to head back to her room. As she rounded the corner of the hall containing her room, Haven spotted Roman leaning up against the wall next to her door.

"Hey!" She called, increasing the pace of her steps.

"Your highness" Roman mock bowed

"None of that" Haven laughed while unlocking her door. Fae had been saying those words to her all day and it was getting old. Although she supposed it was better than the few glares she'd received.

Haven opened her door and beckoned Roman to follow her inside. A smirk took over his face as he pulled a bottle of wine and two glasses from behind his back.

"I thought we should celebrate" He told her

Haven considered for a moment, "I suppose a little wine couldn't hurt"

Opening the doors to her balcony, Haven led Roman to the small table and chair set. They both sat down, Roman poured some wine into a glass and passed it to Haven.

"Thanks," She said, "I'm sorry we haven't caught up before now. With all the craziness I haven't even heard how your tests went"

"Not as well as yours went" Roman joked

Haven snorted, "I don't know if it exactly went well. I did get shot with what I assume was some kind of magic arrow" She raised her glass and took in a large gulp of some sort of cherry flavored wine. It wasn't the best thing Haven had ever tasted but she supposed it would due for a simple catch up with her friend.

"Yeah I got stabbed" Roman commented nonchalantly, as if being stabbed or shot with an arrow was a normal, everyday part of life.

Haven gaped at him, silently willing Roman to continue.

"As I was leaving the festival I came across a woman getting robbed. Of course I intervened. Long story short, the guy apparently really wanted the womans money and I got stabbed for it"

"That's crazy" Haven remarked

"Yeah, I think they just wanted us to prove we'd be willing to do what it took to help someone else, to prove that we would protect our people with our lives"

Haven agreed that that seemed to be the point of the test, although she still wondered how the magic could tell who she was and what her powers were from that alone. Circling back to the topic at hand, Haven asked,

"So what kingdom are you from?"

"Norwood," Roman answered, "Just like Binah originally guessed. It's a collection of islands across the sea. I'll show it to you on the map sometime."

"That sounds nice" She told him

"I think it'll be really cool. I've always loved living by the ocean"

Haven had a moment of confusion seeing as where they'd lived before in North Carolina was nowhere near the ocean. Before Haven could ask what he meant, Roman began speaking again,

"I have seven brothers and one sister. They expect I could be second in line for the throne based on the strength of the water magic I exhibited after my tests. I'll have to wait to find out until I actually go to Norwood and meet my siblings. Apparently we have to face off in some sort of fight to determine where I'll go in line for the throne"

"Wow, that sounds intense. How do you feel about that?" Haven asked, she'd heard that Roman had shown an impressive display of water magic after his tests so she wasn't surprised hearing him confirm it. What Haven was most concerned about was how her friend was dealing with the idea that he might be second in line for the throne. She was overwhelmed by the thought of ruling at the best of times and while she was trying her best to manage her anxiety, some still poked through her defenses.

The idea of having siblings might have appealed to her in the beginning but hearing that she likely would've had to fight them to find her place in line helped her be okay with the fact that she didn't have any.

"I think having a lot of siblings will be fun. Though I suspect they'll mistrust me at first since I am likely to be so close in line for the throne."

"Will you be alright?" Haven's mood dampened when she remembered that in thirty days, Roman would be leaving. Right after her coronation, her friend would leave for his home kingdom to begin his life there.

"Yeah I'm actually looking forward to it." He answered with a smile.

"That's great Roman! I'm happy for you." Haven tried her best not to show her slight disappointment. She wanted to be happy for Roman but there was no denying that she'd miss him. Haven hadn't known him for long but after everything they'd been through together, she felt very attached to him and the friendship between them.

"And don't worry Haven, I'll secure an alliance between our kingdoms before it ever becomes necessary" Roman reached over and put a reassuring hand on her arm. That had not been what she wanted to hear. In fact, she hadn't even been thinking about that.

"You think that could be necessary?" She nervously asked

Roman hesitated before responding and his smile from earlier vanished,

"I think the crown regent has many loyal followers, more than we realize, and he does not want to give up his power. I hope it won't come to a war but if it does, I'll always have your back"

The thought made Haven nervous. She didn't exactly expect smooth sailings with this transfer of power but war? That seemed a bit much. Although having met the crown regent, seeing his dislike of her and how tightly he held onto power, if she really thought about it, war didn't seem like that far of a reach.

Haven gulped down air, "Onto happier thoughts!" She exclaimed. Tossing back the entirety of her wine, Haven let the alcohol settle over her and then reached for the bottle to refill her glass. Roman chuckled, his easy smile returning. He refilled his own glass and asked her how her training had gone with Tasha this morning. Haven happily responded, her mind drifting from thoughts of war to thoughts of her magic. She could feel it brimming just underneath the surface even now. It made her feel special and even a little less homesick.

With a wide smile she told Roman all about her session this morning. He laughed when she told him about how her shadows had gone haywire and had nearly taken out all the fae in a twenty foot radius. Easy smiles followed, helping Haven forget all about the daunting thoughts she'd been having. She held tightly to the hope that it would never come down to a war but Haven couldn't help the nagging feeling in the back of her mind screaming at her to prepare herself for what her subconscious knew was coming.

Chapter Thirty-Seven

The rough material of a picnic blanket scratched Havens nipples as Nik drilled into her from behind. He gripped her hips so hard she swore there'd be bruises. He reached one hand around to rub her clit, earning a loud moan. Nik was working her up to an amazing high. She heard a masculine groan right as she was about to finish. Just a little further she begged, just a little harder.

Haven bolted upright in bed, the sheet clinging to her sweaty body. She'd been having these vivid dreams more often than she cared to admit. Every single time she woke right before the finish line, leaving her body wet and wanting. Every dream frustrated her a little bit more and if she was being honest with herself, made her more pissed at Nik. She didn't even know why. Haven was fairly certain he was not responsible for putting these dreams into her head but nonetheless, they caused even more frustration and anger to bubble up.

Luckily she had not run into him since the festival. She didn't know what she'd do when that happened, would she yell? Scream? Jump him? Haven didn't particularly like the guy but he didn't deserve to be yelled at for something that was likely not his fault.

Determined not to touch herself to thoughts of Nik, Haven tossed back the covers and slipped on some loose pants. Most nights ended one of two ways, either she succumbed to temptation, finishing herself off, or she got up and exercised. Moving around usually helped push the thoughts out of her head. Afterwards, she'd climb back into bed and sleep soundly the rest of the night.

The clock told her it was just after two in the morning as she passed it where it sat on her desk. Exiting through her door, Haven made her way down two flights of stairs and onto the castle grounds. She'd decided to go for a run seeing as she definitely needed the stamina.

The cool night air nipped her arms, the tank top she'd worn for sleep not offering much protection. Her nipples peaked through the fabric but she didn't worry about being seen since no one was ever up this late.

Starting a light jog, Haven made it all of half a lap before a deep voice interrupted her,

"Late night jog?"

Haven turned to see Nik leaning against the castle wall, in nothing but loose sweatpants. Haven cursed her luck, of course it had to be him, the source of her frustrations. It would help if he wasn't stupidly hot and kind of an asshole. That combination normally drew her right in, it never ended well but was always fun while it lasted.

"Want to join me?" She offered, surprising herself. Haven could tell she was thinking more with her downstairs brain than her upstairs one.

"Please," He scoffed "I'm not the one who can barely run two laps around the grounds"

Haven rolled her eyes, she had no idea how he knew that. It wasn't a big secret but the only way for him to have that information was if he or someone close to him had been watching her lessons.

"Prove it" She snapped at him. It would serve him right to end up huffing and puffing just like she was. Haven could picture the smile on her face if that was how tonight ended.

"I don't have anything to prove" He rolled his eyes.

"Sure about that?" Haven taunted.

"Yes" Nik confirmed. Before Haven could reply, Nik was taking off at a run. Haven took off after him, cursing as she tried to catch up.

Haven caught up quicker than she thought she should have. Together they ran and ran, all the way past the gardens and lake before slowing to a light jog on their second pass. The moment was surprisingly peaceful, at least until Haven felt a slight tug on her ankle, pulling it forward and causing her to fall backwards.

"Fuck" She cursed, landing on her back in a puddle of mud.

Nik was laughing incredibly hard where he stood about ten feet away. Haven swore she could see tears coming out of his eyes even in the darkness surrounding them.

"Oh was that funny?" Haven asked, irritation and humor ringing through her tone.

Nik couldn't even respond, he was still laughing so hard. Haven had a sudden thought. Immediately acting on it, she shot a shadow at him, wrapping it around his wrist and pulling.

Haven realized she might have miscalculated either the distance or strength of her power when Nik was launched forward, landing directly on top of her. Nik huffed as he landed but thankfully managed not to crush her.

The shock wore off and now it was Havens turn to laugh. She lifted a hand, covered in mud, and smeared it all down his chest, covering his black tattoos in the thick substance. She wished it wasn't so dark out so she could see them clearer, if only she could convince the moon to shine a little brighter.

"Oh you're going to pay for that" Nik shifted, caging her in with a leg on either side of her waist. He dug his hand in the mud beside her head, leaning in close so he could smear it through her thick red hair. Haven couldn't find it in herself to be pissed that she'd likely have to spend at least an hour in the shower scrubbing it out. Every time she tried to stop laughing, the image of Niks shocked face when her shadow grabbed him popped back into her mind and set her laughing again.

It took Haven a few minutes to get ahold of her laugh. Taking a deep breath and looking up to meet Niks eyes, she found him so close that his chest bumped Havens. Haven watched as his pupils dilated, the air around them changing as he abandoned the mud in her hair. Nik leaned down closer to Haven, his head angled into her neck. She felt his chest rise as he inhaled a deep breath. Haven knew he was likely scenting what had dragged her out of bed.

"Thinking of me?" He asked. All the humor had gone from his voice, leaving behind a rough and scratchy tone.

"You wish" She told him, the words coming out weak and breathless.

He chuckled throatily. Nik shifted the hand besides her head down to grip her thigh, putting all his weight on his left hand. Haven felt the tip of his nose run up her neck, followed by his tongue.

Haven tried to hold back a moan, only a small sound slipped out but it was more than enough for Niks fae hearing. He pulled back, running his gaze down the length of her entire body, an arrogant and purely male smile on his face.

"You are exquisite," He told her.

Haven could see the control Nik was barely holding onto written across his face. He might not want to admit it, he might choose harsh words and seemingly hate her but that did not mean he was not attracted to her.

Havens hips lifted subconsciously, looking for the pressure they were so poorly lacking. Haven didn't feel in control of her movements in that moment. Something about this man, no, this fae, brought out a fierce ache between her legs and a strong desire in her heart.

Before Haven could say anything, Nik shifted their legs, wrapping the one he had his hand on around his waist. He only hesitated a moment before he ground his pelvis into hers. Even through their clothes, the small contact set a fire raging through Haven. Leaning down, Nik burned demanding kisses along her neck and collarbone.

Continuing to grind their bodies together, Nik pulled another moan from Haven. Her hands reached up and twined through the hair at the base of his neck, holding on tightly. If he kept moving like that, Haven felt she could come right there, covered in mud and fully clothed.

"I bet you'd be a good fuck," He told her, pausing for only a second before he added,

"Too bad it wouldn't be worth it"

Niks words ripped Haven from the fog of lust that had descended over her. He immediately pulled away, using his fae speed to basically sprint back to the castle. He left Haven sprawled in the mud, confused, pissed off, slightly hurt and insanely turned on.

Chapter Thirty-Eight

After getting himself off in the shower no less than three times, Nik cursed himself. He found himself slightly panicked over what happened tonight and the thought that they might've been seen. He knew most fae were in bed by about one in the morning but there was always a chance.

Nik hoped he'd been rude enough that Haven would stay far away from him. If she didn't, Nik didn't think he could stop himself like that again. To be honest, he couldn't remember much from their encounter, the feel of her underneath him clouded his brain. When he'd scented her arousal, even through the mud and sweat, he had almost ripped off her pants and taken her right then and there. It would have been rough and hard and not at all how he wanted their first time to go but everything about her seemed to bring out the animal in him.

Even though Nik knew they'd never get a chance to be together, he'd make sure of it, that didn't stop him from fantasizing about the things that could be. Haven was always in his head, the need he held for her was a constant and living thing. It was always there, right under the surface. Sometimes Nik found himself sitting outside of her door in the middle of the night, just to be close to her.

Nik changed into new drawstring pants, knowing Delroy would be by soon.

Speaking of the devil, a crow tapped at his window. Nik used his influence over wind to open the latch and let the crow inside. A cloud of magic swirled around the crow. When it dissipated, his best friend was standing in its place. Delroy walked to Niks dresser and took out a pair of pants to cover himself.

Delroy could turn into a crow, a fact Nik had always been jealous of. Nik was able to turn into a wolf and while that was fun, he'd always wanted to be able to fly. Nik absently wondered what Haven would be able to turn into once she learned enough control over her magic.

"Your father is planning something" Delroy spoke, breaking the silence and pulling Nik from his thoughts.

"Do we know when?" Nik asked

Delroy shook his head, a grim look on his face,

"Just that it'll be soon. We know he's been searching for a way around the rules, something that would let him remain as crown regent instead of Haven taking the throne"

"Has he found anything?" Nik questioned, sitting down on the couch in front of his fireplace.

"No, I don't think so. I think he has the support of at least one council member but it's not enough. As far as I know, Havens arrival mostly stalled the rest of his plans"

"Good" Nik stated.

Over the last year or so, Niks father had been planning something. Nik didn't know what but he did know it was not good. The last time his father had been as secretive and sneaky as he has been lately was right before he took over Shaston, Havens fathers kingdom. Even though Nik hadn't been around when his father had stolen the ruling power in Shaston, he'd heard many stories and they all sounded eerily familiar.

If Nik had to guess, his father was planning to take over another kingdom. Possibly Norwood since it had the smallest army. Nik knew that the king of Norwood would never be intimidated into handing over his ruling power like the crown regent of Shaston had been but if Nik knew anything about his father, it was that he would stop at nothing to get what he wanted. He was likely planning to use the armies from Shaston and Dralia to take Norwood forcibly.

At least, that had been his plan until Haven had shown up. She basically brought down all his schemes, a fact which made Nik infinitely happier. She showed up just in time to save Romans kingdom and she didn't even know it.

Speaking of Roman,

"I can smell him on you" He told Delroy, scenting exactly whose bed his friend had been in before coming to Niks room for their nighty meeting

"Fuck off" Delroy shoved his friends shoulder from where he sat next to Nik on the couch. Nik knew the subject of Roman was touchy at best but that didn't stop him from bringing it up from time to time, especially since Delroy loved tormenting Nik so much about Haven.

Nik pondered how long Delroy and Roman had been getting together, they'd been going back and forth for years now. Neither was willing to admit how they truly felt, although Nik could see how much Roman meant to his friend. Nik constantly wanted to tell either Roman and or Delroy to quit messing around and just be together, especially after feeling how hard it was to stay away from Haven.

Nik hated that pretty much everyone in Havens life was lying to her, Astrea, Roman, even Nik himself, they all had lied to Haven at one point or another. Some might not be outright lies but lies of omissions were still lies

***

HAVEN

The next four days occurred without incident. Each morning Haven got up, trained with Tasha, scoured the library, found nothing, had lessons with Elanor, finishing the days with another run and dinner with Rea and Roman.

The only thing of note was the ball being hosted tonight. The crown regent wanted to celebrate the progress Haven and Roman were making with their training. Not that Haven had made much progress, she still couldn't get the sword from Tasha and was definitely still wheezing by the time they were done running. She had, at least, made some progress with her magic. It wasn't much but it was definitely more than when they had started.

Elanors lessons about ruling a kingdom were also helping fill Haven with confidence about this whole Queen thing. She no longer started shaking when thinking about wearing the crown and ruling over not one, but two kingdoms.

Haven was almost certain that the reasoning behind the ball was complete BS but it gave her a chance to wear a pretty dress and to speak with the council. So far, she hadn't seen any of them around the castle nor did she know how to call a meeting with them. She wanted to impress them, if they were to be her advisors while she ruled then she wanted not only their respect but also their loyalty. She already suspected that one or more did not want her as their queen based off the whispers she'd heard and her limited interactions with them.

Haven definitely wouldn't know half the things she did if it weren't for her gifted fae hearing. It had taken some getting used to at first, she'd overheard way too many things she wished she hadn't. At least now she knew to stay away from the everything stew planned for next Wednesday. The change in appearance had also taken some getting used to, for the first three days she constantly knocked the tip of her tongue on the edge of her newly pointed teeth. Haven still hadn't figured out why she needed fangs but everytime she thought to ask someone, she couldn't find anyone she'd be willing to talk to.

Overall, Haven was still getting used to the changes in her body. Sometimes she ran directly into things, having used her advanced speed without meaning to, but those collisions were becoming less and less as the days went on. The first time she saw a shadow under her skin Haven had screamed, causing the guard at the end of the hall to come running. He'd politely explained how that was a normal manifestation of her magic and that it would likely happen again.

Now, occasionally when she was alone in her room, Haven let her shadows free. The expression of power helped ease the rumbling inside of her begging to be let loose. They often bounced around her room, knocking things over, spilling the ink on her desk and turning on the bathroom faucets. They almost always fixed whatever mess they made but it was hilarious to watch them wander. Haven was also learning to discern the difference in the magics inside of her. She now knew how to summon shadows that were hers and hers only, that didn't do anything she did not command them to, and to summon shadows that moved around on their own, mostly listening to what Haven wanted, but not always. Tasha had been right when she likened that part of her magic to a pet.

So far, her fire wasn't as playful, it was more subdued but just as powerful. She often summoned a ball of fire at the foot of her bed and just watched it exist. It was incredibly beautiful and made her heart fill with something akin to contentment. As of now, Haven couldn't do much that was useful other than moving objects with her shadows or lighting a candle with her fire but it was a world away from where she started. Haven was incredibly proud of herself.

Haven pulled the shadow back from where it had been opening and closing her closet door when she heard a knock at her bedroom door. Not waiting for an invitation, Astrea entered holding a garment bag, presumably her dress for the ball tonight.

"Hey!" Rea exclaimed

"Hey! What have you got for me tonight?" Haven asked, standing from the bed and moving next to her desk where Rea draped her dress.

"Oh you're gonna love it!"

Rea was right, Haven loved the dress. Made out of Emerald green satin was a dress with a deep V connected to an under bust corset that led way to a flowy skirt and high slit. Off the shoulder short sleeves paired with elegant black gloves and matching black high heels completed the ensemble. The dress made Haven feel empowered, sexy and refined. Rea never missed the mark with her dress selections.

Once upon a time, Haven might have felt a little awkward in her body with a dress like this. She wasn't skinny but she wasn't fat either. Haven had decided a long time ago that she was somewhere in between and she needed to be okay with that. Sometimes she'd look at 'curvy' girls and wish she had more meat on her bones, then she'd look at a 'skinny' girl and wish she had less. At the time, she'd just wanted to fit in somewhere, anywhere. Not anymore, Haven was finding more and more that she loved her body just the way it was.

Rea stepped out of the bathroom where she'd been getting ready in a pale cornflower blue dress. It blended almost too well with her pale skin but somehow she made it work and looked amazing. Both girls twisted their hair up, Havens into a loose low bun, strands framing her face and Rea into a Dutch braid that fell to her low back. They were almost ready to take on the night.

Haven pulled out the necklace Binah had given her, fastening it around her neck.

"I wonder why Binah didn't want me to be seen with this necklace," She wondered aloud.

"I know why," Rea stated.

Haven looked up, meeting Rea's eye. Her friend almost seemed guilty.

"Come on, I'll show you" Rea hooked her arm in Havens, leading the way to somewhere that might finally give Haven some answers to her many questions.

Chapter Thirty-Nine

R ea led Haven to the library, a place she'd been about a thousand times. They kept a brisk pace all the way through the stacks, behind the librarian's desk before finally stopping deep in the depths of the library. Where they stopped was dark and dusty, if it weren't for Havens advanced sight she likely wouldn't be able to see two feet in front of her.

Haven glanced around her, finding that they had stopped in front of a large painting. As Rea lit a fae light, Haven immediately recognized the painting. It was the same painting Rea showed her the other night when she recognized her parents. Now that she was looking at a bigger version, Haven knew what Rea was talking about. Around her mothers neck was the very same necklace Haven was wearing.

Touching the necklace, Haven had even more questions than she did fifteen minutes ago. At least she finally had a guess as to why Binah wanted her to keep the necklace hidden. If she'd been wearing it around the castle then someone might have recognized it. Why that was a bad thing, Haven could only guess. Finding out the necklace belonged to her mother also didn't explain why Nik took it the night of the council dinner.

Rea let Haven stare at the painting for all of five minutes before tugging on her arm and saying,

"We've been here long enough, you don't want to be late to a ball thrown in your honor" Haven nodded and let Rea lead her away. She turned and caught one last glimpse at the painting. Haven ingrained the looks on her parents' faces into her mind, they looked intensely happy even with all that had been going on when the painting was created.

They wore wide smiles and glowing eyes, Haven vowed to herself that no matter what happened in the coming days, she'd try her best to wear the same smile. No matter if it came to war like Roman predicted, she'd do her best to never lose sight of her parents' bright smiles and the hope clearly written across their faces.

By the time Haven and Rea made it to the great hall, the ball was already in full swing. Haven let go of Rea, walking over to Roman who was talking to a group of fae, his hands waving in the air animatedly.

"Hey!" Roman called cheerily as she neared him.

"Hey Roman," Haven smiled. Her friend tossed his arm around her and continued his story. Haven caught onto the gist of his tale almost immediately, apparently he'd thrown an ax at a very undeserving fae during his training. The fae he'd almost hit had chased him through the gardens, shoving him into a rose bush that left minor cuts all over him.

Haven took in the way Roman spoke. He slurred a few words, simply plowing through his story. She could tell the wine glass in his hand was not his first. Haven smiled and shook her head.

Looking away from her friend, Haven scanned the room. Her gaze caught on someone leaned against the far wall, shrouded in shadows. Her breath hitched when she recognized who it was. Nik was staring right at her. If she didn't know any better, Haven might've thought there was jealousy written across his scowling face.

Didn't he know that Roman was gay and likely one of her best friends? He had nothing to be jealous about. More importantly, Nik did not have any right to be jealous, not after the way he'd left her in the mud. It wasn't even his words that hurt, although they did twinge a little, it was the way he'd gotten up and left like the moment hadn't even affected him.

Shrugging out from under Romans arm, Haven left him to entertain the group that had gathered. Ridding her thoughts of Nik, she reminded herself of the goal she'd made for tonight, talking to as many members of the council as she could find. Haven desperately needed them on her side. Romans words of war had upset her more than she'd let on. Not a day went by that she didn't think about her kingdoms future.

After a few minutes of searching the busy room, looking at the faces of the couples dancing, listening for any familiar voices and scanning each person by the refreshments table, Haven finally spotted someone she recognized. It was Celia, the woman from the council that had been so nice to her.

Haven smiled as she walked over to where Celia was talking to someone. Attempting to wait until Celia was done with her conversation, Haven stood awkwardly clutching a glass of some sort of wine she hadn't tasted yet.

"Haven, dear, come on over. I have someone I'd like you to meet" Celia called to her, waving her closer. Celia looked stunning in a long flowy red dress that swished around her ankles, it complemented her dark skin perfectly. The sleeves were made of red lace and ended right above her elbows.

"This is Odessa, she's on the crown guard."

Odessa bowed quickly, something Haven hadn't been expecting. It left her a bit flustered.

"Your highness," Odessa smiled, she was tall and lanky with a short blonde bob styled into waves. Her high cheekbones and intense dark eyes stood out. Haven found herself instantly attracted to this girl. Her mind went a bit fuzzy, slowing her response.

Snapping out of her lust induced brain fog, Haven told Odessa, "You don't have to do that."

People bowed all the time. It was something she was getting used to but there wasn't usually the *highness* part. Normally, people just bowed and kept walking.

"But it's true isn't it? You are to be queen." Odessa looked Haven up and down, heat in her eyes. A blush crept across Havens face. Usually, an interaction like this led to some kind of hookup. Granted, it was usually in a random bedroom at a party, not a castle and Haven was a nameless girl and not a princess.

Haven thought to herself that this could be what she needed to get Nik out of her mind. She barely knew the woman standing in front of her but as Haven met Odessa's eyes, she flushed at the obvious heat in them.

"And that's my cue to leave" Celia spoke, startling Haven from her inappropriate thoughts. Haven cursed herself as Celia walked away, remembering what she'd come over for. Odessa and her temporary lust forgotten, Haven turned to call Celia back.

Just as she turned, Haven felt a breeze brush over the bareness of her chest. Looking back to Odessa, she assumed it was her doing. Her assumption was quickly proven wrong when a snake of air began its ascent up her leg. She recognized the feeling of that magic, it was Niks! Dots quickly connected in her brain, she'd be willing to bet that he had tripped her that day in the library when they'd first met and again that night when they were running. Haven guessed he held some sort of influence over air or winds that allowed him to play sneaky games like that.

Haven quickly apologized and turned to look for Nik to tell him to knock it off. Haven barely registered the surprised look on Odessa's face as she walked away. The vine of air was slowly inching its way up her leg.

She couldn't spot Nik wherever he was hiding so instead she made her way to the exit hoping that her temporary departure would force him to leave her alone. The closer she got to the door, the further up Niks magic got.

As she reached the large door, Niks magic brushed the spot between her legs, eliciting a gasp from Haven and forcing her to stop walking. She tried to be quiet but she was almost certain the guard standing by the door heard her. The idea that the guard heard her left Haven incredibly embarrassed and feeling the need to make a quick getaway.

Haven shook off the feeling of Niks magic as best she could and stumbled through the door. Fortunately, as soon as she was out of the room, the air dissipated. Unfortunately, it left a scorching heat in its wake Haven tried her best not to acknowledge.

Haven was very glad she got out before anyone was able to scent what was going on. As much as the guard overhearing her was embarrassing, that would've been worse. As Haven took a deep breath, she promised herself that the next time she had the opportunity, she'd learn how to mask her scent.

Darting down the hall and up to the second level, Haven heard footsteps behind her. She was both afraid it was Nik and afraid it wasn't. As she turned a corner, she ducked into a storage closet. Turning in the small room, Haven backed against a short dresser facing the door. The footsteps quickly passed, Haven had only a second of relief before the steps returned and the door whipped open.

Standing in the doorway was Nik. The expression on his face nothing short of murderous. Haven knew she should be afraid. Instead, all she felt was heat burning brighter and brighter between her legs.

"I could smell you all the way down the hall" He growled, coming straight for her.

Nik's body crashed into hers as he crushed his lips against hers. Shockwaves rolled through Haven, it felt like the world was spinning as he delivered intense, sinful kisses.

Nik pulled back, causing Haven to grumble. She wanted his lips back on hers, now. A fleeting memory of Tasha warning her about all over the place emotions popped into her head before she quickly dismissed it. Haven was fairly sure this was not that but the thought popped into her head nonetheless.

Haven tried to tug Nik back to her. He tutted, bringing a hand up to collar her throat. He only applied the lightest pressure but Haven found herself melting into him anyway.

Nik leaned in close, just as she thought he was going to kiss her again he whispered,

"Were you going to fuck her?"

Confusion pebbled Havens mind for a second before she understood, he meant that guard. Haven needed a second to even remember her name. Once it came to mind, she hesitated to answer Niks question. Haven didn't know the right answer here so she decided on the truth, nodding only once. Haven heard Nik curse under his breath. It sounded like something along the lines of, "Fucking sirens"

Before Haven could get too into what she thought she'd heard Nik say, he tightened his hold on her throat and pulled a needy moan from her.

"Would you have enjoyed it?"

Haven nodded again, hoping he'd get his questions over with and put his mouth back on hers. A fog of lust had descended over her, she didn't want to talk or answer his questions, she wanted Niks body as close as he could get it and his lips back on hers.

A growl rumbled from Nik, the low light coming from under the doorway allowed Haven to see that his pupils were blown wide.

"Would it have been as good as this?" He asked, sliding a hand to the aching spot between her legs. Even through her clothes, that touch had Haven shaking her head repeatedly.

It was the truth. No matter who it was, Haven knew they'd never compete with the way she felt when she was with Nik.

A low laugh sounded from him, Havens only warning before he unleashed himself on her, slamming his lips back to hers. The hand that had been between her legs moved to grip her thigh and hoisted her onto the dresser. Her legs twined together behind his back, he pushed the slit of her dress as high as it would go, exposing her to him.

Nik stepped between her mostly bare legs, molding his body as close to Havens as he could get it. The hand that had been around her throat moved up to clutch her hair. In one pull he ruined the almost thirty minutes worth of work that had gone into pinning her hair exactly as she'd wanted it. Haven literally could not care less, not as Nik began moving his rough kisses down her throat. Pulling himself back to look her over, Nik swore,

"This fucking dress"

Nik moved his hands from her thigh and hair, gripping the opening in the V where it met the under bust corset and ripped. Nik ripped her dress right down the middle, straight to the slit leaving her front fully exposed to him. She would've been mad if it hadn't been so incredibly hot.

Nik spread her legs, Haven leaned back on her palms as she watched him watch her. She knew he could tell how wet she was. Haven hadn't put on any underwear, a fact Nik could obviously see. The insides of her thighs were slick, wetness slowly running down her legs. Even if Nik didn't have a fae sense of smell, the sight alone would have been enough to tell him how turned on she was.

"Holy fucking gods" He said, dropping down to his knees. If Haven was in her right mind, she'd make a comment about him on his knees before a queen.

Nik took one deep inhale before he began devouring her. He had her screaming, moaning and writhing in under a minute. If anyone was nearby they'd certainly hear her. Hell, maybe even the people a floor below could hear her. Although she doubted it with the loud music. Either way, at that moment in time, Haven again, could not bring herself to care.

Nik wrapped one arm around her hip, splaying his hand flat against her tummy, effectively holding her still from where she'd begun rocking against his face. He used his other hand for much more wicked things, easing his mouth at her clit just enough to slip two fingers inside her.

Haven moaned so loudly she had to remove one hand from holding her up to cover her mouth.

Nik smirked into the next glide of his tongue. He used the flat expanse of his tongue back and forth over her clit, in time with the thrust of his fingers.

Havens orgasm snuck up on her, shocking her as she rode peak after delicious peak.

Nik groaned between her legs as she pulsed around his fingers. It was such an indecent sound it made Haven grab his hair and pull him up for a kiss. She tasted herself on his lips, the indecency of that alone had Haven reaching for his belt, wanting him to feel the same pleasure he'd brought her. He immediately snatched her wrist and pulled away.

"Haven wait, I," He pulled away from her, stumbling over his words. The sudden vulnerability she in his eyes tugged on Havens heartstrings.

"What?" She asked gently

"I've never, uh" He paused, "I haven't exactly," He couldn't seem to finish the sentence so Haven did it for him,

"Had sex?"

He nodded. For some reason he seemed unable to meet her eyes.

"Oh" She said, it wasn't a big deal to her, although with the way he kissed you'd guess the man had been around the block many many times. Haven started to talk, to tell him that it was alright and that if he wanted to wait then that was fine. A knock on the door stopped Haven from speaking.

"What?" Nik growled. She couldn't tell what was bothering him so much, was it that someone was interrupting them or had she accidentally made him feel bad about being a virgin? Haven hoped he was just mad that someone paused their little tryst. Either way, if they continued now or if she had to seek him out during the night she'd make sure he knew that his lack of a sex life made no difference to her.

"You father summons you" A voice stated. She recognized the voice as Delroy, the asshole guard that had warned her away from Nik.

Nik pinched the bridge of his nose before looking at her, an apology in his eyes.

"It's fine. Go," She assured him.

He took in the ruined expanse of her dress, smirked and un-clipped the cloak he was wearing before wrapping it around her shoulders.

"Thanks" She spoke softly, she had no idea how she would have gotten back to her room without something to cover up.

Before Nik left, he placed one last quick kiss on her lips, as if he couldn't resist having one last taste.

Haven watched Nik exit, sans cloak. She wondered whether or not this was simply a random jealousy born hookup or if it was going to happen again. She sure hoped it would. Nik was still the asshole who left her in the mud and but she was beginning to see more of him too. Like the boy whose eyes flashed with fear after being told his father had summoned him.

Chapter Forty

Niks mind raced with uncertainties as he followed his friend from the storage closet he'd been with Haven in. He hadn't meant to let slip that he'd never bedded a woman before. While Nik honestly didn't mind that Haven knew, it wasn't something he told a lot of people, or rather, anyone. Nik wasn't waiting for something special but he had his reasons behind his intact virginity. He just hoped he hadn't freaked Haven out or upset her with his accidental rejection.

Nik wasn't sure if he should seek her out later or not, he wanted to speak to her about what happened but he couldn't risk either of them getting more involved than they already were. It wasn't until Nik noticed that his friend was leading him the opposite direction of his fathers office that he was able to pull himself from his thoughts.

"Where are we going?" Nik asked

Delroy was leading Nik in the opposite direction of the ball. Wherever they were going, he assumed his father would be waiting.

"Your room" Delroy snipped

"Why?" Nik asked hesitantly

"Because you reek of sex with a certain soon to be queen"

Nik supposed that made sense. Honestly, his mind was still a little foggy.

Nik smirked at the thought of what they had been doing in that storage closet. Risking a glance at Delroy, Nik grimaced when he saw the scowl on his face.

"I could hear her all the way down the hall" Delroy told Nik, still refusing to look his way.

What Delroy said should have given Nik a pause, no one could know what happened between the two of them but damn it felt good to be the one making her scream like that, to confirm her words from the festival. Nik simply couldn't wipe the self satisfied smirk off his face.

"If you're not careful, someone is going to find out." Delroy told him, "That someone being your father"

Just like that, Niks smirk was wiped away.

They came to the wooden door leading to Niks room. Delroy unlocked the door and entered quickly. Striding to Niks desk, he pulled out a small white crystal and held it out to Nik.

"Thanks" Nik nodded, taking the crystal.

Delroy simply nodded and headed back through the open bedroom door. The pair immediately headed to meet with Niks father.

Along the way, Nik activated the crystal and dropped it into his pocket. It would hide his scent for a while and hide Havens scent on Nik, something he was infinitely grateful for. If his father found out what had just gone on between them, it would make his fathers year.

Even though his chest buzzed with an unfamiliar feeling he had never felt before, Nik told himself he needed to try harder to stay away from Haven. The two of them could not become involved like that again.

Nik did his best to put the memories of her out of his mind for now, instead choosing to focus on whatever ungodly thing his father had chosen to summon him about. As they turned the corner down the hall from his fathers office, Nik finally broke the unusual silence that had descended over him and his friend,

"Let's go find out what the miserable bastard wants"

***

HAVEN

On the way back to her room, Haven walked with a spring in her step. Maybe it was the orgasm, maybe it was finally knowing what Niks lips truly, felt like against hers, either way, she couldn't bring herself to be disappointed about missing out on speaking with the council members at the ball. Not when the memories from tonight would be keeping her warm for a long long while. For now, she just had to change her clothes and then head back to the ball.

Haven hoped no one would notice her outfit change. If they did, Haven had to hope they wouldn't bring it up seeing as she didn't have a proper answer for them. Either way, she was headed back down to the great hall as soon as she was changed, there might still be some fae worth getting to know. Gods knew she needed as many friends as she could get right now.

As she neared her room, Havens feet stalled. A chill crept over her spine, instantly setting off warning bells in her head. Something was wrong, Haven couldn't physically see anything amiss but everything in her was screaming for her to turn the other way and find someone to check things out with. Haven decided to ignore those feelings, instead stepping closer to the door. Even if she could find someone, come up with an excuse as to why she was only dressed in a cloak and convince them to come with her, asking someone to help her check out her room based on nothing more than a feeling didn't exactly scream, 'Powerful Queen'

Everything looked the same as when she left earlier but there was a feeling hanging in the air, like someone had been here not that long ago. Whoever had been down this hall was not supposed to be here, Haven could tell that much.

As far as she knew, everyone was at the ball. No one should've been anywhere near this part of the castle. The only thing of importance in this part of the castle was her room. Romans' room was three halls away, closer to the guards quarters. There wasn't another soul staying in any of the rooms in this hall, a fact that she had found odd at first. At the time, Haven had figured that with everything else taking place, the fact that she had a very private room wasn't important enough to ask about.

Wishing she'd brought her dagger, Haven forced her feet into motion. Creeping the last few feet towards her door, she brought her magic towards the surface. Even though she couldn't do very much with it, Haven assumed she'd be able to shoot her magic at someone and then run if it actually came down to that. Testing the knob, she found it locked, just as she left it. The door still being locked did not immediately take away her hesitance; if someone had the ability to get into her room then they likely could have locked the door behind them.

Retrieving the key from where she'd hung it on her necklace, Haven unlocked her door and eased it open. Quietly stepping inside her room, she found nothing amiss. Haven checked the bathroom and then the balcony, under the bed and in her closet. Everything was just as she left it. Nothing appeared out of place. Furrowing her brows, Haven surveyed her room again. After again finding nothing, she told herself that she was just being paranoid. There wasn't a single sign that someone had been in here. No drawers opened, the balcony doors were still locked, all of her papers and notes were still in the drawer of her desk. Not even the sheets on her bed had been displaced.

Haven took a breath and decided she must be letting Romans words of war and the stress of the past few weeks catch up to her. That had to be what was going on. She repeated the words to herself, attempting to calm her heart. It didn't work very well but she kept trying nonetheless. After all, she couldn't fathom why someone would break into her room if they weren't going to take anything or weren't lying in wait.

Walking over to her bed, Haven intended to remove Niks cloak and change her clothes. She wanted to get back to the ball. As soon as she got within a foot of the bed, immense exhaustion washed over her. Weird, since she hadn't been very sleepy before entering her room. Drifting closer, Haven allowed herself to collapse onto her sheets. She couldn't remember her bed ever being this comfortable. The soft mattress seemed to reach out and hug her, wrapping her in warmth and a false sense of safety.

Havens eyes closed of their own volition. Sleep sounded so good right now, she couldn't remember why she had been worried. There was nothing in her room that would harm her. What was the worst that could happen if she gave into this feeling and let herself take a small nap? Haven couldn't see any reason not to. She couldn't remember why she had been planning to leave her room in the first place.

Haven had one last fleeting feeling of panic before sleep claimed her and everything went black.

Chapter Forty-One

His father really was a miserable bastard. He'd dragged Nik from council member to council member, and even to some of the powerful lords that had come from all over the kingdom to attend the ball. Nik about lost it once his father started on the officials from Shaston. He hated what his father did to their crown regent and seeing the lords from there only reopened that particular batch of hatred. Nik was thankful Haven would be righting that wrong and many others once she took the throne. He knew she didn't know much about ruling a kingdom but with a heart like hers, he had every confidence she would be healing many wounds.

Even if she didn't realize it, Haven was the only one capable of truly returning Drailia to what it once was, a beautiful kingdom full of light and happiness. It had been that way a long time ago while the fae were still in the human realm. Everything had gone downhill after his father took over.

Nik was pretty sure his father was dragging him around to garner support for his bid to place himself on the throne. He hadn't outright said anything but anyone with half a brain could figure out what he'd been alluding to in the many conversations Nik was forced to listen to.

The more backing he had, the more likely he'd be able to take the throne for himself. There hadn't been many that showed any kind of loyalty to his father, only two council members Nik would be keeping an eye on and a handful of other powerful members of Dralian society. Thankfully, no one from Shaston seemed inclined to even listen to what his father had to say.

Unfortunately, Nik knew what his fathers backup plan would likely be when he inevitably failed to legally keep Haven off the throne.

It was why Nik needed Haven to hate him, to absolutely despise him. But he was finding it harder and harder to do things that could cause the kind of hate he needed. Every day he found himself more drawn in by her, spying on her training sessions with Tasha, watching her search the library each day at lunch for whatever she was looking for.

Nik had a pretty good idea of why the pull between them was so strong, he just prayed he was wrong and that he'd be able to garner enough loathing from her to do what needed to be done. That way, when the time came, she'd never agree to marry him.

***

Early morning sunlight streamed through the windows of the castle as Nik walked down the hall, exhausted from his fathers endless posturing. Pausing in an open window, Nik took a deep breath and allowed the early morning sun to calm him. He'd always loved this moment, right before the sun officially rose and morning began. When almost everyone was still asleep and the castle was still.

Nik was on his way to his room, not having gotten any sleep thanks to the fact that his father had kept the ball going until about an hour ago. His plan was to sleep the whole day away, ignoring his fathers order to socialize more with some of the fae that traveled here from throughout the kingdom. His father wanted Nik campaigning, trying to convince others that Haven was not fit for the throne. Nik had no plans to do any such thing. Haven might be young and inexperienced but he knew she could become exactly what this kingdom needed. Watching her lessons, seeing how deeply she cared about the things she was learning told him all he needed to know. Any doubt he'd harbored before going into this had been entirely washed away.

He was just about to turn down the hall that contained his door when a blood curdling scream echoed through the halls. It didn't even take a minute for Nik to recognize the source of the scream and it stopped his heart dead.

Taking off at a run, Nik had only one thought, he had to get to Haven.

Thankfully, Havens room wasn't far. By the time he made it to her door, others were already gathered. It was definitely Haven that screamed. In fact, she was still screaming. The guard that was supposed to be posted at the end of the hall was nowhere to be found. There were a few servants trying to break through the door, plus Astrea. They weren't making much progress. None of them had any powers that could be useful here but Nik did.

"Backup!" He shouted

The five or so fae gathered immediately stumbled away from the door. Nik pulled from his well of power, gathering a large gust of wind in his hands. Throwing it directly at the lock, the door splintered, breaking open.

Releasing a breath of relief, Nik charged into Havens room. It didn't take him long to figure out what was causing her screams.

Her entire room had been ransacked, the desk was on its side, papers and ink scattered all over the floor. Clothes had been pulled out of her dresser and armoire, ripped to shreds and thrown everywhere. The glass from the balcony doors had been shattered, leaving pieces of glass littering the floor making it dangerous to walk on.

Holes had been ripped in the sides of her mattress, feathers from the mattress still hung in the air around the room. The worst was what Nik found when his eyes reached the bed. Haven was sat up against her headboard, clutching her knees to her chest, trembling. She was also covered in blood.

Blood had been splattered all over the bed and her, it dripped down the footboard and gathered in puddles on the floor. One sniff told Nik the blood belonged to a fae, it was also fresh, recent. They'd likely find the body of the guard tucked away somewhere.

Nik inched closer to Haven, not entirely sure how to proceed. She simultaneously looked one step away from a panic attack and ready to rip someones throat out.

Her eyes were wild, the knuckles gripping her legs were turning white. Each moment that passed seemed to increase her heart beat, it pounded in his ears telling Nik that he had to do something quick before she spiraled into a full blown panic attack.

Taking a few small steps, Nik risked Haven clawing him to pieces in her fright. While taking the last step, his foot landed on a piece of glass. It crunched under his boot, thankfully the leather protected his foot from being stabbed by it.

Havens head whipped to Nik at the sound. For a second he couldn't move, not sure what would happen next. When she met his eyes they immediately softened, recognizing him. A tear slid down her face, leaving a trail through the blood spatter. He could tell she hadn't cried until that moment, stuck somewhere between the panic, rage and fright. Nik didn't hesitate in his next move, knowing what he needed to do.

Easing himself onto the bed, Nik sidled next to Haven. Pulling her into his lap, he cradled her close and tucked her head under his chin. One arm went around her back, the other around her legs. Nik was keenly aware of the curious eyes watching them from the doorway, surely this would get back to his father but this was one of those moments where Nik simply did not care. Not as Havens trembling began to subside and her breathing slowly evened out.

Niks eyes strayed across the room, to the wall her desk had been up against. He noticed something he hadn't before, stabbed into the wall with a dagger was a note.

Written in blood it read,

You will never sit on the throne
Nik knew exactly who put it there

Chapter Forty-Two

Waking up covered in blood was not how Haven thought today would begin. Todays plans also did not include being naked in Niks shower, although she wasn't really complaining. Haven hadn't been able to completely calm down while still covered in blood. Nik had seen that and offered his shower seeing as hers had been trashed.

Nik had left to grab some breakfast while she showered and to get an update on what happened. She tried not to think too hard about being naked in his space. The only thing she had on was her necklace, never having removed it last night. When Nik had noticed she was still wearing his cloak, the ruined dress underneath, he'd been quick to stand in front of her so the fae gathered didn't see her naked. At the time, she'd wrapped the cloak as tight as it would go and hoped everyone would think her outfit was also a victim of what happened in her room last night.

Haven watched as blood swirled down the drain, washed away by the soap Nik had grabbed out of her bathroom. Now that her head was clearing, Haven found herself incredibly angry. She quickly figured out that her bed had been the victim of a spell, along with the slash marks and blood. That was probably why she'd passed out before she could even change her clothes. She guessed that someone snuck into her room and cast some sort of spell so Haven would fall asleep and stay asleep. Allowing them to sneak in while she was passed out, rifle through her drawers, rip up her clothes, throw blood all over her and leave a very ominous note behind.

Haven had an idea of who had done it but she had no proof.

The door to Niks bedroom opened. Haven could hear Niks light gait even over the sounds of the water, likely because she was still on edge after what happened. Haven listened to his steps as he neared the cracked door to the bathroom. Once he was directly on the other side of the door, Nik called,

"I grabbed some muffins for when you're done. I also left some clothes by the towel on the counter"

Haven cleared the steam off the shower glass and looked to the countertop by the sink. Sure enough, there was a pile of clothes next to a fluffy white towel. Checking herself over one last time, Haven thankfully found no more blood. It had taken an hour alone to get it all out of her hair. She quickly turned off the shower and got out. Upon closer inspection, Haven found that the clothes Nik left were definitely not hers. He had left his clothes for her to wear.

It made sense seeing as all of her items had probably been destroyed. Still, the idea of wearing his clothes sent heat between her legs. Heat she definitely should not be feeling this soon after basically being attacked.

After drying herself off, Haven began to dress in the dark clothes. They were soft to the touch and still warm as if they'd just come from the laundry. The pants were loose and the shirt hung down to her thighs but at least they were clean.

Walking out of the bathroom, Haven found Nik lounging on a couch. She watched as his eyes heated at the sight of her in his clothes. The muffin he had been about to bite into paused inches from his mouth.

"What did you find out?" She asked, drawing his attention away from her body.

"Not much," He said, looking away from her, "They're in the process of cleaning your room, crafting new windows for the balcony doors and getting you a new mattress"

Haven swallowed when memories of what had happened to her last one surfaced. Taking a deep breath, she walked over to the tray of blueberry muffins and picked one up. She found her way to a chair sitting next to the couch and sat down in it. Beginning to snack on the muffin, Haven tried to come up with some way to thank Nik for helping her and for letting her use his shower. Haven struggled to find something that didn't sound cheesy. For some reason she didn't think he'd appreciate the thanks anyways so instead she chose to just sit in silence. That silence was broken about five minutes later when Nik softly asked,

"Why didn't you wake up when all that was going on?"

"I don't know for sure" She told him, "When I first got back to my room, something was off. I could tell someone had been there but nothing seemed different. Nothing appeared to have been gone through so I chalked it up to paranoia and started to get changed. As soon as I got close to the bed I felt so tired I probably could've passed out on the floor. I could barely hold my head up, the last thing I remember was stumbling onto the bed. Everything after that is black. I didn't hear anything, nothing pulled me from sleep. I didn't even dream. The next thing I knew, I was waking up covered in blood"

Nik nodded his head. "Someone could've placed something on your mattress to make you pass out like that. It could've been a spell or even some kind of crystal"

Haven nodded in agreement, it felt good to have someone else validate her thoughts.

"That explains why you were still in your clothes from last night" He smirked.

The tips of Havens pointy ears turned red, flushing from the memories of being with him last night. She opened her mouth to apologize about possibly making him uncomfortable when he told her that he'd never been with anyone. Before she could get the words out, Nik carefully asked,

"Do you have any idea who might've done it?"

Haven nodded her head. She had a pretty good idea but she would also guess he did not want to hear it.

"You can tell me" He told her, "No matter who you suspect"

Haven hesitated for a moment before making her decision. Opening her mouth she said,

"Your father"

A few silent moments passed, Haven expected Nik to get pissed off. Instead, he simply nodded and looked away from her.

"I suspect the same thing." He said quietly, "He couldn't have done it himself seeing as he was at the ball most of the night but he could have hired someone or had someone loyal to him do it."

His words surprised Haven. She could tell they didn't have the greatest father/son relationship but she hadn't expected him to throw his dad under the bus like that. His next words didn't so much as shock her as they did depress her,

"They found the guards body"

Haven tried to formulate a response. In her head she'd known the blood covering her had to come from somewhere. She'd just hoped no one was actually killed. Haven wanted to find out that the missing guard was injured but still alive. She should have known though, and maybe on some level she did. No one could have survived that much blood loss.

"It was stuffed in a storage closet right down the hall, throat cut" Nik finished

Haven hesitated slightly before asking,

"Why would your father do something so terrible?"

Nik contemplated for a moment, as if trying to decide if he really wanted to tell her, if he really wanted to risk confirming her suspicions. Eventually he met her eyes and said,

"He wants power. More specifically your power. To him, the life of a guard is nothing in the grand scheme of things. He can't kill you, the blowback would be too harsh. He'd be executed. But he can try to find a way to hold onto his power. A way around the rules."

Before Nik could explain more, a knock sounded at the door. Haven recognized the scent on the other side as belonging to her tutor Tasha. She was getting better and better at using her fae senses, it had been awhile since she'd run into anything on accident while trying to gain control over her speed. Her newfound control made Haven incredibly proud. Even if the only person she'd shared her pride with was herself, that didn't make it any less valid.

Tasha knocked again, not even five seconds after her first knock. They were supposed to train today but she'd thought, given the circumstances, it would be called off.

Haven walked over and opened the door, earning a glare from Nik. Before she'd gotten in the shower he had warned her to be extremely careful from here on out. He'd also handed her the dagger Binah had sent, having taken it from the wall before they left.

As soon as the door opened wide enough, Tasha bustled through and shoved a bundle of training leathers into Havens arms.

"Attack or no you still have to train" Tasha insisted, crossing her arms.

"She's had a long day. If she doesn't want to, she shouldn't have to" Nik said, immediately jumping to Havens defense. Tasha rolled her eyes and told him,

"I don't take orders from you, boy"

Nik balked, Haven imagined no one had ever spoken to him like that. His father scared too many people to have someone be so disrespectful. Nik himself was intimidating but not in the same way as his father. You look at Nik and know that if given a good enough reason, he'd kill you. His father, on the other hand, seemed like the kind of man that would kill someone because they sneezed the wrong way.

While she appreciated Nik coming to her defense, it wasn't necessary. She was actually glad Tasha had shown up. Haven needed to work off this excess adrenaline and the only other way she could think of was sex. Training sounded like a much better idea than jumping Niks bones, especially when he was still somewhat looking at her like she might break. Also, he'd probably turn her down. One night did not completely erase the anger and between the two of them.

"It's fine," She told him. Without giving him room to argue, she stepped into the bathroom and changed into what Tasha had brought. Luckily, Tasha thought to bring underwear. Haven imagined the training leathers would rub the wrong way without the barrier of the panties. Actually, Haven thought, they could rub just the right way depending on how you looked at it. She snickered at her inappropriate thoughts.

Tightening the laces on her leathers, Haven gave herself one last word of encouragement and stepped out of the bathroom.

"Alright, let's do this" Haven said, confidence filling her voice. Snatching her dagger off the side table, Haven dropped Niks clothes into empty space and followed Tasha out the door.

Chapter Forty-Three

Haven followed Tasha to their usual training grounds. Unlike other days, Roman was there waiting for them.

"Hey, what are you doing here?" Haven asked as she came to stand beside him.

"Heard what happened. Came to check on you"

"Thank you" She smiled sheepishly. Roman stepped closer, wrapping Haven in a tight hug.

"I'm sorry about what happened," He told her, "How are you doing?"

"Good. I was a little freaked out at first but Nik let me use his shower to clean the blood off. My bathroom is kinda trashed" Haven attempted to downplay how she felt after the attack. She didn't want anyone to know quite how affected she was and quite how much Nik had helped her.

Roman released her and stepped back,

"Nik huh?" He smirked

"Shut up" Haven rolled her eyes, "It was just a shower"

Roman snorted and gave her a look that told Haven he did not believe her. Technically she wasn't lying, the only thing that happened this morning was Nik letting her use his shower. Last night on the other hand, well that was a bit of a different story.

Roman nudged Havens arm and began walking away,

"I'll let you ladies get back to it. Have fun! Don't let her work you too hard H!"

Haven laughed as Roman walked away, other days she might agree with him but after everything that happened today, all she wanted was to work. Haven wanted to work so hard she forgot the way the blood of the guard clung to her skin, the way it smelled, the way it didn't want to leave her skin no matter how hard she'd scrubbed.

"Enough chit chat. Time to get to work" Tasha spoke, breaking Haven's train of thoughts. Haven was grateful to Tasha for preventing her from diving further into those memories. Tasha took off at a run a second later, taking to their usual route around the castle grounds. Haven smiled, relieved to be getting started and took off after her.

"I think today we'll start doing three laps" Tasha told Haven as she caught up to her.

Havens smile fell. They weren't supposed to start doing three laps for another two days. She was barely able to complete two.

This was going to be exactly what Haven wanted, a long and tiring training session.

***

Haven and Tasha parried back and forth. It was almost the end of their weapons lesson. Haven still wasn't able to get the sword from Tasha.

Haven took two small steps back. Tasha advanced with her sword,

"Keep an eye on your opponent's feet, often they will angle their feet in the direction they plan to move"

Haven nodded, covered in sweat and ready to drop.

"With daggers you have to get in close," Tasha continued, "That's usually the hard part, especially when someone has a sword. You have to figure out how to get past their defenses without getting injured in the process. Once you are past their reach with the sword, you gain the advantage."

Tashas sword clanged with Haven's dagger. Ducking down and advancing towards Tasha's body, Havens arm came up towards Tasha's wrist, the one holding the sword. She was attempting to knock into the part of her wrist that would cause a spasm, forcing Tasha to drop the sword.

She had yet to complete this move but today felt different. Maybe it was what happened this morning, maybe Haven had finally started to grasp Tashas training concepts. Either way, as Havens arm connected with Tashas wrist, time felt like it was moving in slow motion.

Haven barely heard the sound of metal clanking against the ground as the sword dropped. Immediate triumph overwhelmed Haven.

"Yes!" She cried, throwing her arms up in the air.

Tasha stepped back,

"Good but remember, a real fight wouldn't be over until the other person was either incapacitated or dead. They still could have tried to get your dagger from you. Or used their hands to hurt you, and if they possess magic then that would be another problem entirely"

"Oh come on Tasha! Let me have this!" Haven whined, she knew she likely sounded like a child but she really needed this win and Tasha was not giving it to her.

"Very well," Tasha nodded, "You did good," She told her, "I guess this means the dagger is now officially yours"

The biggest smile Haven had ever felt stretched across her face. She had almost forgotten that she'd be allowed to keep the dagger once she completed her task. Haven had been training with other weapons but she was best with the long dagger she'd picked up on day one.

Tasha stepped over to the line of other weapons, drawing two sheaths out of a burlap bag.

"Two?" Haven asked

"Pick up your other dagger," Tasha told her. Nodding to where the dagger from Binah laid in the grass.

Haven grasped a dagger in each hand, her training dagger was longer than the one from Binah but they still felt equally balanced in her hands. Tasha finished gathering the sheaths and stepped in front of Haven. Crouching low she said,

"I would recommend wearing your shorter dagger at your ankle and your other at your hip"

Tasha slid down the leather of Havens boot, attaching a small sheath to her ankle. Reaching up, Tasha took the dagger Binah had given her and fastened it into the sheath at her ankle. Next, Tasha showed Haven how to attach her new sheath to her hip with a leather belt.

Haven settled her training dagger into the sheath at her hip, the emerald gleaming in the sunlight.

"You look like a warrior" Tasha told her, a small smile and proud look evident on Tashas face.

Another wide smile spread across Havens face. After the events of this morning, she welcomed the newfound badass feeling she felt after both daggers were sheathed in their new homes.

Haven felt unstoppable and powerful. All of this may have been unexpected but Haven was determined to be the best queen possible for the people of her kingdoms. To honor her father and mother. Whether they lied or not, Haven knew her parents loved her and would be proud of the woman she was becoming.

Haven wasn't given much time to think over her newfound confidence because Tasha pulled her from her thoughts by clapping her hands together and announcing,

"Now onto our magic lesson"

Chapter Forty-Four

It had been three whole weeks since someone broke into Havens room, covered her in blood and destroyed most of her stuff. Everything had been eerily silent since. The staff didn't gossip in the hallways, whenever Rea, Roman and Haven had lunch they didn't talk much. Haven hadn't even seen Nik. Usually she at least passed him in the halls, or even his friend Delroy. Not a peep from anyone. At one point, Haven had even gone to Niks room intending to talk with him but he hadn't been there.

The crown regent had also quit taking meetings. He holed himself up in his office most of the time, only ever coming out when appearances demanded it, not that that was very often.

Haven knew he was planning something, she just didn't know what. The thought frightened her, especially after she officially decided it was him behind the murder of the guard and the destruction of her room.

It was as if the castle could tell something was coming. The closer Haven got to her coronation, the more nervous people became. It had taken all of one hour after she woke up screaming for the entire castle to know what the letter on the wall said. The only person that hadn't changed at all was Tasha. Even Elanor walked on eggshells around her. It was like people expected her to simply keel over and die, like the letter on the wall had been some kind of prophecy instead of a threat.

Haven was determined not to let the fright take hold of her. It had taken all of two days of Haven feeling nervous and jumpy before she decided that if something was coming for her, there was no stopping it. Instead, she needed to be prepared for it. She still went to training everyday with Tasha and her lessons in the afternoons with Elanor. She still searched the library, combing its stacks for answers.

Haven didn't know what else to do so she had decided to do nothing. Whatever was going to happen was just going to have to happen. In her head it made sense, when she tried to explain it to Rea, her friend looked at her like she was crazy.

Thankfully, Haven learned a lot these last few weeks. Her and Elanor were currently in preparation for her coronation taking place in a little over a week. Her control over her magic was incredibly strong, most days she let a few shadows or tendrils of fire flit around her wherever she went. It helped take the edge off and helped the fae milling about the castle to stop looking at her like she was helpless.

For the most part, besides the eerie feeling that constantly hung in the air, everything was going exceptionally well. The more spells she cast, the more she exercised her magic, the stronger Haven became. Except for one bad day when she'd almost burned her eyebrows off, everything had been going the best she could have hoped for. Tasha even recently told her that they'd start incorporating her magic into their weapons and battle training. Even Elanor was impressed.

Haven had learned so much about her kingdom and those surrounding it that oftentimes it felt like her brain was about to explode. She welcomed the feeling, it meant she was one step closer to becoming queen, making her parents proud and serving her people like they deserved.

Excitement wracked through Haven for today's lesson. Recently, Tasha had been teaching her to ride horseback. Today was the day she got to pick out her own horse.

After her coronation there would be a multi day parade Haven would be riding in that went from the castle through the four largest cities in Dralia and then all the way to the capital of Shaston where she'd be staying for at least a week.

Yesterday, the lords of the four major cities had each sent a steed from their stable for Haven to pick from. Whichever she picked would officially belong to her. Anytime she needed to leave the castle, or simply ride through the woods she would take the horse she picked today.

When Haven was being told about all of this, she'd asked about Shaston and why she wasn't already preparing to take over there. At the time, Elanor explained that fifty odd years ago, Niks father forcefully convinced Shastons crown regent to hand over control to Drailia. Since then, while they have remained their own kingdom in name, all the power rested here in Drailia.

After she traveled to Shaston and spent some time there, Haven would return and rule from the castle here in Drailia. Haven didn't like how the crown regent all but turned the people of Shaston into Drailians. He'd erased most of their customs and policies, adapting those from Drailia. Now they celebrated Drailian holidays and events and while the fae did a lot of things in common, it still wasn't fair that the Shastons didn't celebrate all the things they used to simply because the Drailian crown regent took over.

Maybe she could change that when she became queen, Haven thought. If she survived her coronation then one of the first things she'd be doing would be to learn as much about Shaston as she could. Haven hoped she'd be able to return the kingdom to some of its former glory. She didn't know exactly how yet but she knew it was important enough to figure out.

Shaking the thoughts from her head, Haven jogged the last few steps to where Tasha was waiting.

"I can feel the excitement radiating off of you" Tasha told her as they walked towards the stables on the far edge of the castle grounds. It was a large wood building nestled right at the edge of the forest.

"I am," Haven responded, "I've always loved animals"

"Have you given any thought to what your animal form might be when you get to that point in your magic lessons?"

The question stopped Haven in her tracks.

"I can turn into an animal?" She nearly screeched.

Tasha took in the shock on Havens face and laughed, a full bellied, incredibly loud laugh.

"Yes," She told her, "Almost all fae can. Eventually I will teach you how to unlock that part of yourself. Most fae have it happen by accident about the time they turn sixteen but seeing as you were in the human world at that point, there was no one around to teach you. It might be a little harder because of that but I have no doubt you will succeed"

"So I can just turn into any animal?" Haven asked

Another smile played across Tashas face, she was clearly enjoying Havens shock and excitement.

"Not exactly," Tasha began, "By the time we are born and come into our magic it is already decided what our other form will be. You could turn into a bird or a snake, even a dog. The only way you will find out is to do it"

"Can we go ahead and start that lesson?" Haven was pretty sure she knew what Tashas answer would be but couldn't resist asking anyway.

"Be patient, let's take things one step at a time. After you become queen I will start your more advanced magic lessons, form shifting included."

Haven took a deep breath. After the shock of being told she could turn into an animal wore off, she remembered where they were going. Haven tried to let form shifting ease from her mind. She needed to be patient as Tasha had said. Unfortunately, Haven could only be so relaxed about it. She was pretty sure shifting into an animal would be on her mind until she did it.

The sight of the stable up ahead helped put form shifting out of Havens head. The day she changed forms would be a very big day but so was this. Today she would be picking a best friend and partner to carry her wherever she needed to go. She just hoped she picked right.

Chapter Forty-Five

"So, which one are you thinking?" Tasha asked. All day they'd tested out the horses the lords sent. Grooming and riding, getting a feel for their temperaments. As soon as they had initially walked into the stables, Haven was pretty sure she'd had hers picked. It hadn't been about looks, simply the feeling she'd gotten when she walked up to him. She still spent the morning trying each horse but in the end came to the same conclusion from the very beginning. Tasha would not be happy.

"Lord Drummonds" Haven stated, smirking and avoiding eye contact with Tasha.

Tasha rolled her eyes, "How did I guess that? Of course you'd go for the most unruly of the bunch"

Tasha wasn't wrong, Lord Drummond had sent quite the beast. He was easily the biggest with a thick black mane and body to match. All the other lords had sent simple, easy horses in an assortment of colors. One solid white mare, a brown paint and another smaller black gelding. Haven had spent time with each of them, getting to know them and trying to picture herself working with them. Each horse was special in its own way but Haven was consistently drawn to the black stallion from the coastal town of Kithage where Drummond lorded.

Maybe he had sent a different style of horse because he was the only lord to have spent any time with Haven. An official meeting with the lords was scheduled for the day before her coronation but she unofficially met Lord Drummond at the festival before her bloodline test. They had talked for at least half an hour, joking around and generally getting to know each other.

Haven knew Drummond as the short, pot bellied man with kind eyes and a long gray beard. He had two kids and a wife back home. She quite liked him and was looking forward to working with him more once she became queen. Haven hoped that the other lords would be as kind as Drummond had been, although she knew that was unlikely to be the case.

If she thought about it, Lord Drummond likely considered their conversations when he picked this horse to send.

The stallion stomped around in his stall, wanting to be let out. Tasha hadn't been joking, the stallion could be quite unruly. He'd tried to bite the stable hand twice in the last hour. While they had been riding, Tasha and Haven had come across a small creek. The horse proceeded to ignore Havens orders to simply cross. He stopped with all four hooves in the water and splashed around, stomping his front feet and kicking out with his back. Haven had laughed so hard tears came out of her eyes. Tasha had scolded her for letting the horse behave like that but it hadn't taken long for him to finish playing and follow Tasha to the other side of the creek.

Haven stepped up to the animal, running a hand up and down his muzzle and smiled. The horse leaned into her like he was trying to say that he liked her too.

"I'm not even going to bother arguing with you. It's obvious you've made up your mind" Tasha said, exasperation ringing out in her voice.

Haven smiled again, she quite liked her new steed.

"Is this the one miss?" The stable hand asked

"Yes" She nodded

"What's his name?"

Haven thought for a moment before deciding,

"Pluto" It was both the Roman version of Hades, god of the underworld, and the cute little dog from a children's show Haven watched when she was little. It fit him well.

***

After what would likely be remembered as one of the best days of her life, Haven was feeling truly light. She had been given permission to blow off her lessons to get used to her new horse. She'd spent the day exploring the forest and castle grounds with Pluto, laughing when he tried to chase a butterfly and then finishing her day with a picnic down by the lake. It had been exactly what she needed to forget about the stress and anxiety she'd been feeling. Even in normal circumstances, Haven held more stress than most. In a situation like the one she was in with a coronation around the corner and the memory of what she considered a death threat still ghosting her wall? It was safe to say a day of relaxation and little to no reminders of the outside world was exactly what she needed.

The darkness due to the late hour seeped in through Havens balcony windows. Soon after her coronation, she would be moving to the royal rooms on the top floor and while she was excited, Haven knew she'd miss this quaint little room where her life had changed so drastically.

Creeping out of bed, Haven pulled a robe over her chemise. Tonight she had a mission, one that she would not fail in.

Haven was planning to track Nik down and confront him. He'd been avoiding her ever since he'd let her use his shower. Haven was pretty sure the only time she could catch him was when he was in his room sleeping, which was why she'd waited until such a late hour.

Peering down the hall, she found the guard slouched against the wall, likely dozing. There had been one posted around the clock since the attack on her room. Before that, there had been one only during the night.

Haven's enhanced fae hearing allowed the sound of his soft snores to reach her, giving her the perfect opportunity. Not that she needed to explain herself to anyone but she'd rather not have gossip spreading about her sneaking around the castle in the middle of the night.

As quickly and as quietly as she could, Haven made her way to Niks doorway, gripping the dagger she brought with her the entire walk. Once she made it to his room, she tried the door handle, finding it locked just as she suspected it would be. Luckily she had a few tricks up her sleeve, or rather, a few bobby pins. Before he died, her dad taught her some neat tricks. Most of it had been for her safety, like how to get through duct tape holding your hands together if someone kidnapped you and other things she hadn't had a clue why he taught her, like how to pick locks.

Sadness distracted Haven as the wound from her fathers death ripped open. Now was not the time for this, she reminded herself. Haven had to be quick if she didn't want to be caught by anyone other than Nik.

Haven slid two bobby pins into the lock, one bent at an angle, the other straight. Wiggling the top one up and down, Haven listened for the click of the lock. It didn't sound right away, frustrating her and causing Haven to drop one of the bobby pins. Blowing out a breath, Haven pushed a strand of hair behind her ear and picked up the pin.

It took another five minutes of trying the bobby pins at different angles before a click resonated through the hall. Exhaling a breath, Haven turned the handle and silently cheered herself on. Opening the door just enough for her to slip through, Haven hoped that when she did finally get face to face with Nik, he wouldn't be pissed at her for breaking into his room.

Taking a quick glance around his room, she didn't immediately spot Nik. Internally, Haven cursed herself. She didn't know what else to do if he wasn't here other than to wander the halls looking for him. Then she'd stayed up late, risked getting caught and gotten her robe dirty dragging it through the castle halls for nothing.

From what she could see through the open bathroom and office doors, Nik wasn't in either of those places. He wasn't in bed or lounging on the couch. Havens mind flashed with thoughts of Nik with someone else. The thought stung more than she was ready to admit.

A second too late she had the idea to listen for a heartbeat in the dark room. Just as she leaned into that sense, someone grabbed her, shoving her back against the door she'd just snuck through.

"Well well well, what might you be doing out of bed princess?"

Chapter Forty-Six

Nik woke as soon as his ears picked up footsteps in the hall, too used to being on guard for when his father used to show up in the middle of the night to dole out punishments for whatever he thought Nik had done wrong. As soon as he'd recognized Havens scent, his nerves calmed and turned into curiosity.

He had been avoiding her since the night his father paid someone to destroy her room and paint her with blood but it was for her own good. He may not be able to stomach being terrible to her often enough to earn the hate he needed but he could keep her from getting any further attached to him.

He was surprised hearing her picking the lock. It was a very useful talent, one currently in Niks own arsenal, but he wondered how she learned to do it.

Nik heard her drop whatever pin she was using to pick the lock, heard her blow out a breath and continue attempting to pick his lock. An idea popped into Niks head to surprise her just as she'd surprised him. Quickly hopping off his bed, Nik strolled to the wall next to the door so he'd be behind it when Haven opened it. Nik pressed himself into the wall as much as he could, sucking in a breath when he heard the telltale sound of the door unlocking. He was impressed, it had only taken her a few minutes.

The door cracked open and Niks heart sped up as Haven slipped into his room. He watched as she scanned the room, not spotting him. Nik waited until right before she turned enough to spot him before he reached out and grabbed her. Pushing her back against the now closed door, he wrapped an arm around her waist and placed a hand over her mouth.

"Well well well, what might you be doing out of bed princess?"

Nik liked calling her princess. When he was a child, he'd heard Delroys dad call his mom that. While it meant something differ-ent when Nik called Haven that, the fact that she was an actual princess and all, the look of pure devotion on Delroys father's face was one Nik could only ever try to live up to. Not that he'd ever allow himself the chance.

"You're avoiding me" Haven told him, prying Niks hand off her mouth.

"And what makes you think that? Maybe I simply don't like you"

Nik felt Havens body outwardly cringe at his words. The words may be false but if he could be harsh enough then maybe he could get Haven to run back to her room, hating him a little more. Maybe that way she'd be less likely to give in when his father attempted to corner her into a deal Nik knew was coming any day now.

"That's not true. Both you and I know that" Haven spoke strongly, Nik could tell she believed in her words. He could even see the queen she was becoming hidden in the way she spoke. It endeared her to him more than he'd ever admit.

"How do you know?" He asked, tightening his hold on her waist and speaking low into her ear,

"There's lots of reasons for me to dislike you. Even to hate you. You're taking a crown that should be mine, you've got half the council eating out of your hands without doing much work at all, you flit about the castle as if you own the place after having been here barely a month and quite frankly, you are incredibly annoying"

Nik didn't actually believe any of that. Haven had been doing the work, she was earning her crown and doing a damn good job of it. Nik just needed her to believe that that was what he thought. He needed to send her running. Haven looked hurt for only a moment before she steeled herself,

"But what about," She paused, down casting her eyes, hesitating to bring this up. Nik knew what she was about to say and had been prepared for it, finishing her question before she could get the rest of her words out,

"When, in a moment of weakness, I went down on you?"

She nodded her head, an adorable blush rising to her cheeks. Nik could barely see it in the dim light but he knew it was there nonetheless.

"It's simple," He told her, "I won't deny being attracted to you, anyone with half a cock would be. That night was a moment of weakness on my part. I won't be making that same mistake again"

He saw the moment his words hit. Calling her a mistake, that was what hurt. He could feel the tension rising in her body. Niks heart seemed to physically ache but he couldn't relent. Not with everything that was at stake. He needed his words to be enough, he needed to curb this intense attraction between them.

It wasn't just a physical attraction, Nik was borderline obsessed with her and he wasn't sure he was strong enough to stay away. He needed Haven to be the strong one. He needed her to hate him enough to walk away because if she didn't, it could mean the end of the realm as they knew it.

Chapter Forty-Seven

Haven almost screamed in frustration, swearing Nik to hell and back. She couldn't believe he was actually going to stand there and deny every peaceful moment that had happened between them. Yes, most of them were shrouded in something hateful but hate wasn't the only thing between them. In between all the jaded words and snide remarks there'd been soft glances, sweet accidental touches. Haven saw the way he looked at her when he thought no one was looking. She knew he spied on her training sessions and on her library searches. Hate and reluctant attraction were not the only things he felt for her and she was going to prove it.

Haven pressed the front of her body against his, taking in every little reaction. She tilted her face to the side where her lips could connect with the shell of his ear. She heard his breath hitch, felt the pounding of his heart against her chest. Taking a shallow breath, Haven whispered,

"Liar"

Before he could blink, Haven brought a knee up between his legs. As soon as she made contact, Nik released his arm around her waist with a huff of pain. Now that it wasn't pinned to the door, she brought her arm up between them and shoved him further away. Nik promptly grabbed onto the edge of the couch, doubling over.

Taking a moment to step deeper into his room, Haven noticed a silencing candle sitting unlit on his desk. Sending a wisp of fire over to it, the wick caught flame and a thick bubble of unseen magic spread over them.

"How dare you!" She yelled at Nik who was still hunched over in pain. Deciding she couldn't look and yell at him while he was in pain, Haven turned. Now she could see out his window into the night air. She focused her attention there as she expelled her next words,

"How dare you pretend like there's nothing going on here! Do you take me for a fool? Or are you just so arrogant that you think no one could ever notice your stolen little glances or the way you sneak around the library while I'm having lunch, pretending like you're some sort of shadow no one can see!" Haven took a deep breath and lowered her voice before continuing, "I don't know why you are so set against me. Maybe you really care more about losing your crown than I thought, maybe you're afraid dear old dad will come after you for loving someone other than yourself or maybe you don't even know."

Haven finally turned back to him, finding that Nik had righted himself and was looking at her with more emotion than she even thought possible.

"Haven," He started.

"Don't." She told him softly, "If what you are about to say is more lies or excuses then I don't want to hear it. The truth or nothing"

Nik nodded. He paused for a second, contemplating. Taking a step closer, Haven noticed a tear trailing down his cheek. She hadn't meant to make him cry, all she wanted was the truth.

Now that he was a bit closer, Haven noticed something she hadn't before. While she'd been in his room with him shirtless before, there hadn't been a candle lit and she hadn't been able to properly use her enhanced sight. Among the dark lines and swirls of his tattoos were scars, possibly hundreds. Some were small, some were big, long, short, deep, shallow. There were all sorts. There even appeared to be a burn mark or two. Before Haven could say anything, Nik rushed forward, yanking her to him and kissing her roughly.

"You want the truth?" He asked, between kisses. Haven nodded

"Here it is," Nik told her. Reaching to take her hands, he placed them on his chest over a mess of scars, tattoos and his heart.

NIK

The feeling of Havens hands where they gently rested over his heart warmed Nik from the inside out. As much as he loved the feeling of them, he'd placed them there for a purpose. She was about to ask about his scars, a conversation Nik wasn't quite ready for.

Havens lips melded against his, lighting a fire in Niks body and sending whatever hesitations he held out the window. Nik may not have had a plan when he first kissed her, other than to keep her from asking questions he wasn't ready to answer, but now that he had her in his arms, he wasn't intending on letting her go.

Nik pulled at the robe keeping her body from him, slipping it over her shoulders. He paused, tearing his lips from hers and taking her in.

She was stunning, even more so than the night of the ball. That night, she'd been all made up, prim and proper but now here she was, bare faced, in nothing more than a slip of a night dress. Nik knew he'd never seen anything more beautiful. Haven shifted on her feet slightly, giving away her self conscious feelings. Niks brow furrowed,

"You are the most beautiful thing I have ever had the pleasure of seeing." He told her, meaning every word.

A rosy blush appeared across her cheeks and her hands tightened their hold on him.

"Kiss me again" She whispered

Nik obliged, crashing his lips back to hers. Reaching down, he wrapped his arms around her thighs and hoisted her up against him. Her hands moved to knot themselves in the hair at the base of his neck and her ankles crossed behind his back.

Haven tugged on his hair slightly, pulling a groan from Nik he hadn't known he was holding back. Walking them over to his bed, Nik dropped Haven down and watched her bounce on his mattress. Prowling on top of her, Nik found he quite liked having her in this position.

Haven whimpered as Nik placed hot, open mouthed kisses along her jaw and then down her neck. Nik may not have known it then but the sound of her whimpers erased years he spent feeling like he would never be enough.

Haven spread her legs, wrapping them around his waist and pulling his body flush with hers.

The feeling of his cock being so near her wet heat was unlike anything he'd ever experienced. He may be a virgin but he'd messed around with women before and none of them had ever felt like this, quite this *right*.

Nik propped one arm beside Havens head, the other slid down to grip her hip. Next, Niks mouth reconnected with Havens, sending more fireworks throughout his body. Before he could sense what she was doing, Haven flipped the two of them. Her body hovered over where he wanted her the most.

Smirking like she knew exactly what she was doing to him, Haven moved his hands to the edge of her chemise, nodding to give him permission. Nik knew he wanted Haven, it was as simple as breathing to him. He wanted her like the flowers wanted sunlight, like birds wanted flight.

Maybe it wasn't want that he felt so strongly, maybe it was need. Nik hesitated, uniting them like this simply didn't seem right given his plans. Sleeping with her now felt like he would be promising a future he could never deliver. He knew that no matter how much he wished it was different, they'd never be able to be together, to have a future. Nik would make sure of it.

Haven must have sensed his hesitation because she spoke quietly into the silence,

"We don't have to do anything you don't want to"

He nodded. Her hands still rested over his where they were anchored at her hips, chemise in clutch. Stopping didn't seem right. He might not be able to fuck her properly but there was plenty more they could do to quell this desire between them.

His hands tightened their hold on her skimpy night dress. He was tempted to rip the thing to shreds but he had a feeling that after the lust wore off, Haven would be pissed that Nik destroyed another outfit of hers. Instead, he grinded himself against her, earning a feral moan from her.

"What do you want?" Haven asked

"You," Nik responded, "Just you"

Chapter Forty-Eight

Niks words set Havens whole body ablaze. She hadn't come to his room for this but she wouldn't be complaining that it happened. Haven could recognize that Nik distracted her from getting answers to her questions but that didn't make the distraction any less enjoyable.

Haven did not know why Nik didn't want to have sex but she would respect his wishes nonetheless. If he wanted to do nothing then they would, although that wasn't what Niks body language and words were telling her. The way he grinded their most sensitive parts together, how tight he held onto her hips and the slightly unhinged look in Niks eyes all pointed towards his need for release. Even if they couldn't have sex there was still plenty they could do.

It didn't take Haven long to decide what she wanted to do with him.

Inching her way backwards, Haven laid herself between his legs. His hands went from her hips to hair, eyes dilating when he realized what she was planning.

"Do you want this?" She asked him simply.

"I think I need it" He responded.

Palming his cock through his pants, Haven watched every movement of Niks. Moving her hand to his waistband, Haven slid his loose pants down far enough to pull out his cock. Wrapping her hand around the thick base of him, she pumped him once, then twice.

"Is this okay?" She asked.

Nik nodded, his eyes scrunched shut.

"What about this?" Havens tongue darted out, licking him from root to tip.

"Fuck yes" He told her.

Haven smirked. Rising slightly, she closed her mouth around him, earning what would go down in history as the hottest moan she'd ever heard.

It took her a moment to adjust her mouth around him. Once she felt ready, she slowly took him as far as she could to the back of her throat, hollowing her cheeks, and then back to the tip. In and out, she sucked him while relishing in the sounds he was making. Adding her hand back into the mix, Haven moved it in time with her mouth, taking with her hand what she couldn't with her mouth.

It didn't take long before Nik was groaning,

"Haven, I'm close"

Niks grip tightened in her hair. She knew he was trying to warn her but she wanted him to finish right where he was.

"Haven, Fuck. *Ahh*"

Niks eyes rolled back as he came. Haven was thoroughly enjoying the feeling of him hitting the back of her throat. Smiling around him, she swallowed every last drop until he was finished.

Haven pulled her mouth off of him, a slight popping sound rang out as she did and a few strings of saliva spilled over the edge of her mouth. She watched as Niks body sagged back against the bed, sated and calm. She tucked him back into his pants and let Nik use the hands still buried in her hair to pull her up so she was lying on her side next to him.

Haven splayed a leg across his waist, content with her actions. Niks thumb wiped the edges of her mouth, cleaning off the spit and whatever else had leaked out. Nik smiled and then hauled her in for a kiss. This kiss was different, all their previous kisses had been fast paced and full of lust. Now it was slow and sweet, tender and soft. Nik broke apart their kiss to hesitantly say,

"That was," He paused, searching for the words.

"I know" She told him, placing a hand on his chest and laying her head over his heart.

Nik held her tight, enclosing her into his chest. She could hear the frantic beat of his heart as he slowly but steadily came down from his high.

Nik ran a hand over her back, towards the swell of her ass. Slowly, he inched it between her legs towards the apex of her thighs. Shaking her head against his chest she stopped him,

"Tonight was about you" She told him

"Are you sure?" He asked, looking slightly confused.

"Yes I'm good. We've got plenty of time to explore everything else. Tonight I just wanted to make you feel good" Havens mind flashed back to the look on his face right before he kissed her, the sad, broken look he'd worn.

Haven placed a small kiss on Niks exposed chest, he clutched her tighter than she thought possible. If it hadn't been for the fact she was enjoying it so much, she might worry she would suffocate. Although in her mind that wouldn't be the worst way to go.

They stayed just like that, wrapped up in each other for what felt like a lifetime. Eventually Nik broke the silence by saying,

"I'll tell you what you want to know. But after I do, I don't want to talk anymore"

Haven lifted her head from where it was resting against his chest. Making eye contact she asked,

"Are you sure?"

Nik nodded, "Do you want to start or would you rather I just talk?" He asked.

"You can talk" She may have wanted Nik to open up but she knew better than to push. This thing between them, whatever it was, was new and even without the weight of an entire kingdom bearing down on them, the secrets between the two of them made this complicated enough. He would tell her what he could and Haven would be happy with that.

"I've never had sex," He started, looking away from her, "Because I never allowed myself to get close enough to someone. I used to consider picking someone at random and getting it over with but that felt wrong and uncomfortable. I worried my father would hurt or use anyone who got close to me so I simply never let anyone get close. The only exception has been Delroy. I've been friends with him since we were kids and he is the only real friend I've ever had. At one point, I considered the friendship to be a risk. Over time he helped convince me that some things are worth the risk."

Nik smiled, it was a small smile but a happy one nonetheless. His eyes were distant, Haven could tell he was replaying a memory in his head.

"Does it bother you?" Nik asked, drawing himself back out of his head.

"That you're a virgin?"

He nodded

"Not at all," Haven told him, meaning every word.

"Does it bother you that I'm not?" She assumed he'd guessed that fact about her but to have it confirmed and stated so plainly between them sent nerves skittering down her spine.

"No" He told her, "You have every right to make the decisions about your body as you see fit. You could tell me you'd slept with over a hundred different people and my opinion of you would never change."

Haven nodded her head, reaffirming his words in her mind.

"And the scars?" She asked gently.

Nik took a breath, obviously steeling himself to give her this answer.

"My father," He told her. Haven suspected it was something like that but to hear if confirmed had her heart breaking for him.

"It started when I was seven. Sometimes he'd tell me he was punishing me for something I'd done wrong, other times it was to make me stronger. He'd tell me I needed to learn to withstand the pain so I could become a great leader, an even better warrior. He'd mark me with knives, burn me, hit me, do whatever he wanted.

For a long time I believed his words. He was my father, I didn't know any better. Eventually though, I grew to understand that what he was doing was wrong. Other kids never had to deal with their parents striking them, never had to deal with the pity in the healer's eyes when my father told them to only do enough so I wouldn't die but so the scars would linger."

Nik paused, taking Havens hand where it lay on his chest in his and holding it tightly.

"By the time I was sixteen I was big enough to stop what my father was doing. I couldn't though, too afraid of failing and making the punishments worse. Not that they could get much worse but my scared teenage brain hadn't put that together yet. It happened the night before my seventeenth birthday. My father had me standing in front of his desk, my hands flat on the surface in front of me. I'd long stopped fighting him. He stood behind me, a whip in hand, preparing to mark me with it. He cracked it in the air once and when I heard the sound it made I knew I could never let him touch me with it."

Nik took a deep breath. Havens heart cried for him. If she could, she would waltz herself down to the crown regents office and kill him. No muss, no fuss, just a knife straight through to the heart. That way Nik would never have to deal with him again.

"Before he could blink, I turned, using my speed to snatch the whip from him. I ripped apart the leather before tossing it on the floor. I'll never forget the look on his face when he realized I'd finally had enough. In that moment I basked in his fear. He knew I could easily match him in power by that point. I wanted so badly to inflict the pain he had been dealing to me for so long."

"What did you do?" Haven asked softly. Whatever he had done, she knew she'd never judge him.

"I walked out" He told her. She must've worn a confused look because Nik began to explain,

"I was so full of rage. I'd been fighting back against him in the shadows as much as I could. Finding ways to disrupt his plans, even doing simple things like removing the spell on his boots that made them waterproof so when it rained he'd walk around with wet socks. But in that moment, I knew I'd kill him if I touched him. So I didn't. As much as I hated my father I couldn't bring myself to stoop to his level. Maybe that makes me a coward, I really don't know. Others might view me that way but I've never seen myself in that light. I do know that if I had the opportunity today, I don't think I'd make the same choice."

Haven took a moment to let his words sink in,

"I don't think you're a coward," She told him, "If anything, I think it makes you brave. And if you are ever faced with that choice again I hope you make the one that's right for you. No matter what it is."

Nik smiled, a soft and secret smile. Leaning in, he placed a sweet kiss against her lips. When he pulled away she asked,

"What about the tattoos?" Almost every inch of his chest was covered. Black whorls, lines, curves, dots. All different shapes. Some covered his scars, others enhanced them. The work truly was beautiful.

"When I turned nineteen I decided I wanted my body back. I'd been seeing the scars in the mirror for so long. They were a reminder of him, of what he did to me. I started getting the tattoos as a reminder that my body belonged to me. That I was stronger than him, that I survived him."

Haven smiled, taking in the strength of the man under her. She was so proud of him despite knowing him for only a month. Hearing his story only reaffirmed her knowledge of the kind of man Nik was. A strong one, who held demons but didn't let them drag him so deep he could never return.

There was a thread on the edge of her mind that had been bothering her,

"Do you have a problem with touch?" She asked

"No" He shook his head, "Not from others. When I finally told Delroy what had been going on, he hugged me so tight I thought I might suffocate" Nik huffed a laugh, "After that, I realized that his touch hadn't affected me in the slightest, if anything I welcomed the friendly feeling. It didn't take me long to figure out my problem was with my father and no one else. To this day I don't let him touch me. If we're in public I don't let him lead me anywhere. No fatherly hugs, no nothing."

"That makes sense" Haven told him

"I don't want to talk about this anymore." Nik stated, "Ask me something else"

Haven understood. She still didn't like to talk much about her fathers death. It was a different kind of trauma but trauma nonetheless.

"How old are you?" She asked, wondering if he was going to tell her he was actually a hundred and twenty or something since fae were basically immortal.

Nik opened his mouth, "Twenty one" he told her.

"Oh" She responded.

Nik smiled, laughing slightly. He wrapped his arms around her and kissed the top of her head.

"I want to know about you now. Will you answer my questions?" He asked, with the rise of an eyebrow.

"Yes" Haven giggled. She was glad to be moving away from such dark topics, if only because of the lightness that spread across Nik's face with her giggle and the prospect of learning more about her.

The pair talked into the night, sharing secrets, favorite colors, favorite foods and more. Haven told Nik about her fathers death and the betrayal she felt whenever she thought about the fact that her parents hadn't shared any of their past life with her. They got to know each other, as more than just friends. Kisses interspersed the quiet moments, soft caresses led into heady touches. Stopping just before they crossed that final line. Not long before the sun rose, as Haven drifted off into sleep, she heard Nik whisper,

"This would be so much easier if you just hated me" He then kissed the crown of her head and followed her into a restful slumber.

Chapter Forty-Nine

Havens eyes flitted open at the sound of birds chirping and the warmth of early morning light. She was lying on her side with a large weight draped across her hip and a hardness digging into her backside. Niks bed, she reminded herself, she was in Niks bed. She cursed, having no idea what time it was. Tasha would have her ass if she was late for training. Haven scanned the room, finding a clock on Niks dresser. It read eight fifteen. Not late enough to risk strangulation but definitely not on time either.

Haven rushed from the bed, finding her robe lying on the floor. Tossing it on, she remembered to grab her dagger from where she dropped it last night when Nik shoved her against the wall.

Nik groaned from the bed,

"Where are you going?" Sleep coated his voice, making it all too tempting to crawl back into bed. Maybe she'd get more acquainted with that hardness she'd felt earlier. Attempting to shove the thoughts from her mind she said,

"Sorry. I can't be any more late for training"

Haven stole one last glance to Niks bed, where he lay half naked and looking all too cozy.

As Haven rushed out the door, she couldn't bring herself to regret last night. They may not have talked about why Nik wanted her to hate him so much but she could feel the beginnings of something between them. Something strong, powerful and incredibly right.

Rushing down the hall, Haven almost slammed into Astrea who was preparing to knock on her door.

"Hey!" Rea jumped back in fright

"Sorry, just me" Haven reassured her, unlocking the door and leaving it open for Rea to follow.

"Where were," Rea paused before a shocked look unfurled across her face. "Oh my gods!"

"What?" Haven snapped, disrobing and attempting to get herself into her training clothes as fast as possible.

"You smell like him!" Rea whisper shouted, apparently afraid of spying ears.

Haven shrugged her shoulders. "Is that a bad thing?" She asked. She didn't care if the entire realm knew whose bed she had been in last night but she had a feeling that Nik might.

"Yes!" Rea snapped. "Wait here. I'll be right back" With that, Astrea rushed out the door, banging it shut behind her.

Haven threw on her clothes as quickly as she could. She was rapidly running out of time before she was exceptionally late to meet Tasha. Risking a glance in the mirror, Havens whole body heated at what she saw there.

Mussed hair sticking every which way, swollen lips and small bite marks up and down her neck. She looked like she'd been rolling around in bed all night. Which she had. Haven knew she could probably also use a shower, not that she had time for one.

Attempting to tame the rats nest of thick red hair, Haven wet her hair using the small bathroom sink. Next she grabbed a comb, pulling it roughly through the tangles and making the few curls puff up. After the knots were removed, along with a good chunk of hair, Haven tossed her hair in a quick braid. She tied it off with a leather band and prepared to leave her room. Before she could get out the door, Rea came rushing back inside her room.

"Oh good you're still here." Rea closed the door and dropped a few items onto the bed.

"Here take this first" Rea handed her a small white crystal. Haven was only confused for a second before Rea began to explain,

"It'll hide your scent. That way no one will smell him on you"

"Oh" Haven responded, "Is it really such a bad thing if people know we were together?"

Rea gave Haven a sympathetic look,

"Unfortunately, yes. In this realm you have a lot of supporters. Many due to the fact that they've been ruled by Niks father for so long and they don't like it. They don't like his actions, he's smarmy, rude and disrespectful among other things to anyone that doesn't have any powerful influence. That image extends to his son. If people were to find out about the two of you, you would lose a lot of support. Your claim to the throne would weaken. Not that there's anything anyone can do to prevent you from taking your place but they can make it harder. It's not worth it. For now, just take the crystal."

Rea closed Havens hands around the crystal. It felt warm in her hand, she could feel it attempting to press its magic into her. Haven only hesitated a moment before allowing the magic to wash over her. She could feel it covering her like a second skin.

"Good" Rea smiled, "If anyone asks, You're learning about new magics because the crystal won't only hide Niks scent, it'll hide yours as well"

Rea turned to the other object she brought with her.

"What's that?" Haven asked, trying to steal a glance over her Reas shoulder.

"It's a tonic" Rea spoke, turning to hand a small vial to Haven

"What does it do?"

"It's for birth control" Rea told her

"Oh! We um, didn't exactly" Haven could feel the blush rising to her cheeks as her eyes darted anywhere but the direction of her friend.

Rea smirked, "Yeah but you will" Before Haven could respond Rea continued,

"It works for thirty days. You can take it, he can or you both can"

Haven thanked Rea, unstopping the vial and downing it before she could second guess herself.

After Haven finished and handed back the vial, Rea all but shoved her out the door,

"Now get to training before Tasha hunts you down"

***

Tasha was indeed pissed at Haven for being late. She forced her to work extra hard, making her run a fourth lap, do sit ups and crunches until she felt like her non-existent breakfast was going to come up.

Overall the morning had been grueling, causing Haven to do nothing but sit in an old lounge chair she found in the depths of the library after lunch instead of her usual hunt for the diary from Binahs letter. Now she was just waiting for Elanor to show up for their evening lessons. Haven had come to truly look forward to her lessons with Tasha and Elanor.

Her entire world had turned upside down but the lessons helped her land on her feet. She was learning so much about politics, customs and traditions. She also had the confidence she'd be able to defend herself if she was put in a situation that called for it. The blades at her hip and ankle also helped reassure her.

Haven hadn't seen Roman in a few days, he'd told her he would be busy preparing for his travels to his home kingdom. Haven understood, she definitely missed her friend but was hoping to track him down to have dinner with him after her lesson.

A ring sounded through the library, Elanors signal she was ready to begin her teachings. Walking through the stacks, her sore body screaming the whole way, Haven found Elanor at her large desk. Books covered every inch of the surface like normal. Unlike normal, every book on the desk focused on one thing, war.

"What's this?" Haven asked. Originally they were supposed to be going over trade routes and agreements between Drailia and Avenell, another of her kingdoms neighbor across the sea.

"Sit" Elanor said sharply, in contrast to her usual firm but kind tone. The womans long gray hair was pinned high in a tight bun, her dress was a relaxed gray and Haven spotted a blue cloak draped across the back of the chair. Everything appeared normal, except for Elanors tight posture. Something was clearly bothering her.

"What's going on Elanor?" Haven asked, using her best queen voice. Not that it would work on Elanor but maybe it would help the older woman see how unsettled she was.

"Sit child!" Elanor snapped.

Haven sat down and picked up the book nearest her. It was about recent history. Specifically, the takeover of Shaston.

Haven looked up from her perusal of the books when she heard Elanor rustling around in a bag. What she pulled out confused Haven even more. A silencing candle. Elanor moved a book from the center of the table, replacing it with the candle.

"Light it" Elanor told her sharply

Haven sent a wisp of fire towards the candle, catching the wick and igniting the magic. She was starting to get very nervous now. They never used a silencing candle. In fact, sometimes they even invited some of the staff and children to sit in on their lessons. Nothing they ever discussed was a secret.

Elanor pulled another book from her bag and placed it in front of Haven. The title read,

The Creation of Magical Bonds and Ties

"The crown regent has been visiting that book for over a week" Elanor spoke, finally beginning to explain, "He has checked out countless books on magical rules, specifically the ones tying you to the throne. I'm sure you are aware he's been looking for any possible way to keep his position of power"

Haven nodded. She assumed he'd been doing his research, trying to find ways to keep her off the throne. Although she had no proof, Haven was also certain he was behind the attack on her room that took a guards life.

"Good," Elanor told her, "I, along with others, have been keeping an eye on him. We did our own searching, looking for anything he could use against you. At first we believed he was finding nothing as our own searches turned up the same. We have known that he has a back up plan in the event that he cannot find anything and you take over. Unfortunately we still do not know what that plan is."

"So what's with the book?" Haven gestured to the book sitting in front of her. The lack of answers made her nervous, as did her impending coronation. Time was running out for Niks father to make his move. Shadows danced around Havens feet, a manifestation of her nerves.

"We think he might have found something"

Haven sucked in a breath.

"It is my belief that he intends to force you into some kind of magical agreement. Something that would allow him to retain the influence he has. We don't know what, we don't know how he is planning to get you to agree but I know he will not let your coronation happen without attempting something."

"So what do I do?" Haven questioned, trying to get a handle on her nerves.

"As we do not know the exact details of his plans there is not much we can do to fortify against them. For now, I want you to read up on magical agreements. The specifics, the details, everything you can take in. Until he makes his move we are in the dark."

Haven nodded, taking everything in. One thing was bugging her,

"Why all the war books?"

Elanor took a deep breath, Haven steeled herself for what the older fae was about to say.

"The hope is that you will be able to get around, or completely avoid whatever he has planned for you. When you do, I fear our kingdom will fall into war."

Chapter Fifty

Haven didn't remember walking out into the gardens to meet Roman. The entire walk her head rang with Elanors words. According to her, war would be inevitable. The crown regent may not have a lot of support but Haven knew he had enough to cause a problem.

"Hey H!" Roman called out to her

Haven waved. Walking faster towards the table he was sitting at, she hardly noticed the blooming rose bushes along the way. She had barely sat down before Roman was asking,

"Are you alright?"

"I honestly don't know" She told him, a single tear trailing down her cheek. Pictures of war, death and battle flashed through her mind. Normally being able to conjure a picture in her mind was one of Havens most treasured abilities, even when she believed she was human. Now all she wanted was for the images flashing through her head to disappear.

Havens breathing quickened, her hands started to tremble. She knew she was on the verge of an anxiety attack. It had been awhile since she'd had one so Haven figured she was overdue. It may not be quick but normally she was able to calm herself by using deep breathing techniques her last therapist had taught her and wrapping herself up in her favorite blanket.

It often took awhile, sometime hours, before Haven was able to fully calm herself but she always returned to normal. Reminding herself that while it may not feel like it in that moment, everything would return to normal, everything would be okay in the end, also aided her in calming down. She'd once even considered tattooing the words, *all will be well*, across the inside of her arm as a visual reminder of hope for the future.

The problem with her usual solutions was that no matter how many times she told herself everything would be okay, this was the one time she wasn't sure it would.

Romans voice echoed through her mind, as if it was coming from somewhere far away.

"Haven," He spoke calmly, "Breathe, take a breath"

His large hand covered hers in her lap. Through the fog in her mind she could see him crouched in front of her chair. The calming feel of his warm hand helped pull her back to the present. Haven could feel Romans water magic pulsing around her. A cool stream flowed around her ankles, across her forehead and the back of her neck that was exposed thanks to her braid.

The familiarity and comfort her friend offered aided in calming her racing heart. His hand over hers helped stop the shaking. It took a few moments but Havens body returned to normal. At least, as normal as it could.

"Are you alright?" He asked again

"Yeah I think I'll be okay" Haven squeezed his hand and offered a weak smile she didn't really mean.

"What brought that on?"

"Do you think Drailia is going to fall into war after I'm crowned?"

Roman released a breath. Breaking eye contact, he moved to sit cross legged on the ground.

"I honestly don't know. It all depends on the size of the crown regents forces. On just how many fae will be on his side."

Haven was thankful he knew what she was talking about, keeping her from having to explain. The idea that Roman could have been part of the 'we' Elanor mentioned crossed Havens mind. She quickly dismissed the thought, he had come here at the same time she did and had no contact with Elanor since she wasn't his teacher. Plus, he was her friend and Haven doubted he'd keep something that important from her.

"Has that been happening a lot since you got here?" Roman asked, concern evident in his expression.

Haven shook her head, she appreciated his concern but she really did not want to go over details.

"If something like that happens again, will you tell me?"

"You'll probably be in Norwood" Haven tried to keep her tone light but the nervousness about her friend being so far away showed through.

"I'll never be too far away. Whether it's through letters, or by way of a ship to come and visit, I will always be here for you."

Haven smiled, a much fuller and real one this time.

"There's that smile!" He exclaimed, pausing for a second before adding in a lower tone,

"We have the beginnings of a very strong alliance between us. When I get to Norwood I will secure something stronger. Norwoods rulers backed Shaston all those years ago when Niks father took over so we know they won't stand behind him."

Unexpected relief flowed through Haven. Even if it did come to war she'd have allies, people who supported her. That was something she needed to remind herself of more often.

"I feel much better now, thank you"

"Good" Roman said, giving her hands one last squeeze before standing and reclaiming his chair.

"Enough words of war. How is your training going? I feel like we haven't talked in ages!" Haven spoke, trying to move past such hard hitting topics.

"It's been good," He told her, "My magic is coming along very well. I can channel a mean flood, enough to knock my trainer right off his feet!"

Haven laughed deeply. Roman conjured a bubble of water, floating it into the space between them before forcing it to take different shapes. Haven joined the fun, casting tendrils of both fire and shadow to chase around his water bubbles.

They stayed like that for hours, sundown had long since passed but the darkness did nothing to sway them from their spots across from each other, simply practicing their burgeoning magic and spending time in friendly company. Eventually, the laughter winded down, quiet joined in and the cold night air started to seep through their clothes. It didn't take long in the cold for Haven and Roman to end the night with a hug and promises to make more time for their friendship.

Haven exhaled on her walk back to her room, the stress from earlier gone from her body thanks to Romans company. She truly hoped nothing else would pop up tonight to get in the way of her relaxed state. Unlocking and opening her door, it was all too obvious that that was not the way the rest of tonight would play out.

Chapter Fifty-One

"Hello Haven" The crown regent greeted from where he was lounging in her desk chair.

"Hello sir" Haven responded, bowing slightly even though she knew he'd never do the same for her.

He did not deserve the respect she was giving him but she had enough sense to understand that right now he held the power over her. It might not be legal power but Haven was not yet confident enough in her self defense skills to think she could fight off the centuries old fae. She hoped her show of respect and manners would help keep the crown regents temper in check.

"There's no need for that anymore" He told her, not moving from his relaxed position at her desk. The way his unsettling aura suffocated the room had Havens last meal rising in her throat and her body begging to run.

"What do you mean?" She asked

"I mean, we both know how I feel about you and the fact that I would do just about anything to keep you off the throne."

Haven sucked in a breath, at least he wasn't pretending anymore.

"Alright then, what do you want and why are you in my room?" Haven leaned against the door hoping that if he came at her she'd be quick enough to rip it open and dart down the hallway.

"I am in your room because I want something from you" His lips tilted up as he spoke. Haven could tell immediately that this was what Elanor had warned her about. Regrettably, Haven hadn't had time to study any of the books the older tutor gave to her.

"Get on with it then" Haven used her best uninterested voice, the respect she'd shown earlier gone out the window. There was no need to fake anything anymore. If he was going to attack her, polite words weren't going to stop him.

"You are going to marry my son"

Haven snorted in disbelief, "Excuse me?" She liked Nik well enough and was obviously attracted to him, not that she'd ever admit that to his father, but marriage? She was only nineteen and on the verge of becoming Queen to a kingdom she hadn't known existed not all that long ago. The last thing she was interested in was being bullied into a marriage.

"You heard me," He told her while running a hand through his greasy blonde hair,

"Before you are unfortunately crowned you will marry my son, making him the future king. After your coronation you will give him heirs, cementing the DaMarrel line as true blooded royalty"

Haven knew DaMareel was Nik and his father's last name from their conversations the other night. Now she knew what his father had been planning. He probably assumed he could control Nik once he was on the throne even though spouses of the royal line did not have as much ruling power as those born of the royal line. Haven wondered if Niks father had taken that into account. As if he could read her thoughts, the crown regent opened his mouth and let out more slimy words,

"Once you are crowned queen and enough time has passed so that it is not suspicious, you will abdicate your ruling power to my son. Effectively making you a queen in name only.".

"And if I don't?" She asked.

"Then I'll kill everyone you care about," A pretty basic threat but a threat nonetheless,

"I'll start with that servant girl you seem fond of. Then I will move on to that annoying little prince you came in with. After I've brutally murdered them both, I will have someone sent into the human realm to go after your mother. After all, I've already killed one of your parents, what's one more?"

Shock rolled through Haven, causing her to clutch the door-knob behind her. Not to run away but to keep herself from falling to the ground.

Niks father finally stood from her desk chair. Crowding Haven against the door he spoke low,

"Yes you dumb little queen, I killed your father. Not me person-ally, I had someone else do it. It was all too easy. I'd been watching your family for quite some time, all it took was one little snip of a brake line and your father went tumbling over the edge of an icy cliff on his way to pick up your some flowers."

Havens throat dried, she couldn't get a word out. All her suspicions were suddenly confirmed, she knew her father didn't drink and drive like the cops had told her. He didn't intentionally drive over the edge, which had been another suspicion the police had. His brake lines were cut.

Knowing that her dad didn't intentionally leave them, didn't do something so dangerous and reckless, settled something in Haven that had been boiling for quite some time.

"You wanna know the kicker?" He asked, his hot breath rancid against her cheek, "It was supposed to be you in the car that day. I couldn't give two shits about your weak father and mother. Royalty or no, they posed no threat to me. You on the other hand," He trailed off, leaving Haven to fill in the blanks. Her father hadn't been the target, Haven had been. She was the reason her father was dead. The thought brought a pang of agony straight into her chest. She could feel the anxiety and panic creeping over her nerves, just like it had earlier.

Haven was suddenly faced with a choice, could she be the reason her mother and friends died? Haven knew in an instant she could never let that happen.

Finally finding her words, Haven used every drop of malice she could conjure to whisper,

"And what if I kill you first?"

Before Niks father could blink, she unsheathed the dagger at her hip and brought it up between them. As maliciously as she could, Haven aimed it directly at his heart.

The towering man stumbled back, shock etched in his expression. He obviously hadn't been expecting her to fight back.

"I have a better idea," She told him, "How about I kill you right here, right now? I think that might save everyone some heartache."

Haven extended her arm, pointing the dagger at him where he stood. Her position in front of the door gave her the ultimate bargaining chip. If he wanted to leave, he'd have to go through her.

False confidence filled her step forward, backing him further towards the opposite wall. She didn't want to bring herself as close to him as he'd done to her. Even just having him in her room unsettled Haven but she'd have to find the strength to power through.

"Instead of marrying your son and giving up my power, I should just end you. Spilling your blood across my floors would be a good way to avenge my father, don't you think?" Haven spoke low, menacingly, and she meant every word because she was not the reason her father was dead. No matter what the insecurities in her head told her, the reason her father died was standing right in front of her.

"You don't have the guts" He sneered

"Try me" She spit back

The crown regent moved quickly, charging at her. Haven tried her best to remember what Tasha had taught her, ducking out of his way to evade him and attempting to slice as she went. In the end, she was no match for his centuries of experience. She'd lasted all of five seconds before he managed to get the dagger away from her, throwing it across the room, grabbing her neck and pinning her to the door.

Haven clawed at his hand around her throat where he was squeezing tightly, slowly cutting off her circulation. Her shoulders tightened with defeat. His laugh was nothing short of nightmares, the scratchy, grating noise sent chills and trembles of fear down her spine.

"You really think you could kill me? I'll admit, it was brave but remember little queen, you are no match for me. I could kill you right here and now. Snap your neck like nothing more than a twig being used to light a sacrificial fire"

Haven hesitated, her magic was at the surface of her flesh just waiting to be unleashed. She didn't know how that would end and in the chaos, her mind wasn't thinking straight. She was more powerful than him but he had the experience and training she was sorely lacking.

Before the crown regent managed to cut off her air supply completely Haven grit out,

"You need me"

That gave him a pause. The crown regent released his tight grip on her throat, now holding just enough to keep her in place but not to harm her.

"Unfortunately, you are right. For my plan to work I do need you. I need you to stand up in front of a priest, two nights from now, say some ridiculous ancient words and bind yourself to my son."

The crown regent stepped away from Haven. Reaching down, he pulled a knife from his boot. He cut a deep well into his palm, the blood bubbling to the surface immediately. Havens eyes stung from the rancid scent. Grasping Havens hand, he cut an identical mark into hers.

"Make a deal with me" He told her, outstretching his cut hand.

Havens nose scrunched. She really did not want to share blood with the monster standing before her. She hadn't had time to read all of the material Elanor gave to her but she knew whatever she agreed to would be binding. She'd have to choose her words carefully. Slowly reaching out to place her hand in Niks fathers, Haven gasped at the jolt of electricity that passed through her.

"State your intentions to marry my son"

Her heart raced, rapidly climbing towards unsafe levels.

"I will stand in front of your son two nights from now, with intentions to marry."

"In exchange I will not kill you tonight," Niks father nodded his head slowly,

"The deal is done"

Haven could feel the moment the deal took hold, it was an electric feeling that concentrated at the slash on her palm. She had no idea what the consequences for breaking the deal would be but she assumed it would not be pleasant.

Only seconds after his words had been spoken, the crown regent ripped his hand away from Havens and tore out of her room like it was the last place he wanted to be. She did not miss that the crown regent specified he would not kill her *tonight.*

Haven was somewhat disappointed in herself that she hadn't been able to overpower the crown regent but she tried not to be too hard on herself. Afterall, her body was still trembling and her heart was still racing.

A small hopeful smile overtook Havens face, in the rush of what was going on the crown regent must have thought the other things he listed, the power abdicating and children went hand in hand with an agreement to marry.

Haven may not have been in this world long but she knew the fact that she hadn't specifically agreed to those things could make all the difference in the world. She might be stuck in a marriage she didn't plan but she would do everything in her power to ensure the crown regent would feel as powerless and weak as he'd made her feel tonight.

Chapter Fifty-Two

The crown regent left as soon as Haven made the deal with him. The feeling of evil in the air thankfully left with him. Haven could not believe what she'd agreed to.

In her heart she'd known as soon as he'd revealed the truth about her fathers death that she would have agreed to practically anything. At least she only agreed to marriage, the crown regent could've demanded something much worse. She had tried to word her promise as best she could, to leave herself an out, but she was not sure it would be enough. Two nights from now, she was set to marry.

Luckily Haven knew something the crown regent did not. Nik would never listen to his father. Even if he somehow got Nik down the aisle with Haven, Nik would not allow his father to rule over

Drailia and Shaston with them. The crown regent assumed he'd be able to control Nik but Haven knew how much Nik hated his father. He'd never allow that sort of control over his life, not anymore.

Haven desperately needed to talk with Nik but she knew his father would likely be at his room now, delivering the news. Besides, even if the crown regent wasn't there, it was almost two in the morning. Nik was probably sleeping, as Haven should be.

After stripping out of her clothes, Haven drew a bath. Easing down into the deep tub, Haven hoped the warmth from the water would calm her shaking muscles and frazzled nerves.

A low moan sounded from Haven the moment the water covered her skin. It felt amazing. There truly was nothing like a steaming bath to wash away the filth of the day.

Haven must have passed out in her bath because she woke to cold water, shriveled fingertips and a pounding at the door. Haven quickly exited the tub and wrapped a soft white towel around herself, tucking the excess under an arm to hold it up.

Casting a glance at the clock as Haven darted from the bathroom, she could see it was almost six in the morning. Beams of early morning light fell through the balcony doors, the sun just beginning its ascent into the sky.

Whoever was at the door sounded mad, if the frequent and loud pounding was anything to go by. Haven took a deep breath and yanked open the door, finding a very angry looking Nik on the other side. Shoving his way past her, Nik began to shout,

"What were you thinking?"

"Don't be so loud!" She scolded him while closing the door behind him. Haven did not want to yell, she had a slight headache and the idea of conflict this early in the morning only made it pound harder. Apparently Nik did not get the memo because he continued shouting,

"Why on earth would you make a deal to marry me?" He sounded incredulous.

"Maybe I had no choice!" She shouted back. If she had to yell to get her point across then yell she would. Sending out a quick tendril of flame, Haven lit the silencing candle on her desk before continuing to shout,

"Your bitch of a father was waiting here when I got back to my room, he threatened Astrea and Roman. Then he moved on to my mother, proceeding to tell me all about how he'd already killed my father before finally shoving me against the door and forcing me to make a deal for my life!"

A guilty and shocked look crossed Niks face. Had he really assumed Haven made a deal with the devil for no good reason?

"Do you have anything to say for yourself?" Haven snapped

Nik took a moment to compose himself before responding,

"I'm sorry"

Haven nodded, accepting his apology. Maybe if Nik hadn't looked so sad and lost she would have found it in herself to yell some more but in that moment, she couldn't bear to add anymore weight to those already heavy shoulders.

"Why are you so against this?" Haven questioned. She wasn't exactly for the idea of them getting married but her feelings could never equal the broken and disgusted look on Niks face.

"We can't ever be together" He told her, his voice soft and solemn.

"Why?"

"It'll ruin everything. No one will support you if you align your-self with me. So many hate my father, hate me. I could never be a good king. I'm selfish, arrogant, rude, and I don't give two shits what most people think of me. I could never give you what you deserve." He looked away from her, down at his feet not allowing his eyes to reach hers.

Reaching up to cup his cheek Haven asked,

"Do you truly think so lowly of yourself?"

Nik didn't respond but his answer was written across his face, the self loathing he held was so strong it would likely drown him.

"You are worthy" She told him, injecting as much confidence as she could into her voice. He still couldn't meet her eyes.

"You may be all those things you listed but you forgot about everything else, you do care about others. I've felt it when you took care of me after someone broke into my room, I've seen it in the way you smile at the kids running around the castle, I've sensed it in the friendship you share with Delroy. You care about him and you care about me."

Haven reached between them, bringing his hand up to cover her heart.

"You are not the monster you paint yourself to be"

Nik tore his eyes away from the floor, finally daring to make eye contact. A few seconds passed, Haven knew he could feel the pounding of her heart just as she could hear his. Niks eyes trailed down to her lips, nerves causing her to bite her bottom lip. Haven watched his pupils dilate, watched his gaze wander from her lips to the pulse in her throat, further down to the towel that was barely hanging on and then finally back to her face where his eyes met hers one last time before everything changed.

Time stood still as he crashed his lips down to hers, searing a mark onto her heart and into her soul.

Wrapping her arms behind Niks neck, Haven pushed her body into his. Her towel immediately fell away, exposing her naked body.

A low growl escaped Nik when he pulled back to run his gaze down her body, his gaze full of heat.

Niks perusal lingered on the juncture between her thighs. Normally this was where she'd become self conscious, the fact that Nik could see all of her had a blush creeping over Havens entire body. It tinted her cheeks, the tops of her breasts, her elbows and neck.

Nik was back on her in an instant, smashing their lips together, bending down to grab ahold of her thighs and hoisting her against him. Turning so she'd land under him, Nik crashed them down to the bed. Their bodies pressed as close as they could get with Niks clothes still on.

Nik ripped his shirt over his head as best he could with one arm propping him up while Haven went for his belt. The feeling of their bare chests pressed against each other had Haven emitting a low moan. Just the feeling of his bare skin against her nipples had her on the verge of what seemed like the strongest orgasm she'd ever felt.

Nik moved his mouth down Havens neck where he bit and kissed her skin. When he reached the juncture of her shoulder and neck his lips peeled back, exposing his fangs. He appeared to struggle with something for a moment before running the tip of his fangs across her skin. Havens whole body quaked when he did that. The space between her legs ached and pulsed, her toes curled and her magic pulled taunt, ready to explode at any moment. Nik moved on from the juncture of her neck and shoulder, kissing back up her neck and leaving her skin scorching hot and ready for more.

Haven huffed as she struggled with his belt for a moment before Nik reached one hand down to help. Chuckling lightly he asked,

"Something you want?"

Haven could only nod, the pulsing between her thighs had taken control of her brain, halting all rational thoughts.

Nik removed his belt. He leaned back to shrug off his boots, his pants followed.

The fact that they were both completely naked in the same room had whatever rational thoughts left in Havens mind running for the hills. Nik landed back on top of Haven, kissing her mouth fiercely. The feel of his cock trapped between them had spasms shooting down Havens legs. Widening her legs, Haven grinded against him, spreading her wetness and earning a loud groan from Nik.

"You keep doing that and this won't last very long" He told her

"I don't care," She whispered back, "I just want you."

"I want you too" He spoke low, seemingly haunted by the answer.

Reaching down between them, Nik ran his fingers over the apex between her legs. A loud groan escaped him at the wetness he found there.

"All this for me?"

Haven nodded, bringing his lips back to her. His thumb rubbed her clit a few times before he tore his hand away, reaching to grip his cock. He pumped himself a few times before lining up with her opening. He tore his lips away just a fraction to ask,

"Are you sure?"

"Yes. As long as you are?"

Nik responded by pushing into her slowly. Inch by inch he fed into her, breathing ragged and rough. Once he buried himself to the hilt, his hand moved to grip her hip, holding both of them still for a moment.

Fireworks exploded throughout her body as Haven twitched underneath him. Sex normally didn't feel this earth shattering and they'd only just begun. Haven absently wondered if every time between them would feel like this.

"You feel like the heat of the sun after a rainy day, like the cool of the lake after hours of training. You feel like a run through the woods, like freedom and happiness" Nik punctuated each statement with a light kiss across her lips.

A tear streaked Havens cheek as she opened her eyes to glance up at him, finding the look on his face was nothing short of amazement. She was positive she wore a similar expression.

Releasing her hip, Nik twined their hands together. Their lips reconnected as he finally began to move inside of her. The friction on her clit from his body coupled with the insane passion between them had her worked up and ready to come within minutes.

Haven was glad she'd lit the silencing candle before they'd begun. If someone was within earshot there was no second guessing what they were doing. The sound of the wooden headboard banging into the wall was more than enough, add to that the sounds being made by the both of them and it was overly clear exactly how Haven and Nik felt about one another.

Havens sounds and feelings reached a new high as Nik leaned slightly away from her, untangling their hands and using his to press her legs further apart as he continued to drill into her.

Nik left small bruises on her breast as he kissed across it, towards her nipple. The feeling of her nipple in Niks mouth had her clenching around him and on the edges of an insanely intense orgasm.

Haven reached one hand out to her side, clenched in the sheets and the other down to grip Niks ass, feeling how he thrust in and out of her. Raking her nails across him, she was sure she'd left a mark. He didn't seem to care, in fact, he groaned deep and said,

"I'm close"

"Me too" She told him, her words hoarse.

"Let go," He whispered, finally letting go of his grip on her thigh and reaching between them to finish her off by rubbing circles into her clit, "Haven, let go"

Havens orgasm ripped through her body. At this point, she was sure her screams could be heard even over the silencing candle.

Nik grunted as she clenched around him, locking them together and finishing deep inside her.

The two stayed locked together for minutes, waiting for their breaths to even out and their heart rates to go somewhere near normal. When the last of his tremors subsided, Nik pulled out of her and rolled onto his back, taking Haven with him. Her head now lay on his chest, listening to the racing of his heart.

"That was," Haven began

"Incredible" Nik finished. His hand stroked a lazy path up and down her spine, lulling her towards sleep.

Haven tried to pull away, "I need to clean up" She spoke, feeling the evidence of his orgasm leaking down her thighs.

Nik smiled, a purely territorial male smile.

"I'll clean you up," He kissed the top of her head and told her, "Just rest for now. You've got a little while before you need to be up for training"

Haven listened, snuggling back into the comfort of the bed. Nik stood, walking into the bathroom and exiting with a small hand towel. He came back to lay next to her, her on her back and him on his side.

"Spread your legs," He told her softly

Haven widened her legs, allowing him to reach over and wipe away the evidence of tonight.

"You don't have to worry about pregnancy," He started, "I take a tonic that prevents it."

"Me too" She responded sleepily, her eyes fluttering closed.

"Are we going to get married?" Haven asked. Nik didn't immediately respond, allowing her to drift further into sleep. Maybe it was the fright of earlier tonight, sleep deprivation, maybe her mind was playing tricks on her but Haven swore she heard him say just a few words before she drifted off to sleep,

"On my life Haven, we'll never be married."

Chapter Fifty-Three

Closing the door softly behind him, Nik fought against every instinct screaming to crawl back into Havens bed and hold her close. Tonight had been something out of a dream, both a good one and a nightmare. He couldn't believe she'd agreed to marry him. Not only had she agreed but actually bound herself to his father with a deal.

He didn't actually blame her of course, Nik knew what his father was like. He also knew his father wouldn't hesitate to kill everyone he'd threatened given half the chance. Even though she had agreed, you could never be too sure when it came to his father. Nik needed to make sure none of what he was planning fell back onto Haven.

They would arrange a wedding, Nik would be sure everything was just right. From the dress to the flowers and everything in between, it would be perfect. Too bad he'd never make it through the ceremony.

Nik went straight to Delroys room, it was early but he knew his friend would get up as soon as he heard what Nik had to say. Trying the doorknob, it was locked as Nik had suspected it would be. Knocking would be too loud and draw too much attention seeing as Delroys room was smack dab in the middle of a busy hall filled with other guards' rooms.

Taking out the small kit Nik carried everywhere, he pulled out his favorite lockpick and set to work. A longer amount of time than Nik would have liked passed before he heard the distinct click telling him he'd succeeded.

Pushing open the door, Nik immediately felt bad about interrupting the scene before him.

Delroy was laid out on a full bed shoved into a corner of the small room with Roman snuggled next to him. Both were obviously naked and fast asleep. Delroys arm held Roman tight against him, the two of them tucked safely together as Nik had been with Haven only moments ago.

As much as his best friend liked to deny it, Nik knew he felt something for Roman. They'd been hooking up off and on for almost as long as they'd known one another. Every time Roman was in town or Delroy was over in Norwood the pair could be found together.

Of course, both Delroy and Roman claimed they were nothing more than a good fuck to each other. Nik knew otherwise. He saw the soft smile on Delroys face every time Roman was brought up, he may try to deny it but Delroy cared deeply for Roman and vice versa.

Nik almost turned around and left, to let the two of them have their space especially since Roman was leaving soon. The urgency of what happened kept him rooted to the spot.

"Delroy" Nik hissed. He stepped slightly closer and called his best friend again. Nik knew not to get within a few feet of the bed if he wanted to keep his head. Delroy stabbed first and asked questions later, something Nik knew from personal experience.

"Delroy" Nik hissed again. This time he picked up a shirt off the floor and tossed it at him. Delroy groaned in his sleep, rolling onto his side and drawing Romans arm around him. Nik chuckled, he'd never pegged his friend as the little spoon.

Risking his arm, Nik leaned as close as he felt he could to tap Delroys legs. Jostling him slightly, Nik repeated his name, this time a little louder.

A knife came flying at his head. Nik quickly jumped to the side, he hadn't even seen his friend throw it.

"Fuck Nik. It's too early for whatever it is you broke in here for"

Delroy sat up, dropping his head into his hands and rubbing at his eyes. Roman made a noise of discontent, rolling over so his back was to Delroy.

Pink rose to Delroys face when he realized his not boyfriend was still in the bed with him. It was cute.

"Geez you reek of sex" Delroy groaned, searching the bed for his boxers. Roman started to perk up at the mention of sex, rolling back over and trying to snuggle into Delroy.

"I could say the same about you" Nik quipped.

Delroy rolled his eyes, "Yeah but I'm not the one fucking the soon to be queen. Someone who, again, is supposed to be off limits to you" Delroy found his boxers. Sliding them on, he stood and moved around the small room to collect the rest of his clothes.

Delroys room wasn't very big, as were none of the guards. It had a full bed pressed against the back wall in the right corner. A dresser sat to the left of the bed along with some hooks on the wall to hang his uniform. One small window sat in the middle of the wall the head of his bed was pressed against, not providing much early morning light. Thankfully Delroy pulled out a match and lit a silencing candle, providing both light and privacy.

The light woke Roman up, he sat up groaning and rubbing the sleep from his eyes just as Delroy had done. Nik was somewhat jealous of his friend, he wished more than anything to be waking up with Haven in a few short hours.

"What's going on?" Roman asked, keeping the sheet perched across his lap.

"You weren't supposed to spend the night is what's going on" Delroy snapped, there wasn't any heat in his voice though. It was almost like that was what he felt he had to say instead of what he actually wanted to say. Why he felt that way, Nik had no clue and Delroy had never offered up the information either.

"Also, Nik spent the night boinking your friend" Delroy added.

"Seriously man?" Roman questioned

Nik just shrugged, he couldn't bring himself to regret what happened. No matter how things ended, his heart would always belong to her.

"You can smell her all over him" Delroy rubbed at his nose, as if the scent of Delroy and Roman fucking wasn't all over this room.

Most of the time Nik loved his advanced fae abilities. Occasionally though, he wished he could turn them off. Nik would have to run back to his room and find a scent disguising crystal before he ran into someone. If that happened then it wouldn't take long before the whole castle knew his and Havens business. He only hoped Haven did the same.

"I thought we agreed you would stay away from her." Roman said

"Apparently the pull of her pussy is just that strong" Delroy remarked bitterly

"Don't talk about her like that!" Both Roman and Nik snapped

"Sorry, sorry." Delroy held up his hands, "I didn't mean to be a dick. This whole thing just stresses me out."

Nik understood exactly what his friend meant and he felt bad that he was about to pile onto everything else they'd been dealing with.

"My father got Haven to agree to marry me"

Both their heads snapped towards Niks.

"What!?"

"How!?"

"He forced her to make a deal with him. Haven has to meet me two nights from now with the intention to marry" Nik told them, he also filled them in on his fathers threats.

"Shit" Roman swore, a thunderous expression on his face. Glancing at Delroy, Nik found that he wore a similar one.

Silence surrounded the room for so many minutes that the sun had almost officially risen in the sky. It bled into the room all around them, exposing the severe and heartbroken looks on the three males' faces.

"Do you have a plan?" Roman asked Nik

"No," Nik lied, "I think it might be time to start planning a wedding"

Nik could see the suspicion on Delroys face, it was plain as day. Nik hoped his friend wouldn't push him on this, push him to admit the truth. If Nik broke and told his friend the plan he had been holding in his back pocket for a situation like this, Nik knew Delroy would do everything in his power to keep Nik from completing it. Delroy may not understand why Nik had to go through with it, Nik had kept that secret as close to his heart as possible since he'd learned the truth, but he hoped that in time, his friend would forgive him. Nik may never be around to witness that forgiveness but he had hope Delroy would find it nonetheless.

The three of them spoke only a few more words before Nik exited Delroys room, not entirely sure why he'd gone there in the first place. As Nik wandered down the hall towards his room, he let his mind play over the events of the last night, allowing the memories of her to lull him into a calm Nik wasn't sure he'd ever be able to reach again. Once Nik reached his room, he let the memory of having Haven in his arms drift from his mind, filing it away for future use. After all, Nik knew he wasn't going to get a chance to ever hold her like that again, not if he had anything to do with it.

Chapter Fifty-Four

Late morning light streamed in through the balcony doors. Feeling around, it was obvious the bed was empty of Nik. Glancing at the clock, Haven found she had just enough time to get ready for training. She would likely have to sprint in order to make it on time but that was better than arriving late.

A delicious ache pulsed between her thighs as she sat up. Haven smiled to herself, they definitely had some things to figure out but last night helped make things clearer. Nik may not believe he was worthy of being by her side but she'd do whatever he needed to help prove he was. Whether through marriage or more mind blowing sex.

Haven did not need Nik by her side, she knew that much, but the idea of him alone in his self loathing hurt something inside her

Haven couldn't begin to describe. She wanted to help him heal, either for her or for himself.

Haven got ready in record time, slipping a crystal into her pocket to cover her scent before she left. She didn't mind if everyone she came across could scent Nik but she had a feeling he would.

The walk through the kitchens to grab breakfast and then to meet Tasha was quiet. It was early enough that not everyone was out of bed. Those that were, smiled and offered polite waves to Haven. Since finding out who she was, so far, most everyone had been respectful. She had a feeling if she actually went through with the wedding that that would change.

Finishing the last of the roll from breakfast, Haven stopped directly behind where Tasha was standing, waiting for the woman to turn and greet her like she always did.

"Is it true?" Tasha questioned, without even turning around.

"Is what true?" Haven asked.

Tasha finally turned to face Haven, the expression on her face more dire than usual.

"That you're getting married? To Nikolas DaMarrel?"

Haven rolled her eyes, of course people were already gossiping. At least Tasha wasn't being rude about it, like she suspected many others would.

"Where did you hear that?" Haven asked, avoiding answering Tasha's question.

"Some of the higher ranking staff have been talking. Apparently the crown regent is bringing in a priest and having a spot out in the woods prepared for an event that's taking place tomorrow night. A seamstress has also been ordered to fit a marriage gown with your measurements. I've shut down the rumors as much as I could but people won't believe it until you take your place on the throne six days from now, unwed."

"Well that's unlikely" Haven remarked under her breath. Tasha, of course, caught the words.

"Haven Grace Montali Rionach!" Tasha used her stern voice, setting off the warning bells in Havens head that told her to run very fast and very far from an angry Tasha. Tasha even used Havens new name, unsettling Haven further. It was slightly weird, in the human realm she'd thought her name was Haven Grace Moore. Turns out, her parents changed their names to better hide in the human realm. At first she hadn't known what to think about her new name but as time went on, Haven found she quite liked it.

Remembering that Tasha was standing in front of her, pissed off, Haven tried to defend herself,

"I had no choice!" She told her trainer, "His father threatened my friends, my family and then me!"

Tasha's gaze softened slightly, "Why don't you tell the council. They will likely throw him in the dungeon where he can be tried by a court of law."

Haven wished she'd thought of that before making her deal. Although she knew the crown regent wouldn't have simply let her go last night.

"I wish that were possible now. Even if I did, I would still have to marry Nik." Haven held up her hand to show Tasha the new scar where the deal magic had taken hold. Tasha gasped,

"That bastard!" She exclaimed, grabbing ahold of Havens hand and running a finger over the two inch long mark.

"I know. I'm not entirely sure Nik will even show tomorrow night. He's very against the whole thing." Haven stated. She was slightly nervous about what might happen if she showed and Nik didn't. Would the magic binding the deal harm her? She couldn't be sure but she had a feeling Nik would not let her deal with something like that on her own if he could help it.

Tasha ignored most of Havens statement to ask,

"You call him Nik? Is something more going on there?"

Haven could feel her blush rise to her cheeks as memories of last night, along with a couple others flashed through her mind.

"Ah ha!" Tasha exclaimed, "There is something happening. Is that why you come to training using a scent crystal some-times?"

In seconds flat, Tasha had gone from her angry teacher to gossipy friend. Haven knew she'd never speak a word to anyone about whatever she was told so it felt safe to tell Tasha the truth,

"There is something going on. I don't know exactly what, but we did sleep together last night."

Tasha gasped,

"I knew it! I've seen him spying on our training occasion-ally. At first I thought he was checking out the competition, possibly for his father, but after a while I started suspecting something else was going on. He's never exactly wanted the throne, anyone with two eyes and enough sense knows that. I figured if his father wasn't making him report back with your progress then he was likely spying for personal reasons."

Havens blush spread, she had also noticed Nik spying on her sessions with Tasha and Elanor, she just didn't know anyone else had.

"So you are getting married then?" Tasha asked, calmer than when she'd asked a few minutes before.

Haven nodded, "I think so. I know I've been forced into it by his father but I am a little excited. Nik means something to me, I've denied it for awhile and while I probably wouldn't jump straight into marriage I am looking forward to getting to know him more."

Tasha nodded, accepting Havens feelings.

"How do you feel about him possibly becoming king?"

Haven thought for a second before responding,

"I've done enough research to know that he won't have much ruling power unless I abdicate mine to him and I think he'll like that. And as much as my training and lessons have prepared me, I'm looking forward to having a partner in this whole thing. Nik knows all the ins and outs about ruling and I'm pretty certain he would help me when I needed it."

"You know you don't need him." Tasha told her, injecting strength into her voice.

"I know," Haven responded, "I know that I could be a truly great ruler all on my own. I have everything I could ever need right inside me, but I've always believed that there is nothing wrong with wanting a little help or accepting it when needed."

Tasha smiled, "You have figured out something that many take years to learn, if they ever do. It is not a weakness to ask or to need help. In fact, it can even make you stronger. All of the best rulers in our history knew when to ask for a helping hand and when they needed to stand on their own. I think you truly have the makings of a great ruler Haven and I can't wait to see more of the Queen you are becoming."

Haven smiled, a strong powerful smile that felt like it was taking up her entire face. She loved that Tasha seemed to support her no matter what. Especially since she knew everyone else wouldn't feel the same way.

Chapter Fifty-Five

After they finished their talk, Tasha had slipped back into teacher mode, working Haven to the bone for the rest of the morning. Haven was thankful for Tashas lessons but as she sat in the library eating lunch and awaiting Elanor, the aches and pains coursing through her body made her feel anything but.

The longer Haven sat, the more nervous she became about what her tutor would have to say about her impending marriage.

Finishing up the last of her sandwich, Haven quickly dusted a few crumbs off the dress she had changed into and began to wander the library. Walking towards Elanors desk and not finding her there, Haven decided to get a head start on the books already laid out.

After almost a full hour reading about war strategy, Haven began to worry about her late tutor. Elanor was never late. If anything, Haven was the late one.

Footsteps sounded behind her, causing Haven to turn quickly in her chair. Relief flowed through Haven at the sight of her tutor bustling towards her.

"Sorry I'm late!" Elanor apologized as she sat down.

"It's no problem," Haven reassured the older woman, "Is everything alright?"

"Yes, quite! I got caught up talking with an old friend who I thought could help with our little situation." Elanor gestured to Havens hand that was palm down on the table. It wasn't hard to figure out what Elanor was referring to. The deal marking etched into Havens palm seemed to burn as it was so blatantly pointed out.

"How did you find out?" Haven asked.

"One sees things." Elanor tapped her temple and smiled, surprising Haven with her good mood.

"So what did your friend say?"

Elanors smile widened, "Not much, she simply told me not to worry. She was very adamant that everything would work out just fine."

Haven exhaled a breath, she didn't know how Elanors friend had come to that conclusion but it was reassuring nonetheless.

"Alright, let's get started" Elanor hurried on, pushing some books aside as she spoke. Shuffling through the ones laid out before the two women, Elanor picked up a specific edition and handed it to Haven.

"You still think we'll need this?" Haven questioned, in her hand was a copy similar to the book she had been reading before Elanor showed up. It was all about war between fae, about finding weaknesses and exploiting them.

Elanors smile dampened, "Unfortunately I do"

***

Lessons with Elanor ran long. The older fae had tried to apologize again for being late and causing them to be in the library longer than usual. Haven had, of course, reassured Elanor that it was no problem. After all, Haven was pretty sure all that would be waiting for her back in her room was a cold bed.

After grabbing dinner from the kitchens, Haven returned to her room to find her earlier suspicions were not correct, someone was waiting for her when she arrived.

"Hey Rea!" Haven greeted her friend who was lounging on the bed. Setting the plate of mashed potatoes and pulled pork on her desk, Haven tossed herself down next to Rea. It was silent and peaceful for a moment before Rea spoke,

"I heard you're getting married"

Haven sighed, "So everyone has heard then?"

Rea snickered, "No actually, just a few higher ranking members of the staff. I know because the crown regent requested I help get you ready tomorrow. He also requested I give you a fake birth control tonic but I never liked him so I have no plans to follow that particular request"

Haven laughed, the gall of that man astounded her. On a more serious note, she asked,

"Will you help me tomorrow?"

Rea nodded, "Of course. You're going to look amazing!"

"Thank you for not being against this." Haven nudged her friend, "I'm already nervous enough and about ninety percent sure Nik will not show so I appreciate the support."

"I'm sure he will," Rea told her, "Everyone else can say what they want but I know for a fact that he cares about you."

Haven wondered how Rea knew that. As far as Haven knew, Rea didn't have much contact with the crown regents son and Haven thought they'd been fairly discreet with everything going on between them.

"In other news," Rea started, "How's your search for the diary from Binahs letter going?"

Haven told her friend about her failings, about how she was almost certain she'd never find the diary seeing as she'd covered almost every inch of the library at this point. Rea offered to help during lunch tomorrow and Haven gladly accepted.

The pair talked about how Havens training was coming along, her nerves about her coronation in a couple of days and then laughed at the fact that the crown regents big bad plan had been to force Haven into marriage. The threatening note, breaking in and destroying her room, all of it had been orchestrated by him in a bid to remain in power.

Haven guessed that the crown regents plans were the reason Nik was such a jerk when they first met. He had wanted Haven to hate him, to despise him so that she would never agree to marry him. How he knew what his father had been planning, Haven had no idea but she was almost sure he did. She wondered if the crown regent had any other evil plans his son knew about.

Chapter Fifty-Six

Morning training had been hell but Haven was glad for it. It kept her mind off of what was happening three days from now and what was happening tonight, being crowned queen and her marriage to Nik. She didn't know which she was more nervous about. Although, if she was actually honest, she knew exactly which event had her nerves tied up in knots.

Haven knew she would be a great queen, gone were the days of second guessing and doubting herself. She was going to be a kick-ass queen and she knew it. Her biggest challenge would be remembering that on the days her anxiety crept in. What she didn't know was how tonight was going to go. Rea had assured Haven that everything was taken care of but her friend was only able to ease her racing heart so much. It still pounded in her chest as she waited for Rea in the library.

"Hey H!"

Haven turned from where she was perusing a section about ancient fae languages, finding her friends walking towards her. She hadn't expected Roman to come along but Haven welcomed all the help she could get.

"I hope you don't mind, I ran into Roman on the way here and he asked to come along" Rea smiled sheepishly.

"Of course," Haven responded, "Maybe with an extra set of eyes we might have a chance at finding this thing." So far, she'd been searching by herself since she'd found her way into this realm and had come up with a whole lot of nothing.

"Alright," Roman clapped his hands together, "What are we looking for?"

Haven pulled out the note Binah had tucked into the bag she gave Haven. She pointed to the bit about an old diary that would help explain some of the other things Binah had spoken about in her letter. Haven had underlined it after her third day of searching,

Haven, this belongs to you. Soon you will figure out what I mean. Until then, please keep this hidden. Do not show it to anyone.

You are so incredibly powerful. I need you to believe this, to believe in yourself. You are in for a lot in these coming weeks, it will not be the quiet and easy adventure I told you.

For that I am so sorry.

I have no doubt that you will make a wonderful Queen.

I hope they do not get to you before you are able to

come into who you are. <u>There is an old diary hidden deep in the castle library that will help explain.</u>

Please be careful and trust no one.

-Binah

"I think the 'they' she mentioned might have been Niks father. I can't be certain but there's nothing else that makes sense." She told the group.

"Makes sense" Rea agreed

"Where have you searched so far?" Roman asked

Haven quickly explained everywhere she'd searched, from the right side of the library to all the way left and almost through the entire second floor.

"I think we should split up" Haven announced, reading over the letter again.

"Sounds good" Rea and Roman agreed.

The three of them quickly established which sections they'd take and that they'd meet back at Elanors desk in two hours.

***

Over an hour of searching turned up nothing. So far, Haven had searched and re-searched five rows deep in the shadows of the right wing on the second floor.

"Don't let me startle you" A voice called out from the entrance to the section she was currently looking through. Turning, Haven spotted Rea headed down the row towards her.

"Anything?" Astrea asked

"Not a thing." Haven answered. Astrea frowned and shook her head.

"This sucks" Haven sighed, taking a few steps to toss herself down in a cushioned armchair she'd walked past when entering the row.

"Yeah it does," Rea agreed, "Why couldn't Binah have left some specific detail or something. Why be so cryptic?"

"I don't know. Maybe she was worried someone else would find the letter and get to the diary before I could."

"I guess that could be possible," Rea nodded. Motioning for Haven to slide over, Rea sat down in the chair with her friend.

"Do you think we'll ever find it?" Haven asked, sadness ringing through her voice.

"I certainly hope so. You can't ever give up hope Haven." Rea slung her arm over Havens shoulders, comforting her and offering support.

They sat in silence for a few minutes before Rea broke it,

"How are you feeling about tonight?"

"You mean the wedding?"

Rea nodded, "Yes. I know you were forced into it but you seemed excited when we spoke about it before."

"I am" Haven told her. A thought fluttered through her mind, one she'd been trying desperately to keep out. Obviously the sadness showed on her face because Rea pulled her closer and asked,

"What's that face for?"

Haven took a moment before responding,

"My father"

Realization dawned on Astreas face. Haven had been doing all she could since she'd agreed to marry Nik not to think about the fact that her father would not be here to walk her down the aisle. If there even would be an aisle, the whole thing was prepared in such little time and was being kept secret by the crown regent.

"I'm sorry. I know it'll be hard for you, especially considering the way your dad was murdered and all. I'm sure you could ask Roman to walk with you, you're his friend and I know he'd love that you asked him."

Haven barely heard the last of Reas words, she was hung on the fact that Rea specifically said the word, *"murdered"*. Haven hadn't told anyone but Nik how her father had been killed. As far as anyone else knew, he died in an accidental car crash years ago.

"What did you say?" Haven asked her friend, pulling herself from underneath Reas arm and turning to face her in the over-sized chair.

"I said that Roman would surely accompany you down the aisle if you wanted. I think he'd be honored, he-"

Haven cut her off,

"I mean about my dad being murdered. I didn't tell you that." Reas reassuring smile immediately fell, replaced by a panicked look of guilt.

"I-" She started

"I want the truth!" Haven snapped, her temper shorter than normal. Luckily no one else was in the library besides Roman who was somewhere on the other side of the vast space, ensuring this conversation would remain private.

Little things started to add up in Havens mind, comments Astrea had made, how she didn't seem surprised in the slightest after Havens parentage was revealed.

Standing quickly, Haven started to pace. "Have you been lying to me?" She asked, unable to keep the bite out of her tone.

Astrea followed her out of the chair. Haven noticed a slight tremor in her hands. It was obvious her friend was hiding something. Haven had a feeling she would not like whatever Astrea was about to tell her.

She could feel her powers rising to the surface, a shadow knocked a book off the shelf five feet from where she was pacing, the ground beneath her feet began to warm. Thankfully the library had anti fire wards or else her first act as queen would be to announce that the royal library had accidentally burned down.

Roman appeared down the row, most likely drawn by the sounds of shouting and books tumbling. His face pinched when he surveyed the scene before him. His presence seemed to fortify Astreas nerves, allowing her to begin speaking,

"It all started five or so years ago. Me, along with a group of fae dedicated to finding the last of the royal bloodlines and forcing Niks father off the throne, found some incredibly important information. We had finally found exactly what we'd been looking for. It was you Haven, we were looking for you. Unfortunately, we weren't the only ones." Astrea paused, looking to Roman for guidance. He nodded, encouraging her to continue,

"The crown regent found you about a week before we did. At first, nobody knew what to do, should we force you into the fae realm? Should we make contact with your parents? At the time, you were still so young. Because of that, no one would support your immediate claim to the throne and if we brought you here then you'd be in more danger than you already were. In the end, we decided to simply keep an eye on you, keeping you safe, helping you along your way and eventually, when the time came, into the fae realm."

Haven didn't know what to think. Her friend had known who she was the moment they met. Havens mind spun, was that the only reason they had become friends, because Rea knew she would end up queen? If there were fae watching her, then why did her dad have to die? Couldn't they have protected him like they supposedly did her?

Rea exhaled a breath, sitting back down before continuing her story,

"That was the point we officially brought Nik into our ranks, for a while he had been helping us quietly when he could but he was young and untested. He'd made it very obvious by then that he supported our cause and hated his father so we decided the risk was worth it. He began spying on the crown regent, tipping us off whenever he sent minions into the human world to spy on your family. Everything was fairly stagnant for some time. We knew he was planning something, we just didn't know what. Eventually, around the time of your seventeenth birthday, Nik came to us with proof of his fathers plans."

Astrea hesitated before stating the next part,

"He was going to kill you Haven."

Slight shock overtook Haven, she couldn't picture how she'd survived. Niks father didn't seem like the type to let things go when they didn't work out and obviously, seeing as she was not currently dead, his plans had not succeeded.

"We had to stop him from reaching his goal," Rea continued, "Just like we were, the crown regent had been having someone watch you, follow you and learn your routines. He knew that once a month you and your father went and picked out something for your mothers garden. Even in the dead of winter, the two of you found something that would survive in her greenhouse. It was steady and predictable, also the perfect time to attack. We couldn't stop him from going after you but we could stop you from being present when he struck."

Haven let Astreas words sink in, tears gathering at the edge of her eyes.

"I didn't get sick by accident did I?" Haven asked. She could see the truth written in her friends eyes, along with the guilt.

Astrea glanced back at Roman before speaking again. Haven had almost forgotten he was there, witnessing these secrets being spilled.

"We sent someone into the human world, it was actually easier than we thought it'd be. A simple fae herb concoction slipped into the food at your school ensured you'd be sick enough to miss the trip with your father but not sick enough to cause you permanent harm. The poison we used made certain that no humans would fall ill because of our actions."

"What about my father?" Haven demanded, the sadness she felt earlier giving way to anger. She felt her power growing even more around her. She knew why Astrea and her little band of rebels spared her, they needed her, but Haven couldn't fathom why they didn't do the same for her father, especially since he wasn't the initial target.

Astrea at least had the decency to look ashamed as she spoke,

"We knew Niks father wouldn't stop until he had what he wanted and if he found out what we were trying to do, he'd find out who was involved and kill them. You catching a bug and missing one trip could be written off as coincidence but both of you? We knew he'd never believe that since fae rarely get sick, even ones magicless and living in the human realm like your father. We took a gamble that if his plans worked somewhat, he'd be satisfied. In addition, the death of your father drew some awareness to what the crown regent was doing, fae from other kingdoms began paying closer attention which helped to delay some of his other, more nefarious plans."

Haven could barely believe what she was hearing, they just let her father die. Her so-called friend had known exactly what would happen and did nothing. In addition, it seemed as though almost everyone had been lying to her this entire time, having known exactly who she was the minute she stepped into this realm. Rea, Nik, possibly even Tasha and Elanor had all lied.

"What about you?" Haven called to Roman who was standing stock still a few feet away.

He stepped forward, standing directly next to the armchair where Astrea sat. Roman couldn't even meet her eyes as he said,

"Yes Haven, I knew all of it. I'm the one who poisoned you."

Chapter Fifty-Seven

Shock and confusion nearly brought Haven to her knees. In her mind, there was no possible way Roman was the one that poisoned her, he had come into the fae realm at the same time she did and her father died years before that. Unless that was all more lies as well.

"Explain!" She snapped.

"I joined Astreas group when I was only thirteen. I'm originally from Norwood but I came to Drailia often as a child. Even as a young fae I could see the evil in Niks father, it polluted the air around him. My thirteenth birthday was my first in the fae realm, having stumbled here only months before. The crown regent invited my family to the castle here in Drailia to celebrate since I came through the portal here. Of course we obliged, for no reason other than we did not want to anger him. My older sister came with me as I was too young to go by myself. Her name was Nada. During the party she left me entertaining myself with some of the other kids. Hours passed before I noticed Nadas prolonged disappearance. As soon as I did, I grabbed my training sword and went looking,"

Roman paused, Haven could see the horror on his face as he relived old and clearly painful memories.

"I found her strangled and stuffed in a storage closet. I still remember the way her lifeless eyes stared back at me. Her dress had been rucked up around her waist, I could smell what happened to her and who had done it. I immediately went after him, only to be caught by a council member. I frantically explained what happened, they sent word to my kingdom and had me put on the next ship home. I returned with one less sister and one seat closer to the throne.

It wasn't until later that I found out they covered the entire thing up. A few weeks after that happened I found a note in my room from the leader of the rebels, telling me the council member I had spoken to was deep in the crown regents pocket. They hadn't asked anything of me, simply wanting to explain what happened and who they were. I sent a letter back asking to join their cause and the rest is history."

Roman finished explaining, not making a move to wipe the tears from his cheeks. Haven was decidedly less angry after hearing what he had to say but was definitely still confused.

"I'm sorry that happened to you but I don't understand how that led to you sneaking into the human world to poison me."

Roman nodded. Steeling himself, he wiped away his tears and began to explain,

"From that day forward, I worked with the rebels. There wasn't much I could do from another kingdom and so young but I did what I could. I stored important things away from prying eyes, meeting up with other rebels in the shadows to thwart the crown regent. I helped make plans and often went into the human realm to spy when needed. Years later when we discovered his plans to go after you, everyone knew what needed to be done.

I volunteered myself for the job, they needed someone who could be sneaky and unlikely to be recognized if any of the crown regents goons were watching. As I had not officially been back to Drailia since I found my sister dead, I felt I was the perfect candidate and everyone agreed. Too many of the rebels live here and are around him often so they would be easily discovered.

After everything played out, things calmed down considerably. The crown regent couldn't do anything more with so many eyes on him so we decided it was time to lay low. We did that for almost a year before we got wind of some new plans the crown regent had been preparing. We knew it was time to bring you in. A few well placed whispers had the senior trip moved to the mountains where there was a portal into our realm, I joined your school to help nudge you along if you needed it and everything worked out perfectly. You came here and began training to take over as queen. Admittedly, there have been some bumps along the way but we've managed to work most of them out. I'm sorry we couldn't save your father. There was a choice to be made and given the chance, I'd do it over again."

Romans eyes darted between the ground and Havens face, waiting to see what she would do. Would she yell, cry, scream? Not even Haven herself could answer that. She didn't know what she was feeling, she knew she was angry at her friends for keeping all of this from her. She knew she was sad for her father, sad for Romans family and sad for everyone else that had suffered at the hands of the crown regent. In addition, Haven felt betrayed, like she could no longer trust that the friendships they built were true. It was going to take her some time to get over that.

As fae were immortal, she had plenty.

***

After telling her friends she needed some time and that they needed to leave before she started yelling, Haven once again found herself in the depths of the library. She decided to skip her evening lessons with Elanor, not wanting to waste her tutors' time seeing as she couldn't seem to focus on much of anything. She would, at least, do her very kind and sometimes strict teacher the courtesy of explaining why she would be missing out.

Wandering through the stacks to kill time before her tutor showed up, Havens mind whirled with everything that had come to light. Could she blame her friends for what they did? Haven wanted to, she wanted to be furious with them. After all, they were partially the reason her father was killed. Though, in her mind, Haven knew the main reason behind her fathers death would be standing at her wedding tonight as the father of the groom. That fact didn't keep her from feeling the need to track down Astrea and Roman for no reason other than to yell at them for the pain they caused. Haven told herself to put everything out of her mind until after tonight. After her wedding she could get some rest, settle down, and then try to figure out a way to forgive her friends.

If she could make it through the exhausting events of today along with whatever events unfolded by midnight tonight then Haven supposed she could make it through just about anything this realm had to throw at her.

Haven passed the large painting of her parents, her heart tugging at the memory of being here with Astrea. Before she could get too lost down the rabbit hole of her thoughts, Haven tore herself out of her mind and moved away. An unknown magic tugged at her chest, keeping her rooted to the spot a few feet away from the painting. Words echoed in her mind, the soft lyrics of a lullaby her mother used to sing to her, the humming she used to do when working in the garden, the feeling of being rocked to sleep when she was little.

The feeling of magic pressed against her skin. This magic was not coming from Haven, she could feel her own locked inside her. Haven's breathing stalled as she recognized who this magic belonged to. It was her mothers. She couldn't visually see the magic but she could feel its imprint beneath the surface. It was pulling her in, tempting her closer to the painting.

Haven reached out and ran a finger down the wood frame. Something twinged inside her, begging her to continue. Lifting the bottom right edge, a loud creak echoed through the entirely silent library as the painting swung forward. It appeared to be hinged on its left side, allowing it to remain attached to the wall while also offering Haven a view of the back.

Nothing but thin, dark brown paper. There were no special words or symbols etched into the paper. Nothing telling her why her mothers magic had reached out and practically snatched her. Just as Haven was about to push the painting back where it belonged on the wall, she spotted something. There was a tear at the edge of the paper in the far corner, like someone had peeled it back.

Reaching out to tear a small section of paper, Haven held in a gasp. The paper didn't even need to be torn, lifting easily and showing her what was hidden between it and the painting.

A small brown leather notebook sat wedged between the canvas and the paper backing. It was slightly weathered from age but showed no signs of dust or decay. Haven collected it in her hands, closing the painting back against the wall before examining the notebook. The cover was blank, nothing more than simple brown leather with thick string made into x's on its side to bind the pages together. A skinny and long leather strip wrapped around the notebook, keeping it from falling open.

Haven quickly undid the strap and peered at the first page. She almost dropped the book in shock when she read what was written in black ink on the title page.

This wasn't just any notebook, it was a diary. The diary Binah had told her about. Haven finally understood what the older fae meant in her letter when she said that this might help explain some things. Because this wasn't just any diary, it was her mothers diary.

Chapter Fifty-Eight

Haven rushed back to her room, completely dismissing her purpose for waiting in the library to begin with. Elanor would just have to forgive her for missing a lesson without saying anything. This was more important.

While racing back to her room, Haven guessed that the diary recognized the magic in her veins as being related to its owner. She also guessed it didn't call out to her the first time she'd been by the painting because she hadn't been alone.

Haven quickly unlocked her door and scrambled onto her bed, ignoring the dress hanging near her bathroom door. That definitely hadn't been there this morning but it also seemed like a problem future Haven could deal with.

Situating herself comfortably amongst her pillows, Haven tore open the diary. She was trying to be careful with the old and delicate thing but she was also incredibly eager and impatient.

The first few pages were filled with nothing aside from a note stating that the diary belonged to Morana Montali and that anyone who wasn't her would burn under a fiery spell if they dared read her words. Haven hoped being the daughter of Morana Montali would spare her from that fate.

It wasn't until the fifth page that her mother actually started journaling. Haven rapidly began soaking in every word. The beginning of the first entry was simple, stating how the weather was, which council member had irked her and even the hairstyle her lady's maid had done up for her that morning. About half way through, her mother began talking about the war efforts.

Her mothers handwriting changed as the tone of the entries did. While speaking about the struggles she'd been having, fae commanders challenging her, issues about how the humans had begun to outnumber the fae, her handwriting deepened and lost its flowy design. Her mother quit writing with loops, instead choosing hard lines and angles. It was obvious her mother struggled to write about such harrowing things, the pen or quill she'd used dug into the pages and left dents on the next ones.

The following few entries were the same, starting with simple things and ending with hard to talk about topics. There were tear stains on the pages where her mother talked about losing friends, about the pain she felt when burying their bodies. She described the way their skin lost its color, how the blood on the bodies darkened the longer it was left and even the way they smelled after being left out on the battlefronts for days before it was safe to retrieve them.

Multiple times her mother mentioned wanting to go out, to be on the front lines using her powers to help her people. Some of the other rulers felt the same but they were not able to. Their councils all advised the same thing, that they needed to stay back, to save themselves so that when they won this war their kingdoms would still have their rulers.

It sounded like bullshit to Haven, she thought that a ruler should never force his or her people to risk something that they themselves weren't willing to. That was one conclusion she had come to while pouring over different texts and readings with Elanor. Although, from the sounds of it, her mother and the other rulers hadn't been given the choice. Too many were against them and they couldn't simply blow off the opinions and voices of their councils, especially not during such difficult times.

Havens father was one of the other rulers wanting to go out and fight. Her mother detailed their first meeting at one of the many war councils. Robert Rionach was the first to speak up against the members from his council that opposed the royals going out to fight. Her mother had instantly taken notice of her father.

Haven poured through the details about how her mother had taken her father aside after the first war meeting, telling him how she agreed with him and that she thought it was brave of him to speak up like he did.

Her mother thoroughly described all of her fathers features, describing him almost exactly how Haven remembered him. The journal entry where her father first showed up ended with her mother returning back to her rooms at the castle where all the fae rulers were staying, far away from the front lines of the war efforts.

While flipping to the next page, Haven glanced at the clock, noting she had almost an hour left to read until she had to get ready for her wedding taking place at midnight. Her eyes drifted to the closed garment bag hanging by the door, she absently wondered what her dress looked like. She'd let Astrea pick it out since her taste had been immaculate so far.

Forcing herself back to her mothers diary, Haven tried to push thoughts of her friends out of her head. Would they still show tonight? She hoped they would. Haven may be angry with them but she still wanted them by her side.

Her anger wasn't just with them, she was also pissed at Nik for keeping so much from her. She planned to get ready an extra thirty minutes early so she could have time to yell at him about everything he'd kept from her.

Finally pausing all thoughts of recent betrayals, Haven went back to strumming through the pages of her mothers diary. Entry after entry, Haven got lost between the pages. Her mother had detailed so much and the diary wasn't even half over. As much as Haven didn't want to read anything of the sort, her parents had had a perfect first kiss, first date, first everything. Her mother narrated so many scenes between them, scenes Haven definitely skipped over. Her parents may have hid things and lied but there were some lines that should never be crossed and reading about her parents sex life was one of them.

Another thing highlighted through her mothers words was her councils displeasure towards her relationship with the king of Shaston. Apparently it was highly frowned upon for any royal fae to be involved with another royal, mainly due to the fact that if a child was born of that union they would grow to be incredibly powerful. More powerful than most. A chill ran through Haven when she realized that she was that child.

Most outwardly opposed of her parents' relationship was a council member named Evan. He was one of Moranas closest friends and was very opinionated when it came to her affairs. From the way her mother described him, Haven came to the conclusion that Evan had held feelings towards her mom. Feelings her mother did not reciprocate.

Getting up to grab another slip of paper to mark the page with, as she had done with every page she deemed 'not Haven appropriate,' Haven glanced at the clock and startled. It was well into the time she dedicated to getting ready for her wedding.

Closing the diary as gently as she could, Haven dashed to her gown hanging on the bathroom door. A quick mental calculation told her she could make it on time, barely, which meant no yelling at Nik and she'd probably be the last one there but at least she'd be there.

Haven wished Rea was with her. If they hadn't fought, Astrea probably would have shown up to help Haven get ready thus keeping her from being late. Haven couldn't blame Astrea for her tardiness though, that was her own fault. She should have paid more attention to the clock while reading.

Unzipping the garment bag, Haven discovered one of the most beautiful dresses she would ever have the pleasure of wearing. The sheer lace sleeves were off the shoulder and there was a cinched waist and long flowing skirt. It was off white, with lots of beautiful lace details. The skirt of the dress wasn't overly puffy, making it easier for Haven to handle but it still had enough layers to be considered a ball gown.

Rea had picked the perfect dress, Haven hadn't given her wedding dress too much thought in all the recent craziness but now she was glad to have a friend who knew her as well as Rea did, because that's what Rea was, her friend. Probably the best she'd ever had.

Chapter Fifty-Nine

Haven dashed out to the castle stables, planning to take Pluto to where the wedding was taking place rather than walk as she'd originally planned.

She held the skirt of her dress in her arms as she sprinted across the grounds. The castle would surely be rife with gossip tomorrow if anyone spotted her.

Finding Pluto in his stall, Haven quickly brushed him down and saddled him. Leading him from the barn, she hiked up her dress as far as she could with the cinched waist and climbed on. She let him walk for a quick warm up before taking off into the woods in the direction of the clearing Niks father had picked out.

It didn't take long riding at a fast pace before Haven was almost to the clearing. With the moon lighting her way and Plutos strangely good behavior, she was making great time. Maybe Pluto knew how important this ride was, Haven thought. If tonight did not work and they fell into war with the crown regents supporters it would likely be the first of many important rides. The thought caused anxiety to bloom in Havens chest.

Haven sensed the others up ahead, she'd sent her shadows crawling out ahead of her so she'd know when they were getting close. Also so she'd know if she was riding into a trap.

Haven felt a shadow brush against someone's ankle. Whoever it was seemed to be playing with her shadow, reaching down to twist their hand through it.

Riding a little further, Haven sensed no traps, not that she'd know exactly what to be looking for in the first place.

When the clearing came into view, she could see Roman at the edge closest to her. He was the one playing with her shadows. She sent a few more his way, coiling them around his legs. He smiled, causing Haven to smile at the sight of his upturned lips.

As Haven neared him, she dismounted Pluto and gave his black fur a pat. She hadn't thought far enough ahead to consider that now she had a horse to take care of while she was supposed to be getting married. She could ask Roman to hold him but even after everything, she was still holding out hope that he'd walk her down the aisle. Glancing past Roman, she found the rest of her friends standing in the circular clearing. Rea was standing off to the side looking rather lost and Nik was speaking with his friend Delroy, his back turned to her. The crown regent was nowhere to be found but Haven knew it wouldn't be long before he showed.

The 'aisle' was about five feet of trimmed grass with different colored tulips lining either side. An archway stood at the end, created from bent branches with vines and more flowers interspersed throughout.

"You look great." Roman called to her.

Haven couldn't tell whether he was joking or not as she stepped up to him. Smoothing out her dress, Haven guessed he had to be. Her hair was windswept, she had twisted the front pieces behind her head and pinned them into place before she left but she could tell they were barely hanging on. Her small tiara was crooked and some of the fabric on her arms was streaked with dirt from her ride. Not to mention the boots she was wearing had a small hole that had filled with water when she stepped in a puddle on the way to get Pluto.

"I was trying to get here quickly," Haven smiled sheepishly.

"I'm not joking H, you look good."

"Thank you" She nodded

Roman reached up to straighten the tiara on her head. She hadn't put on the crown Astrea left with the dress, telling herself that crowns were for queens and Haven was still a princess. Knocking some of the dirt off her arms and pulling a small stick from her hair, Haven hoped she looked somewhat better.

Gripping the reins tightly in her hand, Haven bounced on her feet with nerves. After what happened earlier she wasn't entirely sure how she was feeling about her friends. She originally planned to ask Roman to walk with her but now, being back in his presence, the anger was starting to resurface. He'd poisoned her, let her father be killed and he'd been lying to her from the moment they met. He must have seen the uncertain anger paired with sadness written across her face because he asked,

"Are we okay?"

Haven took a moment before responding, "I honestly don't know."

Astrea joined the two of them wearing a sheepish smile. It didn't take long before Haven was no longer uncertain about what she was feeling, she knew it was anger along with sadness and the distinct feeling of being betrayed by someone close to you. Or rather, multiple someones.

Nik still hadn't turned towards her, Delroy had glanced over a few times but looked away whenever he caught Havens eye.

Haven silently vowed to try to forget about everything just for tonight. It would be hard seeing as she was about to get married to someone she was incredibly angry with. She knew he was to blame almost as much as Astrea and Roman but the fact he hadn't been directly involved with the death of her father slightly eased her anger towards him.

Taking a deep breath, Haven willed the tension from her body. It's just one night, she reminded herself, just one night. She could go back to being pissed at everyone after the sun rose.

Tuning back into the idle chit chat Astrea and Roman were making around her, she found them discussing why they thought the crown regent was late. It didn't take more than a moment for Haven to figure out that they were joking rather than discussing actual reasons,

"Maybe he slipped and fell and is lying somewhere bleeding out" Roman quipped

Rea huffed a laugh, "We could never be so lucky."

"Well maybe he finally got what was coming to him and was stabbed by a staff member," Roman gasped dramatically, "Maybe we'll all get to have some fun and play murder mystery when we get back to the castle. Then when we find the murderer we can throw them a party."

Both Astrea and Haven snorted. Although it seemed a little insensitive to be discussing someone's murder with their son barely ten feet away but if Haven had to guess, she assumed he'd agree. Nik might even be the one hosting the party.

"Maybe this was secretly all some trick to lure us out here so he could kill us without an audience" Rea jokingly slid her finger across her throat. She knew that her friends were joking but being reminded that Niks father wanted to kill her did not feel good. Her friends must have begun feeling the same way because they settled down, talking idly about her coronation and Romans return to his home kingdom.

Pluto nuzzled at Havens back, forcing her to pay attention to him, not that she really minded. A few minutes passed with Haven stroking his muzzle before her friends quieted suddenly. Turning away from Pluto she saw why,

Nik was standing before her, only a feet away. His gaze was hard and clearly stressed.

"Mind if I have a word?"

Haven nodded, "Of course."

Delroy stepped up, taking Plutos reins from her. She hadn't socialized much with Niks closest friend other than when he was being a jerk to her so she didn't have much reason to smile and thank him but she did it anyway.

Nik guided her out of the clearing into a tight cluster of trees. He stopped once they were out of fae earshot. Haven leaned back against a tree, watching Nik gather his words.

The moonlight glinted off his eyelashes and his face was strained but it did not make him any less beautiful. Haven was suddenly taken aback to the last time they were alone together, Nik above her, thrusting inside her.

She quickly turned her mind to other things, not wanting to start something their friends might overhear. Trailing her eyes over Niks outfit, she found nothing but black. His shirt was black, his pants and cloak were black too. It helped him blend into the darkness around him. Haven wondered if he picked it out for that reason specifically. It clashed somewhat with her gown but she didn't mind. When they first met all they did was clash with each other, their outfits reminded her of that.

"You look amazing" Nik spoke, his voice coming out deep and scratchy.

"Thank you. You do as well." Haven could feel her face flush red, she hoped he couldn't see it but with the strong moonlight and his fae eyesight she was almost sure he did.

"We should talk"

"Uh oh" Haven joked, trying to lighten the mood, "That never ends well"

"Are you sure about this?" Nik asked, ignoring her attempt at humor.

"Of course I am." Haven reassured.

Niks jaw tightened, "So you're saying that if my father hadn't forced you into this we'd still be getting married right now?"

Haven wouldn't lie to Nik. As much as she had been trying to look on the bright side, there was no way to dismiss the fact that she'd been forced into this. She liked Nik, was clearly attracted to him and could even see them ending up together. But there was no denying that if his father hadn't threatened her mom, Rea and Roman, if he hadn't forced her into a deal binding her to this marriage then she wouldn't be here tonight, standing in the dirt in a wedding gown.

"You're right. We definitely would not be getting married right now." She told Nik. He somehow managed to look both relieved and heartbroken.

"We have a lot to work through," She began, "There's all the stuff you lied to me about, your antagonism, the fact that you seem so against me loving you. I mean, we were basically enemies at the start of all this, we are going to have to,"

Nik abruptly cut her off,

"You love me?"

The question startled Haven. She hadn't meant to throw that little piece of herself out there mostly because she didn't know how he would react. Haven still could not bring herself to lie though which is why she responded with a simple head nod. She did love him, through all his harsh words and glares. Through all his soft touches and heated kisses, somewhere along the line Haven Montali Rionach began loving Nikolaus DaMarrel.

Nik crashed his lips to hers, eliminating the space between them and placing a hand on either side of her face. His lips were warm and soft against Havens as they kissed. He pulsed his tongue across her lips, requesting entry. Haven immediately granted it, letting out a small moan as she did. The sound of her moan encouraged Nik as he pushed Haven into the tree she had been leaning against. The rough bark of the tree dug into her back as Havens hands laced together behind Niks head.

The moment was entirely ruined when a voice shouted,

"NIKOLAUS!"

That voice did not belong to just anyone, that voice belonged to Niks father. It was obvious he had made it to the clearing.

Nik pulled away, dropping his hands into Havens. His eyes were downcast but he wore a small smile as he told her,

"I love you too."

Haven didn't have time to process or respond because the crown regent shouted again, breaking whatever was left of the loving and soft atmosphere they'd built around themselves.

"Time to face the music" Haven quipped. Nik didn't smile. Instead, he turned, hand still in hers and led them back to the clearing where they would be tying themselves to each other. The thought didn't scare Haven as much as it probably should, after all, Nik loved her.

Chapter Sixty

In the past, getting married was something Nik almost never allowed himself to consider. Probably because he always assumed he'd end up in a marriage arranged by his father, to someone he didn't know, let alone cared about. Nik couldn't see himself getting along with someone his father truly approved of.

Technically his father had arranged today but Haven couldn't be further from the image Nik once painted in his mind. She was warm and funny, kind and adventurous. Haven could also be badass and lethal when she wanted. Nik was constantly in awe of her, of her strength and courage. If he ever had to pick someone to spend the rest of his immortal years with, he wanted it to be her. Too bad he'd never make it through the vows.

While trudging through the woods back towards the clearing, Nik held Havens hand tightly in his. Her other hand was holding the skirt of her dress off the ground. He hoped it didn't get too dirty, she looked stunning in it. Pausing at the edge of the clearing, Nik took a breath and turned to tell Haven,

"No matter what happens tonight, remember I care about you"

A concerned look crossed Havens face before she asked,

"Is everything alright?"

"Yes" Nik reassured her, the lie tasting like acid on his tongue.

"Are you planning something?"

Haven asked her question softly but Nik could see the steel in her gaze. He knew she'd stop him if he told her so much as a crumb of his plans, which is why he responded with,

"I'm not planning anything. My father is tricky, I just wanted to remind you of my feelings."

Nik smiled gently, nudging her shoulder to help reassure her. He needed her to believe him. Only two other people knew of what he planned, both of which would be arriving later tonight.

Haven softened, wearing a small smile of her own.

"I'm choosing to believe you on this. I know this isn't what you wanted but I won't lie and say I'm not glad we're here. That I'm not glad it's you I'm standing up with because I am." She paused for a moment before finishing, "With that said, if you truly want to back out of this then I understand. We can walk back into that clearing, announce we're not getting married and deal with whatever your father throws at us."

Her words brought a warmth into Niks chest that had been missing for a very long time. He knew Haven cared for him but he also knew this was important to her. She needed this to keep his father from going after her loved ones. He'd already killed her dad and Nik knew his father wouldn't hesitate to go after anyone he thought Haven even slightly cared for. The fact that she was willing to risk that for him meant more than Nik could express in words.

If it weren't for the threats against Havens life, Nik might have considered it. Unfortunately, Nik knew that if he didn't walk into that clearing and at least make an attempt to do what his father wanted then he'd go after everyone in that clearing as a punishment for Niks disobedience. Even though he could get sent into exile, have his powers stripped from him or even be killed if the death of the future queen led back to him, his father was just crazy and arrogant enough to think that there was a possibility he could get away with it.

Who knew, Nik thought, maybe his father simply didn't care about getting caught anymore. Maybe the threat of losing all his sway over the council and all his power over the people of Drail-ia and Shaston was enough to convince him the possible con-sequences were worth it. As much as he may appreciate Havens words, Niks plan needed to go ahead as scheduled. None of this could ever fall back on Haven, he needed to protect her as best he could.

In the back of his mind, Nik knew that his father could end up as the least of their problems if predictions from years past ever began to play out. Nik had never told anyone what that old witch showed him but those memories influenced his every action. Even if his father wasn't the most immediate and pressing threat, a much larger one loomed on the horizon if Nik chose to follow his heart's desire and stay besides Haven. No, Nik needed tonight to go exactly as planned. It might be the only way to save his friends, to save everyone.

"I appreciate that Haven. More than you'll ever know, but it's alright. I want this. I may have been against this in the beginning but the idea of having you as my wife, of getting to spend our immortality together is as frightening as it is exciting and I'm looking forward to it greatly." Nik comforted himself with the fact that that wasn't a complete lie.

"Oh" A sheepish smile spread across Havens face along with a rosy pink blush. Nik hoped that if she ever discovered what he had done, she didn't believe it was because of her.

Nik released her hand and extended his arm, she linked hers through it and together they walked into the clearing. Moonlight shone down on them, casting a beautiful glow across Havens features and the archway they would stand under. Everything looked amazing, Astrea had really gone all out for her friend. Nik hoped Haven would be able to forgive Astrea for lying to her. Haven would need her support after tonight was over and she was crowned queen.

His father stood behind who Nik assumed was the priest at the end of the aisle, like a venomous snake just waiting to strike.

Delroy waited next to Niks spot, Astrea on the opposite side near where Haven would stand. Roman stood a few feet away holding Pluto. Nik knew that Haven had found out the truth about her friends, the lies they told her and the parts they played in her fathers death. For the second time tonight, Nik hoped she'd be able to move past her anger so they could support her and offer help since Nik himself wouldn't be there to do it.

Haven tightened her hold on Niks arm as they neared the beginning of the aisle. Haven hadn't said the words but it was obvious to him that she wanted Nik to walk with her and he was honored to do so.

Time seemed to slow as the pair made their way down the short aisle. Seconds seemed to become minutes, minutes felt like hours. Some sort of magic was taking place, Nik didn't know what was happening but he hoped it wasn't something malicious.

Once the pair reached the end of the aisle, Nik released Havens arm and turned to face her. Taking in her features one last time, Nik committed them to memory.

The priest began speaking but Nik could barely hear the words, he had made his bed and it was time to lie in it.

Chapter Sixty-One

The soft sounds of birds reached Havens ears, she thought it was odd to hear them this time of night but who knew, maybe they had come to see the wedding. As silly as that thought was, it helped to calm Haven down a bit.

Haven forced herself to take in the nervous look on Niks face. He lied to her, she knew that. He was definitely not okay and was definitely planning something. Haven assumed that whatever it was would likely be taking place soon. Nik might have told her that he couldn't wait to spend their immortal lives together but if the look on his face was anything to go by, that had also been a lie. Currently he appeared to be taking in her features and committing them to memory. As if he wouldn't be able to see them after tonight.

Pushing those dangerous thoughts from her head, Haven clasped her hands in Niks and met his eyes. There was so much love apparent in them that she began to rethink everything. Maybe Nik was planning to take on his father rather than refusing to marry her. Haven knew she didn't need him by her side but she wanted him there, for as long as he would stay and if that really was what he planned then she had faith that Nik could win against his father.

As powerful as everyone said the crown regent was, Haven hadn't once seen him use any actual magic. He was likely out of practice from the years spent lounging on her throne. And besides, power wasn't always everything. Haven was a firm supporter of the idea that you had to truly believe in what you were fighting for in order to succeed. While Niks father might believe in what he was doing, it was a selfish belief, one rooted in corruption and greed and, in her mind, that made all the difference.

The nervous priest broke the silence by clearing his throat and announcing that they were ready to begin.

Haven turned to take in the priest the crown regent had forced to perform the ceremony. He was dressed in all white, the rumpled outfit in combination with his light blond hair sticking every which way told Haven he was likely in bed when the crown regent forced him into the forest. She would like to think that he was here of his own volition but the nervous pitch of his eyebrows and the way his eye twitched whenever Niks father moved even an inch told her otherwise.

Suddenly, the birds went quiet, the wind stopped whistling and even the stars seemed to quiet their twinkling in order to pay attention.

"As is traditional in a fae marriage," The priest began, "First, the two of you will exchange rings and vows. Then, I will call upon the beings of our universe to bless this union. Lastly, I will tie your wrists together with a marriage knot, your rings will soak up the power of the marriage knot, leaving a brand and tying the two of you together for the rest of your immortal lives"

Haven panicked for a second when she realized that she did not have a ring for Nik. Her panic was short lived because Rea stepped forward and held a ring out to Haven. Delroy did the same with a ring for Nik.

Haven untangled her hand from Niks and took the ring from her friend. It was cool to the touch and solid in her hand. Silver in coloring, Haven could see some words etched into the inside of the ring but she didn't have a second to read them before the priest continued speaking,

"Haven, you will go first. Place the ring on Niks left ring finger and state your vows."

Haven took a breath, she had thought some about what she might say if forced to recite vows. Public speaking wasn't normally her strong suit and in the short amount of time she'd had to prepare for the wedding she wasn't able to come up with anything. When she tried, nothing sounded right. Nothing she could come up with seemed to fit their passionate and sometimes exhausting relationship. In the moment however, Haven didn't feel the need to come up with anything, she could simply say what she felt,

"Nik, we have not known each other long and we might have been forced here, but that's not what is important. The future we will have, the memories we have made and all the ones to come, that's what is important. Somewhere along our twisted, twining trail full of heated words and thoughtful glances, I fell in love with you and I wouldn't trade that love for anything. I promise to always be there for you, no matter the situation. To love you with all of my heart and to stand by your side in whatever this life may bring us"

A tear trailed down Havens cheek as she finished her vows.

With trembling hands, she slid the ring onto Niks finger. She could feel the power coursing through her veins, see the shadows twining around her feet and singed threads of her wedding gown. She hadn't meant to call her magics to the surface but was glad it happened anyway. Now Nik could see all of her, the shadows and the smiles alike.

Chapter Sixty-Two

Haven was stunning, she might not be aware of it but her powers ignited the moment she started speaking. Nik could feel the warm crawl of her shadows snaking up his ankles and see the little plumes of smoke and fire apparent all around them. He had been doing his best to contain the little fires she kept setting with his air magic by draining the air from certain spots. Even though a forest fire would probably be the least dastardly thing to happen tonight, it still wasn't a good idea.

With her head tipped to him, the strength of her belief in her words written in her eyes and the small crown on her head, Nik thought Haven looked like a goddess.

He might've believed she was one if he didn't know that they were long dead.

The force of her love slammed into him all at once, when she slid that ring onto his finger. It made him want to forget all about his plans, throw her over his shoulder, carry her into the castle, place her on the throne and watch her rule.

She was exactly what their kingdom needed which was precisely why he could never do it. He could never tie her to the poison slowly killing his kingdom. If he did, if he married Haven and took the chance that visions of old would come true and that his father would find a way into power with Nik as the king consort, he'd never forgive himself. He may wish against all hope that he could find a way to stay and be loved by her but he knew it was a fools dream, a selfish and foolish dream.

The slight sound of sticks snapping in the woods alerting Nik to their company as he prepared his words. They were late but he appreciated the extra few moments before his entire world turned upside down.

"Haven," Nik began, "I might have pretended not to like you in the beginning, and you may have actually not liked me but as you said earlier, that's not what's important. This is never something I saw for myself, I never imagined I'd earn the love of someone I care so deeply for, someone I love so deeply."

Nik heard Havens breath hitch at his words.

"Getting to return your love is one of the greatest gifts I've ever been given and I will cherish that until the day that I die"

There was more that Nik wanted to say but decided against it when he heard the footsteps nearing. They were just outside the clearing now, he only had moments before they struck.

Nik slid the ring he'd picked out onto Havens finger, it was a perfect fit. The priest began chanting ancient fae words, calling upon the magic of the realm to bless their union. He didn't get five words out before shouting erupted.

Two large masked men entered the clearing, shouting at everyone to put their hands in the air.

Nik followed the orders, as did everyone except Haven and his father.

Nik felt a magic restricting band being tied tight around his wrists by one of the men's air magic. Perfect, he thought, this was exactly why he'd hired these men over the others he'd been considering, their technique was the best for this situation. It allowed the men to have power over everyone in the clearing without them having to be too close to anyone who might fight back.

Taking in the defiant look on Havens face, Nik panicked for a second. He sincerely hoped she didn't make this too difficult, he didn't know what he'd do if he had to watch her get hurt because of his choices.

Only when one of the men grabbed the priest and held a dagger to his throat did she slowly raise her hands into the air. Nik watched as a band floated to her and wrapped around her hands. She gasped and Nik could tell she was feeling her powers being cut off. Nik took a second to tear his eyes away from the love of his life standing bound before him, finding everyone else standing stock still with magic binds preventing them from fighting back.

The only other person Nik worried about was Delroy, he was a guard and trained to fight with his hands in addition to his magic. It was why he had warned the only two men that knew about his plan to stay away from Delroy. If his friend managed to get near one of them, Nik knew he'd fight like hell to prevent the inevitable from happening.

Chaos broke as one of the men stopped behind Nik. Haven quickly lifted her foot, hooked it behind Niks knee and sent him tumbling to the ground. Everything seemed to be happening at warp speed. He landed just in time to see Haven kick out at the man who was now standing where Nik had been only a moment ago.

The kick landed square in the mans stomach, causing him to groan and double over. As he fell forward, Haven brought her other knee up to land a hit on her assailants nose. Nik would be proud if he wasn't both incredibly worried and pissed. He should have known Haven would go down fighting.

Thankfully, Haven didn't see the other man moving to grab her from behind. Astrea tried to shout a warning but it was too late. Haven was now safely restrained in his arms.

"This is how this is going to go," The one restraining Haven shouted, "You all let us take what we want and nobody gets hurt. Anyone tries to resist and they'll end up with a knife in their chest"

Haven stilled at the mans words.

The man Haven injured pulled himself off of the ground,

"Bitch," He spat. Nik cringed at the words, wishing the men would hurry up so this nightmare could be over.

The man moved to haul Nik off the ground, Nik pretended to struggle before the man holding Haven hostage put a knife to her throat. He had specifically instructed these men to never actually harm her but the sight still sent Niks pulse racing.

"That's right pretty boy, we've got your girl"

The man that had pulled Nik from the ground began rifling through Niks pockets. After he found nothing, he shoved Nik back down and moved onto Astrea. The girl squeaked when he roughly grabbed her, forcing his way into the pockets of the dress she was wearing. Again, he found nothing.

Everything was going according to Niks plan. First the men would attempt to rob them, upon finding nothing, they would get angry and then take Nik as 'collateral' to use against his father.

The men skipped over Delroy, listening to Niks words, and moved onto the crown regent.

"Well, well, well, look what we have here." The injured man waved his knife at Niks father.

"Fuck you" His father spat as the man inched closer.

"Hmm, I don't think so. Little bitch isn't my type"

If it wouldn't give Nik away as having planned this whole thing, he would laugh.

Niks kidnapper grabbed his father roughly and shoved him to the ground. Nik got a sick sense of satisfaction watching that happen.

After finding nothing in the crown regents pocket, the man faked getting angry. He began shouting about how the crown regent and the future queen were supposed to be rich. The man quickly got angrier and angrier, letting his air magic whip around him.

Nik had ordered them to put on a show but this was getting a little unnecessary. Right when Nik was about to fake fighting back, just to move things along, the kidnapper holding Haven drug the tip of a knife down Havens cheek and said,

"Why don't we just take her. Use her as ransom. I bet the kingdom would pay well to have their future queen back"

Shock and nerves coursed through Nik. That definitely hadn't been a part of his plan, he'd paid a lot of money to ensure the events of tonight went as smoothly as possible. They were supposed to take Nik hostage and then never demand the ransom, freeing Nik to disappear into the shadows of the realm. He could see the wheels turning behind the mens masks. Nik would bet they assumed they'd make more ransoming off Haven then they ever would with Nik paying them to fake his kidnapping.

Too bad they had no idea his father would never pay a dime. He'd be able to find a way to keep his power if Haven disappeared and that would suit him just fine. Even now, while being held at knife point, Nik could see the small smile on his fathers face at the thought of having Haven gone.

Nik had just inadvertently solved all of his fathers problems and he had no idea how to fix it.

Chapter Sixty-Three

The brute of a man holding Haven hostage mumbled something under his breath as his partner talked. His grip tightened anytime she moved a muscle. Haven was fairly confident she could escape him if she really tried but he had whispered in her ear about how he'd have his partner slit her friends throats if she kept attempting to escape. He promised to start with Astrea and end with Pluto. His words had quickly put an end to her struggling.

She might have been able to take both men out if it weren't for the ropes around her wrists that were restricting access to her magic. She hated feeling so helpless, she could see the fear written across Rea's face, Pluto kept whinnying where he was being held by Roman and even Delroy looked worried.

Niks father had slowly been inching away, the coward that he was.

She was going to kill Nik once this was over. At first she'd thought this was just a plain robbery, that they were simply in the wrong place at the wrong time. Then she'd wondered how that was possible given how deep into the woods their group was. All it took was one glance at Nik, she'd seen the resignation on his face and immediately known he planned this.

"Why don't we just take her. Use her as ransom. I bet the kingdom would pay well to have their future queen back"

The air around Haven stilled. At first, she'd assumed they might be here to help Nik kill his father, or even kidnap him. She certainly hadn't expected those words to come out of her captors mouth.

The arm holding her captive tightened around her midsection. She could almost feel her captors smile. They probably thought they'd get a lot of money for her but Haven wasn't stupid, she knew that if it was up to the crown regent, they'd never see a dime. He'd simply fake paying for her to appease whatever uproar her kidnapping caused. Hell, Niks father was more likely to pay these men to kill her rather than return her.

Haven frantically scanned the area, she had to figure something out. There was absolutely no way she'd let these men take her.

On her second glance, she caught Niks eye. She could see the worry in them, how scared he was. It was clear as day as was his love for her. For the second time tonight, Haven began to second guess herself. Maybe he hadn't planned this, she thought, maybe this really had been a terrible coincidence. After all, someone who had known this was going to happen or who was in control of the situation wouldn't be so distraught. A single tear fell down his cheek, causing a twin tear to roll down Havens cheek.

"I'm sorry" He mouthed

Haven shook her head, her heart beating frantically against her chest. Whatever Nik was about to do, Haven knew she wouldn't like it.

"Take me" His voice was only slightly audible and she could hear the pain in it.

"No!" Haven shouted, struggling to get out of her captors clutches.

"Yes! I'm the one you want." Niks voice was louder now, full of confidence.

"Why would we take you when we can have something so much prettier?" The man holding her snarled at Nik. He drug the tip of his dagger down her cheek, the same one that had had a tear rolling down it only moments ago. It didn't break the skin but the feeling of the sharp blade caused Haven to still. One wrong move and she'd be crying tears mixed with blood.

"Because you're not stupid," Nik began, "You know exactly what's been going on. If you take her, you'll never see a drop of ransom money. The crown regent won't pay for it."

Nik gestured to where his father had been on the ground. The crown regent was nowhere in sight, Haven would like to think he was going to get help but she knew better. The only person he cared about helping was himself and allowing Haven to be kidnapped would be a great help to him.

"Where did he go?" The bloody kidnapper demanded.

"How am I supposed to know! You're the one who's holding us hostage, his disappearance is on you!" Nik answered sarcastically.

He had a devilish smirk on his face. In seconds he'd gone from what Haven assumed was a tearful goodbye to being an antagonistic little shit to the fae currently holding them hostage.

She'd think it was hot if it weren't for the knife currently being repositioned against her throat.

"Very funny smartass! Maybe we will take you since you seem so keen on sacrificing yourself."

The other man started towards Nik. As he did, a look of relief washed over Niks face. Haven may not like the idea of Nik sacrificing himself but she understood it. Understanding aside, nothing was going to stop her from struggling to get out of her captors hold and shouting,

"No, let him go!"

"Quiet" The man holding her grunted. Haven tried to force her elbow back into his stomach. Unfortunately he dodged her hit but it gave her the opportunity to reach up with her bound hands, grab his wrist and pry the dagger away from her throat.

Just as she slipped out of his grip, air magic slammed into her from the front, forcing her right back into his hold. She knew one of her captors had air magic but she hadn't been expecting them to use it like that.

"You. Can't. Hold. Me." Haven punctuated each word with some kind of jab at her captor, another elbow to the ribs, her heel digging into his foot, she even tried using her fangs to bite into his wrist or arm. Unluckily for her, the dagger made its way back to her throat, forcing her to pause her escape attempts.

A bag was being forced over Niks head where he lay on the ground with his hands tied, forcing Haven back into action, dagger to her throat or not.

"No!" Haven thrashed violently, she couldn't let this happen. No matter what Nik may or may not have planned, she couldn't let these men take him. If he truly wanted to go then they could fight off these men together and then he could leave. They'd tell the kingdom he had been kidnapped, she would fake looking for him to settle the crown regent and whoever else was upset by his disappearance but it would be a lie. As much as it broke her heart, Haven knew that if that's what he wanted, she'd make it happen. No matter what it took.

Haven lurched forward just enough to have the force to slam her head backwards into her captors nose. She nicked her neck on his dagger but with the adrenaline coursing through her veins, she could barely feel it.

He stumbled back and reached up to cup his nose. His arms left her torso. Haven scrambled forward. Just as she thought she was free of him she heard,

"Oh no you don't!"

A hand clutched her dress, dragging her backwards. Before she could make sense of what was happening, pain exploded across her temple and everything went black.

Chapter Sixty-Four

At Astreas screech, Nik released the magic he was using to hold his friends in place. He hadn't wanted to use it on Haven because he knew she would figure out it was him but when she almost escaped the hold of her captor, he had to.

Nik knew that Delroy would also figure out what he had done, and likely already had, but his friend would understand. Delroy knew almost all of the dark thoughts that ran through Niks head, his happiest moments, the saddest ones and the one thing he truly wanted out of life. As soon as Nik held a force of air in front of his friend to keep him from fighting back, Nik knew it was only a matter of time before Delroy understood what was going on.

The fake magic restricting ropes around his wrists dug into his skin as he thrashed, trying to get the bag off of his head. He could no longer hear Havens screaming and it was thoroughly unsettling.

As much as he hadn't wanted to be the cause of her anguished screams he'd take being able to hear it over the eerie silence that now greeted him.

Using his enhanced fae hearing, he picked up her heartbeat out of the pack. He'd spent a lot of time simply listening to it so he could easily tell its unique rhythm from the others. Hearing its faint but steady beat caused relief to wash over Nik.

I'm sorry

He apologized to her at least a hundred times in his mind, unable to speak the words aloud. As he was hauled up and off the ground, bag still preventing him from taking her in one last time, all he could think was,

I'm so sorry

He repeated it over and over in his head, though he knew it would never be enough.

Chapter Sixty-Five

A headache worse than a hangover greeted Haven as she woke from her forced nap.

"Ow," She groaned as she sat up, holding her palm to the wound at her hairline.

"Look who's awake!" Roman spoke softly.

"What happened?" She asked. Looking around, Haven could tell she was back in her room at the castle. Her clothes had been changed into one of her nightdresses and her all but ruined wedding dress hung sadly on a hook on her bathroom door. Roman was sitting on her desk chair beside her bed.

"We'll get to that in a minute but for now, drink this." Roman looked away, grabbing something off of her nightstand and holding it out to her. It was a small cup of water. If it weren't for her scratchy throat and dry mouth she might have thrown it at him. He was deflecting, or at least putting off telling her what she wanted to know. The last time he did something like that he had been keeping the fact that he was inadvertently responsible for her fathers death from her.

"Thank you." She took a sip, it was cool and refreshing going down her throat.

"Of course" Roman gave her a slight smile, he was clearly testing the waters between them and she knew it. Luckily for him she was too tired and felt too much like she'd been run over to bother still being mad at him. Although Haven did wonder what would happen when she was back at her best. Would she still be upset with her friends? It was too much to think about right this minute, especially with something much more pressing on her mind.

"I have to pee" Haven said hurriedly, basically launching herself out of bed. She realized her mistake when she immediately got dizzy and almost fell. Roman reached out and grabbed her elbow to steady her. She thanked him and then did the best she could to dart into the bathroom on unsteady feet.

After tending to her needs and washing her hands, Haven exited the bathroom and sat back down on the edge of her bed. While she was in the bathroom Roman had produced a small plate of food.

"Here, you should eat something." He told her, moving from his spot in her desk chair to sit beside her on the bed.

"If I eat, will you tell me what happened?" Havens memories were fuzzy. She remembered heading out to the clearing in the forest, talking with Nik, walking down the aisle and then not much else. The heavy weight on her finger confirmed something else had obviously happened.

"How about I tell you while you eat?" Roman spoke softly, as if she were fragile. If it weren't for her pounding headache, she might be pissed he was treating her like she'd break.

Haven nodded in agreement. Setting the plate on the bed between them, she scanned the assorted meats, cheeses, slices of fruit and crackers before settling on a couple of grapes that teetered on the edge of the plate.

"What do you remember?" Roman asked.

Haven shook her head, "Not much," She said between bites, "I remember heading out to the clearing, talking with Nik and then walking down the aisle. I don't remember anything after that and what I do remember is hazy. I can recall talking to Nik away from everyone, I remember his face as he spoke but I can't remember the words."

Roman nodded, "That's probably just the concussion. I'm sure your memories will come back to you at some point, probably after you've rested properly."

"Hopefully," Haven remarked, "So are you actually going to tell me what happened or do I need to go and find someone who will?"

Before Roman got a chance to respond, Havens mind conjured a question,

"Where's Nik?"

Roman cringed, the look on his face was enough to tell her something bad had happened.

"Roman what happened?" Haven's voice rose as she talked, "Is Nik alright?"

"I'm not sure." Roman told her, "He's gone H, they took him."

"Who took him?" She demanded

Romans eyes fell to his feet, he couldn't meet Havens gaze as he said, "I wish I knew"

***

After Roman explained, in detail, the events of last night, Haven unsteadily marched herself to the one person who might know something. Pounding on his door, Haven yelled,

"Delroy open up!"

A few moments passed before Haven considered banging on the door again. She could hear movement in the room so she knew he was in there but she did not want to wake the entire hall with repeated knocks.

"I can hear you in there," She called, much quieter than her original tone,

"Please, I just want to talk."

The sound of a lock disengaging met Havens pointed ears before the door opened softly,

"How can I help Her Majesty?" Delroy greeted sarcastically.

In all of Romans explanations there had been a bit about the crown regent being gone. Apparently no one could find him, his office had been trashed when they went looking. The working theory was that he managed to slip away while they were all being held captive, he'd gotten back with just enough time to grab a few of his things and take a horse from the stables before disappearing into the night.

With him gone, Haven had been unofficially crowned as there was no one else with the power to rule. Soon she'd have her coronation, be officially crowned queen and the crown regents absence wouldn't matter. Although Haven had a feeling they hadn't seen the last of Niks father.

Even though she'd pretty much known it was coming, the nickname still caught her off guard. She paused long enough that Delroy tried to close the door in her face. Slamming her hand against the wood, Haven stopped Delroys attempt to get rid of her and said,

"Look, I know you hate me but I need some questions answered and you might be the only one still in this castle that can answer them."

Delroy thought for a minute before responding,

"First, I don't know what you think I can answer for you. I don't know anything about what happened and trust me, I've got lots of questions of my own. Second," Delroy paused, as if debating whether he was actually going to speak whatever was on his mind before coming to a decision and continuing,

"I don't hate you"

Chapter Sixty-Six

Delroys room wasn't anything like she had been expecting, although Haven didn't actually know what she was expecting. Blank and bland walls met with even blander wood furniture. Not a picture in sight, his clothes were neatly tucked away in a dresser, the floors were swept and his bed was made. Haven wondered if he'd been stress cleaning before she showed up.

The only thing marking this room as his was his scent but even that was faint. Delroy had done a good job of making the room seem clinical and impersonal if that was what he was going for.

Upon closer inspection, Haven could smell another scent in addition to Delroys. It was fainter and if she didn't already recognize the scent, she'd never have known he'd been here recently. Romans scent was all over this room. Haven wanted to ask about it but she had a feeling Delroy would kick her out if she so much as mentioned the two of them in the same sentence.

"What did you want to ask me?" Delroy asked roughly, closing the door to his room. He'd told her that he didn't hate her but his tone told another story.

"What do you know about Niks kidnapping?"

Delroy sighed, throwing himself down on his bed and folding one arm under his head.

"Absolutely nothing" He told her, if it weren't for the sadness Haven could hear in his voice she probably wouldn't believe him. She knew she shouldn't take him at his word, sad tone or not, but Delroy seemed to be many things and she did not believe a liar was not one of them. Still, she couldn't help asking,

"Why should I believe you?"

Delroy sat up on the edge of his bed. He looked her in the eye before responding,

"You shouldn't. You're a queen now. Whatever you've been dealing with before now was child's play compared to some of the snakes in the courts. From now on, you should believe no one because trust me Haven, the moment someone has your ear they won't hesitate to tell you exactly what they want you to hear to get you onto their side or to do what they want. And every single one of them is a damn good liar."

Haven swallowed, "That was very ominous" She commented.

"Good" Delroy remarked, his voice softer now. For a second, the sadness and hurt had disappeared from his eyes while he'd been talking. It was back now and it caused Haven to sit down next to him, in an attempt to offer some sort of comfort even though she barely knew him.

"You really don't know anything do you?"

"No"

Haven hesitated before asking, "Do you think he planned it?"

"I'd like to say no, I really would"

"But you can't, can you?"

Delroy shook his head.

She didn't know which theory was worse, that Nik planned his kidnapping rather than staying to fight with Haven or that he really had no idea it was going to happen and was now in the hands of a violent criminal planning to use him against the crown. If the second was true, she didn't know what would happen.

When the crown regent had been in power it was obvious Nik was worth something to the rulers here. With her now in power it was less obvious. Her relationship with Nik was only known by a few, his dad hadn't even known. Although, Haven was certain he knew now. Haven was also sure there had likely been some whispers between some of the workers in the castle but nothing widespread or concrete. A shudder worked through Haven at the thought of what his kidnappers might do if they thought Nik was worth nothing.

Before Haven could get too lost in her thoughts, Deroy reached over and placed a comforting hand on her knee. Softly he told her,

"Don't worry. We'll find him. Whether we have to drag him back from wherever he is hiding or rescue him from some criminal, we will bring him home."

***

Haven closed Delroys door softly behind her. The two of them had talked for awhile, about a lot of things. By the end, Delroy still seemed a little frosty towards her but it definitely wasn't the outright hate she had felt in the past. She'd been in the room so long that early morning light from the sun began peeking in through the windows.

They had decided to send out a tracking party to look for Nik and to have a few of the fae Delroy knew with more questionable contacts put their ears to the ground to see what they could dig up.

Whispers down the hall alerted Haven to the presence of others. Looking down at herself, she cursed. In her pissed off state after Roman finished telling her what happened, she hadn't given much thought to what she'd been wearing when she marched over to Delroys room.

She was barefoot, her black silk night dress hanging loosely around her hips, held up by thin straps that matched the white lace trim along the bottom. It definitely wasn't the most queenly attire to be traipsing around the castle in the early morning. And definitely not the right thing to be exiting a male guards room at this early hour.

She did not want anyone to get the wrong idea about her relationship with Delroy. Haven also had a feeling he would rather be caught dead than have rumors about the two of them spread. And spread they would if anyone caught her leaving his room this early looking like she'd been through hell. She hadn't thought to look in a mirror since she'd woken but Haven would be willing to bet the sight would not be pretty after the last two nights. Being held hostage and knocked unconscious could do that to a girl.

The whispers grew closer, sending Haven into motion. She all but ran back to her room, her feet treading silently on the castles stone floors thanks to her training with Tasha.

It only took her a few minutes running down the corridors to make it back to her room. Luckily she'd passed no one on her trek.

Twisting her door handle, Haven entered her room to find a surprise guest asleep on her bed.

The sight of Astrea curled up on her bed tugged on Havens heart. She was still mad at her friends but at this point, she understood why they did what they did. She just wished they hadn't lied to her about it. Years ago when they knowingly let Haven's father be killed while also poisoning her to prevent her death, they hadn't known her, they were not friends back then. And although in Havens mind it was a pretty shitty thing to do, they had reasons for what they did. Good ones from what Haven could tell. So it wasn't that that upset her, it was the lies, the fact that they had known exactly who she was, known exactly who her parents were and who she'd become. Nik, Roman, Astrea, they had all been lying to her from the moment they met.

The thought soured Havens mood more than she should have let it. Still, she could not bring herself to wake her friend and tell her to leave. She probably came here to check on Haven and fell asleep while waiting for her to come back. Haven crawled onto the bed next to Astrea, she had a few hours to sleep before he had to be at morning training. One last training session before her coronation, before she officially took on the role of Queen.

Chapter Sixty-Seven

The sound of birds chirping woke Haven. Her balcony doors were propped wide open, letting in the soft morning breeze.

"Oh good you're awake!" Rea exclaimed, startling Haven. Rea was setting out breakfast on the foot of Havens bed.

"I wanted to let you sleep for as long as possible but you also need to get a shower before you head to training so it's good that you woke when you did."

The reminder of training snapped Haven out of her groggy, sleep induced stupor.

"What are you doing here?" She asked Astrea. She could tell the question hurt her friend but at present, Haven didn't really care. Mornings and so little sleep always made her grumpy.

"I wanted to make sure you were alright after everything that happened." Nerves were written across Astreas face. Haven watched her pick at her nails, a typical sign of anxiety. Haven immediately came to a decision, she wasn't one hundred percent okay with her friends but at least with Astrea she could pretend. After all, she was pissed at her the least out of everyone. Nik slept with her knowing he'd been lying and likely planning his escape and Roman was the one that actually poisoned her and lied to her the most seeing as he'd infiltrated her school with the sole purpose of making sure she made it into the fae realm.

"I'm okay" She assured Rea, "How about we have breakfast and you can tell me about my coronation dress. I hear it's stunning"

***

Sliding on tall boots over the thick material of her training pants, Haven stood from the edge of her bed and made her way through the bedroom door. The shower she had taken before getting dressed helped her feel immensely better. Her emotions might be all over the place but at least she was clean. Her braid hung down her back as she walked. She'd done her best to keep it out of the shower spray since she didn't usually wash her hair everyday but some of it had gotten wet. Unfortunately they did not have blow dryers in the fae realm, although she assumed someone with air magic could do something similar.

Tasha was waiting at her usual spot on the castle grounds, like today wasn't any different. But it was. By this time tomorrow, she'd be standing in front of the people of Drailia, promising to be a fair and just ruler. By this time tomorrow, she'd have a proper crown to go with the queen title.

"You're late," Tasha told her as Haven approached.

"I know, I'm sorry. I got caught up in the shower. I didn't realize how late it was getting."

Tasha nodded, "Well apparently her highness needs a pocket watch. Lest she be late again."

"It won't happen again" Haven assured Tasha

"It better not, and don't go thinking I'm going to treat you any differently now that you are the queen. You're still my student."

Thank fuck for that, Haven thought. She didn't know how much more she could take of people treating her differently. Almost everyone she'd passed on the way out here had stopped and bowed fully when they saw her. Haven didn't know what to say to that so whenever it happened she'd just kept walking.

"I wouldn't have it any other way." Haven smiled

Tasha nodded, "Alright then, let's get to work"

Tasha took off at a fast paced jog. Haven had gotten used to the exercises, the work with weapons, hand to hand combat and even the magic exercises but she still hadn't gotten used to the running. She could, at least, complete the laps without doubling over but it was still her least favorite portion of her sessions with Tasha.

Their laps took them round and round the castle, all over the grounds and finally back to where they started. Unfortunately, more fae had bowed when they saw Haven running.

"That's going to take some getting used to." Haven commented when they finally came to a stop and grabbed their waters.

After taking down a large gulp Tasha told her,

"You will get used to it. Eventually you might even come to like it, it is a show of respect. It also could calm down after a while. It all depends on what kind of ruler you are."

"What do you mean?"

Tasha looked at her curiously before explaining,

"Normally the bowing slows down as people get used to you. Servants will smile and nod their heads instead of stopping to bow. Especially here in your home castle where you'll get to know most everyone. Of course, in lands beyond and other kingdoms, things like that will continue simply because they do not personally know you and want to show you the respect your position demands. However, if you become a ruler people fear rather than respect, the bowing will never stop because technically it is law to bow whenever you see a ruler and no one wants to be punished for disobeying."

Tashas word gave Haven some hope about the awkward bows ending after awhile but another thing was bothering her,

"I feel like a fraud." Haven could barely speak the words. She'd thought them a few times but never voiced them aloud, they spoke to her deepest insecurities. She wouldn't have said anything if not for the fact that she felt like Tasha would never tell anyone and may even be able to help calm her uneasy thoughts.

"What do you mean?" Tasha spoke softly, sensing the way she felt about the subject.

"I mean, I didn't grow up here. I haven't even been here six months and I already have the crown. Sometimes I don't even feel like I belong here. Just a moment ago you talked about knowing the workers in the castle but I barely know anyone here! I can't name the fae that makes the food or that cleans the halls. How am I supposed to lead them if I don't even know them?"

Tasha didn't skip a beat before asking,

"Do you feel like you're not cut out for the position? That you wouldn't be able to lead your people and take care of them?"

"No" Haven responded. It wasn't that she didn't feel like she would do a good job as queen, she simply second guessed whether she was the right person for the role.

"But I'm from the human world. I grew up human. Just because I was suddenly cast into the body of a fae does not mean I am one." A tear rolled down Havens cheek as she talked. In the past she had considered talking about it with Nik. Astrea always saw the good in her, she never seemed to doubt or question her so Haven worried she wouldn't see where Haven was coming from. Nik however, had similar feelings of his own. Haven could hear it in the way he talked whenever his title was brought up, she could see it in the glares he sent towards his father. It had made her want to seek comfort with Nik. She wouldn't be able to do that now that Nik was missing.

Pushing those thoughts from her mind, Haven met Tashas stare, now was not the time to be thinking about Nik. It wouldn't help anything, the only thing thinking about Nik would do was bring tears to her eyes. She would get an update from Delroy this afternoon. Haven could only hope he'd have good news to share.

"Haven I am only going to tell you this once so I need you to listen and listen well, you are your mothers daughter, your fathers daughter. They were some of the most powerful rulers that ever lived and not only were they powerful, they were loved. Even in times of war, everyone respected your parents, they trusted them and knew they'd take care of them no matter the cost to themselves. I see both of them in you every single day. You have the makings to become one of the greatest fae to ever live if you only move past your doubts and own up to who you truly are. A Queen, and not just any queen, A Fae Queen."

Tashas words filled Haven with confidence as they washed over her. Tasha was right and in the back of her mind, she'd known that. It didn't matter that she'd grown up in another realm, it didn't matter that she hadn't been training her whole life. When Haven looked deep inside herself, she found what had been there all along, power. Power and the ability to use it to make a difference for her people, a good and true difference.

Haven straightened her shoulders, held her head high and assured herself that she was exactly where she belonged. She met Tashas eyes, doing her best to project as much confidence as she could muster. Haven knew that Tasha had seen the change in Haven when Tasha said,

"Good, now let's get to work."

Chapter Sixty-Eight

The rest of Havens training session went swimmingly, both with magic and weapons. Then, on the way to her lesson with Elanor where they had done a trial run of her coronation tomorrow, Delroy stopped her in the hall and told her to meet him outside the crown regents office to look through everything. She knew it was trashed but still hoped to find something, anything, that might clue them in to his plans.

Havens stomach grumbled as she came to a stop outside the door to the crown regents office. Putting her back to the entrance, she looked down the hall, finding Delroy nowhere in sight. She hoped that when he did show up, he brought food.

A moment passed before Haven heard the creak of a door, glancing down the hall she saw none opening. The thought occurred too late that it might have been the door she had her back towards that was opening. A strong hand grabbed her arm from behind, tugging her inside the decent sized room. A yelp left her before her reflexes kicked in and she swung her arm out and behind her, hitting whoever had grabbed her in the jaw.

The hand that had a hold of her let go. She turned just in time to see Delroy use that same hand to cup his jaw where she'd hit him. He was wearing his guard uniform, complete with a leather breastplate. Haven assumed he'd either snuck away from wherever he was supposed to be guarding or was on his lunch break.

"Ow" Delroy groaned

"Sorry" Haven tried to hold back her snicker but in the end, it slipped out.

"Shut up" Delroy snapped, which only caused Haven to laugh more.

"You hit like a fae" He grumbled, finally bringing his hand away from his jaw where Haven could already see the beginnings of a nasty bruise forming.

"Did you expect anything else? After all, I am one." Haven snipped, beginning to inspect the room. Trashed didn't even begin to cover it, all the cabinets were open and papers were strewn everywhere. The desk was even overturned.

"Yeah but you were raised in the human world. I don't know, I guess I wasn't expecting that to hurt so bad." Delroy wasn't rude with his words like she would have expected, if anything they seemed playful.

"Well maybe you shouldn't have grabbed me, you could have just opened the door. I would have seen you and come in."

"But how was I supposed to know you'd swing? It's not like I yanked your hair or something" Delroy jested, wearing a small smile. It was clear he was messing around at this point. Which was good, Haven may have gotten that shot off but she had a feeling that if it came down to it, Delroy could and would kick her ass. Likely without even breaking a sweat.

"You're gonna need ice for that" Haven bantered back

"Already one step ahead of you." He told her while walking behind the overturned desk. Delroy moved things on the ground out of the way and then righted the desk. Picking a basket up off of the ground, he set it on the desk before opening it. Removing wrapped sandwiches and bundled snacks, he set everything to the side before finally pulling out a sort of ice pack that had been on the bottom of the basket, likely to keep the food cold.

Delroy held it up to his face before stating,

"Much better"

"Ha," Haven laughed, "Did you pack us a picnic to accompany our snooping?"

"First, we are not snooping. As you are now unofficially queen, soon to officially be queen, this all belongs to you. Second, I packed ME a picnic. If you wanted food then you should have gotten some before you came here."

He made a good point about everything in this room belonging to Haven. It eased her almost nonexistent guilt about invading the crown regents' space.

She would think Delroy was serious about the food if not for the fact that he was actively handing her a wrapped sandwich. It seemed she might finally be growing on him. She secretly hoped that one day they could actually be friends and he'd tell her about whatever was going on between him and Roman. She was curious about it but not curious enough to find Roman and ask seeing as she was still pissed at him. Plus, Haven wasn't entirely sure he'd tell her.

Haven unwrapped what appeared to be a sliced ham sandwich and began munching while taking in more details around the room. Nothing obvious was taken, although she'd never spent any real length of time here so if something had been taken it likely wouldn't stand out.

She began sifting through some papers on the ground near a wooden file cabinet. Most of what she found was expense reports for the castle and kingdom, papers she had access to and went over often with Elanor. A few minutes of searching turned up nothing special. Mostly just more basic papers.

Turning to where Delroy was searching the other side of the room with his back to her, Haven asked,

"What exactly are we looking for?"

Delroy turned slightly, meeting her eyes for a second before turning back to whatever he was digging through. For a moment she thought he wasn't going to answer her question. Haven almost gave up before she heard his low voice,

"I'm hoping to find evidence that Niks father planned his kidnapping."

"Oh" She responded. Apparently Delroy was dealing with Nik possibly being responsible for his own kidnapping the same way she was, by denying it.

"I don't know why he would have done it, I'm just hoping that maybe we're wrong." He didn't have to say anymore for Haven to know exactly what he meant.

Attempting to change the subject Haven asked,

"What are people saying about it?"

"About what?"

"You know what. One day the crown regent is here, slinking around and putting the fear of the gods into his people and generally doing shady shit. The next day both he and his son are gone with no explanation." Haven tried to use her best joking tone to help ease the tension and it paid off when she heard Delroy snicker. He might deny it had happened but Havens fae hearing certainly heard him. He thought she was funny.

"And how would I know what gossip is spreading?" He asked

"Because you're a guard, don't you hear things?"

"No, no one really gossips around me because they know I'm close with Nik. We tried to make it not so obvious because Nik didn't want his father to know but anyone who paid close enough attention knew it. Fae walking by even quit talking when they see me patrolling."

"Oh, I'm sorry." Haven didn't know why she felt the need to apologize but she did.

"It's fine, not a big deal. I never really cared about what they had to say to begin with."

Haven didn't know how to respond so she didn't. Turning back to the papers she'd been looking through, Haven decided she might have better luck somewhere else, somewhere a little less obvious. Swallowing the last bite of her sandwich, Haven looked around the room until something caught her eye.

In the corner near where Delroy was digging through a cabinet was a plush black armchair. It wasn't the armchair that caught her eye, but rather a slight sliver of paper sticking out of the fabric stapled to the bottom of the chair.

"Hey, look at this." Haven said as she approached the chair.

Bending down, Haven felt around the upholstery on the bottom of the chair. Just beyond the paper that originally caught her eye was a loose sewing pin. Pulling out the pin loosened the fabric enough to slip the paper out.

Haven squinted her eyes in the relatively low light, trying to make out the details. It was a map of Shaston, Drailias neighboring kingdom. It was also the kingdom the crown regent had taken over, where her father was from and where she'd soon be traveling to so she could accept the crown there.

"What do you think this means?" She asked Delroy.

"Hell if I know" He responded.

Haven reached back into the pocket. Feeling a stack of papers there, she grabbed a hold of them. After handing half to Delroy, she began looking through the top few.

Haven moved over to the desk so she could get a better look at them. The room was fairly dark since only one of the sconces on the wall was burning. There were three others in the room but they were very obviously broken. So she could see better, Haven used her magic to summon a ball of flame which she moved to float in front of her, casting light onto the papers spread out on the desk.

"Wow, you're getting good at that," Delroy commented.

"Thanks"

Now that she could see a little better, Haven recognized the papers as maps of other kingdoms and the castles where the royals lived. Some areas were highlighted, mostly entrances and exits.

"Look at this" Delroy nudged her shoulder.

Haven looked over to see what he was talking about. Where she had maps of the other kingdoms here in the fae realm, Delroy was holding maps of the human world. Certain places were marked on the maps. Haven recognized some of them as places the fae used to live before the war with the humans.

"What do you think this means?" Haven repeated her earlier question.

"I don't even have a guess"

A chilling thought occurred to Haven, one she wished she could make disappear.

"What if," She said slowly, "What if the crown regent was planning to take over the other kingdoms like he did with Shaston. The marks on the maps could potentially be weak spots he could use to get into the castles and take over. I know he did it slightly differently with Shaston but intimidation won't work with the other rulers."

A look of horror crossed Delroys face.

"You might be right," He told her, appearing to think for a moment before continuing, "But what about these." Delroy slightly shook the map in his hand, "These are of the human world. How would that help him?"

Haven considered before turning her thoughts into words,

"What if he was planning to take over the other kingdoms so that he could use their armies to infiltrate the human world and take back control? Ever since I came here I've heard whispers about the crown regent and how much he hated that the fae were forced into our own realm and then removed from human history."

"Unfortunately, I think you might be right. Long ago, the rulers had to create our realm because while the fae are more powerful than humans, we are no match for their numbers but since coming here our population has boomed. All seven kingdoms' armies are no match in a war with the humans even with their now advanced artillery. We know the various kings and queens are unlikely to stand behind Niks father but I have no doubt that the crown regent wouldn't hesitate to take their control if he thought he could"

Silence stretched for several minutes after Delroy finished speaking. Haven knew the words they had spoken would likely haunt her thoughts for the rest of her natural life even if they didn't turn out to be true. They had been standing there, agonizing over the papers in front of them and their more unsettling thoughts for so long that the only lit sconce on the wall had gone out. Now the only light allowing them to see was Haven's fire.

"We better hope we're wrong about this" Delroy spoke lowly, breaking the silence.

"Why?" Haven asked, although she felt she already knew the answer.

"Because if we're not then we either need to track down Niks father and kill him, something I'm not sure we'll be able to do without Nik, or we're headed down a very short path towards a very long war."

Chapter Sixty-Nine

Unsurprisingly, Haven hadn't been able to sleep. The beginning of her coronation was in less than seven hours and all she could think about was Delroys words right before they'd left the crown regents office. Another puzzling thing that she hadn't been able to get out of her head was the fact that the office had been trashed. She knew Niks father would never normally keep it that way, he was much too controlling and vain for that, but that meant someone had come into his office and done that on purpose.

Her first guess had been that the crown regent did it before he took off, possibly to throw them off the trail of his plans, whatever they may be. But if that was the case then why didn't he take the papers? Why would he trash the office but leave them behind? Were there more that had been taken? Her other guess was that someone knew the crown regent was planning something and had been looking for proof or details about his plans and simply took the opportunity while everyone was away to break into the office and look around. But still, why trash the office? Unless they had known the crown regent would not be coming back so they hadn't had to worry about covering their tracks.

The whole thing gave Haven a headache which led to her getting up, gathering a snack and a glass of water, lighting a candle with her magic, placing it on the nightstand beside her bed and pulling out her mothers diary.

She kept it tucked away under her pillows, not a great hiding spot but knowing it was there helped her feel closer to her mom.

Haven had been mindlessly reading her mothers words for hours, trying to calm her mind enough that she could rest. Most of the entries were about one of two things, Havens father or the continuing, eventually failing, war efforts. Havens mother had messily scribbled all sorts of notes about war strategies and ideas to help tip the scales towards the favor of the fae. Her mothers entries progressively became more hopeless as time passed.

It all came down to one thing, the humans had so many more warriors than the fae did. Fae human relations had been going downhill long before the war started. In addition to common fertility problems making it hard for fae to reproduce, every so often fae would disappear. These things meant that their population had slowly but steadily been decreasing for years.

Havens mother wrote a passage about how she suspected the humans had been planning for war long before the fae were even able to guess. She also surmised that they were likely responsible for the fae that went missing.

Morana went on and on about their losing efforts and about the terror they were all feeling. It was enough to make Haven decide to put the journal away and go back to trying to get some sleep as soon as she finished the entry she was currently involved in. There were only a few entries left before the journal ended and as much as Haven wanted to know anything and everything about her mothers time as a powerful fae queen, this was downright depressing.

Before she could stop herself, Haven began the entry after the one she planned to finish with. She was glad she did when she read how it began,

We might finally have something to hope for.

Her mothers hopeful and flowy handwriting was back. Haven was glad to see it after pages of depressive and upsetting entries. Haven took a deep breath and let herself reset after those last couple of harsh pages before continuing to read.

Further into the entry, Haven could see exactly what had given her mother, and apparently every other war torn fae some hope,

March 15th 1876,

We might finally have something to hope for.

During todays war council a viable solution to our failing war efforts might have finally been proposed. Not everyone is entirely keen on the idea, myself included, but if it saves our people and gives us the ability to have a future then maybe the dangers are worth it.

The king from Dremid has been in contact with an old magic witch that has given him a spell that might allow us to create an entirely new realm, a purely fae realm. One untouched by humans. This could be the answer so many have been looking for, the solution to our biggest and most present problem.

Unfortunately, it comes with many risks. Risks I'm not certain I am willing to take. Neither is every other ruler but if we don't do something quickly we and our people are likely to perish sooner rather than later.

The spell requires a very large amount of magic and sacrifice from its casters which is why the old witch insisted it had to be performed by royals. Performing this spell will take the majority of the magic from the fae that cast the spell. In addition, the casters will not be able to reside in the new realm with their people.

The Dremid king has an answer for this of course. He has proposed that we sacrifice our power and have our children take our places as king or queen of the respected kingdoms once the new realm is created. Without us.

Of course the Dremid king has no issue with this. He's got five children and another on the way.

Something I'm not sure I'll ever experience.

It's not that I disagree with his idea, I actually am rather impressed. It's just that, as of now, I have no children to take over for me. Neither does Robert, I wonder how he feels about all of this. I haven't gotten to speak with him since the meeting. At which he did not say anything to indicate his feelings on the subject.

For as long as I have lived my courses have always been irregular, not the every six months that most fae women experience. In addition, Robert and I have been together for months now and not once have we used any magics to prevent pregnancy. I'm also certain he noticed the disappointment on my face a few weeks ago when my courses showed up in the middle of the night. He held me extra tight afterwards and I love him for it. As sad as I might be about the possibility of never having children, I cannot allow it to sway my decision about this spell. I know we will be able to come up with something in the interim to fix the issue that not all of us rulers have children so I suppose I need to put that aside for now.

It will take all seven royals to pull this off so all seven of us have to agree. All but one of my council members are entirely for this solution even though they know it means they will be leaving me.. Evan is the only one who disagrees and while I do care about him, his feelings are not something I can take into account at this point. Besides, I am fairly sure that the only reason he is against this plan is because it separates us. Leaving me in the human world with Robert, a fae he hates. Robert is a good man, Evan has no reason to dislike him except that he has something Evan wants.

I have long since ignored Evans feelings which is something I'm not proud to admit but he is a good friend and counselor to me and I would hate to hurt his feelings. However, there is a tightness in my gut that says that if we do go through with this, I won't be sending Evan into the fae world without hearing something from him about how he feels towards me. I am not looking forward to that moment.

I need to talk with Robert and find out his opinion about every-thing. I trust him more than I've ever trusted anyone. I think that's what I will do now, go and find Robert where he is staying in the south tower and tell him about my feelings and see what he makes of them.

-Morana Montalli

Haven flipped the page, finding that that was the very last entry. There were still pages left in the journal but they were all blank, something she definitely had not been expecting. There was noth-ing about her mothers talk with her father or what happened with Evan. It was clear that Evan was likely in love with her mother and she wondered what became of him once the royals created the fae realm and journeyed into their new world.

As far as she knew, none of the current council members were named Evan. Seeing as the current members were still mostly the same, save for a few that had been replaced due to deaths that had been heavily recorded, she didn't know what to make of the whole Evan issue. She supposed that since all of that happened in the past, it didn't matter what happened to her mothers previous council member. Haven had to focus on the here and now.

A tear rolled down Havens cheek at the thought of no more new words from her mother. She missed her horribly. It didn't help that she never got a response to the letter she had sent out in the beginning of this whole thing.

Haven did her best to fight off more tears, being able to read her moms words had helped Haven get through the homesickness and loneliness she had been pretending wasn't bothering her.

Deciding to call it a night, Haven closed the journal and wrapped the small leather band around it before tucking it away. She leaned over, blowing out the candle she had been using to read before sliding down in bed and closing her eyes.

Finishing the diary, while sad, had brought Haven a measure of peace. She believed in her heart that she'd see her mother again someday and she couldn't wait to tell her all about everything she'd learned during her time in the fae realm. Maybe she should try to send her mother another letter, she thought. Haven hoped her mother would be proud of the woman she was becoming, the fae she was becoming, the Queen she was becoming. Gods knew Haven was trying to be proud of herself.

Chapter Seventy

Haven finally managed to fall asleep not long before she assumed the sun would be rising. The bags under her eyes on what was likely to be one of the most important days of her life were unfortunate but Haven didn't regret staying up to finish her mothers journal.

Yawning, Haven sat up and stretched. A glance at the clock told her Rea would likely be showing up any minute. While reading her mothers heartbreaking words last night, some detailing the deaths of a few of her friends and her mothers feelings afterwards, Haven had decided to try to forgive her friends. Truly forgive, not just trying not to think about how badly they hurt her for a night. The wounds ran deep but not having her friends by her side would cut deeper.

As if Havens thoughts had summoned her, a light knock sounded from her door. Calling for Astrea to come in, Haven slid her legs over the edge of the bed and her feet into some slippers.

"Good morning" Rea greeted with a slightly nervous smile as she came through the doorway, leaving it open behind her.

"Morning" Haven responded lightly. She took a breath as she told herself to forgive but not forget.

"What have you brought me for the coronation?" She asked cheerily

A wide smile graced Astreas face, "You're going to love it!" she told her before reaching back through the open doorway and picking something up from where it had been resting against the wall. It was her dress. Clearly too large for a normal garment bag, it simply hung on a hook. Astrea was right, it only took one look for Haven to love it.

The dress was made up of so much lace and tulle that Haven had to stand exactly in the middle between the edge of her bed and the wall to avoid brushing up against something and messing up Reas meticulous work. Some layers Rea smoothed down and others she fluffed, Haven didn't know why Rea did different things to different layers but the end result was something that almost brought tears to both Haven and Astreas faces.

The dress was made of mostly all black material with gold accents. The top half was tight with a keyhole opening and seemed more armor than dress thanks to the stiff metal underneath the swath of fabric. As heavy as the top half was, it flowed very well with the ballgown style layered skirt that had a hidden opening Haven could use to reach the dagger currently strapped to her thigh. The dress had stunning black lace sleeves with bead accents at the wrist and a band that went around her middle finger to keep the sleeves from riding up. A sheer cape connected to the shoulders of the dress and trailed far behind Haven. It had fire embroidered along the edge with different shades of red embroidery threads.

"The black represents your shadows and the red represents your fire." Rea told Haven, while twisting front pieces of her hair back and securing them with pins.

"What about the gold?" Haven asked, smoothing her hands down the plush material of her skirt.

"The gold represents your status as Queen." Rea smiled

"Oh" Haven squeaked. This was becoming very real, very fast. Haven might have some nerves about everything but she knew in her heart and in her head that this was exactly where she was meant to be, she just needed to remember that when the anxiety crept in.

Other than the front strands Rea twisted backwards, the rest of her hair was mostly left alone. It simply trailed down her back in wild red strands. She also kept her makeup simple, a little bit of gold eyeshadow to help her eyes pop, some mascara and a deep red lipstick that matched both her hair and her dress. Rea also gave her a few pieces of jewelry to wear, some dangly black stone earrings and a matching black stone ring that Rea told her Roman had given to her for Haven to wear on her thumb.

Haven didn't know where Roman got the ring but it was beautiful and fit perfectly, she needed to remember to thank him when she saw him in a little while. He was supposed to meet up with Haven and Astrea just before the ceremony began. During the ceremony, Haven would be standing on a balcony of the castle alone except for the priest that would be performing the coronation but she wanted her friends just inside the doorway where they could be close to her. She was glad they didn't mind staying behind the scenes rather than being down in the crowd watching her being crowned.

Haven also decided to wear her mothers necklace that Binah had given to her. It didn't quite fit with the opulence of everything but wearing it honored her mother and made Haven happy so nothing else really mattered.

The last thing Haven had to do was step into the tall black heeled boots Astrea brought for her. After having to hold onto Rea for balance, Haven was able to slip both feet into the boots one at a time. Haven took her hands from Reas shoulders and then lifted up the edge of her dress the best she could since it was rather heavy so that Rea could help her lace the boots up.

"I think we are done here." Rea said after standing up. She brushed her hands together and smiled at Haven.

"Yes, I think we are." Haven confirmed with a smile of her own. She took a minute to look over herself in the mirror one last time. She wasn't surprised by what she saw there but it nonetheless made her heart skip a beat. For what Haven saw while looking in the mirror was nothing less than a Queen, a powerful one.

Chapter Seventy-One

"Do you remember what you're supposed to do?" Rea asked, The two of them stood in the hall outside the room that held the opening to the balcony Haven was moments away from stepping out onto to be crowned queen.

"Yes I remember." Haven nodded.

They had caught sight of the priest who would be performing the ceremony resting on a chair inside the room through the open doorway. Haven was thankful it was not the same priest that Niks father had dragged out into the forest not that long ago. Haven could hear the crowds gathered around outside the castle, there was lots of shouting and cheering. Even without her advanced hearing abilities she probably would have been able to hear them.

All they were waiting on now was Roman, who was supposed to show five minutes ago.

"Good. I'm going to run through things one more time so we have everything straight." Astrea told her. Haven nodded again, listening to Rea tell her exactly how things would be happening.

"First you will step out onto the balcony facing the crowd, remember we are on the highest floor so don't let the height shock you. Next, the priest will call for silence. Then after everyone has quieted he will recite an ancient fae blessing meant to protect whoever has the crown placed on their head. After he recites his blessing, he will turn and remove the crown from where it is resting on a pillar in a velvet lined box. You will turn to him and kneel, he will repeat a few more words and place the crown on your head, thus anointing you as queen. After he does that, you need to stand up and walk to the edge of the terrace and wave to the crowd.

If all goes correctly then they will cheer for you. The final thing that will happen is the priest handing you a ceremonial dagger you will use to cut the palm of your hand symbolizing your willingness to bleed for your people. After this is done the priest will hand you a cloth to wrap up your hand and then you are free to return inside where Roman and I will be waiting for you."

Astrea finished reciting the events that were about to take place and glanced around, looking for their friend. Haven could tell she was also listening for him based on the slight tilt of her head. If he didn't show soon, they'd have to start without him.

It wasn't impossible he had gotten lost but it was unlikely. They were currently on the top floor, which was dedicated entirely to royalty. With the exception of the door to the room they were using for balcony access, all the doors on this floor were closed and locked so Roman shouldn't have a hard time finding them.

Haven allowed herself to get distracted for a moment, this was where she would be staying after the ceremony was complete. In fact, workers were probably packing up her current room this very minute. She would miss her little bedroom but was looking forward to exploring the vast halls and rooms on this floor.

For a moment, Haven lost herself in a memory of that room, one of her very favorites. Her and Niks first time together, their only time together. She had been doing as much as she could not to think about how much she was missing Nik while she waited for news from the search party she and Delroy had sent after him, telling herself that no news was good news.

No matter how hard she tried, he kept popping up in her head, usually at the most inopportune times. Like when she was training with Tasha, trying to fall asleep and apparently, while she anxiously waited to be crowned queen. The thought of him not being here to see how far she had come saddened her so Haven did her best to cast it out, she could bring those thoughts back out when she was alone and had a moment to truly miss him.

Havens thoughts were interrupted when she thought she heard footsteps down the hall. Listening as intently as she could with the crowds filling her ears, she couldn't decide if what she had heard was actually footsteps or the wind or even a very large rat. After all, it had been over a century since anyone had been up here.

The ceremony, while a big deal wasn't the thing she was most nervous about, Roman not showing up was. Just like her and Rea, the two of them had been through a lot and she wanted him here. The thought that he might not show hurt more than she was willing to admit. And then there were the intrusive thoughts. The ones that kept whispering things like, what if he wasn't late of his own volition, what if he had been kidnapped or was lying hurt in a pool of his own blood somewhere.

Haven knew thoughts that began with, *what if*, usually never led anywhere good. In fact, they were hardly ever even close to being right but that didn't mean her heart wasn't stuttering and her hand wasn't trembling because of her friend's absence.

She had just started to pick at the lace on her sleeves, earning a nervous scowl from Astrea when actual footsteps sounded down the hall.

"Sorry, sorry!" Roman called. Jogging to where the pair was standing, he apologized twice more before taking in Havens dress and what was likely a very worried look on her face.

"I'm sorry H, I ran into someone and couldn't get away." Roman rested his hand on her shoulder, trying to comfort her.

"Who'd you run into?" Haven asked

"It's not important, not right now. I'll tell you later, promise."

Haven chose to believe her friend, letting him tentatively wrap his arms around her in a comforting hug.

"Thank you" She whispered as he released her. She already felt much better.

"Does this mean we're alright?" Roman asked

"I don't know," Haven answered honestly, "But we will be."

"I'll take it." Roman smiled, "You look amazing. Now let's get you crowned."

***

The entire coronation had been a blur. If it weren't for the sting of the cut on her palm and the weight of the crown on her head, Haven might not have believed it actually happened. The boom of the largest crowd Haven had ever seen had been deafening, the deep timbre of the priest's voice had been unsettling and the power behind her actions had been captivating.

When Haven had raised her bloody hand to the crowd, she let loose a raw wave of power that earned her even more cheers. In that moment it seemed like everyone in the kingdom was ecstatic that she was finally taking her crown. At least, everyone that had been there. Haven wasn't foolish or naive enough to think that everyone was happy with the shift of power. There had to be followers loyal to the crown regent and Haven had a feeling it wouldn't be long before she came face to face with them.

Haven was currently taking a moment for herself in one of the supply closets on the second floor before heading out to rejoin the celebrations she was sure would carry into the night. If she was being honest, Haven would call what she was doing hiding rather than taking a moment for herself but it was only her in the closet so no one was around to hear her lie.

Thoughts of the last time she'd been in a closet similar to this one surfaced, tugging on Havens heart. Ever since Niks disappearance, there had been a weight on her chest Haven wasn't sure what to do with. Haven wanted, more than anything to be able to speak with Nik, to even see him. While she may try to deny it, constantly playing in the back of her mind were thoughts of him, thoughts that she may never get to see Nik again. Her heart hurt but she had to have hope, hope that one day those search parties would find something, anything that told Haven Nik was alright.

The walls vibrated with the sounds and echoes of people singing and laughing and dancing in the great hall below her. An official ball had begun not long after her coronation with foreign dignitaries and a few royals from every kingdom in the fae realm. Almost every lord from Dralia and most of Shastons villages were dancing and chatting under her feet. They had all been here to watch her being crowned but tomorrow would be when she really interacted with them.

A knock sounded at the door, she assumed it was Astrea since her friend was likely the only one who could have found Haven hiding out in a closet. Both Rea and Roman had separated from Haven not long after the coronation, both for different reasons. Astrea had left to go and find the two of them some snacks and refreshments and Roman had left to greet his family members that sailed in for the coronation. Romans departure had been a reminder that he'd be leaving soon to head back to his home kingdom. Haven wasn't ready for him to leave and she suspected that he wasn't quite ready to leave either but unfortunately he didn't have much of a choice. His family needed him.

The knock sounded again and Haven knew instantly that it was not Astrea. She would never knock again, she'd just come inside.

Haven twisted the door knob, peering out into the hall. She wasn't sure who she expected to be on the other side of the door but it certainly wasn't the small woman standing there.

"It's good to see you again"

Haven smiled, slightly shocked but nonetheless excited,

"It's nice to see you too Binah"

Binah stepped into the storage closet and quietly shut the door behind her.

"Well this is a surprise" Haven commented

The older woman turned to face Haven. A warm smile gracing her features,

"Yes but a pleasant one I hope?"

"Of course!" Haven exclaimed, throwing her arms around Binah, "I honestly didn't know if I'd see you again so this is definitely a welcome surprise."

The older fae laughed and tightened her arms around Haven,

"I'm glad you feel that way but I must admit, I did not come here just to see you get crowned."

Haven pulled back, "What's going on? Is everything alright?"

"Of course my dear, I just came to bring you this."

Binah pulled something from the folds of her skirts. Upon closer inspection Haven realized it was a small envelope. Taking it from Binahs outstretched hand she asked,

"What's this?"

"You'll see" The older woman smirked.

Haven began to open up the letter when Binah stopped her with a hand on her wrist,

"Not yet. Wait until you are alone after the festivities have died down. Trust me when I say that you'll likely need time to process the contents."

Binahs words only made Haven want to rip open the envelope that much more but after taking in the serious look on the older faes face, she chose to listen. Tucking what appeared to be a letter into her dress pockets Haven asked,

"How long are you here for?"

"Not long," Binah sighed, "Right now is likely the last time you'll see me for a while. My garden needs me."

Haven didn't understand why Binah had to rush back home to her garden but she knew better than to question her. Instead she chose to wrap Binah in another hug.

Binah chuckled, "You better get back to the festivities before someone notices you are missing."

Haven pulled back, "I know. I just needed a moment to myself."

"I understand. I'll leave you to it."

Before Haven could stop the woman, Binah whisked herself back out the door, not making a sound as she did. Taking a deep breath, Haven pulled open the door and stepped out into the hall. Binah was nowhere to be found but she did find someone in the hall she hadn't expected to see.

"Hello your majesty" Delroy bowed.

"None of that nonsense Delroy, you know you don't need to bow to me. What are you doing here?"

Delroy smirked, "From now on you will have a guard escorting you wherever you are unless you are in a meeting with the council or have retired for the night. Even then, you will have a guard posted outside your chambers."

Like hell was she going to have some random guy following her around everywhere. Haven opened her mouth to argue but Delroy stopped her before she could,

"Unfortunately you do not have a choice in this. Especially in the beginning. It is law that our rulers be protected at all times. After some time you will likely be able to get the council to agree to let you go places by yourself but until then, you get a guard at all times."

Haven huffed, "I'm the queen now, can't I just change that rule?"

Delroy snickered, "That's not how it works."

Seeing she was not going to get anywhere with him, Haven walked away from Delroy. She'd just have to corner some of the council members and convince them she could handle herself.

Delroy was two steps behind her the entire way to the grand hall, she could already tell that this was not going to work out. At least right now it was Delroy, what happened when it was some random guard she didn't know? What if they were a worse asshole than Delroy had been when Haven had first met him? What if they were the opposite and constantly wanted to talk to her? Worst of all, what if they never quit that annoying bowing? Haven shuddered at the thought.

Pushing those thoughts from her mind as the voices from the great hall became louder, Haven straightened her shoulders and steeled herself. Stopping at the entrance door of the grand hall, she reminded herself that this was very real now and any number of enemies could be on the other side of that door wearing smiles or scowls. There could be a spy for the crown regent or any other enemy she was not so blissfully unaware of. Someone in that room could be plotting to kill her this very minute and she'd never be able to tell.

Chapter Seventy-Two

The bright sun shining through her open window woke Haven from a near dead sleep. Last night, while fun, had earned Haven one hell of a headache. She hadn't drank anything but being around so many loud people, music and general debauchery combined with her lack of sleep ensured she'd be running through her first official day as queen at less than her best.

After the coronation party, she'd been escorted to her new rooms on the top floor of the castle. A simple wooden four poster bed, an armoire, dresser and a door to a large bathroom was all she had found in her new bedroom. At the time, Haven hadn't felt much like exploring any room except her bedroom but she'd been assured she could decorate any of the rooms however she pleased.

Haven walked through the open doorway into what she was calling the sitting room, finding a nice breakfast spread waiting for her on the coffee table. Before she could take a seat, Haven remembered the letter Binah had given her. In her exhaustion last night, she'd been unable to read it.

Darting back into her bedroom, Haven pulled the letter out from under her pillow. Sliding it from the plain white envelope, Haven gasped when she realized what was in her hands.

Dear Haven,

First, I would like to apologize. I'm sure over these last few months you have found some things out about me that I almost wish had stayed hidden.

Please know that your father and I never made it our goal to lie to you. We simply wanted you to ourselves for as long as we could have you. I know it may seem selfish but not telling you about our pasts kept us sane. Even though we knew that eventually you'd end up where you are, we wanted you to enjoy your childhood and teen years for as long as possible. Before we got the chance to tell you, your father passed away. After that, it never felt right for me to tell you. It was always something we planned to do together.

I have no doubt that you will make an amazing queen. Please don't ever doubt my love for you or my confidence in you. I know that if your father were here he'd say the same thing. We struggled for so long to have you and when we finally did it was like we'd been blessed by gods that have long since slept.

I miss you everyday and while it might be selfish of me, I hope you miss me too. Knowing that you are exactly where you belong is the only thing that has made the days easier without you. I hope you are not so mad at me that you overlook my love for you. If ever you need anything, advice, guidance or simply a proverbial shoulder to cry on, I will always be here for you. I may not be able to enter the fae realm myself but if you get a letter to Binah, your words will find me. One day, after all the craziness that your coronation will be and whatever other trials you may face, I hope that you will come back to the human world to visit. I'd love to meet you as the powerful queen I am sure you are becoming.

Know that I am so so proud of you. No matter where the cards may fall and no matter how far apart we are, my love for you will always be present.

I love you Haven

-Mom

Haven stared at the letter in her hands. A tear rolled down her cheek as she folded it back up and tucked it away. She didn't have time to properly process her mothers words but seeing that letter, holding it in her hands and knowing that her mother was alright lifted a weight off Haven's shoulders she hadn't realized she'd been carrying.

Loud voices outside the sitting room pulled Haven from her thoughts.

"Let me in!" A voice demanded, it sounded like Rea.

"No can do miss, you are not authorized to enter the Queens chambers." That would be the guard they'd assigned last night. No matter how hard she tried, the council was not willing to move from their position that Haven needed around the clock guarding.

"Oh come on!" Rea screeched

Haven snickered. She debated letting her friend stay out there for a little while longer. It was slightly petty revenge for her friend's lies but revenge nonetheless. Haven listened to Rea and the guard bicker for a few more minutes before she made her way to the large wooden door that opened to the hall.

"It's alright. She can come in." Haven stated as she opened the door.

The guard, whose name she did not know bowed quickly,

"Are you sure, your majesty?"

"Yes she is my lady's maid and friend. She is always welcome in my chambers"

"Of course." The guard nodded and stepped away from the entryway to let Rea pass.

"How rude!" Rea snapped as she entered Havens rooms.

Haven laughed at her friend, "He's only doing his job"

"You're enjoying this aren't you?"

Haven snickered, "Only a little"

Rea rolled her eyes, taking a moment to look over Havens new rooms. Although the entire top floor were technically Havens rooms, the rooms they were in now were her personal rooms. The rest were various meeting rooms and an office. There was even a war room with a large map of the fae realm. As much as she didn't want to admit it, Haven had a feeling that room would be getting some use at some point soon.

"This is nice, albeit a little boring." Rea remarked, standing by the fireplace. The sitting room held a couch, coffee table, a small dining area, a balcony, the door to her bedroom and bathroom and a large stone fireplace.

"I know I need to decorate but it doesn't feel so urgent, especially since I'll be leaving soon for Shaston anyway."

"Yeah I get that. Have you decided who's going with you?" Rea asked, sitting down on the couch near the coffee table and fireplace.

"I figured I'd have to have some guards. If Roman wasn't going back to his kingdom I'd ask him but he leaves the day before me. Other than a few of the council members, the only other person I'd want going would be you." Haven had an idea for someone else she'd hoped would go but she hadn't asked him yet so she didn't want to say anything. She hoped to find him sometime today, between all the meetings being held and to festivities still going on.

Rea sucked in a breath, "You want me to go?" She asked.

"Of course," Haven stated, sitting down next to Rea on the couch, "I'm going to need a friend."

"I'd be honored" Her friend responded, wrapping her arms around Haven.

Haven smiled, "I'm glad. I don't think I could handle all the bureaucratic nonsense without you."

Rea huffed, "Yeah I could see you getting mad and 'accidentally' knocking out some poor lord who was pissing you off."

"Good thing you'll be there to stop me!"

Chapter Seventy-Three

After a headache of a day, meeting with all the lords and royals from other kingdoms, Haven was ready to collapse on her bed and sleep for about three days. If she'd have known being Queen forced you to talk to so many people, she might not have accepted the crown.

Unfortunately, there was still one more thing on her to-do list for the day before she could collapse into her bed and sleep. A knock at the door told her she wouldn't have to wait long to take care of it. She'd already let the guard outside her room know to let him pass when he showed up.

"Come in" She called

Delroy opened the large door, entered the sitting room and closed it behind him.

"You wanted to see me?" He asked

"Yes," Haven nodded, "Are there any updates on Nik?"

Delroy shook his head, a defeated look on his face, "No, not even a whisper of his whereabouts."

Haven shoulders slumped, she stood from the couch and walked to the open balcony doors. The night sky was lit up with what had to be hundreds of thousands of stars.

"That's disappointing."

"Yeah it is." Delroy responded. Coming to stand next to Haven, she could tell how much this was beating him up. She knew he likely felt abandoned and heartbroken, as she did.

"We'll find him." She assured

"Maybe he doesn't want to be found"

Delroys words hurt but Haven couldn't deny she'd been thinking the same thing. There was no trace of him, nothing in the local villages, no whispers about a prince being taken hostage. Worst of all, there was no ransom, no demands for his safe return. The more Haven thought about it, the more she decided what happened that night had been Niks doing.

With her thumb, she rubbed her left ring finger where a black ink tattoo banded around it. She'd taken off her wedding ring but the black ring hadn't gone away. During the day, she used makeup to hide it, to hide her connection to him. Haven doubted Nik had meant to let it get that far, to let them actually be wed. Or maybe Nik had thought nothing final could happen until after the priest used the wedding ribbon to tie them together.

Whatever Niks intentions had been, she assumed he had failed. Haven assumed he meant to leave them behind without a trace.

"What is that?" Delroy asked, noting her anxious movement.

Haven stretched her hand out to Delroy, showing him the black marriage ink.

"Wow,"" He remarked, "Something tells me he hadn't meant to let it get that far."

"I felt the same"

"At least we know he's still alive." Deloy commented

"What do you mean?" She asked

"The only way that mark can be removed is through death. The magic that binds the two of you together is strong even though the ceremony went unfinished. Not even cutting off a finger could remove it. The tattoo would simply move to another finger." He explained.

"Wow" Haven wrapped her arms around herself. It was a small comfort to know that Nik was still breathing but a comfort nonetheless.

A few minutes of silence passed before Haven decided to get to the real reason she asked Delroy to meet her,

"Would you be interested in becoming my personal guard?"

"What?" Delroy turned to her.

"Well, since I have been unable to get around the council when they say that I must be guarded at all times, I figured it would be better for me to have someone I don't completely hate and somewhat trust following me around. I already picked one other person so that the two of you can take shifts but I want you to be my main guard. You'd need to move your chambers to one of the spare rooms on my floor as well as travel to Shaston with me."

Delroy was silent for a moment, forcing Haven to blurt out,

"You can say no. I won't hold it against you. No one knows you're being offered this position so it's entirely up to you. Take a few days to think about it if you want."

"Are you sure you want me?" Delroy began, "For one, we barely know each other. I know you didn't like me in the beginning and it was obvious I didn't really like you either. Two, I'm not even a higher ranking guard. I mostly patrol and help keep things running smoothly in the castle."

"Don't belittle what you do and who you are," Haven told him, "What you do is important and if I didn't trust that you could do this then I wouldn't have asked you. About the whole, us not liking each other thing, I think we can move past that, don't you? Especially if we are heading where I fear we are. I'd rather have someone I feel I can trust guarding me. So, will you do it?"

Deloy didn't hesitate, "I'd be honored."

Haven nodded. Things were silent for a moment, the two enjoying the peaceful night air and quiet before Delroy asked,

"When you say, where things are heading, do you mean?"

"War," Haven finished for him, "I know in my heart and in my head that the crown regent is not going to let things go that easily. And if what we found in his office is any indication, this has been going on longer than I've been alive."

Delroy nodded, "I agree, I've known the man since I was a child and never once have I seen him give up on something. He is a horrible man willing to do horrible things to get what he wants. Worse, there are fae out there who will support him, who will be right by his side as he does those horrible things."

Attempting to lighten the mood even slightly, Haven said,

"You know it's funny, I've been around the man for months, he could become the largest hindrance to the future of the realm and I don't even know his name."

Delroy thought for a moment,

"Evan, Niks fathers name is Evan."

A chill crept over Havens spine and her blood ran cold as she realized just how far the crown regents, or rather Evans, hatred ran. If he had been the Evan from her mothers journal, the one that had been in love with Morana then there would be no stopping him.

Images flashed through Havens mind of blood, tears and death. Death of her loved ones, death of her people. She was frightened for them and for herself. If there were any gods listening she prayed they'd aid them in this bloody journey.

Chapter Seventy-Four

As pieces of the puzzle fell into place, Evan couldn't help but be thrown back in time. Back to the moment everything good in his life ended.

Todays the day, he thought. Today the witches spell would be cast and the new realm would be created. Today, he would finally confess his feelings for Morana. She'd welcome him with open arms and they'd stay in the human realm together. Leaving one of the other council members to take his place as crown regent. Morana had offered him the position yesterday and while he'd been honored, it wasn't the one he wanted.

Evan made his way down the hall, towards Moranas room. He knew the way by heart at this point. Finally coming to a stop outside her room, Evan found it completely silent. Not unusual, she most likely had lit a silencing candle, useful if this went how he wanted.

Taking out the key Morana didn't know he had, Evan unlocked the door. Pushing it open, he instantly knew that the speech he had planned would be going to waste.

Lying on her back, Morana had her legs spread wide with the devil himself between them. Her head was thrown back in pleasure as Robert thrust into her.

It only took a second for Morana to notice him. Evan took in the panicked look on her face as she jumped up and pushed Robert off of her. Confused, Robert turned to look, finding Evan there in the doorway.

Morana wrapped herself in a sheet and climbed off the bed. Evan snarled as she neared him, he could smell the evidence of her affair all over her.

"What the fuck do you think you're doing?" She shouted

"Get out!" Robert yelled from behind her but Evan would not be intimidated by rats like him. Standing his ground Evan responded,

"What am I doing, what do you think you're doing? Allowing him between your legs, you have better taste than that. What about us!"

"What about us Evan? There is no us." Evan could see she was trying to soften her words but it still didn't matter. The woman standing before him was a traitorous whore.

"You bitch!" He snarled. Reaching out to grab her, he wrapped his hands around her neck and twisted to shove her against the wall. Morana clawed at his hands, attempting to shove him off. Robert grabbed Evan from behind, ripping him from her and throwing him down on the ground.

Robert hit Evan over and over again before Morana finally pulled him off. Evan spat blood on the floor before rising. Very slowly he looked the two of them over, both covered with a now bloody sheet and looking like they'd been put through a tornado.

"You'll pay for your actions!" Evan spat before exiting through the open doorway. He could hear Morana beginning to cry as well as Roberts comforting words.

Once upon a time he'd considered Morana to be the love of his life and long before that, Robert had been his best friend. Not that Morana had known that of course. Robert had cast him aside as soon as he'd taken his throne.

He'd make them pay, he'd make them both pay.

Evan absently thought about the night after everything in his world had come crashing down. He wondered, if he hadn't made a deal that stripped so much from him, would he have been able to move on from that night, from her? Evan didn't think so, even in the little pieces left of his black heart he knew he'd never have been able to move on from Morana. Even if he hadn't sold his soul to the devil in attempt to rid himself of the pain, Morana would have lived inside his head for as long as his soul was still in this realm.

Now that he was nothing more than a vessel for others to use as they pleased, Evan knew there was no changing what was coming. He hadn't had complete control over his actions in centuries and he wondered, if he did, if Evan was able to get himself away from his mental captors, would he even bother to try to change what was coming? Or would he just let the cards fall as they may?

Casting the useless thoughts from his head, Evan dragged himself back to the present. There was no getting out of that deal he'd made so long ago and he knew it.

The sounds of the loud tavern below him rose up to greet Evans' ears. Just because he was in hiding didn't mean he couldn't indulge in some of life's luxuries. Taking a large drink of some of the worst whiskey he'd ever had, Evan thought back on how much he had accomplished since he'd found Robert and Morana in bed together. The death of Robert being one of his prouder moments and one of the only times he'd felt alive in over a century.

Evan only had a few more tasks to complete before he could finally reach his goals and take what the voices in his head told him were his. The death of that little brat being high up on that list. Evan couldn't look at Haven without seeing her mother and unfortunately, her father. She was a perfect mix of the two.

Soon, he'd be able to take her down, take the kingdom for himself and then the rest of the realm. After that, he'd take the one thing he wanted most, Morana. He'd show her how weak Roberts daughter was, how easily she crumbled under Evans efforts. Then together they'd release horrors never before seen and take back what was never supposed to be given up in the first place, the human realm.

A Note to the reader:

Thank you, thank you, thank you! If you've gotten this far, or even if you randomly picked up this book and opened it to this page, I cannot thank you enough. This book is the culmination of years of hard work, tears, dreams and late nights. I have always dreamed of creating a world for people to disappear into when they need a break from reality. No matter why you need that break, I will be forever grateful that you chose my world to disappear into. Words cannot fully explain how much this book means to me (ironic, I know) and how much your support of it means. From one book dragon to another, I will forever appreciate you. Here's to dreams being fulfilled!

Sincerely,

Lillie Jean Andrews

Acknowledgments

First, to my mother and grandmother, thank you for your relentless support and cheerleading. Without you guys, I am fairly certain I still would have written this book but I'm not sure I would have ever had the courage to publish. While there are some parts of this book I hope your eyes never touch, I love you!

Second to my bestie, Amy, thank you for never judging me and being there when I need to vent and thank you for always being willing to give me a hug even if it's over the phone from hundreds of miles away!

Lastly to my beta readers Gianna and Solmary, you guys truly helped me turn this book into what it is today. You guys gave me feedback when it was desperately needed and helped me turn this novel into something I feel deserves to be on shelves! You guys are the best!

About the author

Lillie Jean Andrews is a born and raised Florida girl. While you might not find her at the beach, she can be spotted at the springs or cozied up in bed with a novel. She loves travel, horseback riding and has been writing since her early teen years and reading since long before that.

She adores chai tea, cowboy boots, handwritten journals, cypress trees, otters and stickers. She is a mama to one unruly pup named Hannah and although she doesn't always succeed, she tries her best to always see the good in each and every day.